B.O.Q.

B.O.Q.

AN NCIS SPECIAL AGENT FRAN SETLIFF NOVEL

N. P. Simpson

 JOHN F. BLAIR, PUBLISHER *Winston-Salem, North Carolina*

JOHN F. BLAIR,
PUBLISHER
1406 Plaza Drive
Winston-Salem, North Carolina 27103
www.blairpub.com

Cover image: Vladimir Piskunov/E+/Getty Images
Cover Design by Brooke Csuka

Library of Congress Cataloging-in-Publication Data

Simpson, N. P.
  B.O.Q. : an NCIS Special Agent Fran Setliff novel / By N. P. Simpson.
    pages   cm
  ISBN 978-0-89587-616-4 (alk. paper) — ISBN 978-0-89587-617-1 (ebook) 1. United States.
Naval Criminal Investigative Service—Fiction. 2. Women—Crimes against—Fiction. 3. Murder—Investigation—Fiction. I. Title.
  PS3619.I5636B67 2014
  813'.6—dc23

                        2013039143

10 9 8 7 6 5 4 3 2 1

Printed in Canada

THIS NOVEL IS DEDICATED

to everyone who has ever lived or worked at Camp Lejeune. You've been lucky enough to be among some of the sharpest, wittiest people in the world.

CAST OF CHARACTERS

Naval Criminal Investigative Service, Camp Lejeune Field Office, and family

Special Agent in Charge Arthur Boyette
Special Agent Fran Setliff
Special Agent Peter Rumley
Special Agent Rodney Walker
Elva Walker
Special Agent Hank Bunn

Marine Corps Base, Camp Lejeune, and family

General David Wallace, Marine Corps commandant
Colonel Ralph Schoengraf
Brigadier General Amesly Johnson, base commanding officer
Theresa Johnson
Wallace "Wally" Johnson
Colonel Bob Knightdale, chief of staff

Marissa Knightdale

Colonel Mel Hampshire

Major St. Legere, General Johnson's staff secretary

Captain Rhonda Baptiste, aide to General Johnson

Captain Patsy Wilson

Carolyn Holdsclaw, General Johnson's personal secretary

Captain Vic Maldonado, special assistant to the United States
    attorney, Office of the Staff Judge Advocate

Commander Kevin Terry, Navy psychiatrist

Private First Class Jervet Harriman

Charmaine Roundtree, civilian director of Human Services

Daily Observer staff and family

George Griffin, editor

Ann Markham Buckhalter, former columnist

Lieutenant Colonel Gary Buckhalter, Marine Corps retired

Libby Buckhalter

Dierdre Buckhalter

Dale Buckhalter

Lowell Mapp, military reporter

Clay Konnecker, police reporter

Vance Aygarten, former military reporter

Others

Nita Highlock Donning

Hugh Donning

Paul Donning

Gifford Pfeister

Jane Sherbourne

B.O.Q.

ONE.

SUNDAY

Naval Criminal Investigative Service special agent Fran Setliff drove to the fatal-incident scene as cautiously as surging adrenaline and a jabbing bra underwire allowed. Victoria wasn't so hot at keeping things secret after all.

She slowed and dimmed her lights at the Sneads Ferry gate so the Marine guard could read her base sticker before waving her through. She assumed that however the dead woman at the Camp Lejeune Bachelor Officers' Quarters got that way, her body had already been taken to the Naval Hospital morgue. If the Navy doctor acting as medical examiner had pronounced the body dead, that is. According to regulations, the victim wasn't really dead until the Navy doc said so. Fran had heard of a case in which a corpsman had to perform cardiac resuscitation on a decapitated body for twenty minutes because the medical examiner got stuck in traffic.

She wondered if the crime scene at the B.O.Q. was disorganized or organized—or, as a fellow agent put it, "splatty or natty." Fran's experience with gore was limited to crime-scene photos she'd seen as part of her sixteen-week course at the Federal Law Enforcement Training Command at Glynco, Georgia. It was truly mind-boggling what people could do to each other. Of course, she'd witnessed a few unappetizing sights during the two years she spent in the Sylacauga, Alabama, police department before going back to school. But the split scalps and non-lethal gunshot wounds she'd seen were the results of plain old foolishness. People drinking, doping, fighting, fornicating, and aggrandizing themselves. Most of the time, as soon as libidos and tempers cooled and sobriety settled in, the perpetrators wished they'd done things differently.

It was the same kind of idiocy that had led her to marry Marlon. Even after she stayed upright long enough to realize Marlon had multiple character flaws, she intended to stick it out. But then she caught him in Grandmama Pattle's harp-back rocker at three o'clock in the morning—buck-naked as when he made love to Fran three hours earlier—performing verbal cunnilingus on some giggly woman at the other end of the telephone line.

After they divorced, Fran turned over enough new leaves to mulch all of Coosa County. She earned a degree in psychology and criminology, on the reasoning that the demand for good people in law enforcement wasn't going to let up. "There'll always be jackasses in this world, so I'll always have a job," she assured herself.

She heard about the Naval Criminal Investigative Service from a classmate who'd just finished a hitch in the Marines as a military policeman. The Marines she already knew about. Her dad had freeze-dried a few of his toes in Korea and still headed up his reserve unit's annual Toys for Tots campaign. He had his old dress blues retailored to wear to her wedding. There was no expiration date to being a Marine.

The classmate explained that NCIS was made up of civilian agents who investigated serious crimes on Navy and Marine Corps bases. Fran's ears had pricked up at the civilian part because, frankly, getting back into a polyester uniform had all the allure of a hog lagoon. Which ended up being an irony because the white shirts, blue suits, and black shoes for NCIS agents were as much a uniform as camouflage utilities.

She told herself she was fitting in well at Lejeune. She had the kind of baby-sister cuteness—freckles, curly hair just this side of auburn, big brown eyes—that wouldn't repulse anybody but didn't make many circle back for a second leer either. She was sort of a femme non-fatale. Fran was vain enough to be proud that she looked terrific without any clothes on, but she hadn't known how to work that information into her civil-service application. Though not tall, she was extremely fit. That was part genetics and part having five brothers with whom to work out the pecking order. In her basic law-enforcement class, she'd earned the nickname "Monk" because she could scurry up a rope with simian ease. And she could do five pull-ups from a straight-arm hang without kipping. She was a one of a kind: the only female NCIS special agent at Lejeune, bound and determined to bring honor to her gender.

The thirty-six other special agents at Lejeune were assigned to such areas as crimes against persons, narcotics, and theft of government property. Fran was assigned to white-collar crime, which mostly involved bad checks and shoplifting at the Base Exchange but had been known to include investigating contract kickbacks totaling thousands of dollars. Lately, computer hacking was becoming a component of all of the above. But when something especially noxious happened, like a dead woman at the B.O.Q., the special agent in charge would schedule an all-hands meeting like the one slated for that very evening. Beforehand, all available agents were encouraged to visit the incident scene and soak up general impressions.

Fran assumed base commanding general Amesly Johnson already

was informed and digging a damage-control trench. It was the worst possible scenario, from a public-relations standpoint: dead woman in an officers' guest suite on base. Fran wasn't yet clear on whether the victim was active duty or civilian, but if she was a legitimate guest at the B.O.Q., she was either an officer or an officer's dependent. And base officials liked to preserve the notion that womankind was well protected within that residue of Southern chivalry known as the commissioned ranks.

Fortunately for investigators, the several buildings comprising the Bachelor Officers' Quarters were not on a main artery through the base. That stretch of Seth Williams Boulevard mostly served the two-story houses and shady lots assigned to families of field-grade officers.

By the time Fran parked (illegally) on the street in front of the Officers' Club, the entry drive to the adjacent B.O.Q. buildings had been cordoned off. Two MPs were diverting resident rubberneckers through the feeder road between the day-care center and Engine Company 4 of the base fire department.

No civilian media yet. But Fran would bet anything that reporters were already cluster-bombing their whiny selves next to the main gate. But they wouldn't dare try sidestepping base protocol. It was two years since Operation Desert Storm had liberated Kuwait and shooed Saddam Hussein back to Iraq, yet the strict controls on press access to the base that went into effect during that conflict had outlasted it.

Fran figured the military reporter at the local paper, the *Daily Observer*, knew better than to do any reckless nose-thumbing. As the only civilian daily in a circulation area that was almost all military connected, it had to do a dainty dance. If a subscriber wasn't a Marine, he or she was the daughter, nephew, or widow of a Marine. Or a retired Marine. Or a USO volunteer. Or all of the above. Notable exceptions included the publisher, editor, and military reporter for the *Daily Observer*. Which meant reporting anything negative about the Corps ran the risk of making the paper appear hostile or insensitive to the Few and the Proud.

Oh, Lord, Fran thought as she tiptoed through pine needles and bark mulch. *The commanding general's here.* His official white Plymouth with star-studded red flags on opposite sides of the hood was in his reserved spot at the main entrance to the O Club. The sergeant who served as his driver was standing alongside, neck stretched out like he was readying himself for the hangman. Something next to the river had his full attention.

Holy shit! The chief of staff, too! Their presence meant her boss's arterial pressure would be off the charts. He hated having to tolerate tours of a possible crime scene by personnel who were not responsible for the investigation. There was too much chance for contamination.

Officially, Special Agent in Charge Arthur Boyette had the authority to keep God Almighty away from a potential crime scene. But in reality, stopping a commanding general would be as laughably futile as Wile E. Coyote trying to stop that oncoming anvil. Fran smiled just to imagine the request: *General, I must insist you keep your distance from my crime scene. Might I respectfully suggest you return to your quarters and screw yourself with a 155-millimeter shell casing?*

TWO.

Fran stopped at the yellow tape barrier surrounding the newly erected command tent. The flap facing the B.O.Q. was rolled up, but she hesitated to step over the crime-scene tape without letting whomever was in charge know she was there.

"Setliff! Another weekend without a date?" Special Agent Peter Rumley popped his head out of the shadows and motioned her around the tape. His remark wasn't meant as an insult, merely an observation. It was a given that any woman near a Marine base who didn't have a date wanted it that way.

"Look where dating got you, Rum." Rumley was the father of five. "Anybody identified the victim yet?"

"Not officially. Her husband's been notified and is on his way. He's a retired lieutenant colonel. They live outside Raleigh."

"How'd she die?"

"Not sure yet. Drowned is a good first guess."

"Drowned? I thought she died in her room."

"That's a good second guess. She was found this morning by a five-year-old staying there." He pointed out the center building facing the parking lot. "The little girl was on the pier with her dad, a captain. He was going to take the kid to Burger King for breakfast while Mom slept in. The kid was running back and forth. Dad was mostly just standing by, letting her blow off steam before they got in the car. Suddenly, the kid started jumping up and down, yelling for her dad to come see, said she'd found a mermaid. Dad went to where the kid was, looked in the water, and saw a woman's body floating face up, with only her legs sticking out from under the pier."

Rumley and Setliff walked as near the water as they could get without impeding the Military Police photographer triangulating on the pier.

"I don't know much about water," Fran said, "but the current looks brisk. Couldn't she have floated down from somewhere else?"

"It doesn't look like she came far. Apparently, her hair was tangled in an old crab trap whose buoy lines had wrapped themselves around one of the pier pilings. The water's not more than chest-high there. Seems like she could have pulled herself loose. As it was, the captain tried to pull her out. Thought maybe she was still alive, said he had to tear out some of her hair to get her free of that trap. By that time, the kid woke up the wife, and she helped haul the body up on dry land. Once they took a look, they knew there wasn't much point starting CPR. The wife had already called 911, which got relayed to the MPs and the hospital. The dead woman had a room key in her pocket. Her ID was in her purse, in the room."

Took her key with her but not her purse, Fran thought. That meant she planned on going back to the room. And she hadn't planned on going far.

"I didn't see the body," Rumley continued as they slow-motion hurdled the lines bracing the command tent, "but word is it was pretty banged up. Whether that happened before she hit the water or after is yet to be determined. We're checking her room on the chance she died there. Come on. I'll walk you through. Just stay on the paper, okay?"

Instinctively, they walked up the newsprint-covered stairs with hands raised, stick-'em-up style, so as not to risk touching the walls. Not that the print crew was likely to find anything useful. Presumably, thousands of visible and latent prints covered the stairwell.

Rumley chuckled. "The captain's wife is from El Salvador. The MP she talked to on the phone asked her how she was so sure the woman in the water was dead, and the wife told him she grew up in guerrilla territory. Saw more corpses than a mortician. I bet she did, too."

They both snapped up against the wall as their mutual boss, Boyette, and General Johnson came toward them. Just as Fran had thought, Boyette was fit to be tied. Not that the general would be able to tell. The only giveaways were Boyette's knotted jaw muscles and the pulsating red patch between his eyebrows. Any more obvious signs of stress were as unthinkable to Boyette as an off-center Windsor knot. He was nitpicky almost to the point of absurdity, which in his job wasn't all bad. He was also humorless and had a voice like a dentist's drill overdue for some WD-40. But he was a 180-degree improvement over the man he had replaced, who, rumor had it, tried to save the troops from associating with Jacksonville prostitutes by monopolizing them himself.

Boyette was prissy and anal, yes. But Fran would bet her retirement he was incorruptible. His word was as good as a signature witnessed by an order of notary nuns. And he wouldn't take a rubber band out of the supply closet without filling out a triplicate chit. But his fussy rigidity and pointy shoes put some agents off. They liked their superiors to have slick edges and a little dandruff. Fran was not among them. Still, as Grandmama Pattle would say, Boyette's mother must have had pickling brine in her womb.

The general, by contrast, radiated relaxed authority. Johnson was six foot five. His thick, cropped hair was reddish gray. His hazel eyes were set deep in wrinkles earned on parade fields where sunblock wasn't regulation. He sported a few scars Fran recognized as skin cancer excisions. A faint web of magenta veins fanned out over his cheeks and substantial nose. Normal warrior wear and tear. His physique was that of a man whose commitment to fitness predated his commission. He had pitched semipro ball and occasionally showed off a still-smoldering curveball in benefit games. The total package, Fran had to admit, was impressive.

Word on the street was that Johnson was being groomed as the next commandant. The street Fran got that word from was a major she had spent a few fumbly dates with before an ex-girlfriend showed up to restake her claim. Fran was skeptical about the commandant part. She gathered that being commanding general of Lejeune was like being relegated to the elephants' graveyard. It was where old generals went to wave their trunks a few more times before retiring to chase bad golf shots all over Virginia and Maryland. That was usually true, the major had explained, but Johnson had taken over Camp Lejeune as a personal favor to the current commandant, after Johnson's predecessor fell out of a twenty-five-mile company hike to have a fatal heart attack.

The scuttlebutt was that Johnson was well connected politically and expected to command the Second Marine Division in a year or so. Second Marine Division was the Corps' version of Valhalla and a traditional steppingstone to the commandant's job.

In the present circumstances—touring a possible crime scene— General Johnson was of course more subdued than usual. He greeted Fran by her first name, a distinction she took with a grain of salt. Fran knew that the general, who had no women on his command staff, took special pains to notice female officers and civil servants. She suspected he was trying to counteract buzz that suggested he was less than happy about women's expanded role in the Corps.

Fran and Rumley allowed themselves only a moment to bask in General Johnson's charisma before leaning into the room assigned to the dead woman. The evidence collection people were poring over the carpet, square foot by square foot. They used stainless-steel combs and swatches of transparent tape. Sometimes, the most effective techniques were the simplest. This one was much like removing fuzz balls off an old sweater. But there seemed to be little fuzz to collect. Nothing in the room appeared as if it had been sat on, walked on, or reclined on.

"Looks like even the dust mites in this place practice good hygiene," one of the evidence collectors remarked. "And the bedroom's just as neat. Purse on the desk, suede backpack in the middle of the bed, unzipped, with the usual overnight-stay ladies' stuff. There's a little makeup kit by the bathroom sink, but aside from one hand towel that was used and refolded, nothing's been touched. Oh, except for the plastic bag."

"Plastic bag?" Rumley said.

"Yeah, a white plastic bag. It was taken out of the bathroom wastebasket and left on the bed. It had corners poked in it, like somebody put books or a box inside. Whether that happened before or after the victim checked in is anybody's guess."

"Fran, this is Warrant Officer Baumer," Rumley interjected, "fresh from Twenty-Nine Palms, California. Anybody hear anything, warrant officer? From the next room, maybe?"

"I don't think anybody was in the next room, or in any other room in this building. She had the whole place to herself. Unless she had a visitor, of course."

"Maybe it was just some kind of accident," Fran offered.

"Well, that would sure make the general happier than the alternative. But it don't seem like something a middle-aged woman would do, does it? Fall in the river in the middle of the night and drown." The warrant officer's knees popped like vacuum jars as he rose to his feet.

"How do you know she was middle-aged? Did you see her ID?" Fran asked.

"Educated guess. Retired colonel's wife, I heard. If she's wife number one, she's probably forty at least."

"At that advanced age, could have been natural causes," Fran mumbled, then did a slow, thoughtful turn in the doorway.

The only auras Fran believed in were the kind that appeared when contact lenses caught high beams at a spooky angle. But the room did have a melancholy feel to it. She realized what she was sensing was an expensive, intensely floral perfume. The room smelled like a funeral home. She passed the observation on to Rumley, who sniffed, then smiled.

"Yeah. Funerals. Weddings. They both smell like that."

Fran stayed to observe the stoop-labor criminology while Baumer and Rumley took a smoke break. When she began to experience vicarious back spasms, she, too, left the building, passing Baumer on his way back up.

Rumley motioned her over to a compact car that looked gray-green under the parking lot lights. Techs were patting it down inside a secondary taped-off perimeter.

"That's the victim's Camry. Since you're so attuned to smells, you might detect the horse."

"Huh?"

"Baumer said the car smells like horse. Or horseshit. Is there a difference? No kidding. Not so's a normal person would notice, maybe. But Baumer's got one of those super-sensitive noses. He can tell you what the boss had for dinner last night just by getting a good whiff of whichever stall he read his morning paper in. The guy's legendary."

As she and Rumley walked away from the parking lot, they passed an MP delicately collecting the cigarette butts sprinkled around the entrance to the B.O.Q. building where the dead woman had stayed. Smoking was prohibited inside the building, so smokers staged themselves on the steps and flicked butts in a semicircle on the sidewalk. Fran found it hard to believe any killer would pause for a smoke after dumping a body in the river, but she had long ago resigned herself to the capriciousness of criminals. If Jeffrey Dahmer could keep a victim's head in his refrigerator alongside the olive loaf, anything was possible.

Ogling all those old butts and seeing Rumley tap a fresh cigarette out of the pack brought back the familiar craving. After six smoke-free months, Fran had no intention of ever lighting up again. She did, however, allow herself the pleasure of walking close to Rumley and breathing deeply of sidestream.

"Well, Rum, what do you think?"

They'd crossed the street in silence, giving themselves some physical and mental distance from the B.O.Q.

"Those guys?" Rumley blew smoke toward the agents loading evidence cases into the official Cherokee that would transport them to Lejeune's NCIS field office. "Spinning their wheels, probably. The medical examiner will decide it was an accidental drowning. All their little glassine bags will go in storage for a while, then get shit-canned. That's what General Johnson is hoping for." He exhaled a ribbon of toxins. "Most of what we do ends up being a waste of time anyway. That's the nature of the business. Twenty dead ends for every off ramp. I can live with that. I just don't like the idea that a dumbass general might be trying to direct the flow of traffic."

"Jeez, Rumley, that's the most metaphor you've ever crammed into one of your depressing speeches."

"You asked, little girl. So, what do you think?"

"Maybe it's just the aura of horseshit and funerals, but I'm sensing the general's not going to get what he's hoping for."

THREE.

The Naval Criminal Investigative Service at Camp Lejeune shared a building with the Provost Marshal's Office. The provost marshal was the Marine officer, typically a colonel, in charge of the Military Police. The arrangement was logical because MPs usually were the first to arrive at a crime scene, even if the case ultimately became the responsibility of NCIS. The arrangement was not, however, popular with agents.

Accommodations for Arthur Boyette and his investigators, on the second floor, were austere, to put it kindly. No matter how many times base workers painted the bulkheads the requisite nuthouse green and waxed the buckled linoleum floor, the place smelled like the boys' locker room at a mold-ridden middle school. NCIS was slated for slicker quarters, once renovations at old Hospital Point were complete. The facilities shuffle was an ongoing dance at any military base.

One thing about Boyette's meetings: They were sure to start on time. Fran got a chair only because another agent had eaten four burritos for dinner and had been warned he could stand in the hall or get a note on his fitness report about his "social awareness."

It's like a gathering of the law-enforcement clan, Fran thought proudly. The one room at the field office big enough to qualify as a "conference room" was wall-to-wall agents and MPs.

Boyette was at the lectern, one pointed toe tapping against its scuffed base. He was snapping his pointer like a Dickensian schoolmaster against one of the few real blackboards left in the First World.

Fifteen special agents were squeezed shoulder to shoulder on folding chairs. Colonel Bob Knightdale, General Johnson's chief of staff, was sitting up front near Boyette, presumably representing the general. He had the good chair. No duct tape crisscrossing torn vinyl for him.

The provost marshal, Lieutenant Colonel Jimmy O'Dell, was unconsciously knotting hangman's nooses in every venetian blind cord within his reach. Even among Marines, celebrated for their one-of-a-kind characters, Top Cop O'Dell was a standout. For years, he had sold homemade hot sauce out of the PMO. Buyers of "North Carolina Napalm" were assured that 10 percent of every purchase, after expenses, went to the Navy Relief Fund. Nobody ever asked about the other 90 percent. As provost marshal, O'Dell had no real role in the investigation; NCIS automatically assumed serious cases. But as a courtesy, and to assure the rumor mill was not O'Dell's only source of information, the base's top cop was included in some NCIS briefings. To his credit, O'Dell was reliably discreet about official business.

Also present were the Joint Public Affairs officer, Lieutenant Colonel Garland Chek, and Captain Vic Maldonado, who worked for the staff judge advocate.

Chek would have the thankless job of defanging bad news and passing it on in the form of bland press releases. There was no way to pretty-up this one, even if the death was accidental. If it wasn't, the most the general could wish for was a successful investigation yielding an expendable perpetrator, preferably a civilian. If the perpetrator was a Marine, the base would just have to roll with it and be grateful if the culprit hadn't been awarded a good-conduct medal or recently been handpicked for some special assignment.

Because Marine lawyer Vic Maldonado also acted as special assistant to the United States attorney, he would be the prosecutor if the death involved foul play and the accused was a civilian.

In the matter of Vic Maldonado, Fran tried not to get all squirmy with frustration. His lushly swarthy looks made him perfect fantasy material for a woman raised in a family of freckled towheads. In the blink of a feverish eye, he could alternate fantasy roles as sheik, gaucho, and Polynesian fire dancer. His eyes were clear and lustrous as high-viscosity motor oil, his hair as clean and shiny as Corfam. If these weren't sufficient swoon stimulants, he was also a damn decent guy.

Fran was first drawn to him when their respective agencies had volunteered to help children participating in the Special Olympics, held at the base's main parade field. What impressed her about Maldonado was how completely at-ease he was. How thoroughly he enjoyed himself. She herself felt mostly pity, both for the children and their parents. Captain Vic Maldonado was either a better person or a better actor than she was.

The only other time she'd spent more than thirty seconds in his presence was at a criminal justice seminar at which he lectured about search and seizure. He had asked her out for a cup of coffee afterward, but some obligation forced her to refuse. He hadn't asked her out again. Admittedly, a cultural chasm yawned between them. He wore a pinkie ring, for instance. In Alabama, that was on par with a man buying his skivvies at Frederick's of Hollywood. Grandmama Pattle would think his greatest disadvantage was his place of origin, New York. Grandmama Pattle once remarked that Yankees talked too fast to make good husbands. "A man who talks that fast just naturally says more things he can't take back."

Fran knew only that Maldonado was as unlike ex-husband Marlon as a man could be. She had wasted a few hours since the seminar plotting how she could get the handsome lawyer to ask her out again. Eventually, she gave up. He'd probably noticed her in the first place because, to him, she looked like an exotic example of *Redneckus backwaterus*.

Maldonado was not particularly popular. Most Marine lawyers weren't. In the Corps, any male not in a military specialty based on shooting, larynx crushing, or eye gouging was considered a second-stringer. She'd often overheard legal officers referred to by that most condescending of Marine epithets, "faggot."

Everyone in the conference room except for Chief of Staff Knightdale, who looked tired and troubled, was emotionally wired. Here before them was the opportunity to take everything they'd learned and work wonders in the name of justice. It was also a prime opportunity to really fuck up.

Arthur Boyette didn't waste time with motivational drivel. To Boyette, anybody who needed motivating was a liability waiting to be weeded out. As usual in big cases, he had included everybody in this initial meeting. He wanted to avoid the elbowing for position that could poison an investigation if everyone wasn't clear about his area of responsibility.

"The victim's name is Ann Markham Buckhalter. A white female, forty-two years old. According to her driver's license, she was five foot six and weighed 130 pounds."

Which means she really weighed 140, Fran thought. She jotted that number down.

"Mrs. Buckhalter was married to Lieutenant Colonel Gary Buckhalter, who retired from the engineer school eighteen months ago. Both Colonel Knightdale and General Johnson knew the Buckhalters personally. I'm sure a number of others still on active duty knew them, too. Maybe even somebody else in this room. I offer my sympathies to all."

He dipped his chin to Knightdale, who responded in kind.

"Please be aware of this when you conduct your interviews. You may be speaking to someone who bunked next to Buckhalter in Officer Candidate School or was an usher at his wedding. Be even more tactful and genteel than you usually are."

Scattered smirks at that one.

"After Lieutenant Colonel Buckhalter retired, they bought a house in Raleigh. He is at the hospital officially identifying his wife as we speak but will be available for an interview later this evening. I've spoken to him briefly. He says his wife left for Lejeune at about noon Saturday. They have one child, a fifteen-year-old daughter, Deirdre.

"The clerk who was on duty when Mrs. Buckhalter checked into her room is a retired staff noncommissioned officer named Tom Boatwright. He says the woman arrived yesterday afternoon at 1500. She didn't seem upset or agitated in any way. Apparently, Mrs. Buckhalter stayed on base once a month or so. Boatwright is putting together a list of specific times and dates.

"The clerk, Boatwright, had seen her often enough to know her by name when she signed in. In the past, he said, she'd mentioned stocking up at the commissary, stopping by the PX pharmacy to pick up prescriptions, and, once, meeting an old friend. He said she was always alone when she checked in and, although he wasn't there when she checked out, the log shows that was usually late Sunday morning."

Fran was taking notes that would be legible only to herself. Several of the agents had microcassette recorders running. So far, nothing Boyette had said about the victim was extraordinary. Including Mrs. Buckhalter's staying at Lejeune by herself. Contrary to the stereotype of the browbeaten camp follower, most of the officers' wives Fran had known were independent and tough as pig iron under their Liz Claiborne sportswear. The wailing women who showed up on the television news every time a unit was deployed to somewhere dicier than, say, the base bowling alley were invariably married to low-ranking enlisted men. They were often young women with few resources, little education, and practically no idea what their husbands did for a living. The kicker was that, meanwhile, the husbands, while expressing sometimes genuine regret at being separated from their wives and children, had that unmistakable gleam in their eyes. "Stick it in! Watch him bleed! *Oo-rah!*" They were already easing one combat-booted foot out the door.

Fran had heard that retirement could be a shock for couples used to lots of spaces in their togetherness. It might be worth asking why Ann Buckhalter had chosen to spend the night at Camp Lejeune instead of driving home.

"Until we are absolutely certain this death was accidental, we're going to proceed as if foul play may have been involved." Boyette's dental-drill voice bore through her reflections. "I'd rather we get accused of overkill than of underestimating the seriousness of the case. If you haven't seen the room where she was staying—716—and familiarized yourself with the area where the body was found, please do so.

"The desk clerk on duty at the B.O.Q. last night was Mrs. Bonita Arbalaez. I know Mrs. Arbalaez. She is the wife of a sergeant currently stationed in Pusan. She is four foot eleven in all directions and teaches my son's catechism class at Infant of Prague. One of you will be assigned to take her official statement. Be gentle. Make her walk through everything she did, heard, saw, said, and sensed. You might have to join her in a few Hail Marys, but just play along.

"Also," Boyette continued, "we will interview every Officers' Club employee and guest who was there last night. Get the club manager to pull all the checks and charge-card receipts and club tabs. I want everybody. Start from the top, so we won't end up duplicating efforts.

"Mrs. Buckhalter made one phone call from room 716, about thirty minutes after she checked in. The call was to the Naval Hospital office of Commander Kevin Terry." Boyette nodded toward an agent in the front row. "Walker, I'm putting you in charge of this one. Keep in mind that Commander Terry could be an old friend of the Buckhalters, and you may be the first he hears about the death."

So, the Navy's in it now, Fran thought. Commander. Naval Hospital. That meant doctor, dentist, or chaplain. It was unlikely the victim had called Terry in connection with medical treatment. Retirees and their dependents were so far down the priority list nowadays that military doctors rarely saw them. Only active-duty personnel got tinkered with by the Navy. Retirees got Tricare—Medicare for the mustered-out.

Most likely, Ann Buckhalter would have gone to a private doctor for any health problem. It was possible Commander Terry was a chaplain, although it seemed unlikely Ann had driven all the way from Raleigh on a Saturday afternoon just to get her soul serviced.

"Mrs. Buckhalter had a press card in her purse. Apparently, she is—was—connected to the *Daily Observer*, here in Jacksonville," Boyette said. "Setliff, I want you to take this one, but first I'd like to give you some deep. In my office."

Nobody in the room so much as twitched. They didn't dare. "To give deep" was Boyette's way of saying "to give unofficial background information." Boyette was immune to double entendres. Or he was the greatest straight man since Bud Abbott.

"Stand by for a few minutes after we adjourn here," Boyette told her.

"Certainly, sir."

Shit. Fran stifled a spurt of disappointment. If she had to be included in this one, she would prefer a role with a little more voltage. She already knew why Ann Markham Buckhalter had a press card. She had been a highly visible member of the local media. Two years earlier, when Fran first came to Lejeune, Ann Markham was an editor and columnist for the paper. Her maiden-name byline explained why Fran hadn't realized who Ann was at first. It wouldn't be much of a surprise if Ann had kept a few ties to the *Daily Observer*.

Fran had just started to pound her peg into a comfortable hole at her Lejeune job when Ann Markham resigned from the paper to write a book—something for children, if Fran remembered rightly. That must have been about the same time Ann's husband, Lieutenant Colonel Buckhalter, retired. The paper had rerun Ann's "most popular" columns for months after her departure. Fran had scanned one or two until all that sappiness sent her blood sugar into the coma-sphere. The columns were mostly maudlin goop about how a Marine's wife should be "the star shining over your soldier-of-the-sea." Sort of Norman Vincent Peale getting it on with Molly Pitcher. Atop a manure pile.

Fran hadn't been impressed with Ann Markham, columnist.

FOUR.

MONDAY

Boyette's meeting lasted until midnight, although the number of participants dwindled as one and then another was excused to set up interviews. By the time Fran and Boyette walked down the hall to his office, she was on her fourth mug of coffee and experiencing caffeine flashbacks. Her tongue was coated with sludge, and her contact lenses felt like Frisbees. She didn't know why she kept drinking the damn stuff. Drinking coffee when she was tired just made her really alert to how tired she was.

Boyette looked pretty zonked, too. The fluorescent overhead light did its dirty work on both of them. He sat, then preemptively apologized before propping his feet on his desk. He'd been standing for five hours, he explained. She sat across from his desk, although she'd have preferred to stand. She'd been sitting almost as long as he'd been standing.

His phone began ringing immediately.

"Yes, I know who she is," he said, plaiting his eyebrows together with his fingers. "Let's assume that's peripheral for the moment. If we can leave a little breathing room between the two incidents, it'll be easier on the family and us as well. Okay. Sure." He hung up and forwarded the line to voice mail.

"I'm sorry to keep you, Fran. To the point: Have you ever met George Griffin? No? Well, I guess the world's not necessarily that small. Griffin is editor of the *Daily Observer*. That means he's the one with final say over what appears in the paper. I can't convince the general that Paul Vogelsang—Vogelsang is publisher—does not know diddly-squat about what goes on in the newsroom. Just because he's the one who represents the paper at golf tournaments does not mean he makes editorial decisions. Griffin is the brains. Vogelsang keeps tabs on the money. As long as there's money to keep tabs on, Vogelsang is happy to leave everything else to Griffin."

Fran must have had a surprised look on her face, although it could have been caffeine overdose.

Boyette gingerly shifted his feet. "The reason I know about this is because I used to head up public affairs for a dysfunctional city police department. I learned a few things about the newspaper business out of self-preservation. Griffin is the person you need to talk to. Word is, he's a fair man. But he has only a secondhand understanding of the military. He and our public affairs guys have locked horns once or twice. Which is to be expected. They want all the grit and grime. We don't want anybody to know there is any grit and grime."

Fran had heard of a few clashes. What the base Public Affairs Office was peddling that the civilian media weren't buying was the idea that any bad publicity about the Corps threatened military morale. Which threatened readiness. Which threatened national security. Which threatened world peace. Which threatened the Star Fleet, she supposed. That explained why the story about a Marine being court-martialed for a series of sexual assaults got front-page coverage in the *Daily Observer* and a tiny inside paragraph in the base's paper, the *Globe*. In fact, after reading the base's version, readers couldn't be sure whether the guy went to Leavenworth for a dozen rapes or mooning some teenagers in the park.

"Should I call Griffin directly or go through Public Affairs?" Fran asked Boyette.

"Call him directly. Just let our guys know what you're doing. But don't get drawn into discussing any particulars with JPAO. They're not part of the investigation." Boyette pulled off his glasses and pinched the bridge of his nose. "Approach this interview like a minefield. I believe Ann Buckhalter was feeding Griffin information about Lejeune she wasn't authorized to share."

"What makes you think that, sir?"

"Hell, it's obvious. Prophylactics made by porcupines couldn't have as many leaks as this base. We've got privates calling the paper complaining because base housing won't let their six Rottweilers live in their cracker-box quarters with them. More serious, we've got women calling the paper instead of the MPs to report their Marine husbands are beating them up. And even more serious, we've got people privy to confidential military information who never outgrew being the third-grade tattletale. Mrs. Buckhalter had a special reason for passing dirt to the paper. It was career enhancing."

He raised his palms in response to Fran's raised eyebrows.

"I don't want to speak ill of the dead. No matter what she did, she didn't deserve to end up like this. But I want you to know what you're walking into. During the Gulf War, the local rag, with zero correspondents in the Middle East, knew more about troop movements than Schwarzkopf himself. The press people had the good sense to hold their water until base Public Affairs gave 'em the go-ahead to print, but it was obvious they knew more than they could have gotten through official channels. Ann Buckhalter was the only officer's wife in the newsroom at the time. She was also one of the liaisons for the Support Our Troops committee in town. So she got invited to a lot of Key Wife teas at General Ostman's quarters. Where, I suspect, Mrs. Ostman relayed the latest she'd heard from her husband in Kuwait City."

Key Wives had acted as information checkpoints for other wives in their husbands' units during Desert Storm.

"If that's true, Mrs. Ostman wasn't very savvy," Fran said.

Boyette shrugged. "She probably viewed Ann as a fellow Marine wife, somebody who put the Corps first, like she did. I didn't know Mrs. Ostman, but I've heard she played the part of empress consort to the hilt. If her husband felt she was enough of an unofficial co-commander to be privy to intel, then she, in her role as spokeswoman for him, felt authorized to decide what to share and whom to share it with." He kicked his chair back from the desk. "Knowledge really is power, Fran. And loose lips really do sink ships."

"What about Lieutenant Colonel Buckhalter?"

"What about him?"

"Didn't he have any idea all this double-dealing was going on?"

"Buckhalter was buried at the engineering school at Courthouse Bay, part of a course restructuring team. Buckhalter was far, far away—literally and figuratively—from the units involved in the war."

"But wouldn't he know what Ann was up to? Didn't he and his wife talk to each other?"

Boyette smiled. "She was literally and figuratively far away, too, I expect. Engineers aren't known for their pillow-talk skills, Setliff."

Fran glanced toward the window. Outside, some of the MP drug-sniffing dogs fired off sharp barks from their kennels.

"I know you're as exhausted as I am," Boyette said, swinging his feet to the floor with a grimace. "But there's something else. Something I don't think the paper's gotten wind of yet. Apparently, Ann was much more protective of information related to her own family."

"Sir?"

"Ann had a fifteen-year-old daughter. Deirdre. Until about a month ago, she was just another retired officer's kid who showed up regularly at the base stables. Horse crazy, like a lot of girls that age. Her feelings for the place may have changed when an MP cruiser found her running across Stone Street at 0100 with a Marine in close pursuit. She was screaming. Her clothes—and his—were 'in disarray,' as they say."

Marines were routinely pulled from their permanent jobs for six-month assignments with Morale Welfare Recreation. Those in the Fleet Assistance Program—FAPS—acted as gate sentries, staffed the base gyms, worked at the animal shelters. Some of the duties were especially desirable for particular Marines: weightlifters and bodybuilders readying for competition who needed more hours in the gym or, in the case of the stables, Marines sharpening their rodeo skills or wanting to organize a mounted color guard.

"The Marine, Private First Class Jervet Harriman, is restricted to barracks," Boyette said. "He may be charged with carnal knowledge—statutory rape, in the civilian world—or he may be charged with rape."

"Good God, sir, shouldn't he be in the brig?"

"He was. For a couple of days. Then his battalion commander convinced the magistrate at the brig to turn him over."

"Pretty unusual, isn't it, considering the seriousness of the charges?"

"It's an unusual situation all around, Setliff. Harriman's not denying something happened. He says the Buckhalter girl told him she was seventeen and that one of her girlfriends backed her up. But Deirdre's father has been pushing hard to hurt this guy. He claims Harriman should have known how old Deirdre was because he helped keep track of sign-ins at the stables and had seen her ID many times."

Fran could see why Ann wouldn't have shared this particular on-base episode with her fellow journalists. "What was Deirdre doing there at that hour? I assume Harriman didn't kidnap her."

"Kidnap her? Hell, he doesn't even own a bicycle. Oh, she admits meeting him voluntarily. Deirdre was supposed to be spending the night on base with a girlfriend—no doubt, the same one who lied to Harriman about Deirdre's age. The friend lives in one of the Capeharts on Cukela Street, within walking distance of the stables. Deirdre sneaked out. Met Harriman at the corner of Stone Street. They walked to the stables. Nobody was there at night. A couple of dogs, who'd know Harriman, of course. Harriman claims he and Deirdre were making out by mutual consent. Yes, he thought they were about to have intercourse in the empty stall. Suddenly, she started screaming, pushed him off, and ran out of the barn. He went after her. Not to force her to continue the act, he says, but to calm her and keep her from hurting herself."

"And she says?" Fran asked.

"That's why no charges have been filed yet. She's told more than one version of what happened. She claims she doesn't know whether they had intercourse, that he hurt her, that he didn't hurt her. She told him to stop, she didn't tell him to stop."

"Was she injured?"

"The medical exam said no, except for the kinds of superficial bumps and scratches you'd get from rolling around bare-assed on hay. She claims she was a virgin until that evening. Years of competitive horseback riding make that a difficult call, too. No semen inside her, however. . . ."

"Sir?"

"The Marine was wearing a, uh . . . used condom when the MP found them. Harriman swears he ejaculated before penetration. And that there was no penetration."

"Is that likely?"

"He's nineteen, Setliff. Driving over a pothole could make him ejaculate."

"You seem ambivalent about this, boss."

"I myself haven't spoken to any of the parties concerned. But Harriman's sergeant apparently went to bat for this guy. He told the investigator Harriman is as tender as veal. Hasn't shown concern for anything but the girl's well-being ever since it happened. He's even offered to marry her, for God's sake. On the other hand, the agent who interviewed Miss Buckhalter says—unofficially, mind you—that she's one of the most beautiful girls he's ever seen. Also, one of the most loosely woven basket cases."

"And Ann knew about this, of course."

"Of course. But there hasn't been a query from the paper, despite its fondness for stories about Marines who rape. That suggests Ann kept mum. Or that Griffin knows and has held back, out of concern for Ann's feelings. With Ann dead, he may decide to forge ahead. Anyway, I wanted you to know what's going on in case he starts poking around the Harriman matter when you talk to him."

"Good Lord, sir, do you think Ann was so upset about what happened to her daughter that she threw herself in the river?"

"I guess anything is possible. But think about it, Setliff. If she loved her daughter, would she bail out just when the kid needed her most?"

Fran blinked frantically, trying to juice up her gummy contact lenses.

"Go home, Setliff. Get some sleep. Arrange that interview with Griffin. Tape it, if possible. Report back to me by phone before typing it up or talking to anybody else."

ooooo

It was 0100 when she pulled off the Swansboro exit ramp. When she slowed for the light at Bellflower Street, it occurred to her that the newspaper might be open. Didn't the presses run in the middle of the night? A little detour wouldn't make her eyes any baggier in the morning.

Yep. Floodlights on. A trio of smokers puffing away beneath an over-hang on the side of the building. A couple of beat-up delivery vans with their motors idling. She considered stopping but decided against it. In twenty minutes, she'd be home. She'd call from there.

As soon as she locked the door behind her, Fran scraped the con-tacts off her parched eyeballs and fumbled blearily for her bedside phone. She knew the number because it was on all the *Daily Observer*'s vending machines. The same prefix as hers, followed by the four digits that spelled "news." Cute. The number rang enough times for Fran to start dozing before someone picked up.

"Newsroom," a man's voice said.

"Is Mr. Griffin there, please?"

"Hold on."

Unbelievable luck.

"Griffin here. May I help you?" A good voice. A Southern voice. A bourbon-and-burning-pine-knots voice.

"Mr. Griffin, this is Special Agent Fran Setliff with the Naval Crim-inal Investigative Service. When would it be convenient for me to talk to you about Ann Buckhalter?"

"Ms. Setliff, you read my mind. We just got word the base Public Affairs Office is putting out a press release tomorrow morning. All I got in response to my query this evening was that a woman was found dead in the Paradise Point Bachelor Officers' Quarters." Bourbon and wood smoke fanned by nervous energy. "We're pretty shook about this thing."

How did you know the dead woman was Ann? Fran wondered. "Is there a time tomorrow when we can meet?"

Fran braced herself for a little territorial hedging. But no.

"Yes, of course. If you hadn't called, I planned to call you. I agree it's important we talk. Can you be here at eight?"

She didn't push Griffin for more information, preferring to get an-swers from people she could see. And she was just too damn tired. She'd been up since four, when her cat had awakened her by sucking on her ear. Fran suspected the cat was brain-damaged, but with a cat, diagnosis was tricky. She hadn't minded getting up so early because she assumed she'd be able to take a Sunday-afternoon nap. She wouldn't make that mistake again.

After ambushing the cat in the laundry hamper, she locked him in the utility room. If he started regressing to kittenhood in there, he would just have to suck the gas valve on the water heater. At that point, all she wanted was to sleep undisturbed for what was left of the night. She peeled off her pantyhose and shucked her jacket before collapsing onto her bedspread. She could feel makeup settling in her pores like tub caulk and the plaque on her teeth rising like yeast, but she didn't care.

The room began to shift, mirage-like. For some reason, she was levitating above a general's staff car, tethered to the car's red flag by her hair, wrapped in a ruffled bedspread that flared around her feet like a mermaid's tail. Whoever was in the car wasn't paying attention to her. "A woman's body was found in the river," she insisted to the heedless driver. "She worked for the newspaper, and things are still cozy with them because she tells them secrets. Her daughter was maybe raped by this nice young Marine who can shoot at a pothole with hardly any provocation. The daughter is a knockout but lost her virginity to a horse, sir. Sir?"

Fran floated free and drifted into peaceful insensibility. It was all good until her alarm went off at six.

FIVE.

Some agents claimed it was best to make interview subjects come to Lejeune, where, uneasy in the unfamiliar setting, they might feel intimidated and blurt stuff out in an effort to please. But Fran figured people were as likely to be intimidated into blurting out lies as the truth, so what was the point? On the other hand, less anxious subjects might slip in a few truths without even noticing. She therefore preferred to interview people in their natural habitat.

She'd driven by the *Daily Observer* building many times but had never been inside. The place was amazingly unsecured. She walked right in the front door and through a dark, empty lobby. Even the lights on the artificial Christmas tree were turned off. According to a sign posted on one interior door, the business office did not open until nine. She couldn't resist jiggling the handle to confirm that that department, at least, was locked. Nothing else was. Glass doors stenciled with "Classified Advertising" and "Marketing" were actually ajar.

By contrast, the glass door to the newsroom framed an almost hallucinogenic light show. A dozen eerily lit computer screens projected flying toasters, psycho-spirals, and shooting stars into the surrounding murkiness. In the far corner of the cavernous room, a glass-walled cubicle glowed like an aquarium. She assumed the man in the see-through office was George Griffin. He looked up when the newsroom door gave out a gasping wheeze as Fran opened it.

From a distance, Griffin's thick, well-groomed hair and rounded face could have belonged to a twenty-something. But as he got up and came toward her, one hand extended while the other hit a bank of switches that turned on the overhead lights, Fran doubled her first estimate.

Griffin's smile was ingratiating, his eyes a baby-rattle blue. He led her into the see-through aquarium, where he offered her a seat on a butt-sprung red vinyl couch. He sat in a swivel chair behind his desk and began unconsciously to rock. Fran had seen the mannerism before. It was good old nervous energy and not symptomatic of anything pathological. An observer, however, could get seasick trying to maintain eye contact with one of these perpetual motion machines.

Fran had decided not to use a tape recorder. She found the gizmos distracting. When she used one, she tended to keep glancing at the damn thing to make sure she flipped the cassette over in time.

She and Griffin got through the too-bad-about-Ann stuff quickly. Then came the mental tossup for which of them got to pump the other for information first. Fran won. After all, her team had the deceased and soon would have the autopsy. She was in a much better bargaining position.

"When I spoke to you last night, Mr. Griffin, you not only knew there was a body but that the dead woman was Ann Buckhalter. How did you come by that information?"

"Educated guesses. Our military reporter, Lowell Mapp, knew Ann planned to stop by the paper this weekend. She often did. Ann still wrote an occasional piece for us. When he didn't hear from her, Lowell assumed she'd changed her mind or gotten tangled up somewhere else."

Fran scoured Griffin's wide-open face. *No irony intended,* she thought.

"The next day—yesterday—our police reporter heard the MPs call for help over the scanner. White female. In the river. Paradise Point. Code whatever. Dead."

Fran knew the provost marshal would piss buckshot over that. A constant code-breaking contest went on between the local media and the Military Police. Unlike the civilian police, whose codes dated back to Hammurabi, the MPs frequently changed theirs, expressly to avoid what had happened here: the newspaper finding out about something before the base Public Affairs Office put out an official press release.

What worked in the base's favor, according to the MPs, was the natural tendency of reporters to be lazy. They didn't want to look up the code every time something unfamiliar came over the scanner. And because dispatchers usually sounded emotionally flat-lined, listeners couldn't tell whether or not they were relaying something earth shaking. A squirrel down someone's chimney? Someone's neighbor disembow-eled? The vocal inflection was the same.

The weak link in the base's strategy was local civilian law enforce-ment. Because criminal activity so often crisscrossed both civilian and military turf, it was necessary for each to know the other's codes. But the civilian police were much more laid back about the press. They pulled up the drawbridge only when their own department's competence was in question. They didn't take it personally when John Q. Citizen did something repulsive. The Marine Corps took everything personally.

"What made you think it was Ann they were talking about over the scanner?" Fran asked Griffin. She'd sunk so deep into the butt-sprung couch, she thought she might need a giant shoehorn to get out.

"Another educated guess. And a gut feeling. Ann usually stayed on base in a B.O.Q. guest suite when she came down for a weekend.

And I remembered her joking about being 'the only woman on the island' most of the time. Plus, she hadn't called like she said she would. It wasn't like Ann to change her plans without telling anybody. I guess I took a shot in the dark—God, what an asinine thing to say! Was it a gun? I don't know how she died."

"Me neither."

One skeptical eyebrow shot up. He paused mid-rock.

"Honestly, Mr. Griffin, I don't know. I expect Public Affairs will release information about the cause of death after the autopsy is complete. Maybe later today."

Griffin restarted his chair. "Our police reporter passed the word to our military reporter, Lowell Mapp, who was at home. Lowell called me and then, at my direction, put in a query to Lejeune's Public Affairs Office. I spoke to you last night before I had heard anything from Public Affairs. But my suspicions had already been confirmed. Ann's husband, Gary, called me late yesterday afternoon. He said an MP had been sent to Raleigh to pick him up and drive him to Camp Lejeune. I guess the idea was that Gary would be too upset to safely drive himself.

"I'll tell you this, Ms. Setliff. I don't think Gary would have called me if he hadn't been extremely unhappy with NCIS. I can't say I blame him, although I understand your agency's position, too. He said they wouldn't tell him a darn thing except that Ann was dead. He got to see her only once, briefly, when he identified the body. For all he knew when I talked to him, she died from a heart attack, an aneurysm, a poison dart. I can imagine the possibilities that went through his mind. Unless, of course, Gary just wanted me to think he was in the dark. You know, because he was somehow involved in Ann's death. That sounds like quite a stretch to me, but I can see that investigators would have to consider it.

"I told Lowell not to contact Public Affairs again until we get their press release. There's no reason to. I expect the TV news will announce

Ann's identity long before we can get it in print. Anyway, at least in the
A section, we plan to deal with it as a personal loss to the newsroom,
rather than a police matter.

"Oh, I did have the presence of mind to pull a file photo of Ann, the
one we used to run with her column. She hadn't changed much. I hope
I don't sound callous, Ms. Setliff. Everybody here who knows what happened is pretty shook. Ann was smart, intense, tenacious. It's unreal to
think she's dead. Jesus, her poor kid!"

"Can I see the picture?"

"Sure. I left it on the light table."

She followed him into a small room adjacent to his office. It could
have been the entrance to a mine shaft, for all she could see from the
doorway. Then he flicked the switch that converted a glass-topped table
into a square of bright light. He laid a jeweler's loupe on top of a mounted slide already in place and stepped aside so Fran could take a look.

She'd forgotten how good looking Ann Buckhalter was. Volumi-
nous dark hair, tousled just enough to err on the professional side of
casual. Smooth skin. Light-colored eyes whose feline shape was exaggerated with eyeliner. Great teeth in a carefully arranged smile.

"How well do you know her husband, Lieutenant Colonel Buckhalter?" Fran asked Griffin.

"I know Gary only in that superficial way you know coworkers'
spouses. You see each other at the company Christmas party. You speak
if you pass in the parking lot. If you're asking if I noticed anything unusual about him, the answer is no. Buckhalter always seemed like an
okay guy to me."

"Can I have a copy of this?" Fran held up the slide.

"I'll have one printed for you as soon as a photographer gets here.
Should be about ten. I'll send it by courier, if you want. In care of the
field office?"

She put the slide back and followed Griffin out of the darkroom.
Two people were coming through the newsroom door—a thirtyish

woman carrying a small picnic cooler and a younger, heavyset man wearing a battered Army surplus fatigue jacket. The woman chirped good morning at Griffin as she wriggled out of a plaid all-weather coat. She sat at the desk nearest the door, bending sideways to push the cooler underneath. The young man came straight toward Fran with a crooked smile and an outstretched arm. He had been expecting her.

"Ms. Setliff, this is Lowell Mapp. He covers the base for us," Griffin said. "Lowell, Ms. Setliff is with the Naval Criminal Investigative Service."

She shook the young man's hand. The handshake lacked the practiced solidness of Griffin's. The reporter went for the old thumb hook. And his palm was oily.

Lowell Mapp was a surprise to Fran. Many military reporters were former service members themselves. They tended to retain, or at least mimic, a military bearing. Mapp lumbered, smelled like Texas Pete and Marlboros, and shaved haphazardly. His hair was long enough to tuck behind his ears, which he did with annoying frequency. That might explain the oily palm. He was wearing baggy jeans and no tie. The fatigue jacket would rankle those on his beat, and not because it was stenciled "US ARMY." Military gear worn by grown men who'd been no closer to combat than the mosh pit at a rock concert was a no-no. Most unforgivable of all, Mapp was about thirty pounds overweight. He was every gunnery sergeant's dream candidate for the Fat Patrol. In an organization rabidly focused on self-discipline, failure to maintain a lean physique could be literally degrading.

"Lowell's been covering the base for about six months," Griffin said. "Graduated from J-school at my alma mater year before last. Now that he's here, we can get down to business. What say we go into the publisher's conference room? Sally Jo, will you field my calls 'til I get back?" He directed this to the chirpy woman with the cooler. She responded with a backhanded salute.

Fran was taken aback. She thought she and Griffin *had* been getting down to business. Had they just been warming up?

The conference room was down a short paneled hall off the lobby. It was a windowless room with little more in it than a long table, multiple mismatched chairs, and a hot plate with coffeepot. The longest wall was covered by a mural depicting an aerial view of Onslow Beach.

Fran was further taken aback when Griffin locked the door. He sat down directly across from her and leaned forward as though he wanted to be sure she heard him and yet could keep his voice low.

"It hasn't been easy for Lowell," Griffin began, "taking over a beat that had been covered by a longtime reporter who was also a retired Marine. A beat that also had a ghost reporter—Ann. Jesus, there I go again! Sorry, Ms. Setliff. I never realized how many figures of speech refer to death."

"Sex and death, coming and going," Mapp mumbled to the mural.

Griffin either didn't hear or chose to ignore the remark. "Let's say that Lowell's period of adjustment has been unusually challenging."

A haircut would improve his chance of success, Fran thought. *So would knocking off the inappropriate asides.*

"What I'm about to tell you won't make any of our jobs easier," Griffin said. "But I've decided that, because the information may have a bearing on a possible murder investigation"—he waved away Fran's gesture of protest—"and I emphasize the word *possible,* I'm going to let you decide what to do with it. I hope for everybody's sake that the information is 100 percent irrelevant to Ann's death. I warn you, you won't be any more popular for hearing this than we'll be for telling it."

What a buildup! Fran wouldn't have left that room if Captain Maldonado were standing outside the door with a five-carat diamond and a Barry White CD. She had a hunch whose two-star name was about to come up.

"I don't want you to think Ann looked for axes to grind," Griffin said. "She had an unbelievable number of contacts, civilian and military.

People confided in her, things they wouldn't tell me or a chaplain. Most of it was unverifiable or libelous or ludicrous. The more promising stuff, she'd bounce off me—and, more recently, Lowell. Once in a while, she got on to something wire-worthy."

Griffin nodded at his reporter, who humped his chair closer to his boss and duplicated his covert posture.

"Ann called me this past week," Mapp said. "She said she'd gotten a tip that a lawsuit had been filed against the Navy months ago. The suit alleges that Lejeune's commanding general—General Johnson—reorganized the base command structure solely to avoid having a woman on his staff."

Fran's first reaction was amazement. How could a lawsuit filed against such a conspicuous person as a Marine Corps general be kept quiet so long? Her second reaction was, *Oh, shit!* She'd have thought, *Oh, fuck!* except that Grandmama Pattle would have launched a bar of Lava soap down her throat all the way from the afterlife.

Griffin read her reaction correctly. "We're not a big paper, Ms. Setliff. Our circulation is less than twenty-five thousand. We don't routinely send a reporter to the fed building in New Bern, on the chance that somebody may have filed a lawsuit that has local interest. The New Bern paper is even smaller, so it's not surprising this got past them, too."

"Did Mrs. Buckhalter say who tipped her off?"

"No. There are a number of possibilities. After all, lawsuits are public record. Anyway, that's why she was going to meet with Lowell or me this weekend. To hash out the best way to tackle this."

Mapp smiled, but his eyes chopped through Griffin like a Ginsu knife. The greasy reporter thought he had a proprietary interest in this scoop, Fran realized.

There well might be such a lawsuit. Fran knew General Johnson had reorganized the base command structure soon after taking over. That was no secret. Official word was that it was a cost-cutting move.

"Mr. Griffin, certainly this would be an embarrassment to the general. But like it or not, a lawsuit is a matter of public record. It's bound to come out sooner or later."

Griffin raised both palms in the classic gesture of defense. "And for all I know at this point, the suit may be baseless, no pun intended. But there's something else I think you should know. Last night, Lowell told me that Ann also said she might be able to provide us with the audiotape of a staff meeting. During that meeting, the general said he didn't want women in command positions. If there is such a tape, it would cost him a lot more than embarrassment."

Embarrassment! The Marine Corps already was accused of entrenched misogyny, which a commanding general was supposed to vehemently deny at every opportunity. Fran flashed back to Brit Lit 101. For a commanding general to state that he didn't want women in any command position was the equivalent of Henry II saying he didn't want that pesky priest Becket muscling in on royal turf. Johnson's comment, like Henry's, would be construed as an order by anyone subordinate to him. The consequence would be fatal—for a woman's career, anyway. And the political fallout would be humiliating. Johnson would draw criticism from every politician hungry for women's votes. His chances of taking over Second Marine Division, much less becoming commandant, would dwindle to nothing. How ambitious was he? And didn't Ann Buckhalter have any qualms about taking a career-busting swipe at a general?

Fran's dad had told her about the huge barrels used by troops in Vietnam to collect and burn human waste. The Vietnamese local assigned to this detail was called the "Papasan Shit Burner." Fran felt like she was about to get a new NCIS job title: Mamasan Shit Burner.

"Lowell was more enthused about the tape than I was," Griffin continued. "Frankly, I have some reservations. The paper isn't equipped to authenticate a tape or pay experts to do it for us. However, I expect the lawyers for whomever filed the lawsuit against Johnson would be delighted to try and prove such a tape was real, and would have the resources, too."

Griffin cleared his throat. "I'm a little embarrassed to admit it, but I almost hoped somebody else—TV, maybe—would get hold of any such tape first, so we could do follow-up instead of breaking the story. And yet that wouldn't have been fair to Lowell if it were legit, would it?"

"And now, Ann's death, unfortunately, gives it a few extra twists." Mapp spoke in undertaker tones, but Fran could have sworn she detected a sparkle in his sidewise glance.

She nodded noncommittally. Further comment on the tape matter would be unwise until she talked to Boyette.

"Which brings us back to our original topic," Fran said. "Just so I can say I covered all the bases, no pun intended"—she smiled at Griffin—"would each of you please describe your activities this past weekend? Mr. Mapp?"

Apparently, Mapp had prepared for this one. "Call me Lowell, okay? Saturday, I got up about ten. I had the late shift this weekend, so I slept in. At about noon, I went to the Laundromat at the strip mall near my house. I got home in time for the kickoff, Carolina and Virginia, at two o'clock. The game ended between four-thirty and five. Then I drove to work."

"Where do you live?"

"At the beach. Salter Path. Two-ten Sharkstooth Lane. It takes me forty-five minutes to get to work."

"Who else was working that night?"

"The wire editor, R. J. Barefoot. Vicky Sobel and myself—we were the duty reporters. Clay Konnecker was on call for cops. Pat Lynch was sports. The intern, a kid named Rick something, was helping him. Carolanne Parr was photographer. Must have been a half-dozen more in the pressroom."

Griffin interjected, "I can get you a list of everyone here that night. The whole staff, if you like."

"Thank you. Could you also identify everybody at the paper who worked directly with Ann or socialized with her?"

"Sure. My turn?"

Griffin told Fran that he and his wife had driven to Chapel Hill Saturday for the game Mapp watched on television. They went to a restaurant afterward and then to a friend's house. They left Chapel Hill at about eleven and stopped by the paper on the way home, at about one in the morning—just before press time.

"Lowell told me he was a little worried because Ann hadn't called or come by," Griffin said.

"I wasn't worried, exactly. More disappointed. I wanted to get on the lawsuit story as soon as possible, but it wasn't urgent. I wasn't going to go with it until the base had a chance to respond. The suit was already months old, so I figured a few more days wouldn't matter."

Someone knocked at the conference-room door. "Excuse me, George," a muffled voice said. "It's Sally Jo."

Griffin got up and opened the door to a face grimacing in mock contrition.

"Sorry. I know you asked not to be disturbed," the woman whispered, "but the publisher is on the phone. He insists on talking to you."

Griffin excused himself and followed the woman out, closing the door behind them.

Fran quickly rewrote parts of her notes that might be indecipherable even to herself later on. She suddenly realized Mapp was staring at her. She stared back. She could have sworn that, just for a second, the look he gave her was full of lethal intent. Then he quickly plugged in a sweeter expression. *He's not really bad looking*, Fran thought. If his features belonged to someone with an entirely different personality and wardrobe, they might even be attractive.

"What did you think of Ann Buckhalter, Mr. Mapp?"

"Lowell. Mr. Mapp sounds like a grade-school teaching aid." He grinned.

She reciprocated.

"I thought I was damn lucky to know Ann. She was very generous with tips. Information. Insights. When I got out of J-school, I went to work for a biweekly in the boonies. It was an okay first job. One of those small papers where everybody has to do a little of everything. This job was a definite step up for me. I wanted the county government beat, but Griffin offered me the base. I knew zip about the military. In fact, I'm just now starting to think I know what I'm doing. I may never stop being pissed off at the Public Affairs Office, having to jump through their mindless hoops. Why can't I just call the general's office when I want to know something? I mean, if you want to know something about Turner Broadcasting, you call Ted Turner, right? You may not get through to him, but nobody thinks you're committing an act of treason for trying."

"I'm curious. Why did Griffin give an important beat to someone who wasn't interested? And didn't know the territory?"

Mapp shrugged. "Griffin's a great guy. Fair to a fault, I'd say. But he's got a few biases. I think he likes having a reporter who graduated in the top 10 percent of his class at the University of North Carolina's J-school handling the paper's most visible beat. Besides, journalism is the lowest-paid form of garbage collecting. And let's face it, this town is an armpit. Griffin may not have had a lot to pick from."

"So what's the draw?"

"Not many get to start at the *Washington Post*. If you've got talent and make connections, you won't stay where you start for long."

"And Ann?"

"To me, her talent was having connections."

"But you got the bylines."

"She was okay with that. A lot of base brass suspected she was a part-time mole. If she'd written anything other than pro-military pro-paganda herself, it would have confirmed their suspicions. And then all those little green rats would have been afraid to tell her anything. It's a Mafia mentality. You can come down on other family members, but never discuss the family business outside the family."

"If that's true, why didn't Ann feel disloyal?"

"Look, you're asking me to speak for her, and I really can't. I always assumed she wanted it both ways. She wanted to be a poster girl for the Marines. But she liked getting her digs in, too. Even in the best of families, there's somebody you'd like to stick it to."

Always looking on the sunny side, huh, Mapp? Fran thought. "How did you feel about her personally?"

"I liked her. She had a terrific sense of humor. A lot of the time, we kept the newsroom TV tuned to CNN with the sound turned down. She'd improvise really funny commentary—you know, topical stuff—to go with the video. Crack us all up." Mapp tucked a stray strand of hair behind his ear for the umpteenth time. "If you're asking me if I had any prurient interest in Ann, the answer is no. She was an attractive woman, sure, but she was a lot older than I am. To me, she was a coworker and a mentor and a source. Sometimes, she intimidated the hell out of me. I always had the feeling she'd give me after-school detention if I screwed up."

Fran smiled. "What's the next step for you professionally?"

"Ann opened my eyes in a lot of ways. I'll always be grateful for that. The first few weeks I was here, I bitched about my beat to any-body who'd listen. I told Griffin I thought the Joint Public Affairs acro-nym, JPAO, stood for 'Just Plain Assholes Office.' Then, one afternoon, the old girl really let me have it. She made me realize that being the little frog next to a big pond had its advantages. Ann reminded me that Camp Lejeune is the biggest Marine base in the world. Things happen there that have international impact. Thousands of lives can be put on the line in a heartbeat. Millions and millions of tax dollars are tied up there. The beat's got blood, guts, guns, glory, and kinky sex. What other small-town paper could offer a new reporter all that? She was right, of course. If I can't make a rep for myself here, I won't do it anywhere. And I'm determined to be one of the exceptions. I'm going to have a big-enough name to actually make money in this business. Camp Lejeune is a great place to build from."

Fran was impressed. She hadn't heard such an impassioned speech since Marlon tried to convince her a woman couldn't get pregnant if she was on top.

SIX.

Fran usually bounced her reports off fellow agent Peter Rumley before showing them to their boss. But considering the sensitivity of what she'd just learned, Fran was glad Boyette had ordered her to save the results of her interview with Griffin for his eyes only.

She ran into Boyette when she stopped by the Base Exchange on her way back to the office. He was shopping for something to relieve a cold sore. Fran was looking for tweezers. Her last tweezers had lost their pincer power when she used them to remove a shredded scouring pad from the garbage disposal. If she went much longer without tweezing her eyebrows, people would start checking her out like a woolly caterpillar, trying to see how bad winter was going to be.

The basics-only section where the two agents met was set apart from the upscale main showroom that offered tax-free Tommy Hilfiger shirts, Giorgio perfume, and Waterford crystal. Fran found her boss jerking a copy of *Penthouse* out of the startled hands of a preteen boy. She stifled a smile. The steamier publications were supposed to be sealed in plastic, on their own special shelf, secured by a flip-down panel known as a "beaver dam." But it was impossible to keep troops from scouting out the strong stuff. And sometimes they were careless about putting it back behind the dam. An elderly retiree passing by a full-color, in-flagrante rag on her way to the Maalox could spoil a base store manager's whole day.

"Little bastard's in my son's catechism class," Boyette grumbled as he jammed the magazine back in place. "Good morning, Setliff. Through with the editor already?"

"Yes, sir. But I need to talk to you. I think we're about to open a can of Guinea worms."

Boyette sighed. "Let's go sit in my car. Hang on while I pay for this." He held up a multipack of Blistex.

Fran realized she was getting hungry and glanced at her watch. Not yet eleven. Had she eaten breakfast? Did a handful of Raisinets and café au nothing count? She thought about buying a hot dog from the sidewalk vendor but knew Boyette hated anybody eating in his new Saab.

Boyette slowed his pitter-patter pace. For a second, Fran thought he was stopping to look at a mid-aisle Christmas display. But he was cutting narrowed eyes at the entrance. Fran followed his gaze, looking for the target of his withering stare.

"I guess it's never too cold for tank-top patrol," Boyette muttered.

Provost Marshal O'Dell and a silo-sized MP were storming the main entrance, on one of their routine missions to rid the Base Exchange of exposed armpit hair. Base regulations prohibited men from wearing running shorts, tank tops, and most other PT gear in the exchange. A notice posted at all store entrances explained the regulation. For Marines, however, a posted notice had all the force of dryer lint. General Johnson had encouraged the MPs to enforce the dress code after standing in line behind a Marine private wearing only a Speedo and a young man's perpetual semi. But some, including Boyette, thought the base's top cop himself should at least pretend to have something better to do.

When they reached his car, Boyette offered to turn on the heater, but Fran said no thanks. She didn't need her eyeballs to be any crispier than they already were.

She started by telling Boyette about the friendly reception she had gotten from Griffin. He'd struck her as sincere. Of course, pickled okra also struck her as appetizing. She flipped through her notebook to help resurrect the conversation. If Boyette was disappointed that she hadn't used a tape recorder, he didn't say anything. His only reaction while she spoke was to poke his tongue against the cold sore, then recoil from the taste of Blistex.

After she finished, he silently massaged the ostrich-skin steering-wheel cover for a few seconds, then abruptly started the engine. "I need to talk to legal, Setliff. Surely, the staff judge advocate and Captain Maldonado know about this, even if we didn't. Can I drop you anywhere?"

"No thanks, sir." She had a hot dog piled with chili and onions waiting for her. Tic Tacs to follow in triplicate.

Boyette lowered the automatic window on the passenger side. "Oh, Setliff."

"Yes, sir?" Fran ducked to window level.

"For the time being, don't discuss this, even if someone else brings it up first. I'll try to get back to you before the end of the day."

"Sure, boss. Good luck."

SEVEN.

Fran's office consisted of a gray metal desk separated from other agents' desks by black felt dividers framed in aluminum. It was as frill-free as the newsroom she'd just visited. Reporters, however, weren't electronically frisked before coming through the inner door. And they didn't have to maneuver through encrypted code before opening a computer file.

She was typing in her report when Peter Rumley came in. Her screensaver was set so that if she lifted her fingers from the keys for more than three seconds, her screen went solid red. She lifted her fingers.

"How's it going?" she asked, smiling.

Rumley always looked as if he'd been ninety-six hours without sleep or a change of clothes. Maybe sleepless nights accounted for the five kids. Or five kids accounted for the sleepless nights.

"Going according to plan. Not confirmed, but I heard that Ann Buckhalter went into the water alive and drowned where she went in. No ligature around the neck. No gunshot or knife wound. Tragic mishap? Suicide? In shallow water? With the Morehead bridge a short drive away? Oh, and the victim was wearing makeup. Recent pedicure. High heels. Would a woman put on makeup and high heels and then do something that would absolutely guarantee she would not look her best when next seen?"

"High heels? To walk out on a pier?"

"More like dressy sandals, I guess, but definitely designed for looks, not comfort. Or the weather. And she was wearing just one shoe. The other is missing." He absently scanned Fran's foundation-free freckles. "Anybody at the newspaper give you a hard time?"

"Total sweethearts. I wish I had more to share. It was a dry run." *Not a total lie*, she thought. *My throat went dry the minute Griffin mentioned General Johnson.*

Rumley walked away but immediately returned, frog-walking his chair from his cubicle to hers. Apparently, he was the one in need of friendly feedback today.

"I talked to the victim's husband for a few minutes last night," he said.

Fran looked up in interest, fingers still raised.

"Lieutenant Colonel Gary Buckhalter. Forty-eight years old. Looks like the pencil-pusher he is. Tall. Thin. Lousy posture for a Marine. Wire-rimmed bifocals with lines. Made it hard to read his expression. Maybe there wasn't one to read. I didn't expect him to be all-to-pieces. Still, if somebody kicked him in the gut, I bet he'd double over. So, why didn't he show some reaction to getting gut-kicking news just a day ago? He now works as a part-time consultant for ACCA, a multinational electronics corporation. He and Ann were married for twenty-one years. They have one daughter, Deirdre, fifteen. The girl goes to a private high school in Raleigh. Tuition must soak up half his retirement pay. The Buckhalters also had a son. The boy was not much older than Deirdre. Died of leukemia when he was nine. Do you think Buckhalter went all-to-pieces over that one? He retired just two years after being promoted to lieutenant colonel. Had to have a knee replaced. An old injury complicated by osteoarthritis."

"Is Buckhalter's time accounted for the night of the murder?" Fran asked.

"Yes and no."

"Come again?"

"He says he was home. Daughter Deirdre left the house with a girl-friend and the girlfriend's parents early Saturday. The group was go-ing Christmas shopping, then to a movie. Buckhalter said Deirdre was picked up before Ann left for Lejeune. The girl got home about 2300 Saturday. But her bedroom is in a garage apartment, so Buckhalter did not speak to her when she got home. He was awake—in bed reading a book, he says. He heard the car drive up and heard voices, normal part-ing chit-chat. Then he heard the car drive away."

Isn't that slack, under the circumstances? Fran thought. *Wouldn't a concerned father who believed his daughter was recently raped at least look in on her?*

"Buckhalter says he didn't see Deirdre again until Sunday at about 1000, when she came into the kitchen to get something to eat. They spoke briefly—typical monosyllabic parent/teen stuff. He told me he hadn't heard anything from Ann, but didn't really expect to."

Fran generated a mental timeline.

"So, theoretically," Rumley continued, "he could have driven the two and a half hours to Lejeune, drowned his wife, then driven two and a half hours back to Raleigh. Possible, but not likely. I mean, even if he left the house in a frenzy to kill, wouldn't he cool off considerably in two and a half hours?"

"Richard Speck didn't cool off until he ran out of student nurses," Fran pointed out. "Buckhalter could have spent the drive building up a head of steam, picturing what his wife might be up to. Who she might be up to. Did he seem uncomfortable about Ann's spending the night at Lejeune without him?"

"Not that I could tell. But like I said, the guy's tuck was tight. He told me Ann did that once a month or so, which agrees with the guesthouse record. She would spend Saturday afternoon at the paper, according to her husband, or in the microfiche room at the public library. Sometimes, she had dinner with somebody she knew from when they were stationed at Lejeune. Female or couple friends. She didn't like to drive at night, Buckhalter said. So, since it gets dark early this time of year, she'd get a room on base, do her shopping at the exchange and commissary on Sunday morning, then drive home."

"Sounds reasonable to me."

Rumley shrugged. "Or a great cover for monkey business. Oh, another thing, Fran. I talked to that retired gunnery sergeant who was doing desk duty when Ann checked in. He said she got that room only because somebody else checked out unexpectedly. Which brings up the possibility the original occupant was the intended victim. If Ann was a victim."

"I thought the whole building next to the river was unoccupied except for that one room. And yet they cleaned a recently occupied room for Ann, instead of just giving her one that was ready to go?"

"Not a room, a VIP suite." He raised and lowered his eyebrows waggishly.

"You're getting ahead of me, Rum. Anything of interest about the original occupant of Ann's room?"

"Only if rank-pulling and intrigue appeal to you. The person who had the room before Ann is a pregnant captain. Six feet tall. Hair shorter than mine. Bigger neck, too. Her quarters had just been painted. She couldn't stand the fumes. Puked every time she opened the front door. She planned to stay in the guesthouse until Monday. Supposedly, she got a VIP suite because of her delicate condition—you know, closer to that healthy river air. Truth is, her daddy is some undersecretary for the chief of Naval Operations. That could definitely get a few strings pulled. Anyway, when she dropped by her quarters Saturday morning, she kept her breakfast down, no problem. So she went back home. Trust me on this. There's no way somebody could have mistaken dainty Ann for that woman." Rumley chuckled. "The whole time we were talking, the desk clerk—Boatwright—was sweating like a bottle of beer in a Vieques bar."

"Is he a suspect?"

"Only of bending the rules to impress Buckhalter's sexy wife. His alibi is tight. Saturday-night mass at Francis Xavier with the wife and kids. He was sweating because he took it upon himself to grant Ann a special favor or two in the past. His boss and Mrs. Boatwright might want to know why."

"What favors?"

"Nothing any other dumbass wouldn't do. Contrary to base regulations, he sometimes let her stay in a VIP suite and fudged the information on the books."

The four VIP suites were reserved for visiting dignitaries. Members of Congress. NATO officials. South American dictators. Pregnant Marines with connections.

"Boatwright didn't see any harm. The rooms have to be cleaned periodically whether they're used or not, he said. He was just trying to score points with a good-looking customer."

"Did he, um, *score* any points?"

"He swears he never even shook her hand. I expect he's telling the truth. Even if she was the type, I don't think he'd be *her* type. Uncle Fester would be his celebrity look-alike, not Burt Lancaster." He noted Fran's puzzled look. "*From Here to Eternity*. The officer's wife and the virile noncommissioned officer. Don't you got no culture?"

"My coonhound ate it. What about Officers' Club employees?"

"Haven't heard. Boyette's scheduled another all-hands meeting for 1800. Maybe we can fill in a few bald spots then."

Special Agent Rodney Walker came in shoveling down a Dairy Queen Blizzard with a pink spoon.

"How can you eat that thing this time of year?" Rumley asked. "Makes my head ache just to watch you."

"Remember who you're talking at, Rumley. In Chicago, nobody even bothers to put on socks in this weather."

"Or wash them either," Rumley shot back.

The two men ambled away from Fran's cubicle. She smiled fondly at their backs. Among her peers, they were her favorites: Rodney Walker, the only African-American at the Lejeune field office, and Peter Rumley, the most reproductive.

Fran finished her report, encrypted it, emailed it to Boyette, and secured her machine. Not knowing what else to do until she heard from her boss, she decided to go to the Officers' Club and see how the evidence boys were getting along.

"Dumbass!" Rumley shouted from across the room. She heard him smack his forehead with his palm. "I forgot. I'm supposed to coordinate. Setliff, you're gonna interview the Navy commander. The guy Ann Buckhalter called from the guesthouse the night she died. Commander Kevin Terry. Doctor Commander Kevin Terry. Psychiatrist."

Fran's voltage meter shot off the dial. "Do I need to make an appointment?"

"Nope. The commander's administrative assistant said Terry will be available after three. Know anything about psychiatry, Setliff?"

"Isn't that the branch of medicine that never cures anybody?"

"Yeah. You'd have to be nuts to see one of those guys."

Fran rifled her desk drawer for soda money. *Damn*. Why hadn't she cashed a check while she was shopping?

Rum's head popped up over the black flannel. "Looks like Commander Shrink was part of Ann's Lejeune routine. Going by the guesthouse phone log, Ann called either Terry's office or his home just about every time she came down. Don't know yet whether she called him from Raleigh, too. He lives at Emerald Isle. Alone. Been divorced six years. The ex-wife is in Annapolis."

"I ask one thing of you, Rum. From this point on, no matter what I find, there will be no couch jokes in my area. That goes for euphemisms, too, including sofas, davenports, and chaise longues."

"No problem. The last one especially. If I can't spell it, I don't joke about it."

ooooo

Fran showed her ID at the reception desk in the echoing hospital lobby. A Navy petty officer directed her via her choice of spiral staircase or elevator.

Fourth floor. Discreetly set apart. She got in the elevator with a nurse sporting a ponytail and a Doc Holliday mustache. His aqua scrubs were littered with clip-on toys, mostly Looney Tunes characters. She bet he was headed to the fourth floor. He was.

She followed his bootied footsteps past a set of stainless-steel doors. He immediately disappeared to the right, through an interior door equipped with security buzzer and reinforced window.

Straight ahead was the cool, plant-filled grotto that served as a reception area for the psychiatric out-patient suite. Only two people were in the area, a Marine with a splinted nose and a woman with legs thin enough to twine together like pipe cleaners. They sat on opposite sides of the room, the woman anxiously peeking from behind a copy of Forbes, the Marine dozing. When Fran came in, his swollen eyes flickered open, then closed again.

A head covered with tightly braided blond hair shot up above the reception desk, followed by big blue eyes, a perfect smile, and the black polyester uniform of a female corpsman.

"Why, you must be the special visitor Commander Terry is expecting," she chirped at Fran. "He said to show you right in. Now, watch your step. They just buffed our floor. Isn't this weather just wonderful? So bracing!"

She practically twinkles, Fran thought. *A slap in the face to every miserable jerk who comes through that door.*

Rear end bouncing briskly, the perky corpsman led Fran down a short hall to a closed door with an engraved plastic nameplate: Commander Kevin Terry, USN.

Terry's office was so small, Fran was nearly struck midsection by the extended hand of the man in the double-breasted uniform. It was a large hand belonging to a large man.

Most Navy doctors were about as military as the skipper on *Gilligan's Island*. If they came out of their military indoctrination seminar with a fifty-fifty chance of saluting the right people, the Navy was happy. Their services were too highly prized to quibble. This doctor, however, was squared away. Insignia, ribbons, and buttons were where they should be, and fingerprint-free. The haircut was regulation and highly becoming.

"Special Agent Setliff, Naval Criminal Investigative Service. Thank you for seeing me, Commander Terry."

He offered her the plusher of two pub-style chairs. When they both were seated, her knees were less than a foot from his.

"I apologize for the close quarters, Agent Setliff. Our conference room is in use, and I have a patient waiting in my consulting room."

"It's all right, Commander," she said, canting her squeezed-together knees as far to the right as possible. "I won't keep you long. Let me start by offering my condolences. I understand Ann Buckhalter was a personal friend or a longtime patient, I'm not sure which. Perhaps you can clarify that."

"Neither, really. Ann and I were friends, but not personal friends. Lately, she may have decided we weren't even friends. Certainly, we were longtime acquaintances. I was an acquaintance of Lieutenant Colonel Buckhalter, too. But my connection to the Buckhalters was based mostly on our shared concern for their daughter, Deirdre. Ann and I spoke regularly, that's true, but only in conjunction with the girl's treatment. Ann herself was never my patient."

Why would a fifteen-year-old girl need a psychiatrist? Bulimia? Drugs? Sexual promiscuity?

"Ann's daughter was your patient?"

He nodded. "Still is, I assume. There were times I suggested Ann herself might benefit from counseling, but she resisted the idea." He smiled. "She said there were limits to what she wanted to know about herself."

"You had not prescribed any medication for Ann?"

"Good God, no. Did she die of some kind of overdose?"

"I don't think that's been determined, Commander. And Deirdre? Have you prescribed medication for her?"

"I'm reluctant to discuss her at all, Agent Setliff."

Fran didn't press. "Did you plan to see Ann Buckhalter this past weekend?"

"See or at least talk to. Saturday, she called me and left a voice message. I erased it. I'm sorry. I had no way of knowing it would be important. She said she was at the B.O.Q. and asked me to call her when I could."

Why would a psychiatrist erase a phone message so quickly? From a patient's parent for whom he had recommended counseling? Seemed a little too reactive to Fran.

"Did she sound agitated? Depressed? Different?"

"No. Of course, most people don't sound natural talking to an answering machine anyway. But nothing about her voice struck me as unusual."

"What time did you get the message?"

"Not until about 1730. I was here reviewing study data most of the day, but the switchboard was screening my calls. Unless the duty chief thought it was urgent, he knew not to disturb me. It was just after 2000 when I called her back. There was no answer."

His glance cut away from Fran's face. She noticed he had dense, feathery eyelashes. There was gravity in his body language and voice, but his emotional pitch seemed flat. A professional affectation?

"When did you leave the hospital, Commander?"

"Not long after I called Ann."

"Where did you go?"

"Home."

"You didn't drive by the B.O.Q. guesthouse to see if she was there?"

"No. I assumed that if it was an urgent matter, she would have said so in her message. I thought she didn't answer because she was out with friends. I had no idea when she'd be back."

"Do you often work on Saturday, Commander Terry?"

"Often? No, it's a bit unusual. I don't schedule patient sessions on weekends. Occasionally, the brig may want to have a prisoner evaluated for suicide risk, or a patient might need a change in meds. But remember, the Naval Hospital does not provide long-term psychiatric care. Active-duty personnel who need it will probably be discharged from the military. Dependent family members must go to a civilian doctor."

"But if that's the case, why are you treating Deirdre, a retiree's daughter?"

Terry lightly tapped the fingers of one hand against a stack of books. "I see I'm not going to be able to keep Deirdre out of this." He sighed. "I began treating her years ago, while her father was still on active duty. I hadn't seen her in a year until I began treating her again a few weeks ago."

"Please start at the beginning, Commander. Can you give me an idea why you started seeing Deirdre? She must have been just a little girl then."

"I was assigned to the same ship as Gary Buckhalter. As a matter of fact, I worked for him, in a sense. We were part of a joint exercise with the Army. The small group of medical personnel on my team was administratively attached to Gary's unit. My team was one of the first trials of a Psychiatric Intervention Team organized to aid war refugees, hostages, recaptured POWs. I was a lieutenant commander then, which, I'm sure you know, equates to a major in the Marines. Gary was still a major but had just been selected for promotion to lieutenant colonel, so he was my senior. It was his first joint exercise. I thought that's why he seemed uptight about it. It was a double first for me: first time on a ship, first time working with the Army. Gary's and my duties were in such different areas, there weren't many opportunities to interact on a personal level."

"So, how did you get to know the Buckhalters?"

Terry paused. "Gary was extremely religious."

Fran lifted an eyebrow.

"I mean, Agent Setliff, that he was—at the time—one of those officers who think their mission is to close the gap between church and state. Frankly, his proselytizing got old real fast. Then one of the chiefs told me Gary's son had died less than a year before. Apparently, the boy suffered terribly in the months before his death. And I later learned Ann was left to deal with it more or less by herself. Gary coped by immersing himself in his job and church work, refusing to accept the inevitable. He was convinced God was going to make his boy well. When the boy did die, Gary's religious fervor only intensified. Life after death was the only way he was going to get his son back."

"Did you talk to him—professionally, I mean?"

"No. Gary would have laughed at the idea that psychiatry could offer him anything religion couldn't. He found his own treatment. When Gary coerced troops into prayer meetings, he thought he was doing them the biggest favor imaginable. Some of them agreed. Those who didn't kept it to themselves, for the most part."

"I'm struggling to figure out how this gets us to Deirdre, Commander."

"We're almost there. During one of Gary's homilies, he talked about how his daughter—then only nine—had been 'spiritually enriched' by her brother's death. He said she had become more mature, obedient, thoughtful. But from the way he described her 'mature' behavior and 'thoughtful' silences, I knew the girl was presenting symptoms of depression. Gary also mentioned that his wife—against his wishes, he said—was taking their daughter to grief counseling at Lejeune's Family Services Center. Coincidentally, at that time, I was setting up the protocol for a long-term study: 'Effects of Military Deployment on Dependent Juveniles Presenting Symptoms of Depression.' A colleague of mine also involved in the study was stationed at Lejeune then. I asked him to arrange for the girl to be treated at the Naval Hospital instead of the Family Services Center. I wanted to include her in the study."

"It's hard to believe Buckhalter would okay such a thing," Fran said.

Terry smiled weakly. "I didn't discuss my intentions with Gary. After my colleague at Lejeune began treating Deirdre and getting an extremely good response, he discussed the study with Ann."

"How long after?"

"A year. Eighteen months."

"Commander, I don't know much about medicine, but I find it hard to believe you could include a minor in a study without a parent's consent."

He smiled again. It was the smile policemen give cranky individuals who tell them they don't have the right to shine those big old flashlights into the backseats of people's cars.

"I expect you could make the case that I didn't follow policy. But the girl was not formally included in the study until I did have Ann's consent. By that time, Deirdre had improved enormously. Ann was grateful for what she saw as my contribution to that improvement. The study didn't wind up until a year ago. Which is why I continued to see Deirdre on an infrequent basis up until that time. My colleague had to bail out, two years into the study. High blood pressure. Disenchantment with military medicine. He went into private practice in Seattle. But his case notes were government property, so I retained access to those."

"What did Deirdre think about the study?"

"I'm not sure how much she knew. She was always cooperative. She's a good kid. It's a shame she has to deal with the loss of her mother, on top of everything else."

Fran gave herself a moment to mull. She'd get back to "everything else" after she followed the current chain of thought.

"I know you said Ann wasn't your patient. But just as an observer, how well did Ann deal with the loss of her son?"

The commander's jaw muscles contracted. "We spoke about it only twice. Once, I cautioned her about her tendency to idealize the dead boy. She was deeply offended. Frankly, I was stunned by the intensity of her reaction. She even threatened to withdraw Deirdre from the study. The other time it came up, Ann mentioned she had wanted to have another baby after the boy died, but Gary wouldn't hear of it. She said Gary felt the death was the will of God. For him, having another child would be like trying to undo God's will."

"I'm surprised the marriage survived at all."

Terry shrugged but said nothing.

"You said you recently started treating Deirdre again. Why was that?"

"Agent Setliff, I've been stretching privacy ethics for much of our conversation. I'd like to confer with my boss before discussing Deirdre further. I will tell you I doubt very much that Ann's death has anything to do with the reason Deirdre resumed treatment. I admired Ann. She was brilliant and charming, but she could be as impulsive and hard-headed as a four-year-old. It wouldn't have been out of character if she simply decided to take a moonlight swim in the river. I'm sorry she's dead. But if there's anything at fault here, it's probably Ann's own judgment."

Time to lob one out of left field, Fran thought.

"Were you and Ann ever sexually intimate?" Fran suspected there had been at least a spark between two such good-looking, self-important people, one of whom was impulsive, the other of whom stretched ethics.

No doubt about it, the commander squirmed. And cleared his throat. "I've debated with myself whether to be frank about this. It was a lapse I deeply regret. Yes, Ann and I were intimate for a brief period during Gary's last tour. It ended by mutual consent."

This was an ethical stretch that could have ended in a court-martial for the commander. Having sex with another officer's wife was "conduct unbecoming." Having adulterous sex with a minor patient's mother was downright shitty.

So why had Terry decided to tell Fran? Either his conscience was bothering him or he suspected Ann might have confided in someone else who'd squeal on him. If the confession didn't come from Terry himself, it might look like he had more to hide than adultery.

For the moment, Fran wasn't interested in the details.

"Do you know if Ann had other extramarital affairs?"

Terry gave Fran a quick, strained smile. "Agent Setliff, we weren't teenagers. We didn't compare notes on past relationships. At our stage of the game, things like that didn't matter. But I will tell you this: Camp Lejeune has the world's shortest grapevine. If she had extramarital history, I probably would have heard about it. Oh, once in a, uh, playful moment, she said if promotions were based on men's understanding of women's needs, I'd be a general officer. And a general officer she knew would be a private. But I didn't take it seriously, and, no, I didn't ask her which general officer she had in mind."

Was Terry throwing out that tidbit to divert attention from himself? Or to take a shot at . . . ? How many generals *had* Ann discussed her "needs" with?

"Was Ann in love with you?" It was clear to Fran that he had not been in love with her.

He relaxed, then shrugged. "She never said she was. The only time we talked about our relationship—after it was over—she said we'd been like sandpaper, smoothing down the rough spots in each other's lives. That's as good a description as any."

"What kind of rough spots were you going through, Commander?"

His pupils contracted. "I was . . . at a professional crossroads. I was up for promotion. I was seeing changes in military health care I didn't like any better than my colleague did. I was seriously considering leaving the Navy. My private life wasn't rewarding either. Early midlife crisis, you might say." He chuckled softly. "The pop psychiatrists get it right once in a while."

If Terry and Ann Buckhalter had done all this sexual sanding and then gone back to being casual acquaintances, it showed amazing sophistication on everybody's part. Terry had been able to get therapeutic sex and still hold on to his interesting specimen—Deirdre.

"Are you involved with someone now, Commander?"

No smile, just an annoyed compression of the lips. "I can't see how that . . . Well, yes. Of course there is a woman in my life. A real-estate agent, absolutely no connection to the military. I occasionally take her to a movie or out to dinner. Sometimes, I take her to official functions. She was my date for the Navy Birthday Ball this year."

"May I have her name?"

His jaw tightened. "Jane Sherbourne. Gold Ribbon Properties. Pelletier Street."

"Was Miss Sherbourne—it is Miss?—aware of your relationship with Ann?"

"Why should she be? That was old news. Jane knows I'm not

interested in a permanent commitment with anyone. I don't think she is either." He braced his hands on the arms of his chair and leaned toward her in preparation for rising. "I'm afraid I must get to my patient, Agent Setliff."

Fran noted that he did not offer to talk with her at some other time.

She descended from the fourth floor by elevator and took a side trip down the blindingly glossy hospital corridor to the cafeteria. After getting in line for a turkey sandwich with a half-pint of milk on the side, she carried her tray to a table by the wall of windows overlooking the emergency entrance. A couple of male corpsmen in green scrubs passed by, echoing each other's laughter and spinning their plastic trays on upturned fingertips.

Fran popped out the carton's lip, splattering milk just as she'd done every day in grades one through six. She flipped through her chicken-scratch notes.

So, why did Ann Buckhalter call Commander Terry that afternoon? And when he tried to return her call and got no answer, why wasn't he a whole lot more curious about what she was up to?

EIGHT.

Fran called Rumley from a secured phone in the hospital pharmacy. He wasn't in the office, so she talked to Rodney Walker instead.

Walker had been taking statements from Officers' Club personnel who worked the night Ann died. Two club employees, a bartender and a Filipina waitress, remembered seeing Ann. The bartender said she'd come in with a mid-sized plastic bag full of something. Ann put it on the counter for only a few seconds before moving it to the foot rail. It was flat, like a thick book, and she had used her feet like bookends to hold it in place.

"He says he didn't get much of a look at it. But he didn't think she was using it as a makeshift purse, because she never opened it. She took her wallet out of her jacket pocket. The bag was white, but he was sure it wasn't a bag from the Base Exchange because it didn't have that red logo on it."

"Mighty sharp-eyed barkeep," Fran said.

"Well, you know how it is. Slow night. She was good looking. He was looking."

The waitress, Walker said, got only a glimpse of Ann when they passed through the lobby at the same time. She remembered Ann was pretty and wore cute high-heeled shoes. Strappy, she said. Too cold for those shoes, she'd chastised Walker, as if he'd made Ann wear them.

Everybody else at the club except for a teenage busboy was fully accounted for during the evening. The teenager, son of a deployed first sergeant, had acted extremely nervous. Like he was hiding Jimmy Hoffa's remains in one of his jawbreaker-sized zits. The kitchen manager told Walker the busboy was a pain in the ass because he had a habit of disappearing for a few minutes every hour or so. And he wasn't ducking into the head; the kitchen manager had looked for him there repeatedly. Walker suspected the boy was slipping out to smoke grass. He had the sly lurch of a regular user. Not to mention the bloodshot eyes and excessively minty breath. But the busboy insisted he hadn't seen anything the night Ann came in. Not even Ann. His excessive nervousness wasn't necessarily significant, as far as the Buckhalter case was concerned. The kid must know that bad things could happen if the MPs found out about the grass. His whole family could be kicked out of base housing. In military families, when it came to drug violations, the sins of the children were visited on the father. And the first sergeant's homecoming would not be a happy one.

The other interesting thing Walker had to share with Fran was that it had been established, from her stomach contents, that Ann died of drowning within eight to twelve hours of being found. She'd made their job easy by eating the lime rind in her gin and tonic.

"Funny," Walker said after Fran gave him the basics of her interview with Commander Terry, "it seemed like such a straightforward case. I didn't think we'd come up with a half-dozen people to interview. The

B.O.Q. was practically empty. The club was practically empty. In the end, I figured we'd decide Ann Buckhalter had a few too many, fell off the pier, got snagged by a crab trap, and drowned. If she struggled, there was nobody to hear her. But now, loose threads seem to be hanging off just about everybody."

"And Boyette hates loose threads almost as much as the provost marshal hates exposed armpit hair in the PX," Fran said.

NINE.

TUESDAY A.M.

The parking area behind the PMO acted as a kind of greenroom, where MPs and NCIS agents about to exit or enter the building often paused to do a little leg pulling and ass grabbing, sometimes literally.

Fran was one of the first arrivals Tuesday morning, having awakened bright eyed and bushy tailed after six solid hours of sleep. Her curiosity was immediately piqued by the two other greenroom occupants, who were leaning over the hood of a car on braced arms, shoulder to shoulder, heads conspiratorially close. Warrant Officer Baumer was just coming in, judging by his fresh shave, and Staff Sergeant Gutten was checking out, judging by his 0600 shadow. Both faces practically radiated schadenfreude. Some higher-up must have had an embarrassing interaction with law enforcement.

She couldn't resist walking in a direction that allowed her to eavesdrop.

"Didn't mention mor'n twice his daddy's a general," she caught Gutten telling Baumer with a snort and a chuckle.

"Whose daddy's a general?" Fran chimed in, grinning. "Good morning, gentlemen."

Gutten's jaw tightened, but Baumer dipped his chin at the staff sergeant and winked. "She's one of us."

Fran wondered whether Baumer meant she was "one of us law-enforcement types" or "one of us Southerners."

In any case, it was Baumer who greased the conversational skids. "Staff Sergeant Gutten here came upon a single-vehicle accident at Autumn Oval last night, or this morning, to be more precise. The driver was a sixteen-year-old male whose military ID said his name was Wallace Charles Johnson. Young Wallace's sponsor is Brigadier General Amesly Johnson, commanding general, Camp Lejeune."

Autumn Oval was the small, prettily landscaped traffic circle that separated senior officers' quarters from those assigned to generals.

"Good Lord! He wasn't hurt, was he?" Fran asked Gutten.

"I don't think so, ma'am, but I got EMS to carry him over to the Naval Hospital so they could give him a once-over. He was conscious but did seem a little disoriented. I couldn't say whether that was on account of head trauma or alcohol or drugs or what."

Fran couldn't conceal her surprise. Alcohol? Drugs?

Baumer glanced at his watch, then nudged Gutten. "Go on and tell her the whole story. Might be useful to NCIS, in case of any repercussions."

"If you don't mind, Staff Sergeant," Fran added. "You're the one with firsthand knowledge. I'd love to hear your observations." She loaded as much mush and molasses into her drawl as she could at that hour.

The MP said he'd been on routine patrol when he heard the sound of an impact from Autumn Oval. "It was 0115. It wasn't metal on metal, more like the sound a Bush Hog makes plowing through a thicket. Then I heard a voice, a male voice, yelling, 'Fuck! Fuck! Fuck!' Just quotin' him, ma'am. He didn't sound in pain, to tell the truth, just pissed off. I expected to find an older man from the sound of the voice, but teenage boys can shift up and down in pitch. Especially if they're excited.

"When I got to it, the Jeep was at a forty-five-degree angle with the driver's-side wheels in the ditch. It was dark out there, all those shade trees and all. The engine was still running, the headlights off. In fact, it was rocking in place. When I pulled up, I had the idea for a second that rocking was the recoil of somebody climbing out the Jeep and kicking off against the roof before running away. But I didn't see but one person, and he was leaning out the passenger-side front window, tossing out pieces of shit—debris—over the hood into the shrubbery. It was a kid, face white as lard. I radioed in the plate number and asked for medical assistance and a backup car. I figured I'd let the backup deal with whatever was being pitched over the side. By then, the kid had pulled himself out the window. He was a little wobbly on his feet, scared, quiet. No cussing. Just squeaking and moaning.

"'Staff Sergeant Gutten, Military Police,' I said to him. And I asked if he was injured. He bent over and grabbed his knees like he was trying to fight off a faint, but said, 'No, I'm okay.' I managed to get the door open far enough to reach in and turn off the engine. Took a look inside the backseat and cargo bay. Outdoor gear, mostly water-related. Banged-up canoe paddle, carabiners, nylon rope, scoop and casting nets, overturned ice chest. I asked to see some identification and the registration for the car. He patted his jacket until he found his wallet and then looked up at me for the first time. He had this goofy smile, like he was about to puke on me and was apologizing in advance.

"The name didn't ring a bell right away. Wallace Charles Johnson. We got more Johnsons on this base than privates, no pun intended. Sixteen years old. Valid license. Then I dug the registration out of the glove compartment, where he told me to look for it. Quarters Four. Holy shit! Who lives in Quarters Four? None other than the commanding general, also name of Johnson."

That explains the schadenfreude, Fran thought.

Gutten must have read her mind. "Now, there's a certain satisfaction in knowing generals' kids get in the same kind of scrapes as the rest, but there was a moment I kinda felt sorry for young Wallace."

"You figured his old man was really going to lay into him?" Fran suggested.

"Not that, so much. When I was grubbing around in his glove compartment, a beat-up photo fell out. It was a few years old, so I didn't recognize the kid right off. But it was him, all right, with some lady. His mom, I guess. I thought that was funny, a big kid like that carrying around a picture of himself with his mom."

"His mother died of cancer a year or so back," Fran said.

"Yeah, that come to me after I had a second to think. Thank God I remembered the CG is a widower. I put that picture back in the glove compartment so fast, you'd have thought it was on fire."

"Did you give him a field sobriety test?"

"Yes, ma'am. And he failed. He'll probably claim in traffic court that he was too shook up by the accident to think or walk straight. I didn't see no bruises, but that didn't mean he wasn't hurt. I saw an accident once where this dead gunnery sergeant was sitting behind the wheel without a single hair out of place. Ribbons still on straight. They told me later that under that squared-away uniform, his aorta was ripped clean away from his heart."

"Did you ask if he was alone in the car?" Teenagers rarely got drunk and went for a spin by themselves at that hour. Maybe he'd already dropped someone off.

"Of course, ma'am. He didn't answer right off the bat, because he was trying to get his nice jacket off before he blew chunks all over it. But after he puked up everything he'd eaten since kindergarten, he said, several times, that he was by himself. And that was about it. He whined about not being able to find his cell phone, and I said I'd call his father for him. He got really quiet after that."

"At least you didn't put him in your cruiser before he puked," Baumer pointed out.

"That's my one regret," Gutten shot back. "Now, I won't get to make some lance corporal scrub vomit out of an official vehicle."

He dropped the smirk and turned back to Fran. "About that point, the backup and the EMS van drove up. I ordered the MP to follow the van to the Naval Hospital and be sure the boy got a blood alcohol test."

Wallace Johnson could refuse to take the test, of course, but that would mean automatic suspension of his driving privileges. And if a beer can or a roach clip showed up in the bushes at Autumn Oval, it was unlikely anyone would bother with the forensics necessary to tie it to the CG's son. Fran figured the incident might be settled by a gentlemen's agreement down the line. But nobody better count on Staff Sergeant Gutten being one of the gentlemen.

TEN.

TUESDAY 1430

"But why me, sir?"

Fran blurted this to Boyette a split second before she realized how infantile it sounded. And in Vic Maldonado's presence, too. She might as well have poked out her bottom lip and stamped her little feet. Why didn't she just go back home and marry her web-toed first cousin, Goober Ray?

"Um, excuse me, sir. Let me rephrase that. It's just that I'm probably the least sophisticated agent here, politically speaking. I still get woozy if I see too much scrambled egg on someone's hat."

"Cover," Maldonado corrected her.

She looked at their deliberately vacant expressions. Then the light dawned. What did she have that no other agent had? Ovaries, of course. She straightened her shoulders and sighed. Inwardly, anyway.

"Won't your choice look a little obvious?" she said.

She was in Captain Maldonado's office, which was almost as austere as Boyette's. More books. Less caked floor wax in the corners.

Fran had not been surprised to learn that base legal was aware of
the lawsuit claiming General Johnson reorganized his staff expressly to
exclude women. The surprise was that there might be a link between
the lawsuit and the dead woman in the New River. That was on a par
with discovering there might be a link between your baby-sitter and an
international child pornography ring.

Maldonado was half-sitting on the end of a low bookcase. His
sturdy, well-groomed hands were folded between his knees. One high-
sheen Corfam dangled above the floor.

"Obvious is good," he said. "It's dicey enough that the general is
named in a sexual discrimination suit. To have his name come up in
a death investigation is a thousand times worse. It's important, Setliff,
that we be prepared to account for our handling of all aspects of this
case. Not just because we want to cover our butts—that's a given. We
must be able to reassure the public we didn't take any shortcuts around
the truth because a commanding general's name came up."

Boyette nodded. He might tiptoe around General Johnson to pro-
mote family harmony. Yes, General Johnson could make heads ache at
Boyette's agency, but he couldn't make them roll. Boyette did not report
to the base commanding general. He reported directly to Naval Criminal Investigative Service headquarters in Washington.

"We don't want it to look like the old-boy network protected the
general in any way," Boyette said. "Or even that his statement might
have been unintentionally slanted because it was taken by a male agent.
Frankly, a woman needs to be involved in this, Setliff, and you're it."

In other words, Fran thought irritably, if I can squeeze a sex-change
operation into my schedule, I'll be off the hook. Is there a Jiffy Penis franchise
in Jacksonville?

Not for the first time, Boyette seemed to read her mind. "Important as the gender consideration is, I wouldn't ask you to do this if I

didn't think you were capable. You say you're politically unsophisticated. Good. That will give you objectivity. I thought your handling of Commander Terry was super. And Vic will give you ample deep on the discrimination suit, so you won't be walking in cold."

Fran was feeling too pouty to work up an inner giggle. In fact, if she hadn't been rattled by the prospect of interviewing the general, she might have welcomed the chance to turn all fifteen watts of her charm on her favorite lawyer.

"Yes, sir. I assume you've already set this up. How much time have I got to prepare?"

Maldonado glanced at his watch. Bad sign. "An hour and a half. The general is expecting you at four. I'll be there, too, at least when things get rolling."

"If a follow-up interview is needed," Boyette added, "I'll send Rumley with you. Of course, what we're all hoping is that this will blow over quickly. It should. Unless there really is a damaging audiotape and the newspaper decides to do something with it. Or the autopsy indicates Ann Buckhalter, allegedly in possession of that inflammatory tape, died from something other than an accidental drowning."

ooooo

Alone with Captain Maldonado at last, Fran felt surprisingly at ease. He had the kind of self-confidence that was contagious instead of intimidating.

"Does General Johnson know about the tape?" she asked him.

"Alleged tape. The tape may be a bluff, to stoke a settlement. Yes, he's been briefed about it, but remember, there wasn't much to tell. Even if a tape exists, it may be worthless. Who made it, and why? Is it inaudible, incoherent, edited? All that would have to be clarified before a judge could declare it admissible in court."

She asked him to explain the lawsuit. "Keep it simple, Vic. Leave out the *whereins* and the Latin parts."

"Not even a single *actus reus?*"

"Nope. No *e pluribus unum*s or *coitus interruptus*es either."

He chuckled, then shifted into lawyer mode. The suit had been filed by Charmaine Roundtree, he explained. Roundtree was the civilian director of Human Services for Camp Lejeune and had a staff of more than two hundred people. She attended the general's staff meetings, just like the Marine officers who served as assistant chiefs of staff. Before General Johnson reorganized the command structure, Roundtree's civil-service rating had been the equivalent of a lieutenant colonel. But when he put Roundtree's department under Manpower, she became subordinate to Manpower's boss, a male civilian. She found herself shut out of staff meetings and also hit an unexpected glass ceiling. She was no longer eligible for promotion. There was no higher rating for her new job than the one she already held.

"Were any men bumped off the ladder because of the general's reorganization?" Fran asked.

"No. And that won't help the general's case. But the big issue is motive. Did General Johnson move this woman just so she wouldn't be part of the inner circle? Or, as he says, to save the taxpayers money?"

Fran mulled this. "Vic, just out of curiosity, what's your impression of the general's attitude toward women?"

"Women as Marine officers?" Maldonado gave her a wicked smile. "He'd as soon use his rifle on one as his gun."

She got the bawdy allusion. Recruits were taught not to refer to their rifles as guns. This was reinforced by repetition of a traditional ditty: "This is my rifle (point to firearm). This is my gun (point to pecker). This is for shooting (point to firearm). This is for fun (point to pecker.)" The recent increase in female recruits had not inspired revised lyrics. It was assumed that many women Marines wouldn't take offense at being presumed to have peckers.

"Lovely," Fran grumbled. "Don't apply for a spot on his defense team."

"Seriously, Setliff, I personally have never heard him make a sexist remark. If anything, he seems a little puritanical. He once chewed the ass of a lieutenant colonel who told a couple of—how shall I put this?—pussy jokes at the annual Field Grade Follies. The jokes followed a chaplain doing a soft-shoe routine with his teenage daughter, and a major's wife singing a Gordon Lightfoot medley."

"Good for him."

"Don't pull down your banner just yet, Susan B. Just because the general stands ready to protect women's delicate ears from dirty jokes doesn't mean he's going to protect their right to be warriors."

"But we're not talking about warriors here, Vic. Civil servants don't carry bayonets and M16s."

"Ah, but it's the principle. If you don't believe women can handle authority as well as men, it doesn't matter whether bayonets are involved. I expect that's what Mrs. Roundtree's attorneys will say."

Maldonado pulled a toothpick out of his middle desk drawer. Fran braced herself for disillusionment. There were a few things lust and Corfam couldn't overcome. Not many. But a few. Seeing the lust object pick lunch from his teeth was one of them. But Maldonado didn't. He used the toothpick to free a tuft of lint from the double-barred insignia on his shoulder. He did put the toothpick in his mouth eventually, but only to clamp it between his teeth.

"The general has women on his personal staff," Fran noted. "The nice-looking blond captain. The one with great legs and bad skin."

"That's the general's aide, Captain Rhonda Baptiste. Glorified errand girl. Arranges the general's personal transportation. She seems like a good officer. Serious. Keeps a low profile. Then there's Carolyn Holdsclaw. A civilian. She's the general's personal secretary. Handles his unofficial correspondence. As opposed to his staff secretary, a male major, who takes care of his professional correspondence."

Fran pictured Mrs. Holdsclaw. Somewhere between thirty and sixty and built like a pontoon.

"They are it, as far as the general's female staff is concerned."

It was a beautiful late-fall day, bracingly cool and sunny with a light breeze. Farther north, such a day could have passed for spring. They decided to walk to Headquarters Building, which was less than a hundred yards from base legal.

A parade flag wrestled against its rigging in the center of the building's circular drive. A ship's bell and two antiaircraft guns mounted in cement served as military-style lawn jockeys. The building was surprisingly accessible, Fran noted, like the newspaper offices. She and Maldonado walked into a large cathedral-high lobby divided by a curving staircase. Sparkling glass cases contained displays of Marine Corps memorabilia. At the top of the stairs was a red-carpeted landing big enough for official ceremonies.

The general's staff secretary, Major St. Legere, was waiting for them, grinning like a mule eating briars, as Grandmama Pattle would say. The major had no chin and less grammar. He delivered his mangled syntax in a voice that sounded like dead leaves trapped in an exhaust fan. But he was far from stupid.

"Just remember, Special Agent Setliff," he warned Fran with a wink, "flares illuminate both sides of the battlefield. While you're figuring the general out, he'll be figuring you out."

"That would be too big a job for me, Major, and not much of a challenge for the general," Fran replied with a grin of her own.

St. Legere greeted Maldonado with a nicotine-coated handshake and led them up the stairs. To the right of the landing was a long hall decorated with portraits of former base commanding generals and sergeants major. The hall to the left honored past commandants and sergeants major of the Corps.

They proceeded to the left and down the hall, past the base inspector's office, past the offices of two assistant chiefs of staff, to the end suite. St. Legere quickly introduced them to the general's aide, Captain Rhonda Baptiste, and his secretary, Carolyn Holdsclaw.

The general's chief of staff, Colonel Bob Knightdale, came through his open office door when he heard them and offered to tell the general they were there. The colonel didn't make it to the general's closed door, however. Johnson bounded through it like a rambunctious St. Bernard. He loped around the agent and the lawyer, slowing only to drop a folder onto Mrs. Holdsclaw's desk and pound Vic on the back. He approached Fran with such vigor that she nearly took a defensive step backward. But he stopped short of her comfort zone, bridging it instead with an outstretched hand.

The man could be three feet away, Fran thought, *and still knock you over.*

He herded Fran and Maldonado into his office, where he sat and told them to do the same, all the while maintaining a smile big enough to span a ravine. The light from the window behind him accented the bright auburn scattered through his graying hair. His desk was framed by two flag stands capped with brass eagles, one supporting an American flag, the other a scarlet Marine Corps flag fringed with gold. The walls showcased expensively framed personal photographs, as well as the plaques units traditionally presented to commanding officers when they departed. Johnson's collection also included the head of a tiger bagged in 1971 by Montagnard tribesmen in Vietnam.

He looked at Fran, then at Captain Maldonado. "I won't trivialize this serious situation with small talk. I realize time is precious. Please proceed."

If that's how he wanted it, Fran was glad to oblige. "General Johnson, did you know Ann Buckhalter?"

He nodded. "Yes. I met the Buckhalters when Gary and I were both at Second Fleet Support Service Group. This was almost ten years ago. I was the commanding officer of Headquarters and Service Battalion, just selected for promotion to colonel. Gary was the commanding officer of Eighth Engineer Support Battalion. I knew him and Ann pretty well because there were so few other officers in the group."

"Would you describe him as a good friend?"

"No, not really. But from what I saw and heard, he was a good officer. I knew he was a newly reformed drunk—a recovering alcoholic, I should say. By the time I met him, he was as straight-arrow as they come. The worst thing I ever heard about him professionally was that he could be inflexible. That seemed like fairly small potatoes to me." The smile incrementally shrank as he spoke. "But he was not a particularly likable guy. The standing joke was that when he signed the pledge, he promised to give up his sense of humor, too. I felt pretty bad about the jokes when I found out he had a son recently diagnosed with leukemia. Going through a nightmare like that can rob anybody of his sense of humor. I know. I lost my wife to cancer two years ago after a long, hellish battle. You think you understand, but you really don't until your own family goes through it."

Fran wondered if the general knew about the photo his son kept in his glove compartment. No call to bring that up, or the accident on Autumn Oval.

"And Ann? Mrs. Buckhalter?"

"Ann was terrific looking and very outgoing. She was certainly more of an extrovert than Gary. But the other officers' wives didn't seem to like her much. She gave the impression she thought she was too independent, too worldly for the Officers Wives' Club activities. My late wife, Theresa, tried to smooth the waters. She was a natural-born mediator. But the line was being drawn then between housewives who saw themselves as a critical part of the Marine Corps family and wives who wanted to distance themselves from their husbands' careers. Ann Buck-halter was one who wanted to distance herself, except when it served her purposes."

"What do you mean, sir?"

"During the Gulf War, Ann wrote tearjerker columns for the civilian newspaper about being a Marine Corps wife. It struck some of the other wives as hypocritical. The only time she was active in the Officers Wives' Club was during Desert Storm. Once that was over, she no longer participated. Matter of fact, I think she even got some kind of state press award for those columns."

"Was Ann flirtatious?"

"Oh, only in a harmless, charming way. I never saw her cross the line. Career officers of both sexes tend to marry people who know how to behave."

True, Fran thought. But there were exceptions. Like a certain major's zaftig wife who had to be ordered to wear a bra under the cobweb-thin tops she favored for trips to the Base Exchange. Nipples disconcerted the tank-top patrol even more than armpit hair, which the zaftig frau had also sported.

"When was the last time you saw the Buckhalters?" Fran asked.

"I saw Gary at Colonel Biggers's retirement last fall. We spoke briefly. At that time, I hadn't seen him since his own retirement. I don't recall Ann being with him."

"And the last time you saw Ann?"

"I caught a glimpse of her in the commissary parking lot a month or so ago. I can't pin the time down any better than that. Sorry. I waved, but I don't think she even saw me."

Fran thought the general's pupils had contracted ever so slightly when he answered the last question. And he was blinking less often. The St. Bernard had been replaced by a Doberman.

Until this point, Fran had only been taking notes. She now took a microcassette recorder from her briefcase and held it up. The general nodded, assenting to its use. She pushed the record button and said the date, the time, and the names of everyone present.

"General Johnson, will you describe your activities this past Saturday?"

"I got up at 0730, late for me. I took my black Lab, Bilbo, out for a jog, following my usual route—Seth Williams Boulevard to Stone Street, Stone Street to Brewster, around the golf course, and back to the generals' housing area. I was back by 0900. I fixed breakfast for myself and my son, Wally, made a second pot of coffee, and sat on my sun porch to read the newspaper while I ate. I showered. At 1000, I walked to the golf-course clubhouse to discuss next year's tournament schedule with the manager. I hit a few balls at the driving range while I was there and then walked home. I did some paperwork while I watched the Virginia-Carolina game. Kickoff was at 1230. I took several phone calls during the game. I don't know the exact times. I expect Southern Bell could give you that. One was from my son, to tell me he was going out to Onslow Beach with a pal. Didn't know when he'd be back. One was from my chief of staff, Colonel Knightdale. Oh, and one call was from a woman, a schoolteacher named Susan Ratchford I go out with occasionally. I had planned to take Susan to dinner that night. She called to cancel because her seven-year-old daughter was sick—a sore throat or something. You shouldn't have any trouble verifying all this. After the game, I brought in the mail. The mail included my bank statement, so I balanced my checkbook. I then took Bilbo out for a walk down by the river. Went as far as the gun club and the tennis courts."

The tennis courts were about midway between the general's quarters and the B.O.Q.

"I tossed an old tennis ball around for Bilbo to chase. Came home. I wrote a letter and watched the news on NBC. Fixed myself a tuna salad sandwich. Watched about half of *A Few Good Men* on cable. Couldn't sit through the whole thing. Ridiculous. Corporals reporting to colonels! Where the hell were the noncoms?" The pupils expanded. And he chuckled. "I'm a stickler for accuracy."

Fran's heart picked up the pace. The general's recitation was now approaching the time frame of Ann Buckhalter's death. So far, he had a remarkably detailed memory. And he was right. Everything he'd said thus far could be verified.

"After the movie, I walked Bilbo again at about 2100, this time around Autumn Oval to St. Mary's Street, around the golf course, and back. It was a fine night, but it had turned colder than I expected. I remember wishing I'd put on a heavier jacket. Oh, yes, I saw Colonel VanHouk come out of his quarters to close his garage door. I don't know if he saw me. After I got home, I read for a while, went to bed, and read some more. Lights out. That's it." Johnson gave a wry chuckle. "The irony is, it was the first Saturday in weeks I didn't have some kind of official function to attend."

Fran heard Maldonado shift in his chair and clear his throat. Round two coming up.

"General Johnson, Captain Maldonado has briefed me about the lawsuit filed by Charmaine Roundtree. We've been told that Ann Buckhalter had an audiotape that supports Mrs. Roundtree's allegations. On the tape, you allegedly state that you do not want women on your staff. We've also been told that Ann planned to give that tape to a civilian reporter the night she died."

The general's nostrils flared. "Captain Maldonado has told me about the alleged tape. I doubt it really exists. Oh, maybe somebody taped me saying something that a person with an ax to grind could claim showed a bias against women. I am not seriously concerned. I am confident that Ann's death had absolutely nothing to do with Roundtree's lawsuit. How could it? Wasn't it an accidental drowning?"

He directed the last question to Captain Maldonado, who was

looking at the tiger head. The last Fran heard, investigators hadn't reached any conclusions about the cause of death. Was the general trying to indicate what he wanted them to conclude? Was King Henry hinting they should mosey back over to the cathedral?

It occurred to Fran that Maldonado might really be there as the general's unofficial attorney, protecting Johnson's interests, as well as the integrity of the investigation. And if those conflicted? Where did that leave NCIS, exactly?

"The investigation is not yet complete, sir."

The silence went on a beat too long. During that time, the general's expression took on an annoyed coldness.

"Special Agent Setliff, I've been in the Marine Corps nearly thirty years. It's been my vocation, my avocation, my family, and my religion. But at some point, unless he's a complete jackass, a Marine realizes that his career, like everything else, must end. That career can end with a bang or a whimper, but it will end. I'll probably be long retired and forgotten by the time the Charmaine Roundtree lawsuit is over. But I assure you, as commanding general of this base, I have never done anything that was not in the best interests of the Corps."

Fran jumped, startled, when Johnson's arm shot across the desk. He jabbed at the stop/eject button on the tape recorder.

"I want to tell you a little story, Agent Setliff. A few years back, I was an assistant chief of staff at Camp Butler, Okinawa. A young girl, a Japanese national, was raped and beaten nearly to death in Naha City. She kept telling the police, "*Kokujin, yunifomu.*" Black man. Wearing a uniform. Because most of the black men on Okinawa were U.S. servicemen, and most of them were Marines, Okinawan officials demanded fingerprints and a photograph of every black Marine on the island. Corporals. Colonels. Every single one. Whether or not he was anywhere near Naha City on the day of the assault.

"I'm sure you're aware of the political thin ice involved. We want to keep our bases there as long as possible. The Okinawans want their beachfront real estate back. And the brutal truth is, some years, the only violent crime that takes place on Okinawa is committed by American troops.

"This particular incident couldn't have happened at a worse time. The commanding general of Marines on the island was in Hawaii, tied up in top-level discussions about a situation in Korea. The chief of staff asked me for advice. We decided to cooperate with the Okinawan authorities. He and I agreed that our relationship with the Okinawans was more vital than any inconvenience to some of our troops.

"We told our black Marines that they would not be ordered to let the Okinawan police photograph them, but that their cooperation would protect our mission. Of course, no one wanted to risk being sent home with a black mark against him—unfortunate choice of words. I actually went with a black lieutenant colonel who worked for me— as fine an officer as I've ever known—when he was photographed. He showed great restraint. I was ready to wring the neck of the little, slick-haired, bowing bastard they sent to take the pictures. My father is a Pearl Harbor survivor, for God's sake.

"For the first and only time in my career, Agent Setliff, I was ashamed. Ashamed of my leadership. Ashamed of the Marine Corps. I have never—I repeat, never—made another decision I was ashamed of."

Fran finally dared to breathe. "Did they catch the girl's attacker?"

"Yes. He was a seaman on a Nigerian freighter. He was wearing mismatched military-surplus clothing when he assaulted her."

Fran thanked the general for his patience and waited for him to stand so she and Maldonado could, too. On her way out, she noticed a framed photo of a curly-haired boy being tightly embraced by a woman with thin arms and hands that must have been plumper when she first wore the chunky engagement set that fell over the first knuckle of her ring finger. A companion photo showed an older version of the boy, this time alone and scowling into the sun. He was kneeling in the prow of a sleek green whitewater canoe with "Semper Fi" stenciled on the side.

ooooo

When she stepped outside Headquarters Building, Fran felt the shaky relief of a kid leaving the principal's office.

"Well?" Maldonado asked. "How do you think it went?" He put on his garrison cap and shoved his hands in the pockets of his jacket.

"Am I talking to friend or foe?" she asked sourly.

"Friend, of course. What makes you think that's even in question?"

"I just had the feeling in there that you were acting as some kind of . . . buffer."

"So? A buffer protects one side as well as the other. Listen, I've got a proposition for you. You check in with your boss, and I'll go back to work. When you can cut yourself loose, call me and we'll go scope out the bears."

"There's a game today?"

"You're cute, Setliff, you know that? And philosophically speaking, I guess you're right. In life, there's always a game somewhere. But I'm talking about four-legged bears."

"Is this like the old come-on about submarine races?" Her sunny side was coming back up. "I heard that a sailor inviting a girl to the submarine races is like a civilian inviting her to see his etchings. Bear watching sounds like the Marine variation on the theme."

Fran was kidding. She knew numerous black bears roamed some of the remote training areas within Lejeune's 110,000 acres. So many were on the loose that the base issued bear-hunting permits. She had heard the animals weren't shy either. An MP who had taken part in a rugged overnight exercise told Fran, "The critters were so friendly, some of the guys thought they were gonna end up engaged." She smiled, both at the recollection and at Maldonado.

He gave her a friendly frog-punch. "No master plan, lady. Once in a while, I just like to drive out to the boonies at night and observe. It's professionally useful. Gives me more insight into hairy unpredictable things."

Fran laughed. "You should meet my cousin Eustine."

ELEVEN.

If it had been anybody but Vic Maldonado, Fran would have backed out.

By 2230, after she finally caught up with Boyette and transcribed notes and tape, she was so tired she was seeing things in triplicate. Boyette allowed her to skip his second all-hands, but he told Rumley to fill her in on Ann Buckhalter's preliminary autopsy results and to show her the photos of Ann's body taken at the Naval Hospital.

Ann hadn't suffered much apparent damage. Because she had been submerged, there was no lividity. She had some silt and plant debris in the corners of her eyes and mouth, and silt thickened with blood plugging her nostrils. Superficial bruises were on her cheek, brow bone, and one arm. Evenly spaced scrapes along one cheek, and a bald spot in the most convex part of one eyebrow. She could have gotten those injuries banging against the pier piling or struggling to disentangle herself from fishing line and crab pot. The water at the end of the pier was not much deeper than Ann was tall. If not for the entangling debris and a rusty fishhook nabbing her down jacket, she might have popped to the surface like a cork.

More interesting were the scraps of paper clinging to her skin and wet hair. Fran asked Rumley if they were flotsam from the river. He didn't think so. The scraps were twenty-pound laser-printer paper, all with torn, not cut, edges. Similar scraps were found adhering to the pier pilings and in the crevices between the planks. One was still clutched in Ann's hand. It appeared that she had been trying to destroy something.

"Love letters?" Fran suggested.

"On laser-printer paper? Not very romantic. And from the quantity, the writer would have to be long-winded."

"Blackmail, maybe?"

"Naw. That would call for brevity even more than romance would."

Some of the scraps had computer printing on them. Unfortunately, the paper was biodegradable and had started to disintegrate as soon as it got wet.

Fran sighed. Grisly police photos didn't move Fran nearly as much as this kind, in which the victim was relatively unscathed. It was like Ann was almost alive. So near and yet so very, very far.

"Tox isn't complete," Rumley told her, "but indications are that Ann had some itty-bitty marijuana fragments in her hair, too. Pressed into the roots above the ear with the missing earring."

A pothead? That didn't sound in character with what Fran knew about Ann Buckhalter. She looked up at her fellow agent in surprise.

"Tox prelims show no illegal drugs in her system. Just food, a prescription antidepressant—paroxetine, I think—and legal adult beverages. But it does appear she acquired the marijuana fragments about the same time as the paper scraps. Details and hair follicle analysis to follow."

She started to push the depressing photos toward Rumley.

"I've saved the best for last," he said, and pushed them back. "Ann's most serious injuries were under her hair. She had multiple unexplained blunt-force injuries on the crown and left side of her head. No skull fracture. Nothing that could have been fatal or probably even left her unconscious, but too serious to be explained by an underwater run-in with a crab pot or a pier. No splinters either."

"You mean she was struck on the head before she went in the water?"

"*Au contraire*. Whatever she was struck with hit her after she was underwater. The blows drove microscopic bits of river life and paint right into her scalp. She didn't live long after that, although the cold water makes it a difficult call. All we know for sure is that drowning was the cause of death."

Fran picked up a photo showing the left side of Ann's head. Yes, she could see discoloration and swelling in the mastoid area. The discoloration darkened, then disappeared into the hairline. Whatever blows caused the head injuries might explain the missing earring, possibly knocking it out of the earlobe. By contrast, the right-side head view showed no comparable discoloration but clearly showed a silver hoop set with tiny bits of glittery marcasite.

"Hold on. Did you say paint? The pier isn't painted, is it?"

"Right. And it wouldn't have been this kind of paint anyway. Tiny flecks of high-tech black and green vinyl paint and an even tinier fleck of clear spar varnish."

"Considering all the boats going up and down the New River, the flecks could have washed up under that pier from just about anywhere, anytime."

"Sure. Or they could have come from whatever struck Ann Buckhalter on the head as she was about to die under that very same pier."

ooooo

Fran decided not to go straight home and brood about loose threads and blunt trauma all evening. She would grab her chance to be alone with Vic Maldonado. She just wished she could take a shower and change clothes first. Under the fluorescent light in the field office women's room—a converted utility closet—her face was the color of overcooked egg yolk. She scrounged some blusher from the Military Police lost-and-found locker.

Maldonado drove a Miata with a tan vinyl top. The long stretch of highway, pitch black except for the headlights, was soothingly monotonous. The rustle of his coat—he had changed out of his uniform—the graceful thrust of his hand as it shifted gears, the lovely wail of Linda Ronstadt through the car's top-quality speakers, all were a feast for romance-starved senses. The woods rose up on both sides of the road, as crisply defined as strokes of India ink on blue display board. A handful of stars twinkled through bleary clouds.

He did most of the talking. He told her his parents had managed a small municipal children's park while he was growing up. His father maintained the rides and a small petting zoo. His mother sold tickets and supervised the ride operators and vendors. Maldonado and his brother and two sisters got to ride everything for free. But they had to help out by picking up trash and scraping gum off benches. At least his dad rented portable toilets whose cleaning was included in the lease. The kids had to clean up only the incidental revolting messes, not the routine revolting messes.

Later on, when Vic was in high school, his father got a desk job with the recreation department and his mother went back to school for her teaching certificate. Vic went to NYU and spent two undergrad summers in platoon leaders' class at Quantico, thereby earning his officer's commission. He went through Columbia Law School as an inactive second lieutenant in the reserves. Specialized in civil-rights law. His brother studied computer programming at a community college. His older sister was a sister. A nun. The other was human resources manager for a pharmaceutical company.

Fran was relieved his family background was no more upscale than hers. She just wished she didn't have an ex-husband in her bio.

He asked why she had gone into law enforcement. She explained that she'd wanted to be a cop of some kind ever since she was a little girl—from the day she watched deputies pour jugs of pea-green moonshine, garnished with straw and the occasional carcass of a still-smiling frog, down a storm drain in front of the courthouse. "Those deputies are doing God's work," her teetotaler grandmother had raptly announced. And Fran had decided that pouring moonshine down a storm drain might be just the thing for a religious woman.

"I was a very self-righteous ten-year-old," she said. "I had so many perfect-attendance pins for Sunday school, my dresses looked like dart-boards when they went in the wash."

Maldonado laughed. It was a clean, meaty laugh.

Abruptly, he shut up. He turned off the ignition and craned his neck over the steering wheel. She craned, too. All she saw at first were some dumpsters eerily illuminated by a floodlight mounted on a telephone pole. Next to the dumpsters, some big, lumpy bags of garbage rustled in the breeze.

Maldonado twisted toward her and lowered his head close to her shoulder. Fran flashed back to middle school, when Bobby Bristlethorpe snaked his arm over her breast in the balcony of the old Loew's Theater. She reflexively leaned away—as she had then—before realizing Maldonado was reaching between the bucket seats to get something out of the back. When he turned around, he was holding a billy-club-sized flashlight. He clicked it on and aimed it through the windshield, sweeping it over the dumpsters.

Fran's eyes followed the beam. "God Almighty!" she gasped. In the shimmery runner of light, the lumpy bags grew wriggling snouts and beady, blinking eyes. The snouts projected from shaggy heads the size of tractor tires. Fran thought she counted six.

Apparently, the smell of human flesh didn't appeal to them. Or scare them either. After a few indifferent glances in the direction of the Miata, the big animals returned to snuffling through refuse they had pulled from the dumpsters. Pizza cartons and ration trays seemed especially enticing. One bear lifted a liter plastic bottle over its dropped jaw to catch a few dribbles of Mountain Dew. Another stood on its hind legs and rubbed happily against the projecting lip of the dumpster door.

"This beats all," Fran whispered. "They're making such a mess! I'm surprised the game warden doesn't make people lock the dumpsters."

"No good. Bears are smart. They could open a bank vault if a couple of rancid Whoppers were inside. Anyway, from the base's point of view, it's cheaper to clean up after the bears than man a dumpster security detail."

Fran folded her legs under her. Without the motor running, the car was chilly.

"Cold?" he asked. "Want to go?"

"Oh, no! I wouldn't miss this for anything."

He stretched his arm behind her shoulders and pulled her closer. It didn't do a thing for her cold feet, but the rest of her felt as spark-prone as two sticks being rubbed together.

Suddenly, one of the bears bellowed, shook its massive head, and smacked a second bear with a front paw. The object of contention was a KFC bucket. The second, smaller bear backed away, then quickly lunged at the attacker, peeling back its upper lip to expose long, yellow teeth. The mingled grunts and growls ricocheted among the metal walls of the open dumpsters, sounding like steel drums played in hell. She felt a prickle of fear.

The two bears exchanged swipes. Then the larger one shoved the smaller one in the direction of the Miata. Fran and Maldonado froze. The smaller bear circled behind the car, using it as a barricade. It paced in increasing agitation, bellowing at every turn. The bigger bear tracked the pacing with a swaying head, then lumbered to within a few yards of the car. It stopped short directly in front of the hood and slowly rose on its hind legs, sniffing the air with a slimy snout.

The two people in the car didn't breathe. She instinctively pressed closer to Maldonado, who gently squeezed the back of her neck as a gesture of reassurance. With his free hand, he clicked off the flashlight. She hoped that was because bears didn't see well at night and he was expecting the animals to be drawn back to the floodlight once the area around the car was dark. The bigger bear dropped to all fours. But the one at the rear of the car started grunting excitedly and butting the rear bumper. The little car rocked like a toy boat.

"Oh, Jesus," Maldonado whispered. "The ice chest! I left the ice chest in the trunk."

Fran didn't understand but was alarmed by the tone of his voice.

He squeezed her neck a little harder. "I haven't washed it out since I went shrimping."

Their eyes met and locked when they heard a grating sound. The bear was trying to bite through the Miata's bumper to get to the shrimp smell. *A bear is eating Vic Maldonado's car!* Fran thought wildly. She glanced up at the convertible top and realized with horror that their heads were shielded by only a piece of plastic. It might as well have been Handi-Wrap.

Something in the smaller bear's changed vocalization alerted the bigger bear. It shuffled toward the noise to get a better look. *God, no!* The car might withstand a little roughhousing from one bear, but two—or six!—could work it over like a paper shredder. The bear that had been chomping the bumper sprawled over the trunk. Fran thought she was going to vomit when she heard the sound of ripping vinyl behind her. She slunk in her seat in a ridiculous effort to shield herself under the mini-dashboard. Inadvertently, she kicked her purse. And the nausea abated sharply.

"Vic, I've got my nine-millimeter," she said softly.

Maldonado looked startled, then smiled wryly. He shook his head. "Get it out, but let's try something else first. Buckled up? Hold on to your skivvies, Setliff."

She grabbed the console with one hand and the door handle with the other, the pistol under her instep. She pressed her head against the neck rest and imagined herself on the Big Bad Wolf at Busch Gardens. He started the engine and threw the Miata into reverse and then immediately into drive. The bear behind the car was thrown off balance and possibly singed by the exhaust pipe. It ran bawling into the trees, shrimp forgotten. Maldonado then executed the fastest three-point, two-wheel turn in Miata history. Fran opened her eyes long enough to see the bigger bear's head jerk back in surprise. It gave one reverberating growl before dropping to the ground and hurrying off in the same direction as its sparring partner.

"You okay?" Maldonado said when they were safely back on the highway. "Jesus, I'm so sorry. That was the stupidest thing I've ever done, I swear to God. I've been out here a half-dozen times, and the bears never came anywhere near the car."

"Did you bring a trunk full of bear bait those times?"

"I did say 'stupidest,' didn't I?" He patted the interior roof of the car. "Those guys could have ripped open a ragtop like a bag of Fritos." He shook his head, chuckling. "What was I worried about anyway? I forgot I was with a cop. I'm not sure how a nine-millimeter would work against a bear, though. If you didn't drop it with the first shot, it might have got really pissed off."

Fran started to laugh, too. It was mostly the nervous laughter of relief, but that was okay. Relief was a highly underrated feeling.

"Vic, when I stop having flashbacks, I'm going to thank you. I haven't had so much fun since I used to watch my brothers shoot water moccasins out of the trees." She was laughing for real now. "Being scared shitless definitely makes for a memorable evening."

"No kidding? Out of trees?"

"Sure, city boy. Water moccasins like to sun themselves on branches hanging over creeks and rivers. I guess the water acts like those reflectors movie stars use to get a tan. Oh, Vic! I wonder how much damage they did to your car."

He shook his head ruefully. "I'm not too eager to explain this to my insurance agent. He better not ask why I didn't get the other guy's name."

She laughed harder. He grabbed the back of her neck and pulled her toward him, playfully bouncing her cheek against his shoulder. *The man can do more with a neck*, Fran thought, *than most can with inner thighs*. He didn't release her before quickly pressing his lips against the top of her head.

They reached the turnoff to the base's industrial area, then passed the steam plant. The clock was running. If she wanted to find out more about him, Fran reminded herself, she'd better start steering the conversation.

"I've told you about my unnatural union with Marlon. What about you? Ever been married?"

"Nope."

"Come close?"

"More than once, I'm embarrassed to say."

"Really? Ever been officially engaged?"

"That, too."

"When?"

"Currently, as a matter of fact."

Currently? She hadn't seen that coming. A girlfriend, maybe, but a fiancée? Fran was too surprised to ask for details. He, however, volunteered that her name was Monica, and that she lived in Wilmette, Illinois.

Thank God he didn't volunteer a description of her gorgeous hair or whatever the hell else Monica had. Probably tall. Slinky. Perfectly symmetrical C-cup. Wore thong underwear and never once felt like a cellulite incubator with a permanent wedgie.

Crap. Why didn't Fran just stick a KFC bucket on her head and let the bears make hash out of her? She was too wasted to disguise her disappointment. Why bother? But if Maldonado noticed that all of a sudden she'd run out of perkiness, he didn't show it.

She turned up the volume on his CD player and glumly focused on the concertina wire spiraling by her window. She couldn't shake the feeling of his fingers on the back of her neck. Or his lips on her fuckin' hair. *You just let that Lava fly, Grandmama.*

TWELVE.

WEDNESDAY

Dull-eyed and droopy-tailed, Fran drove to work an hour early, for no good reason she could think of. She chose the roundabout way, through the officers' housing area. Joggers with reflective strips on their jackets were trotting across the Wallace Creek bridge. Fran noticed that the bridge's Don't Feed the Alligators sign had been taken down. She hoped that meant alligators were no longer cruising the waterway between the creek and Gottschalk Marina. At least the base's bears stuck to the boonies.

Like buckshot drawn to a magnet, Fran couldn't stop herself from pulling into the B.O.Q. parking area next to the pier where Ann's body had been found. She kept hoping the atmosphere around the death scene would send up some kind of supernatural smoke signal.

The yellow tape was down. The command center tent had been struck. One MP vehicle was parked across two spaces in the middle of the pavement. She greeted the occupant, an MP cuddling a coffee thermos the size of a beer keg. His utilities were so heavily starched that they crackled when he rolled down the window.

He told Fran that a fingerprint team from the State Bureau of Investigation had spent the night in the suite where Ann Buckhalter stayed. The state agents needed the dark to use luminol. Fran was willing to bet the blood-detecting chemical hadn't revealed any stains connected to Ann's death.

The only other lively thing the MP had noted was a little girl who must be staying with her parents in the B.O.Q. building on the opposite side of the street. She'd ridden off with a giant plastic owl in her bike's basket. One of those decoys meant to scare off crows. Made a couple of early commuters do a double take, he said.

Fran drove slowly back up Charles Street, past the Officers Wives' Club Child Care Center. Only the children of officers could use the ranch-style facility surrounded by a ten-foot chain-link fence. The center was funded by Officers Wives' Club dues and fund-raisers. The child-care center for children of enlisted Marines was in an enlisted housing area. It was funded by the base's Welfare and Recreation Department. The social and financial distinctions of rank were stamped on military brats at an early age.

Cars parked alongside the center were disgorging small children. Two women were unloading babies from car seats. Two others were in the playground area, talking with their heads close together. Fran bet herself they were discussing the retired lieutenant colonel's wife found in the river. She mentally paid herself off when one of the women jerked a thumb in the direction of the B.O.Q. and the other gave an exaggerated shudder.

Fran's eye caught a young woman wearing an oversized sweatshirt and workout leggings. Her hair was clipped to the top of her head. She was standing at the fence, apart from the other women, with a small boy. The boy was hopping excitedly from foot to foot, watching a klatch of rotund rabbits nibble grass on the opposite side of the chain link. The rabbits, longtime golf course residents, were oblivious to the squealing child.

Fran recognized the woman. Blond. Bad skin. Great legs. Captain Rhonda Baptiste, General Johnson's aide. Fran eased off the road and leaned out the window.

"Good morning, Captain. Your little boy? What a cutie pie. We met yesterday, remember? NCIS special agent Fran Setliff."

"Sure. Hi. Please, call me Rhonda."

"And I'm Fran. I didn't think the general ever let you leave Headquarters Building."

"It's almost true. My son thinks I mostly come out in the dark, like Dracula. Looks like you get an early start, too."

Without makeup, Rhonda Baptiste's complexion problems were more obvious. But she also had a kind of rough-cut prettiness. Her smile, directed at the little boy, was nice. Her teeth were as outstanding as her legs. Fran wondered if Baptiste's parents had been willing to spring for orthodontia but not Accutane.

"This is Jeremy," the woman said, tousling the boy's hair.

Jeremy tackled his mother's knees, throwing her off balance against the fence. She laughed. He grinned.

Fran didn't envy the captain her job. An aide didn't actually have to shine the general's shoes, but he did have to facilitate their being shined. *How does a female aide's role differ?* Fran wondered. She doubted Captain Baptiste had to stand by with Johnson's head scrubber while he took a shower, like she had heard one general's aide did. The plus side of being an aide was having the opportunity to regularly suck up to top-level people. The only contact most captains had with generals was a sweaty handshake in a receiving line. The captain did all the sweating, of course.

As Rhonda Baptiste and her son headed toward the door of the child-care center—young Jeremy gamely racing a toddler on a Big Wheel—Fran decided to take full advantage of her chance meeting with Baptiste on neutral turf. She found a parking spot and waited.

A few minutes later, Baptiste came out of the center sans son. Fran caught up to her walking toward her car. The captain looked melancholy. It occurred to Fran that leaving a child every morning for the pleasure of coddling a general might be a wrenching experience for a mom.

"I can't imagine how you juggle all those hats and still come up with a happy, healthy kid like Jeremy. I can barely manage to keep my cat alive."

Baptiste kept walking but slowed. "Is this going to be a professional discussion?" the captain asked. "You must know I'm aware of your agency's theory that there's some connection between the general and that woman who drowned."

Fran stepped in front of her so they were eye to eye. "No theory. He doesn't deny it. Okay, Captain. I'm going to be as blunt as a ball-peen hammer. Until this investigation is officially closed, I'll think about Ann Buckhalter a lot. I'll think about her while I'm flossing my teeth. I'll think about her in the checkout line at Food Lion. I'll think about her during foreplay, if any such activity takes place. But I don't pitch bogus compliments to people smart enough to see through them. It's simple, really. My colleagues are all men. I wouldn't mind having a few acquaintances at Lejeune who aren't."

Baptiste sighed, then smiled. "Sorry. You're right. It's not easy fitting into a new mold. I know."

"Isn't your husband a Marine, too? Does that help?"

"Yes. He's a great guy, and we've been lucky. We haven't been geographically separated yet. But it's inevitable, if we're both going to put in our twenty. My husband, Steve, is due for an overseas tour next summer. I could pull mine at the same time, but I'd like to stay with

General Johnson as long as he's at Lejeune. I want a career with the Corps. General Johnson can help me make the most of it, if he wants to. But anybody who thinks you can fit a child into your career as easily as you put another key on your key ring is nuts."

"Well, you seem to be better than average at keeping it all a-jinglin.'"

Baptiste opened the trunk of her car and took out a perfectly pressed women's "Charlie" uniform, skirt and tunic. No utilities for Johnson's people. She hung the bag in the backseat.

"Thanks. Bottom line: I'm here because I'm motivated. There are things I would change. I believe things will change. Any organization's got room for improvement, right?" Baptiste unzipped her fanny pack and tossed it into the front passenger seat. "My turn to be nosy. The investigation into the drowning—how is it going?"

Fran hated having to be evasive, after the captain had been so frank. "It's the early stages for this one. We agents focus on our assigned facets of the investigation and leave it to the bosses to put the whole thing together. You never met Ann Buckhalter, did you?"

Baptiste shook her head. "I don't even know what she looked like. Attractive, I hear. Rumor is that she was shoved in the river by a jealous boyfriend. Or a jealous husband."

"Not a segue from that, I promise, but did you know Mrs. Johnson? I noticed the photos of her and their son in the general's office."

"No. But people who did know her still get misty when her name comes up. I think she did a lot of nice things for people without expecting anything in return, not even recognition."

"A sad loss, then. Well, I should head to the office. Really nice talking to you, Rhonda."

The two women got into their respective cars and went their respective ways. Fran wondered if Captain Baptiste would tell the general they'd run into each other. What would he make of it? It had been an honest-to-God coincidence, but she doubted he'd believe it.

THIRTEEN.

As soon as she got to work, Fran regretted coming in early. Boyette was sending her to Raleigh. She could have avoided the rush-hour snail-slog if she'd hopped directly onto Highway 24 instead of coming on base first.

Her mission was to assess the Buckhalters' living situation and wheedle permission to look through Ann's home office. She didn't have much chance of getting a search warrant. If Buckhalter said no, that would be that.

The drive to Raleigh was painless as long as she could fight off pedal fever until she got past the speed trap in Richlands. Once she hit Interstate 40, the speed limit was seventy.

She had been to Raleigh often enough to have a good idea where the Buckhalters lived even without Boyette's directions. She called Buckhalter from a restaurant just off the beltline. She didn't want to give him much advance notice. As far as possible, she wanted to see the house as Ann last saw it.

Fran was pleasantly surprised when the woman who answered the phone—Gary's mother—insisted Fran come right over. At that point, she felt a stab of guilt. She was dropping in on a family preparing for a funeral. *Merry Christmas, y'all.*

The house was an attractive ranch at least twenty years old but well kept, in a subdivision of similar houses. The pearl-finish Thunderbird in the driveway was a recent model. Fran supposed Ann's Camry was still in the impound lot at Lejeune.

Gary Buckhalter was leaving as Fran arrived, but she didn't get the feeling it was to avoid her. He still had a regulation haircut, she noted. Most men who had any hair left when they retired let it grow out. He looked annoyed, but Fran didn't read too much into it. She told him investigators hoped that something in Ann's office might "clarify" what happened the night she died. It sounded pretty lame, but Buckhalter waved Fran in like the necessary evil she was. He introduced Fran to his mother—a rosy dumpling of a woman, mid-sixties, maybe, in a shiny lavender jogging suit—and said he'd be back in about an hour.

The woman fluttered and hovered, chatting awkwardly for a few moments before showing Fran which room had served as Ann's home office. Fran couldn't make her understand she was a federal agent but not an FBI agent.

A bit more fluttering and she withdrew, leaving Fran to take a closer look at a display of family photos. Buckhalter was a man who had a hard time smiling for the birdie. He looked particularly disgruntled in an informal group shot that showed him in an open-collar shirt. Ann, on the other hand, was full of sexy glee in a fiesta-pink sundress. She gazed at the camera with smiling, parted lips. Between them, a child who must be their daughter, Deirdre, grimaced self-consciously over barbed-wire braces.

Most of the pictures were of Deirdre. Many also featured horses. Tiny Deirdre in a velveteen hard hat standing next to a shaggy Shetland. Middle-sized Deirdre in snug riding coat and snugger pants, leaning over the neck of her mount, patting the red ribbon hooked to his bridle. Teenage Deirdre preserved in airborne elegance going over a jump. Fran admired the girl's proficiency. And guts. To Fran, a horse was sixteen hundred pounds of nervous jitters. One thing was clear, especially in the recent photos. Like her mother, Deirdre was a looker.

The house's furnishings were the typical military-family mix of East and West: Asia's Seven Lucky Gods sitting alongside Williamsburg pewter on a Victorian end table; rattan papasan chair and La-Z-Boy recliner backed by a Korean rosewood screen. In the corner of the living room was a pile of battered boxes marked "Christmas decorations." Fran wondered if anybody would have the heart to put them up.

Ann's office did not appear to have been tidied recently. Week-old dates on her "Far Side" desk calendar hadn't been discarded. A CD encyclopedia was still in the open slot of her computer tower. A few stray paper clips and a stained coffee coaster nested in a light layer of dust.

Two small file cabinets were in the office. Fran gave the files a quick thumb-through, but nothing unusual caught her eye. One cabinet held an archive of press clippings, business expense receipts, and old notes. The other held accordion folders, each labeled, containing research material on more recent projects.

Gary's mother came in the room just as Fran was getting ready to look in Ann's desk. Would Fran like a cup of coffee? No thanks. Did Mrs. Buckhalter—Bev—know where Ann kept her audiotapes? The woman said she didn't know but would ask Deirdre. Fran heard Bev Buckhalter calling to her granddaughter as she walked down the hall. A few seconds later came the *thump, thump* of athletic shoes on uncarpeted stairs. A stunningly pretty teenage girl with carelessly combed hair appeared in the doorway. She looked calm, but it was the exhausted calm of somebody who was all cried out.

"Deirdre, I'm Special Agent Fran Setliff with the Naval Criminal Investigative Service. I'm so sorry about your mother."

The girl smiled weakly. She shifted from foot to foot, slowly slink-ing—that was the only way to describe it—into the room.

"Thanks. It's been pretty awful. If I didn't have Gamma Buckhalter, I couldn't stand it. They had to put my other grandmother—Mom's mom—on tranquilizers. She can't even drive a car yet."

"Have they set a date for the funeral?"

"Saturday, I think. The Naval Hospital is supposed to release Mom's . . . body on Friday. It's just going to be a memorial service. Mom is being cremated." Deirdre swallowed hard but didn't tear up. "She used to say she wanted to be cremated because it was silly for a shriveled-up old body to take up good ground space. But it's kind of, you know, weird like this. Mom wasn't old and shriveled up."

Fran nodded. "Deirdre, I hate disturbing you and your family this way. But it's really important that we find out as much as we can about what happened."

"It's okay. It doesn't matter. I can't stop thinking about it anyway. God, if I just hadn't, if I didn't . . ." She waved her hands helplessly.

Deirdre wasn't aware Fran already knew about the alleged rape at the base stables. Better to let it stay that way, for the time being.

"Your mother's death was probably just a terrible accident, Deirdre. Nothing you did or didn't do would have changed anything. I want to look through your mother's things—her work things—to see if there's anything else we should know. Do you know where she kept her audio-tapes? I know she taped some of her interviews, like I do."

Deirdre hesitated. Her eyes shifted away from Fran. *Is she just reluc-tant to let a stranger touch her mother's things?* Fran wondered.

"Mom uses . . . used a microcassette recorder. One that fit in her purse. It runs those little-bitty tapes." The girl pointed at the desk. "I think they're in that bottom right drawer."

She was right. The drawer held a recorder and multiple clear plastic bags filled with tapes. A gummed label on each bag identified the tapes according to the names of the persons interviewed. Most of the bags also had dates.

One bag's tapes related to a committee planting dogwoods at the site of the Beirut Memorial. Another contained an interview with the first female general in the Marine Corps. Yet another was of the Charlotte lawyer heading up a fact-finding commission on base expansion.

Two of the bags were labeled "Answ. Mach." Fran noticed that Ann had one of the old answering machines that recorded messages directly on to a microcassette tape. It also allowed easy recording of phone calls, an advantage for a writer like Ann.

Fran asked Deirdre if the tape currently in the machine had been changed since her mother's death. It had not. Would she please remove it for Fran? She would.

Fran placed each group of tapes on top of a separate evidence collection bag, just in case she got the okay to take them with her.

"Deirdre, did your mom talk to you about projects she was working on?"

The teenager had collapsed, flexible as cooked vermicelli, onto a velvet ottoman.

"Not really. Not while she was working on them, anyway. After the story ran in the paper, we might talk about it. It used to bug me when we were at Lejeune and people would make such a big deal about her column. A counselor told me I was jealous of the attention she got." Deirdre sniffed. "I guess kids think they should get all the attention. You know, I never realized it before, but Mom and I mostly talked about stuff I was interested in. For me, that's horses. When I was little, I begged and begged them to get me a horse. But I understand now what a big expense that would have been. I used to argue that I could pay for a horse myself. I could earn money cleaning out stalls, working in the tack shop. Pretty stupid. Just getting a horse shod costs more than I'd have earned in a wee—"

The chatter stopped so abruptly, Fran turned around to look at the girl. Apparently, she wasn't all cried out. Tears were threatening to overrun the beautiful eyes.

"I miss him so much," Deirdre whimpered.

Him? Fran started. *Good Lord, she can't be talking about the Marine she claimed raped her, or tried to rape her, or whatever the hell it was she claimed.*

"Manila Bay," Deirdre said tenderly. "I used to exercise him and groom him and feed him and lunge him. I bet by now he's forgotten everything we did together."

Fran, choking off a smile, was glad Deirdre was staring at her own fingers stroking the thick carpet. Rape or no rape, Deirdre was still a baby.

"I didn't have the heart to go back to Camp Lejeune for a while," she sighed, wiping her eyes. "I've been riding at this private stable here in Raleigh. It's okay, but I don't know anybody there yet."

Fran didn't say anything.

"Manila Bay belongs to this woman who's in Japan with her husband. I got to ride him whenever I wanted, in exchange for helping take care of him." She looked up at Fran with a lopsided smile. "Dad is supposed to go to Lejeune tomorrow to sign some papers. Do you think he'd let me go with him and ride Manila Bay while he's doing that? Do you think anybody would think it was weird, me going there? I mean," she added hastily, "so soon after Mom died?"

Fran tried not to show her surprise. It was understandable that a teenager, even one who had just lost her mother, would want a little diversion. But one would also think that, for this particular teenager, the base stables would have such a bad stench, figuratively speaking, she'd never want to go back. Horse love must be an awesome emotion.

She couldn't imagine Gary Buckhalter allowing Deirdre to go anyway. Unless he saw it as a way of letting her confront her fears and defuse them. Fran hadn't gotten the idea Buckhalter was the kind to delve into his teenage daughter's psyche, but she could be wrong. She had thought Marlon was sensitive, and he turned out to be as emotionally impervious as vinyl siding.

"I don't know if tomorrow is a good time—for your dad, I mean—but whenever you get there, I think it'll be okay," Fran said. "If Manila Bay can help you through this, more power to both of you. Maybe I should say more horsepower."

Deirdre rolled her eyes and giggled. A nice, normal teenage giggle.

"I'm sure everyone will understand," Fran said. She changed the subject when she found a charge-card receipt from the Base Exchange in Ann's desk. "Did you ever go to Lejeune with your mother after your dad retired?"

"Sure. We'd go shopping, or she'd drop me off at a friend's house on base. I got my driver's license two weeks ago. Mom promised I could do the driving next trip." Her voice trailed off.

"Oh, you're sixteen now?"

Deirdre nodded.

Fran wondered if that would affect the case against the Marine she had accused of assaulting her. A miss was as good as a mile in a statutory rape case, she supposed. Nearly sixteen was still fifteen.

Fran's eyes flickered over the dark screen of the computer centered on the desktop. "Are you guys on the Net?"

"Of course."

"Do you know your mom's email address?"

Deirdre nodded. "Mom used email a lot. I asked her why she didn't just email stuff to the newspaper instead of driving all the way to Jacksonville. She said she needed to recharge her 'journalism batteries' in a real newsroom."

Passing along hot tips face to face also avoided leaving an electronic trail, Fran knew.

At Fran's request, Deirdre turned on the computer, accessed the Internet, and opened Ann's email file. No password needed. There were two unopened messages, one from lena_and_ricky@earthlink.net, the other from uncletooter@aol.com.

"Oh, crap. Nobody's told them about Mom yet," Deirdre moaned over Fran's shoulder.

Nothing in the outbox, and the email history cache was empty. Ann must have cleaned out her files before she left for Lejeune.

Fran had the girl open Ann's document directories. The material was similar to what Fran had seen in the two filing cabinets. No red flags. Fran let Deirdre shut the system down.

Disappointed by how little she'd accomplished despite the long drive, Fran was mulling her next move when she heard Gary Buckhalter return. She tried to eavesdrop on the exchange between Buckhalter and his mother but couldn't make it out. Seconds later, he appeared at the door to Ann's office and told Deirdre to go help her grandmother. Deirdre shrugged docilely, sprang up on her long legs, and left.

Buckhalter looked at the bagged tapes. "Did you find what you were looking for, Agent Setliff? I'm sorry I wasn't here to help you."

His words were cordial enough. His tone? Not so much.

"I'm the one who should apologize, Lieutenant Colonel. I would appreciate your permission to take these microcassettes with me. I'll get them back within a day or so."

Buckhalter hesitated, lips pursed in annoyance, but finally said, "Take whatever you need. Just write out some kind of receipt, will you? So I don't forget where things are."

"Of course." She looked out the window at an empty bird feeder. "Nice house. Did you move in right after you retired?"

"Yes. We were lucky to find it. Real-estate prices in this area have skyrocketed."

Fran was aware he was touching the back of her arm, discreetly steering her out of the room. She discreetly dragged her feet.

"I've heard that moving back into civilian life can cause culture shock after twenty-some years in the military."

He gave a cheerless laugh. "I got my wake-up call when the bank's loan officer asked me which rank was higher, a major or a sergeant major. Most of the civilian world doesn't know the difference and doesn't care."

"Lieutenant Colonel, were you ever concerned about Ann's safety when she was at Camp Lejeune by herself?"

"Never. Lejeune was like our own backyard. If I worried at all, it was about the drive there and back. I could imagine her being in an automobile accident, but something like this? Never."

Fran scribbled out an itemized receipt for the fourteen microcassettes as they slowly moved down the hall and on to the front porch. His hand was positioned on the door handle, ready to shut it between them as soon as she handed him the piece of paper. But Fran had one more topic she was determined to touch on.

"Navy commander Kevin Terry. Ann called him Saturday. Is he a friend of yours and Ann's?"

Buckhalter glanced over his shoulder into the house. He did close the door, but with both of them on the outside. Snatching the receipt from her hand, he leaned his face much closer to Fran's than was comfortable for her. Behind the lined bifocals, his eyes were the mottled brownish gray of a rattlesnake skin.

"Listen carefully, Special Agent Setliff. I know what you're fucking getting at. Yeah, he was a friend of Ann's. He sure as hell wasn't one of mine. I don't have any respect for Commander Terry, either as a man or a doctor. I doubt Ann cared what I thought, and she didn't have to clear any of her friends with me. And I'll answer the question you're itching to ask. Yes, I knew. I knew about her and Terry."

"You didn't mind?" Fran blurted out.

The look he gave her was withering. But it was too late to rephrase the question.

Buckhalter took her not so gently by the elbow and quasi-frog-marched her down the porch steps to her car. The driveway was separated from the adjoining yards by a high privacy hedge. No neighborly assistance would be forthcoming should he decide to throttle her.

Fran fumbled at the touchpad that would unlock her car, dismayed that she'd handled Deirdre so well and Buckhalter so poorly. She was trying to think of something to say that would neutralize his anger when he surprised her by stepping back and speaking calmly, almost in a monotone.

"You see, I didn't think I had the right to condemn her. I wasn't always there for Ann. She resented me for it, and I couldn't seem to make things right again." He took a carefully controlled breath. "I liked to think Ann was just using Terry to work her way through a screwed-up stage of her life—like I once used alcohol. Better a boyfriend than booze. Sooner or later, she'd get it out of her system and we'd hit some kind of balance. Anyway, that's what I hoped."

"She told you about her relationship with Terry?"

"She didn't have to. She'd come back from Lejeune wearing a honeymooner's glow. Once in a while, I'd even get some of the erotic overflow." His smile was bitter and wrenching. "It didn't take much to figure out who was responsible. She mentioned him just a little too often. Talked to him on the phone just a little too often."

Did Buckhalter want Fran to feel sorry for him? Baring his soul to a stranger seemed out of character for the engineer. On the other hand, how would a retired lieutenant colonel typically behave after his unfaithful wife's body was fished out of a river?

"It doesn't sound like you were worried she'd leave you."

He turned away from her, absently ripping sprigs from an overgrown holly. "I don't think she was planning anything along those lines.

And I sure as hell know he wasn't. Years ago, I got the idea that Terry had only one special person in his life, and that was Kevin Terry. Anyway, Ann would never have done anything that would make her look less than perfect in Deirdre's eyes."

"Do you think Commander Terry could have done something to hurt Ann?" Fran intentionally didn't specify the kind of hurt.

Buckhalter snorted. "He didn't care enough about her to hurt her." Fran must have looked startled. "I mean, I don't think he had strong enough feelings about her to fuel a crime of passion."

"Lieutenant Colonel Buckhalter, your mother said the memorial service is Saturday. Will that be here in Raleigh?"

"No. What's left of Ann's family is in Michigan. We're flying out Friday night. I think it bothers Deirdre that Ann is being cremated. But frankly, I wouldn't know where to bury her. We've moved around so much, I'm not sure where home is. For most of our life together, the Marine Corps was our home." He smiled. "But they've evicted us."

ooooo

Fran drove back toward Lejeune with a brand-new Chieftains CD pumping through her speakers. She favored Tejano music in hot weather, Gaelic in cold. The Tejano was in good supply at the Base Exchange. The Chieftains were not. Which was surprising considering the high percentage of Irish-American officers in the Corps. Daugherty. Downs. Kelley. Cathcart. McGowan. Mourne. One couldn't cross a parade field without tripping over Irishmen, orange and green.

But Fran had discovered the Chieftains on her own. The traditional pipes and fiddles made her homesick for central Alabama. Where she once rassled with her barefoot brothers and caught night crawlers and ringworm at the same time. Who wouldn't get a little choked up?

FOURTEEN.

Fran's interview with Lieutenant Colonel Buckhalter yielded one important bit of information. Contrary to what Commander Terry thought, Buckhalter knew darn well that Ann had been cheating on him. And something else. Buckhalter had sounded as if the affair was recent—ongoing, maybe. Terry had implied it was long over.

She had intentionally avoided one question: Was Buckhalter aware that Ann had started taking Deirdre to see Terry again? Fran wanted to confer with her boss before risking more of Buckhalter's wrath. Or inflicting more pain.

She dreaded the task of listening to the fourteen microcassette tapes. Fortunately, Fran had a good ear for high-speed playback. She figured she could always hire herself out as a Chip 'n' Dale interpreter if the law-enforcement thing didn't work out. Another mitigating factor: She could listen to them at home, where she could incinerate her quads on the step machine at the same time.

A quick once-over for pending cases at the field office, then she'd check out for the day. Eight-pounders missing from the base bowling alley. A racist message hacked into the school superintendent's staff newsletter. She'd call her boss from home.

Her purse was already on her shoulder when her desk phone rang at 1630 on the button. The voice at the other end was male and briskly to the point.

"Keep an eye on your mailbox, Special Agent Setliff. You're going to be getting something that's relevant to an important matter."

Fran reacted brilliantly: "Huh?"

The caller hung up. *Shit.* She hit the redial button. It rang, rang, rang, forever rang. She searched a reverse locator site on the Internet. A public phone in Swansboro.

She kept repeating what the voice had said, writing it down as she mumbled. Mailbox. Something "relevant to an important matter." That was pretentious syntax for a crank caller. The mailbox part made Fran think of a letter bomb. But why warn her to keep an eye out for it? Which case, anyway? The word *important* wasn't necessarily helpful. What was critical to one person might not be worth an eight-pound bowling ball to somebody else.

Whoever had called knew her personal extension, something not just anybody had access to. The man's voice sounded phony, as if he'd made a halfhearted effort to disguise it. She tried to place it geographically, but the best she could do was eliminate everyone south of Virginia, and New Yorkers, if they all sounded like Rudy Giuliani.

She abstractedly drummed her fingers on the plastic bags holding Ann's tapes. What if the caller was talking about a tape? *The* tape. The tape Lowell Mapp had been expecting to get from Ann the night she died. The tape Fran knew damn well wasn't in any of those plastic bags in Ann's desk. Ann would never have stowed it so offhandedly.

But wait! Even if there was such a tape, and even if the mystery caller was indeed referring to that tape, why would he pick Fran to get it? She hoped that being chosen as the recipient didn't have anything to do with ovaries.

FIFTEEN.

WEDNESDAY EVENING

Instead of bugging out early, Fran was pacing the linoleum when she heard Boyette's voice on the landing. She had caught a bad case of what Grandmama Pattle called "nerve-chiggers" waiting for him to show up. What was standard operating procedure if a politically explosive audiotape showed up in her mailbox?

She hurried to flag down Boyette before someone else did. He was giving a parting handshake to a white-haired SBI criminologist whose name she couldn't remember. In situations like this, the all-purpose "sir" was invaluable. The SBI agent, a retired Marine, had stopped by Lejeune on a dual mission. He wanted to give Boyette a preliminary report on evidence collected at the Buckhalter death scene, and he wanted to make a stop at the base liquor store. On base, liquor was tax-free.

After the three exchanged pleasantries, Boyette signaled Fran to stand by while he walked the criminologist downstairs. She waited impatiently by the back hallway window.

When Boyette returned, he began by tersely noting that, as Fran had expected, the SBI had found no blood in the room or hallway of the building where Ann had stayed. "Any injuries she had, she probably didn't get inside the B.O.Q.," he concluded.

He practically waved off the peculiar phone call Fran had received. Before they got to that, Boyette said dismissively, he needed to caution Fran about something else. She braced herself. Surely, he wasn't going to say something about her and Vic Maldonado. No. This had a much higher pucker factor.

General Johnson had been making inquiries about Fran, Boyette said. Ostensibly, the general was impressed by the professionalism of the agency's sole female. The timing of the general's interest, however, made Boyette queasy. Once a commanding general put his foot into something, it was hard for him to take it back out. She must be especially careful about everything she said outside the agency, he warned.

Fran started feeling queasy herself. But she was relieved, too, that her boss was watching her back.

Abruptly reverting to the subject of the tape, he advised her not to listen to any recording that fell into her hands by an unorthodox route, including her mailbox. She must not place herself in a position where she could be blamed if the tape was damaged. Plus, it might be wise to have someone from base legal, or even the chief of staff, present the first time it was played.

Boyette cautioned her not to get too excited about the mysterious phone call. She was jumping to conclusions, he said. More likely, considering Fran's area of expertise, somebody had taped his coworkers conspiring to steal government property. Wasn't she investigating some missing bowling balls? Or maybe some officer was pissing off his clerk by making that clerk type book reports for the officer's fifth-grader.

Boyette was so unflappable, he made Fran feel like a frantic fifth-grader herself. After he pitter-patted away, Fran scuffed out a few more irritated turns in her cubicle and admitted he was right. She was mostly relying on a strong gut feeling. To Boyette, that was like a passenger on the *Titanic* relying on Dramamine.

She sublimated the gut feeling about the tape into a gut yearning for dinner by the time she got to her car. She was examining a new-found bumper scrape when Agent Hank Bunn walked by.

"I don't care how hard you rub that puddle-jumper, Aladdin, it ain't gonna turn into a Corvette," Bunn said.

"Good. I can't afford to play radar tease with state troopers like you do," Fran shot back.

Hank Bunn's tarp-covered 1988 pace car straddled two parking spaces at the far end of the lot. The tarp and the pristine custom paint job beneath it were courtesy of the contractor who had spray-painted the water tower across the street without factoring in wind velocity and direction. Or noting the vintage Corvette parked thirty yards away behind a chain-link fence and some lacy shrubbery. Fran hoped the contractor would forget about the incident before that water tower needed painting again, and that she would remember which space Hank had been in at the time.

ooooo

Some days, the commute seemed endless. But Fran enjoyed living at the beach. Hurricanes were the big liability. Only one road connected Atlantic Beach to the mainland. And it seemed like old State Road 58 got washed out every time somebody took a piss in the ocean at high tide.

Fran's lot boasted no palm trees or pili grass. Her house of weathered cedar shingles was built on pilings, its back deck extending over a marshy inlet. Below were a carport and a storage room that held her washer/dryer and the boxes of stuff that seemed to follow her everywhere.

She realized that anybody who could find out her extension number at the field office also could figure out where she lived. She was glad her mystery caller planned to leave his surprise at the end of her gravel driveway in her little black mailbox, planted at an unnatural angle due to a monster storm that had crashed through a year earlier. There were lots of nooks and crannies in that storage room below the house. And Fran had always been that downcast kid left with an empty basket after the Easter egg hunt.

Her cat greeted her with his leg-rubbing routine. *Why you and nobody else?* Fran grumbled, patting his arched back. She fed the cat and herself before tackling Ann Buckhalter's tapes. She'd let the fat-free hot dogs and coleslaw settle before getting on the step machine.

She had one thing to be thankful for. Because Buckhalter had voluntarily given Fran the tapes, she was spared the rigmarole of checking them in and out of the evidence locker. She juggled the plastic bags, deciding which ones to play first. There just had to be a pony somewhere in all that shit.

Two hours later, she had given up on the pony and was just hoping to stay awake. The tapes were numbingly boring. If she had a nickel for every time somebody said "you know" or "like," she could have bought herself a Corvette like Dunn's. She had to hand it to journalists, Ann Buckhalter among them. At least in law enforcement, there was a cut-the-crap attitude that discouraged people from droning on. No way could Fran have faked two hours of rapt interest while interviewing some woman about the parasite threatening the dogwoods at the Beirut Memorial.

Fortunately, a few of Ann's interviews were considerably shorter, leaving large portions of several tapes blank. Fran saved the two

answering-machine tapes for last. One was recorded when Ann lived at
Camp Lejeune, making it at least two years old. Why had Ann saved it?
Maybe she planned to reuse it. Or maybe she just wanted a reminder
never to cover another Officers Wives' Club performance of *Little Black
Dress*.

The reporter who had the base beat before Lowell Mapp had left a
couple of messages. So had editor George Griffin and police reporter
Clay Konnecker, who urged Ann to get to the scene of a street prostitu-
tion bust before a dead ringer for Rosanne Barr cackled her way out of
processing.

The last tape Fran listened to was the one she had asked Deirdre to
remove from the machine. Sensing the home stretch, pony or no pony,
Fran perked up.

The first half-dozen messages on the tape were from or for Deirdre:
a girl named Sandy; a girl named Beth; the guidance counselor at Deirdre's school; her dentist's appointment clerk. Those were followed by a
message from George Griffin for Ann, a message from a mortgage bro-
ker urging the Buckhalters to refinance their home—cut short—and
an extended interval of silence.

But then, as Fran was about to press the stop button, a child's voice.
So guileless and sweet, it could have been Tiny Tim about to bless us,
every one. "Hello? I want, um, I'm trying to find that lady that works
for the, um, the *Daily Up-server*." A fumble of the receiver and a child's
noisy sigh.

*Probably some kid writing a school report about female journalists with
dysfunctional families*, Fran thought.

"Could you help me? Did you ever hear of, um, a lady named
Highlock? This guy that's, uh, you know, staff of chief officer? If you
call me, I can tell you something important about them. Bye."

Staff of chief? *Okay*, Fran thought, *kids mix things up*. Could be the
child meant a Navy chief on somebody's staff, or even the newspaper

staff. Didn't Jimmy Olsen call the editor of the *Daily Planet* "chief"? Or had the child meant to say "chief of staff"?

Fran replayed the message until it played by itself in her head. And it wasn't just the words that held her attention. "A lady named Highlock?" The wording sounded as if the child was hinting at hanky-panky between a chief and a lady named Highlock. But that was lascivious grown-up thinking. The voice sounded way too childlike to be dishing dirt.

She prayed to God the child wasn't an abuse victim who had finally worked up the courage to tell somebody. But why would he—or she—call Ann? Maybe it was a brother or sister of one of Deirdre's friends. *Shit.* The poor little thing had forgotten to leave a number. He—or she—was probably wondering why Ann never called back.

According to the tape, the message had come in on a Thursday at 6:05, but it could have been weeks ago. Apparently, Ann erased some messages and saved others, like most people. But that made it nearly impossible to establish a chronology. Fran set the tape aside to share with Boyette and tried to put the voice out of her mind.

She took a long shower, pausing occasionally to ambush her cat by flicking water over the rod onto his head. He disliked water but couldn't resist coming into the bathroom to swipe under the shower curtain at the mouse-like tips of her toes. Fran could have sworn he gritted his teeth every time he was beaned by one of her mini water bombs. Why didn't he just stay out of the line of fire?

Fran flashed back to Deirdre, a teenager wanting so much to return to the base stables, even though she claimed she had the worst experience of her life there. Some things were like magnets. Depending on which end was up, they could either attract or repel.

SIXTEEN.

When she got out of the shower, she discovered Vic Maldonado had called and left a message. She hadn't heard the phone because the exhaust fan in her bathroom roared like a wind tunnel. He said he wasn't calling about anything urgent or official. He just wanted to know if she'd suffered any "ursine" flashbacks. In fact, he was thinking of naming his first daughter Ursine in honor of the occasion. Would she call him back when she had a chance?

Not on your life, damn engaged Yankee, Fran thought. *Okay, the fact that you called gives my shriveled-up ego a boost. And thanks for assuming I know what* ursine *means, even if you do mock Southern names in the process. But I'm a heap smarter than my cat. I know how to dodge bullets, especially emotional ones.*

She mixed herself a rum and Coke and went out on her deck. She was barefoot and wore only a pair of flannel boxers and a short terry-cloth bathrobe. It didn't matter. With the light off, her deck was dark as coal tar. The nearest house, across a strip of marsh, was invisible except for a single yellow porch light. The only time she saw interior lights or heard any commotion from that direction was on weekends. A second home, probably. Her neighbors to the left and right were screened from view by a sand dune and a pine thicket, respectively.

She leaned into the lovely, cool air flowing over the deck railing and slipped her arms out of her robe, letting the top fold down over her tied belt. The wonderful, tingly feeling of emerging goose bumps spread over her bare skin, drawing her nipples up tight and hard. This was a pleasure she allowed herself once in a while, when the air temperature was just right. She raised her chin and forced her shoulders back sharply, like the figurehead on a ship. There was an erotic element to her little ritual, certainly, but the pleasure predated her awareness of the sensuous potential of breasts.

When she was young, she and her brothers would race into a summer's day with bare feet, bare, bug-bitten legs, and bare backs and chests. She remembered the identical downy whorls between each pair of shoulder blades as she scampered behind Rusty and Baron. The three of them were virtually genderless, especially since Fran's hair had been pixie-clipped for warm weather.

Then came the summer her mother went to the hospital to bring forth brother number three. Fran's aunt Libby came to help with the older children. Her first morning in charge, Aunt Libby grabbed Fran's arm as she was barreling shirtless through the door and insisted she "put on a top" before leaving the house. Fran called for Rusty and Baron to come back, assuming they must put on tops, too. But Aunt Libby waved the two boys on, laughing and shaking her head.

When Fran later joined her brothers, wearing a ruffled halter with a scratchy tie at the neck, she knew something had changed forever. By the time her preoccupied mother again took charge of their household, Fran was as self-conscious about going out of the house without a top as she had been indifferent before. She now had a gender. And hers had to wear a top.

But not on my own private back deck, baby, she thought. *I am one with the genderless breeze.*

Maybe because her mind had drifted to the memory of childhood, Fran thought again of the wistful little voice on the tape. She decided to stop by the base stables the following afternoon, on the chance Deirdre would be there. If so, maybe she could tell Fran who had left the message about the Highlock "lady" on Ann's answering machine.

A gust of unexpectedly chilly air prompted her to wrap her bathrobe back around her bare torso. As she tied the sash, she shivered and had the unsettling feeling she was being watched. Ridiculous. No one could possibly see her there on the overgrown blackness of her deck. Not without night-vision goggles, anyway.

SEVENTEEN.

THURSDAY

Weekday mornings were quiet at the base stables. The only activity visible from the street was in the pony ring, where sullen little Shetlands trudged a circular rut, burdened by euphoric preschoolers.

Two horse cultures coexisted at Lejeune's stables: Western scruffy and English stuffy. Neither came cheap.

The Western camp was comprised of the Marines temporarily assigned to work at the stables. They favored jeans, pointed-toe boots, and raft-sized saddles. In their spare moments, they might practice for rodeo competitions or even organize a mounted color guard for parades. The color guard was an off-and-on project because base horses came from several sources and the quality of their training varied. Some had been signed over by financially strapped former owners. Others had been brought down from Quantico's base stables in response to Lejeune's greater demand.

Unlike the Marines, most of the adolescent girls who took riding lessons on base were enamored of English saddles, sausage-skin jodhpurs, and velveteen hard hats.

It was nearly 1300 when Fran slowed for the Horse Crossing sign on Stone Street. The Jeep Cherokee belonging to Agent Rodney Walker's wife, Elva, was parked by the tack-shop door. Elva must be there with her daughter. Fran realized school kids were on Christmas break. Rodney joked that he and Elva spent more money on horses than a couple of racetrack touts. It was worth every cent if it kept daughter Ginelle horse-crazy instead of boy-crazy for another year or two.

Fran waited, turn signal blinking, while a string of novice riders crossed the street toward the area set aside for guided trail rides. A couple of the trail riders were Marines who looked like they'd never been nearer to horseflesh than the pet food aisle at the grocery store. They were finding it hard to look macho while gripping their saddle horns with white knuckles. The Marine horseman guiding the group of greenhorns was wearing a weather-beaten hat and a smirk. He deftly steered his horse around a pair of nervously giggling female riders. Meanwhile, the horses were rolling their eyes at each other as if to say, *Who are these assholes, anyway?*

Fran turned and parked under a mile-high pine tree. She spotted Elva immediately, hanging over the jump-ring fence. Ginelle was in the ring, looking self-confident on a big bay. She directed her mount over a low jump and cantered to the opposite side of the ring, where two other girls were waiting their turns. The instructor, a woman wiry as a whipsnake, wore a hand-shaped Panama pulled down over her eyebrows. She barked at Ginelle, telling her that her stirrups were too long, before ordering the next girl to make her horse trot.

"She talks to those kids like they're in boot camp," Elva grumbled when Fran walked up.

"Well, somebody's doing something right, El. Ginelle looks terrific." Fran's words turned that frown upside down.

"Thanks. Say, what are you doing here? Somebody stealing hay?"

"No. I thought Deirdre Buckhalter might be here. I went by their home in Raleigh yesterday, and she said she might come down with her dad. She is really hooked on some horse named San Juan Hill or Bay of Pigs or something. Sad situation. Deirdre seems like a nice kid."

Elva looked over her glasses at Fran. "It's the nice ones that cause the most trouble. Yeah, okay, it is sad. In any case, I wouldn't know Deirdre Buckhalter if I saw her. She's a couple years older than Ginelle. I did see some kids that looked to be about that age back by the tack line."

"Keep those heels down!" the instructor bellowed at a student. Fran winked at her friend, miming a couple of exaggerated goosesteps as she walked away.

She headed in the direction Elva had indicated, past two barns and toward a covered area where five horses were tethered. She'd seen enough Westerns to know what a tack line was. Three of the horses were being groomed and saddled in preparation for lessons. One old dun mare was standing alone, motionless except for a flicking tail.

The door to the tack room was open. Fran stepped into the cool gloom. The wall in front of her was hung with bridles and cinches and saddles and dusty hard hats. To the right of the wall, a giggling Deirdre straddled a narrow bench. Her outstretched boot was between the knees of another girl, who had her back to Deirdre. The object, Fran guessed, was to remove Deirdre's tight knee boot. Its mate already lay on its side under the bench.

Both girls glanced up when Fran approached. They had the plastered-down hair left by exertion and snug-fitting riders' hats. Even with helmet hair, Deirdre was beautiful. The other girl looked like a painted egg.

Deirdre squelched her giggle when she recognized Fran, as though ashamed of enjoying herself. When Fran smiled, however, Deirdre smiled back.

After apologizing for forgetting Fran's name, Dierdre introduced her to the chunky, dark-haired Beth Amans. All three laughed when

Deirdre's foot suddenly popped out of the boot, throwing Beth off balance. Fran squatted on an overturned bucket while the girls knocked dirt clods off the boots and put on rubber muckers.

"These are getting too tight," Deirdre complained of the leather boots. "But I just got them three months ago. Dad'll have a cow if I ask for another pair."

Although Fran suspected Deirdre was in the best bargaining position with Dad she'd ever be, she said nothing.

"Come one, Deedee," the Amans girl said, brushing off her grass-stained jodhpurs. "I have to put Guam in her stall."

Deirdre got up, too, but hesitated. Which stall was Beth taking Guam to? she asked. Fran caught the note of anxiety, but Beth was oblivious to it, as well as to the relaxed exhale that followed her answer. It appeared that as long as Deirdre stayed away from a certain barn, she was okay with the base stables.

Beth's brisk exit ahead of her friend allowed Fran to draw Deirdre aside for a moment.

"Deirdre, I listened to your mother's tapes last night," she said quickly but softly. "There's one message I didn't understand. I thought you might know what it was about."

"What? Oh, okay."

Fran told her about the "Highlock" message, going so far as to try and mimic the voice.

Deirdre was uninterested. "It doesn't mean anything to me. I never heard of anybody named Highlock. I don't even know anybody named Locke."

"Yes, you do!" Beth Amans yelled from where she was untying the dun mare. "Tanya Locke."

Little pitchers have ears like Mount Palomar, Fran thought.

"Oh, yeah," Deirdre admitted. "But I'm really sure I don't know anybody named Highlock. Not in Raleigh or here either."

Fran already knew nobody living at Camp Lejeune was named Highlock. She'd even checked the alternate spellings Highlocke and Highloch. Nor was there anybody by those names in the Raleigh phone book, nor in any of the places the Buckhalters had been stationed.

All in all, Deirdre didn't seem like the kind of teen who was likely to conjure up a rape or, for that matter, need years of counseling. But as Grandmama Pattle would say, "Just 'cause the wind ain't blowing right now don't mean the barn ain't blowed away."

The girls departed. Fran headed in the opposite direction, out the far end of the barn and into another. Horse barns were pretty much as she remembered. Stalls. Straw. Shiny greenish piles of shit. Flies of the same color and almost as big. Not so many this time of year, though.

She walked out the far-side door of the second barn, into the sunshine. A scowling but good-looking young Marine was to her left, wrapping the legs of a big, docile gelding. The Marine had a cigarette clamped between one eyetooth and his lower lip. Partly blocked from view by a wheelbarrow full of grain pellets, he didn't see Fran or the redheaded teenager staring at him over a dividing wall. The redhead was fourteen-year-old Marissa Knightdale, daughter of Colonel Bob Knightdale, General Johnson's chief of staff. Fran didn't envy the Knightdales their next few years of child-rearing. Marissa was as well developed as an eighteen-year-old and, reputedly, persistent as a battering ram with boys. That and the flaming red hair made her hard to miss.

Seemingly unaware he was being mentally gobbled up by an under-age girl, the good-looking Marine was busy muttering to himself about somebody named "Fucking Asshole." Fran wondered if he was familiar with other FAPS who worked, or had recently worked, at the stables. PFC Jervet Harriman, for example.

She stepped into Marissa's line of sight, cocked her head at the Marine, and inquired about what he was doing.

He squinted up at her from under a tightly rolled felt brim. His hazel eyes were shaded by feathery black eyelashes. No wonder Marissa was ogling.

"Pardon, ma'am? Oh. I'm wrapping this fella's legs for a trip to the beach."

"The beach? Why? Does he need to work on his tan?"

The Marine smiled through a stream of cigarette smoke. "I wish. Got a VIP staying in one of the staff officers' beach houses. He wants to ride on the beach. Why don't he get himself a nice beachball to play with?"

"Is it such a big deal, taking a horse to the beach?"

"That's not it, ma'am. It ain't good for horses. Running on the sand. They sink in too far, and it stretches their tendons. And they're not used to it. Makes 'em stumble."

Onslow Beach was a beautiful stretch of North Carolina surf and sand that fell within the boundaries of Camp Lejeune. Parts were used for amphibious training exercises, but much of it was reserved for recreational activities.

Fran bent down and stage-whispered toward the felt brim. "VIP? Come on. Who is it? The commandant?" General David Wallace, the Marine Corps commandant, had been known to visit the base without public announcement.

The Marine laughed and flicked his cigarette butt into the dirt. He took his hat off—not enough hair to get plastered down—and fanned it over his knee. "Sorry, ma'am. I'm not at liberty to say. Would if I could. You the mother of one of these kids?"

"I couldn't afford to be their mother."

He grinned, then returned to his task and let the scowl slide back into place.

Fran caught the movement of Marissa Knightdale's beckoning finger and walked toward it. The finger backed away, leading Fran from the barn. She'd met Marissa once, at a change-of-command reception, but she doubted the girl remembered her.

The bouncy redhead scanned the area theatrically—no one in hearing range—cupped her hands around her mouth, and leaned close to Fran's ear. She reeked of piña colada lip gloss. "You guessed right! It is the commandant."

Fran's eyebrows shot up all the way to her widow's peak. She wasn't shocked by the intel itself, but by its unauthorized source.

"Who?"

Fran must have looked dumbstruck. Or just dumb. Marissa snickered.

"Don't you know who the commandant is? You a high-school dropout or something?"

Being patronized by a fourteen-year-old snapped Fran out of her shocked stupor. "Oh, I know who he is. I'm just wondering how you know so much about his schedule."

"I overheard my dad talking to my mom about it," the girl said smugly. "Trust me. I know stuff. My daddy's a full-bird."

And if he knew he was supporting a motor-mouth mole, he'd be horrified, Fran thought. This little pitcher had Mount Palomar ears *and* a big mouth.

Marissa started to say something else but stopped short. Her jaw clenched as she looked past Fran's shoulder with an expression that would have made a cobra shudder. Fran turned to follow her gaze and saw Deirdre Buckhalter pause beside the open barn door to rake her boots over a boot scraper. She took no notice of Marissa and Fran. But the hazel-eyed Marine, leading the nicely wrapped horse out of the barn, gave Deirdre an innocuous fleeting look. Fran thought nothing of it, but it sent Miss Knightdale into a splotchy-cheeked fury.

"What makes her think she has a right to every cute guy?" she sputtered at Deirdre's unmindful back. "Hasn't Suzy Super Slut got enough people in trouble already?"

"Yeah, and her daddy isn't even a full-bird." Fran couldn't resist the jab but regretted it immediately. Who was supposed to be the grownup here?

Fortunately, Marissa was again diverted by the hazel-eyed Marine, who had stopped at a tack-line trough to let his big old charge take a big old drink. She flitted up and down the tack line, patting sequential flanks, determined to get his attention. He seemed determined to ignore her. He had plenty of common sense, Fran suspected, and knew to steer clear of nymphet noodle heads. Why hadn't PFC Harriman been as sharp?

Fran picked her way through the manure minefield to a soda machine outside the stables office. Had she learned anything useful, other than that Marissa Knightdale was a blabbermouth and that her parents should do a better job of supervising her eavesdropping? What other beans had that kid spilled?

She passed the Walkers at a distance but limited contact to a wave and happy thoughts. Rodney had joined Elva and Ginelle at the corral fence, and their family huddle was too darn cute to barge in on. Special Agent Walker loved his womenfolk, no doubt about it. But he also probably swung by the stables once in a while to catch a glimpse of his paycheck before it was converted into road apples.

EIGHTEEN.

"Dependents are like STDs," Boyette said matter-of-factly when Fran told him about the security breaches at Marissa Knightdale's house. "Containment depends on everybody keeping what they've got to themselves."

Boyette already knew about the commandant's unofficial visit, of course. The provost marshal would have let him know. No matter how unofficial or sub rosa the visit, the commandant required a special security detail and accommodation flourishes worthy of the man at the top of the heap. Schweppes tonic water in the fridge. Tahitian Orchid air freshener in all the heads. Oh, and the bedside table stocked with his favorite candy. Fortunately, NCIS was not on the front lines of Operation Almond Joy.

Boyette said he'd think about the best way to put a flea in Colonel Knightdale's ear. Meanwhile, she should stand by—maybe get a

Buckhalter toxicology update from Rumley—while he made a phone call.

"I have something for you to do, so don't wander off."

ooooo

Rumley greeted her with a strained smile. His chronic TMJ was giving him a fit. But he insisted that not talking at all would just make things worse.

"Ann Buckhalter had both alcohol and the antidepressant paroxetine in her system," he mumbled. "She ate not long before her death. The food and alcohol in her gut were what she bought at the club." Using a raised finger, he enumerated his points in the air. "We haven't found out where the paroxetine came from, but it wasn't a disabling, much less a lethal, dose. No more of the drug was found in her room or car. Neither Ann's doctor in Raleigh nor, according to you, Commander Kevin Terry had prescribed any meds for Ann or her daughter. But that doesn't mean it was stolen or came from a forged prescription. Some women pass prescription drugs around like cookie recipes."

"I don't think Ann had any women friends," Fran said.

Rumley shrugged. "Minute traces of marijuana were found in her hair, but none in her body, including hair follicles, and none in the room where she stayed. All indications are that Ann fell—or jumped—off that pier. She got tangled in some crab-trap lines and drowned. At this point, only three loose ends are keeping Boyette from announcing the death was accidental. One: the missing contents of that white plastic bag, which was empty when we found it in the B.O.Q. room but contained something—according to the bartender—when she was in the O Club bar. Two: all those pieces of torn paper found clinging to her body. Maybe she tore up something and threw it in the water. A suicide note, maybe, that she changed her mind about leaving. Or maybe she just went into the water in an area where there happened to be a bunch of paper debris. And three: those nonlethal blunt-force injuries to her head that we know she sustained after she was in the water. We don't know what—or who—caused them. Still, does any of that scream 'crime' at you, Setliff? Couldn't it be whispering 'misadventure' instead?"

"What if somebody pushed her in?"

"We've got nothing pointing to that, Fran. But for the sake of argument, even if somebody did push her in, that isn't a crime. Prisons would be full of eight-year-olds."

"What about pushing somebody in the water and making sure they can't get out?"

"How? By making sure a loose crab trap washes under that pier— weeks ago, maybe—and gets snagged by some even older fishing line? And by making sure Ann Buckhalter wears her hair down instead of up that night, so it gets snarled in the trap?"

"I just hate ambiguous outcomes, Rum."

"Yeah, they're almost as bad as wishy-washy outcomes. But another important ingredient is missing in your recipe for a crime: a motive. That's usually where we start. Why would somebody want this woman dead?"

"Jealous husband?"

Rumley shook his head.

"Officer boyfriend afraid he'd be court-martialed for adultery?"

"They'd have to kick all those eight-year-olds out of prison to make room."

"PFC lusting after Ann's daughter?"

"He was restricted to barracks."

"Gen—"

She'd nearly brought up General Johnson and the incriminating tape Ann was supposed to have had. But the drowning and the tape were still unrelated matters, as far as NCIS was concerned. The tape was connected to a lawsuit, not to a death.

Rumley stood and took his lower jaw in both hands. Wincing, he pushed back and forth like he was trying to pry a door off its hinges. Fran knew exactly how to relieve what was ailing him. She was a natural-born chiropractor. Dig in a thumb here, lift and pull there. But she had no intention of offering her services. Her golden rule was, Don't touch the boss or fellow agents anywhere you wouldn't want them touching you. She'd seen too many young women pat, pick lint from, and lean against coworkers, with bad results. She wasn't giving anybody an inch unless she was prepared to accept every inch he had. Maybe she'd make an exception if someone needed the Heimlich maneuver.

"I'm going to run get a Dr Pepper. If the boss asks for me, tell him I'll be back in two shakes of a sheep's tail. Can I bring you something? Ibuprofen?"

Rumley shook his head and lip-synced, "No thanks."

Fran trotted down the stairs and across the street. At the far end of the motel-style enlisted barracks was a Quonset hut that served as a tiny seven-day store. There wasn't any Diet Dr Pepper in the cooler, so she bought a Diet Cheerwine instead and trotted back to the field office building. Boyette met her downstairs, relieved her of the Diet Cheerwine, and handed her an unmarked legal-sized portfolio.

"I've arranged for you to meet the general at"—he flipped up his lapel and peeled off a sticky note—"Onslow Beach. Unit 6, the full-colonel-and-above unit. That's the one farthest from the bathhouse. The general is there making happy talk with the commandant, but he's expecting you. You have forty-five minutes to get there."

What the . . . ? Forty-five minutes! Fran sniffed her sleeve for attar-of-horse and checked the bottoms of her shoes.

"Captain Maldonado's going with you. I need the general to sign the transcript of the interview you conducted and Maldonado sat in on. He can witness the signature. On your way over, the two of you can give the transcript a once-over and see if you agree it accurately reflects the taped portion of the interview."

ooooo

She didn't see Maldonado until she reached for her door's keypad. He was standing by the left rear bumper, hands folded in front of him like a fig leaf, a file folder and red nylon ditty bag tucked under one armpit. His expression was blank.

She stifled the involuntary zing of pleasure she felt at seeing him and plugged in a little paranoia. Why hadn't Boyette sent Rumley to witness the signature? Rumley had actually helped her with the first draft of the transcription and was a notary, for God's sake. Was it Boyette's idea to send Maldonado, or someone else's? And why the rush? The one thing she was sure of was that her boss wasn't throwing them together in an effort to match-make. Boyette was as sentimental as a clogged sink.

"I smell a fix," she grumbled as she backed out of the parking space.

"Special Agent Setliff, I swear I have not been fixed," Maldonado said.

"It's not a joke, Vic. I don't need legal oversight."

"Maybe it's the CG who needs the oversight."

"Great. Cryptic and evasive. You must be a terrific lawyer. Just happened to be passing by? Staff judge advocate wants you out of his hair for a while? General Johnson wants you in mine?"

He looked genuinely surprised. "I'm following orders, just like you. Hey, I thought we were friends. Why all the hostility? And why didn't you return my call? I'm the man who saved you from being mauled by bears, remember?"

"You're the man who put me at risk of being mauled by bears," she snapped. *And mauled my heart immediately thereafter.*

She added lamely that she'd been busy. She wasn't good at the old romantic bob-and-weave. She flashed back to a song Grandmama Pattle used to sing: "I'd rather be in some dark holler, where the sun don't ever shine, than to see you another girl's darling, and to know that you'll never be mine."

She willed herself to focus on the upcoming assignment. A drive to the beach. A chance, maybe, to meet the commandant. Her dad would get a kick out of hearing that. She would not let herself look into Maldonado's beautiful, dark eyes. She wouldn't look at that cute upper lip either. Eyes straight ahead. Personal issues tossed.

Maldonado did not attempt to draw her out again. He busied himself sampling every radio station on the dial, eventually settling on Bob Seger. He whistled along, oblivious to how grating and off-pitch he was. Fran hoped his God-awful warbling would drive the lovely Monica nuts.

NINETEEN.

The unpaved road leading to Onslow Beach was blocked. The beach was closed to general traffic for the season.

Fran didn't have to get out. A man dressed in a red sweat suit with "USMC" stenciled in slick yellow letters across the chest was waiting for them. As soon as her Wrangler pulled up to the chain, the man screwed his cigarette butt into the sand and hopped up from the embankment where he'd been squatting. He unhooked the chain and waved them through with a big grin, telling them to pull over just beyond. In the rearview mirror, she watched him replace the chain and retrieve a beer can from a cinder-block stile.

"Who is that?" Fran asked.

"That's Colonel Ralph Schoengraf, CO of the infantry school," Maldonado said. "He's kind of a play date for the commandant. They go back a long way."

He rolled down his window. Fran noted that the man with the bristly white-blond hair approached Maldonado's side of the car instead of hers.

"Good evening, Colonel Schoengraf. This is Special Agent Fran Setliff."

"How's it going, Vic? Nice to meet you, Special Agent Setliff."

Schoengraf reached his hand through the passenger-side window and across Maldonado. Fran took it.

"Let me jump in my Jeep, and I'll lead you in. Wouldn't want the security detail to think you were some of the commandant's groupies."

They parked behind the bigger of two rustic but well-kept bungalows. An MP with an M16 and a holstered pistol stood between the buildings smoking a cigarette. A second MP was posted on a dune, scanning the area with binoculars.

Fifty yards away, just close enough to be recognizable, General David Wallace, commandant of the Marine Corps, was ankle-deep in the surf, looking intently to his right, hands on hips. He wore a sky-blue windbreaker and dark khakis rolled up to the knees.

Schoengraf said something to the nearer MP that got lost in the wind. The MP's response was to hastily bury his cigarette in the sand and readjust the angle of his utility cap.

General Johnson was waiting for them inside the beach house, which was comfortably furnished with sisal area rugs, upholstered rattan furniture, and a sixteen-bottle wine cellar. He offered them a beer, which she and Maldonado declined and Schoengraf accepted.

"I'll see if the four-star would like one," the colonel said, and left.

Johnson signed the transcript so readily, Fran assumed he had previewed a copy. He asked her about the Buckhalter investigation, and she gave him a sketchy summary of the toxicology report. Professional bobbing and weaving she could handle.

In a matter of minutes, he was steering them back out the door when Fran's eye caught a pair of seagoing canoes bouncing in the surf.

It was those boats, unnoticed by Fran earlier because of a fence-topped dune, that the commandant was watching so closely. He and Schoengraf gave the boats' occupants a cheer and an energetic thumbs-up when they raised their paddles to stage a mock pugil-stick bout.

"My son, Wally, and one of his friends," Johnson said, following her gaze. "Wally is quite the paddler. Expert fisherman, too." He frowned. "Dammit. I can order those boys to put on a PFD, but I can't make 'em keep it on, no matter how loud I bark."

"What can they catch out here, sir?" Maldonado asked.

"Oh, pompano, sea mullet, blues. Lots of pinfish, flounder. Follow that little brick walk down toward the beach and take a closer look, if you want."

They walked no farther than the tip of the dune, however. Schoengraf spotted them and motioned them forward, but Maldonado gestured a reluctant decline and pointed at his watch and the portfolio. The commandant paid them no mind at all.

From the dune, Fran clearly saw the two teenage boys, each in a high-riding canoe. The boy closer to shore, in a red canoe, was awkwardly trying out a scoop net. The other, in a green canoe, was several yards farther out, throwing a bunched-up net so expertly that it opened into a perfect circle before it sank out of sight underwater. His skill reminded Fran of a rodeo cowboy tossing a lasso over a steer's head. Soon after the net—edged with small weights and connected to the boy's wrist by a line—sank, he drew it up like a gigantic drawstring bag. One yelp of triumph over a successful catch, and he paddled over to the red canoe, where he dumped his net's contents. The boys fist-bumped before drifting apart.

Fran was so charmed by the scene, she was reluctant to turn away. But what happened next jolted her enough to make her stumble off the brick walk. The boy in the green canoe, whom she'd now positively identified as Wally Johnson, slowly stepped onto the gunwales of his pitching canoe and stood. Perched there, toes curled over the opposite top edges at the boat's widest point, he rocked gently back and forth. His arms were perfectly relaxed at his sides, swinging slightly with the motion of the boat. Fran was amazed at the boy's agility.

But the human teeter-totter bit was just his warmup. He then sat on the backless seat in the bow and crouched forward, grasping the gunwales at the point where they were as far apart as the width of his shoulders. Stiffening his arms and extending one leg and then the other, he pressed himself into a handstand. He held the demanding pose for several seconds while his audience, including the MP on the dune, whooped in admiration. Fran whooped along with them. The boy in the red canoe just shook his head and grinned. He'd probably seen the performance before.

The aquatic gymnast pulled off his cap, revealing a thicket of damp curls. The body was that of a lean, muscular teen, Fran noted, but the face was the same little guy cuddling with his mother in the photo in General Johnson's office. Wally Johnson was difficult, she'd heard, and might be on his way to a school for problem boys. But for a few seconds there, he was the most amazing kid she'd ever seen.

ooooo

Fran was mildly disappointed she hadn't been able to meet the commandant but also relieved when the O-6-and-up beach cottages disappeared from her rearview mirror. Vic was, apparently, ready to let his regulation hair down, too. He flipped off his garrison cover and began unbuttoning his shirt. The late-afternoon sun gave his undershirt a pinkish glow.

"What are you doing?" she asked, smiling. "Checking yourself for senior-grade cooties?"

"Take a right toward the all-ranks area, will you? Dammit, Setliff,

I've already worked ten hours today. We're at the beach. How's about we use the scenery for something pleasant?"

"Like skinny-dipping? Count me out. You're probably as irresistible to sharks as you are to bears."

She felt a little giddy, like people do when they've just escaped a high-stress situation. She giggled when he pulled up a trouser leg. Men's exposed shanks were the funniest things in the world.

"Maldonado, don't you dare take those shoes off in my car. I get enough sand in it from my own driveway. Last time I went home, I took my mama for a drive and she asked if I was dating an Ay-rab."

She turned off the engine. Though they were both laughing, Fran had the sense to realize Vic had planned for this. That's why he'd brought along the ditty bag. He now reached into the backseat for it with one hand while unsnapping his web belt. He pulled out a pair of faded baggies and, looking fixedly past her, took off his uniform trousers. He put the baggies on over a pair of knit boxers.

Fran sat half in, half out of the car, looking at him with frank admiration. The wind ballooned his T-shirt up over his chest. Under the regulation polyester had been more of that beautiful golden skin. And a belly covered with just enough smooth black hair. He emptied the ditty bag with a snap, forcing out a heavy gray sweatshirt that he pulled over his head.

He looked at her, frowning. "Even an Ay-rab would think you're overdressed, Setliff. Can't you at least unbutton a cuff or something?"

She decided to analyze his mixed message later. Using the brake as a shoehorn, she levered off her pumps and braced her feet against the dashboard so she could wallow out of her panty hose. That was as unbuttoned as she was going to get. If she took off her jacket, she might get unsightly arm-hair-raising goose bumps.

He hauled her up beside him. To steady himself, he dug one of his feet into the sand, bumping against one of hers. They both looked down. Her toes had a few flakes of three-month-old nail polish. His big toes each had a crabgrass-like tuft of hair on the middle joint. They laughed again.

She wasn't sure whether he released her hand or she took it away. They walked down the plank path over the dune with their hands at their respective sides.

Barely discernible in the distance, a man was jogging with a prohibited unleashed dog. Nearer to them but still out of earshot, two women appeared to be hobbling along the shore, hunched over canes. Upon further inspection, they were really raking at the sand with bamboo back scratchers, searching for shells. Fran was glad she was wearing a narrow skirt instead of pleats. She wouldn't want a wind gust to flash the fact that her underwear was strictly granny gear. Warmed by a whole day of golden sunshine, the breeze felt wonderful chasing around her thighs. And walking barefoot in her Anne Klein suit seemed so bohemian. She knew her hair looked like a bag lady's, but she didn't care. His hair was funny, too, blown against the direction it was combed.

Occasionally, he sidestepped and playfully jounced against her. And if she didn't hear something he said, he would pull her toward him for a lips-against-ear repeat. At one point, he fell to his knees and burlesqued trying to dig out a lightning-fast mole crab. When she laughed at him, he swatted at her bare legs with sand-encrusted hands. She hopped out of range and then hopped back. They must have looked like idiots. Or, as Rumley would say, dumbasses.

Maldonado sat back on his haunches and squinted up at her. "Did you know the Japanese use mole crabs in sashimi?"

Fran wrinkled her nose while considering the idea. "Well, if you think about it, they're not so different from crawdads."

"Good point. It's all in what you're used to. Did you know they don't eat cheese in China? Smells like vomit, they think."

She chuckled. "But they don't gag at the smell of ten-thousand-year-old egg?"

The discussion of exotic food brought the suggestion from Maldonado that they slip out the Sneads Ferry gate and get something to eat before heading back to Mainside.

What's going on? Fran thought. Why did every assignment with Maldonado segue into something dangerously date-like? Was he toying with her feelings? That would be a mean thing to do, and she didn't think he was a mean man. Or did he find her so unsexy that he viewed her as a female eunuch, the perfect companion for a man who was going to marry somebody else? No. She didn't buy it. If his feelings were neutral, why did he put his hands on her so damn much? Why did he stretch out their eye contact to the breaking point?

She was sure of only a couple of things. She was enjoying herself. And fiancée or no fiancée, if she ever had the chance to supplant the memory of Marlon's twitches, lunges, spasms, and fart-filled groans with the Maldonado version, she might jump at it. Being engaged was not the same as being married. Or so she'd keep telling herself.

He must have interpreted her sudden thoughtfulness as a reluctance to leave the beach. He sat and then lay back on the sand, hands behind his head. What was she to do? Stand there, letting him look up her nostrils? She stretched out beside him. Both squinted blissfully skyward.

She was studying a super-suggestive cloud when he suddenly sat up. Following his gaze, she saw with horror that the shell she was loosely cupping in her hand was sprouting hairy legs and stalks that ended in beady eyes. She scrambled to her feet, dropping the small hermit crab into the sand with a squeal.

Maldonado laughed. "Know what you are, Setliff?"

"Yes. Do you?"

"I know you're refreshing. Not naive, but not jaded. God knows, you're not pretentious. Whoever is with you doesn't have to waste energy trying to get past the bullshit."

She appreciated the praise but couldn't help feeling let down. They were the kind of compliments her brothers might give her. Or each other.

"Come on. Let's go eat," he said, pulling her to her feet.

ooooo

After a dinner that included overcooked but well-seasoned shrimp and lots of workplace anecdote swapping, Fran let Maldonado out of her car behind base legal. He said good night with a quick, eunuch-worthy kiss.

TWENTY.

Rumley was the only agent in the field office when Fran got upstairs. He buzzed her through the security door, where her appearance elicited a double take. He asked her if she'd run her hair through a cotton-candy machine and, seeing her bare legs, narrowed his eyes. Loudly, he sniffed the air around her.

"I'll sort them out for you," she said. "Horse. Salt water. Shrimp shells. Melted butter. Female pheromones. Result? Bad hair, good time."

Rumley smirked but didn't question her. He was her friend, not her girlfriend.

She was picking up her phone to call Boyette when she heard a commotion from the sidewalk outside. Despite the cool evening air, the window at the front of the building was open. Rumley was subject to more hot flashes than the Mid-South Chapter of the Elvis Presley Fan Club.

The commotion included several agitated voices, male and female, but no scuffling or obscenities. Probably not Marines. Fran glanced at her watch. It was after ten o'clock. Her agency had been keeping second-shift

147

hours lately, but the Provost Marshal's Office was usually quiet on a Thursday night. Especially on an off-payday weekend. She secured the envelope containing the signed transcript inside "Knoxette," the mini-vault Boyette used for after-hours material connected to active cases.

The noise from downstairs grew louder and moved toward the back entrance of the office. Fran walked to the landing window to see what was going on. Three MPs were herding a group of what appeared to be juveniles up the concrete ramp to the duty desk. The teens were alternately protesting and laughing. They looked and sounded drunk.

Two girls. Three boys. *Well, well. What's this?* Fran squinted through the window screen. One of the detainees was Lowell Mapp, the reporter she'd met at the newspaper office. She took the stairs two at a time and cut through the MP reception area, closed for the day, so she could question the duty officer before the rowdy group came inside. An MP staff sergeant she knew was watching them through a reinforced glass door.

"What's going on?" Fran asked.

"Evening, ma'am. Same old, same old. Bunch of young peckerwoods partying in an outlying training area, not far from the Onslow Beach turnoff. Lucky we got to 'em before they got behind their wheels and killed theirselves. The complicatin' factor is that two of them boys belong to Colonel Moser and one of the girls is a master sergeant's kid. Other girl belongs to God knows who. Says she's a retiree's kid but lost her ID in the woods somewhere. The colonel's older boy and the civilian are the only ones old enough to drink. Far as we know, anyway. Our luck, the one without an ID is really the commandant's daughter."

"The commandant doesn't have a daughter."

"Well, that's good."

"Who reported them?"

"Little bastards built a fire. A colonel named Schoengraf called from one of the officers' beach houses. Spotted the smoke as he was leaving."

Schoengraf, the commandant's play date. "Staff Sergeant, I think I recognize the civilian male." Fran said. "Can I talk to him?"

"Let me find out how vomitous he is. If he ain't raped anybody, they'll probably just escort him off-base anyway."

The staff sergeant went into the soundproof room where the five were now sitting. One of the girls had stopped laughing and started crying. Daddy must be on his way.

Lowell Mapp was fingering an unlit cigarette and looking daggers at the black female sergeant questioning him. The sergeant consulted with the staff sergeant and apparently told Mapp he could leave. He must have made the breathalyzer cut. Mapp didn't quite jerk his driver's license out of the female sergeant's hand. Good thing he didn't. The MPs had two short-term holding cells. The walls weren't really coated with human blood, but by the time the sergeant would have gotten through with Mapp, he'd have sworn on a stack of stylebooks that it was.

Fran assumed nobody had recognized Mapp as a reporter and that he—wisely—had decided not to name his place of employment. She approached him as he picked up the receiver to a public telephone by the exit. He smelled of dirty laundry, upchuck, and wood smoke. His eyes were bloodshot and glittering with malice. The fun part of being tanked was long gone, and the surly stage was setting in. Fran bet he was a hairsbreadth away from saying or doing something that could cost him his job. She wanted to grill him before that happened.

"Looking for a lift?"

Mapp's head whipped around at the sound of her voice. He forced a crooked smile. "Jesus, Special Agent Setliff to the rescue. Is this a small fuckin' world or what? Sorry. I mean thanks. My car and my cell phone are at Shelton Moser's house, M.O.Q. 2314. I should have known better than to hang out with an idiot like Shelton."

"Lowell, I don't think you want to be anywhere near the Mosers' quarters tonight. Or to drive past the gate sentry and risk ending up in here twice in one night. I'll be glad to take you home."

He rocked on his heels. "Yeah, I guess you're right. Would you drive me to the newspaper instead? Clay Konnecker is working tonight. I'll crash in the back of his truck. When he gets off, I'll have him bring me back over to get my car."

Fran remembered Konnecker was a retired Marine. His truck's base sticker would get him through the gate without a fuss.

"Good plan. We better clear out. Fireworks are about to start."

Colonel Moser was charging up the ramp. He didn't even glance in Fran's direction as he blasted through the door. The Moser boys did not look happy to see their father.

Fran repressed the urge to drape her passenger seat with a mat before Mapp sat on it. The reporter was defiling a shrine, sitting where Maldonado's vastly cuter butt had nested, but Fran didn't see any point in offending the reporter before she quizzed him.

"Where do you know these kids from? Aren't they a little young for you?"

"Shelton was one, two years behind me at UNC. Same fraternity. He's on academic probation this year. Home with Mama and Diddy for winter break. He saw my byline in the paper, called me. Probably bored with Lejeune's resident turds. We've gone out for beers a few times. His little brother has the brains in the family, and he's not smart enough to know you don't make a fire upwind of dry grass. Little brother just found out he got some dipshit scholarship to UNC-Greensboro. Shelton thought we should celebrate. I should have trusted my instincts. Nothing good ever comes of me driving through that fucking gate. Knuckle-dragging asshole MPs acted like we were smoking crack. Shit, we had the fire put out by the time they got there."

"Who are the girls?"

"Little brother's girlfriend and some friend of hers. Both too stupid to live."

"Well, maybe they'll be smarter when they grow up. I take it you didn't tell the MPs you're the military affairs reporter for the *Daily Observer.*"

"Shit, no. I made Shelton and his brother promise not to say anything to the girls either. It's a safe bet they never read a newspaper. One good thing from all this: I got a great idea for a story. What happens to retarded gorillas? The Marines make MPs out of them."

He cooled down when they pulled on to Main Service Road, but not before he shot a middle finger out the window in the direction of the Provost Marshal's Office.

"You're pressing your luck, Mapp."

"What luck?" He threw his head back against the neck rest and closed his eyes. "So, anything new on the Buckhalter case?"

"You know I can't discuss that."

"How about General Johnson's lawsuit? Anything there?"

"Ditto. No can speak."

"Doesn't hurt to ask. You're pressing *your* luck even being in the same car with me without clearing it with Public Affairs." He gurgled an unattractive little laugh. "No news on Ann's mystery tape, the one supposedly made at a staff meeting?"

"Nope. Any more scuttlebutt about it at your end?"

"Uh-uh."

"Maybe she was just fooling with you, Mapp. Throwing you a red herring to distract you from something even juicier she was working on."

The look he gave Fran could have eaten through sheet metal. "She knew better than to jerk me around. I don't like being played."

"Hey, I'd watch the tone, if I were you. We're talking about a woman who died under unexplained circumstances."

"Well, that's a shame, okay? But I'll tell you what's easy to explain. Why I'm not pulling my hair out over it, and haven't noticed anybody else doing it either. Griffin, maybe. But he's a pussy anyway. Sure, I learned a lot from Ann, but you can't trust people who are messed up emotionally. And she was reaching the certifiable point fast."

Fran repressed her growing revulsion. He was making her skin crawl, but she wanted to clarify a few things before unloading him.

"I heard it was Lieutenant Colonel Schoengraf who called the MPs. Did he tell you to put out the fire?"

"I wouldn't know Schoengraf from Shinola. Nobody showed up except the black dyke in the squad car and some other MP who must have trotted over from Onslow Beach. I told you, the fire was out before they even got there. A chest of ice, a few cans of beer, and it was all over."

"Except for the underage drinking part."

"I ain't underage. Anyway, Very Special Agent, are you telling me you never had a drink until you were twenty-one? I bet you didn't wait until then for much of anything. You have a knowing look."

He reminded her of Marlon, who used to say he could tell whether or not a girl was a virgin just by seeing how she walked. As if the first-comer left a permanent impression, like a footprint in wet cement. She didn't respond. He was starting to unnerve her more than a little, maybe because she was tired. The evening had been so lovely until Lowell Mapp came into it. She looked at her odometer, urging the numbers to turn over. Less than a mile to go. He opened his eyes and turned sideways in the seat so he faced her.

"You've been such a sweetheart, I'll let you in on a tip I got a couple days before we all were distracted by Mrs. Buckhalter's tragic death. I haven't even told Griffin this yet." Mapp closed his eyes and wagged his tongue from one corner of his mouth to the other. "I'm looking into the possibility there's a little dope-smuggling ring running grass up and down the New River. Marines on the air-station end, dependents on the Lejeune end."

Fran flashed to the traces of marijuana on Ann's body. Not enough to give a cricket a buzz. She didn't doubt there were dependents and Marines smoking pot on base. Still, a "smuggling ring" the MPs hadn't caught wind of? More likely, somebody was trying to land somebody they didn't like in a whole heap of woe.

She caught Mapp's triumphant leer out of the corner of her eye. She'd hold her applause until the end, thank you.

"Wow. Sounds like a mellow version of the Medellín Cartel. I'll be watching for your byline." She tried for a withering smirk. No good. She just didn't have the face for it.

"I figured you for a girl who likes to watch," he chuckled, and closed his eyes again. "Want to help me with my exposé and make it a double byline?"

"I'd rather have a double bypass."

He shrugged. A minute later, he was snoring and drooling. *Dammit.* If she had to roll him out of the car when they got to the newspaper, it was going to be directly behind the biggest delivery truck she could find.

Fortunately, he was able to roll himself out.

As much as she hated adding another forty-five minutes to her workday, she couldn't resist returning on-base and circling through officers' housing. She wanted a look at Mapp's car.

The lights were on at quarters 2314, Colonel Moser's residence. Aside from the scuffle of deer hooves when her headlights swept over the wooded end of the cul-de-sac, the street was quiet. Two cars were in the Mosers' driveway, and a Toyota hatchback was parked on the street. The hatchback had a grimy windshield with a UNC decal and a bumper sticker that said, "The *Daily Observer*, Take on the World!" The plate was a vanity—NCJSKUL. A girl could be too stupid to live and still figure out the hatchback was Mapp's.

TWENTY-ONE.

Fran's second wind had diminished to a glassy-eyed calm by the time she pulled into her driveway. She had just enough energy left to pet her cat and sweep up the cereal he had dumped on the floor, defying her efforts to make the kitchen counter off-limits.

She leaned against the bathroom tile with her eyes closed while she took off her underwear. She kept them closed in the shower while she scrubbed off the day's grime. She had just stretched her toes into the cool tucked corners of the sheets when she realized she'd forgotten to floss. Her dad knew a sergeant who had to give up opening beer bottles with his teeth because he forgot too many times to floss. She decided to risk it.

Fran had reached that stage of semi-hypnotic sleep in which dead relatives ask why the cat is clawing at the candlewick bedspread when she heard the crunch of footsteps near the end of her driveway. She woke up, fully intending to do nothing but listen until the steps moved on. It was kind of late to walk a dog, wasn't it? She smiled drowsily. Maybe a vampire was walking his bat.

She snapped to full alert when she heard the creak of metal. Somebody was fooling with her mailbox. She glanced at the bedside clock. Nearly 0230. She raised her head to get both ears off the pillow. The next thing she heard, a muffled cough, brought her bolt upright. The cough was from the carport area. She wouldn't have heard it except for the air vent in her carport laundry room. Her bedroom's vent was directly above it. If she had a fire pole, she could have slid right down onto the cougher's head.

Fran was really awake now. There might be an innocent reason why somebody was making her mailbox creak at that hour. It sat on a public street. An insomniac neighbor could have been out for a stroll and jostled it. But she couldn't think of a single reason why a second person would be in her laundry room. One frightening possibility was that the person near the mailbox was a lookout for the person in the laundry room. A burglar and a burglar's aide?

She got out of bed as quietly as she could and slipped her feet into fifteen-year-old Weejuns. She was wearing only a super-sized Bama football jersey, but she figured anybody who saw her would be too struck by the nine-millimeter to notice her clothes.

She did not turn on the lights. She wanted to get a look at her visitors, if she could. Without the lights, the moonlit yard was brighter than the inside of the house. Gun in one hand, big-bopper flashlight in the other, she moved quietly through the living room to her front door. The door opened on to a screened landing and the stairs leading down to the carport. It was the only door to the house, except for the sliding glass door to the balcony.

Fran looked through the peephole. No one was on the landing. She carefully unbolted the door and pushed it open as far as it would go with the chain still latched. As she was maneuvering one eye past the molding, she heard a car pull up in front of the house. A door opened and shut, and then the car backed down the street. She heard hastily shifted gears and the rumble of acceleration. The car turned a corner and drove off toward the highway. All she'd seen was the headlight beams. She assumed whoever was in her yard and laundry room had been picked up by whoever was in the car. The wheelman. She moved onto the landing and flicked the switches that controlled the lights at the top and bottom of the stairs. She tried to think of anything valuable and easily pilferable she stored in the carport. Nothing.

The street and yard were absolutely quiet. She switched on the flashlight and swept the beam to her right. It illuminated only the screening around the stairwell. Aimed straight ahead, it revealed her empty driveway and the red blur she knew was the flag on her mailbox. *Shit.* She'd forgotten to bring in her mail.

Fran was still holding the gun, but in a more relaxed grip. She was eight steps from the bottom when the wooden stair tread she was standing on shuddered violently. She lost her balance and fell backward, landing painfully on her tailbone. She dropped the flashlight as she grabbed for the railing. She held on to the gun but banged the heel of her hand sharply against the stair.

Someone raced from under the stairwell out of the carport, disappearing to the left. From his height, bulk, and stride, she guessed it was a man wearing soft-soled shoes. From his speed and agility, she guessed a young man.

Momentarily stunned by the pain in her lower back, she stood immediately, rubbing the spot as she straightened. She snatched up the flashlight and pressed her back against the wall, gun pointed toward the ceiling. Gun raised, she ran down the remaining stairs and to the far corner of the carport. She stuck her head around the wall a second too late to get a good look at whoever was scrambling over the embankment that separated her yard from her neighbor's. He disappeared into the heavy shrubbery, setting off a relay of barking dogs. Fran didn't even consider pursuit. Chasing a prowler who was possibly armed through a dark neighborhood at 0200—nearly 0300—in the morning wouldn't be smart for somebody who'd forgotten to put on her glasses and was too tired to see straight anyway.

Fran walked cautiously around the carport, turning on both miserably inadequate lights. Everything that should be there was. Nothing was missing. But her visitor had left something. It was under the stairwell where, she supposed, she and the nine-millimeter had surprised him.

She picked up the Zippo lighter and turned it over in her hand. It was decorated with a Foghorn Leghorn sticker that looked the worse for wear, as if it had endured years of abrasion moving in and out of rough pockets.

Fran realized the guy under the stairs had intentionally rammed them, hoping to distract her—throw her off-balance, maybe—before she saw him. That explained one guy. But what about the other? Was there a connection between whoever had been fiddling with her mailbox and whoever had been skulking around her carport? If the guy at the mailbox was just some insomniac whose wife had come looking for him in the car, maybe the guy in the laundry room was a run-of-the-mill Peeping Tom.

There wasn't a woman living alone who hadn't been plagued by that kind of creep. Some guys sprang their best boners by watching unsuspecting females do something sexy, like clip their toenails or load the dishwasher. Maybe this one was queer for football jerseys. In any case, the coast was now clear. Whoever it was probably wouldn't be back.

Fran stopped in front of her mailbox and stared at it. Wait. She might have been worrying about the least dangerous part of the scenario. Maybe somebody had planted something unpleasant in her mailbox. Like a pygmy rattler. Or a bomb. In her job, she had given a few irrational people reason to feel spiteful.

Using a length of clothesline from her laundry room, she made a quick bowline knot and draped it carefully over the steel handle on the mailbox door, then slowly backed across the street, taking up the slack. When the line was taut and she was crouched behind a dense azalea, she gave it a firm, steady tug.

The mailbox door popped open. Nothing went boom. She directed the flashlight beam into the box's black metal gullet as she approached, squinting. Something was inside, but she couldn't make it out. She waited a few more seconds, then leaned her head down to the opening.

Snorting at her own paranoia, she took out a promo for pizza take-out, one of those gun-nut catalogs everybody in law enforcement got, and a notice that she was preapproved for a bank card. Also a letter from her mother, a corner of which was stuck in a metal seam. Fran grabbed the letter's long side, brushing her knuckles against the metal wall. She felt something projecting from the curved top of the box.

She jumped back. *I could call Boyette*, she thought, *and have him muster the bomb squad. However, if I wake half the base and it isn't a bomb, I'll look like the agency's biggest dumbass, as well as its only female.*

She decided to risk ending her life as splatter art. She pried the object loose with a fingernail. It was a small, square package, completely covered in shiny green packing tape. A nickel-sized magnet had held the box in place against the metal.

Fran's scalp crawled with excitement. She was ready to bet all nine of her cat's lives she knew what was in that box. A microcassette tape. *Oh, shit.* Why hadn't she thought of that before she took it out? Now, her fingerprints were all over the damn package. And anybody else's were smeared. She stood there in her driveway, holding the little box at arm's length like a dirty diaper, debating whether or not to call Boyette immediately. She decided she better.

Boyette's wife, Abby, answered the phone. Fran apologized for disturbing her. As usual, Abby was politely distant. Middle-of-the-night phone calls were the price she paid for the thrill of being married to Boyette. The man himself was initially gruff but soon caught a little of her excitement. He told her to keep the box close at hand but not to unwrap it. He would arrange an official unveiling in front of appropriate witnesses.

Fran put the tape inside an empty Band-Aid box and tucked it under her pillow. If she was wrong and it contained a delayed-action explosive, at least nobody would argue about whether or not she should have an open casket.

Before she went to sleep, she remembered the lighter. She'd left it on her kitchen counter next to the big bopper. She'd also forgotten to tell Boyette about the Peeping Tom.

TWENTY-TWO.

FRIDAY 0800

Boyette had handpicked the subdued group in the conference room. It included the base staff judge advocate, Linwood Petrie, and Boyette's most senior agent, Milt Touchberry. Touchberry had been out of the loop the past month, recovering from gallbladder surgery. Also present: Colonel Bob Knightdale, General Johnson's chief of staff. Boyette and the staff judge advocate had discussed including Knightdale. In the end, they had agreed there was less potential for misunderstanding if someone from the base CG's office was present.

Fran felt nearly as eclipsed in that group as she had in General Johnson's office. Every man there was years ahead of her in professional experience. Every man there was old enough to be her father.

Fran was present because she had been the first to hear of the tape they expected the mystery package to contain. And of course, she was the one to whom the package was delivered. If any questions arose about either of those events, she was there to answer them.

Everyone at the table was trying to maintain a bland expression. But curiosity can be as compelling as lust, and just as hard to hide. They were all horny, wanting to get at that tape.

Boyette had not touched it himself. Nor had he encouraged anyone to expect anything earth-shaking. But because of all the preliminary conjecture and drama, he was setting himself up for real embarrassment if it turned out to be a pirated tape of a Frankie Valli show.

At Boyette's request, MPs had let bomb-sniffing dogs take a whiff of the package before it was opened. The dogs weren't impressed. Boyette had also videotaped the unwrapping. This was accomplished by a gloved agent using surgical scissors. If Boyette hadn't covered all his bases, it wasn't for lack of effort.

He asked Fran to shut and bolt the door. He showed the men the evidence bag containing the pieces of green tape. He showed them the small plastic case the tape had been in. No visible marks or latent fingerprints were on the green and white label. He showed them the tape itself, a high-grade Maxell. He handled it with a pair of jeweler's tweezers.

Boyette fumbled only once, when he put the tape in the player backwards. He reversed it and pushed the play button. The volume was set at mid-range.

As one, the five people around the table leaned toward the black tape player. The first sounds were overlapping conversations from an indeterminate number of voices. But they soon sorted themselves out. Like dominos, the men at the table sat back, one after another, as they recognized voices.

Fran could identify only three, but the context made it clear who the other speakers were. One was Colonel Knightdale. The other men at the table smiled uncomfortably when Knightdale silently raised his hand in recognition of his own voice.

It was also easy to figure out where the tape was made, and at what time of day. General Johnson had a cuckoo clock on the wall behind his desk at Headquarters Building. The Bavarian-style clock, handmade in Seoul, was tacky-cute. Instead of a cuckoo, a bugler popped out of the teakwood housing. The pendulum was a globe and anchor. It chimed Adjutant's Call on the hour and bonged on the quarter-hour. The clock could be heard chiming on the tape. Fran identified the sound quickly enough to count the chimes. Nine. General Johnson's calendar would pin down the date. He did not hold regular weekly or even monthly staff meetings. Most base divisions and departments were more or less autonomous. The general's ass-kicking and ass-kissing sessions were usually one on one. He did all the kicking. Somebody else did the kissing. Johnson called a staff meeting only when the agenda was important to everybody. These infrequent meetings were carefully documented.

In addition to Knightdale, the first part of the taped conversation included four of the deputy chiefs. Provost Marshal Jimmy O'Dell and the civilian who headed the Manpower division were among them. Fran wasn't sure why, but she felt relieved that no one from the staff judge advocate's office was on the tape.

Hearing the familiar voices made her feel like an eavesdropper. It was like they were all outside a closed door, listening in on a party they hadn't been invited to. Except for Colonel Knightdale, of course. He had been invited. That made his situation awkward.

Not that anybody on the tape was saying anything shocking. The only obscenity so far had come from the provost marshal. He used it in reference to the then-upcoming NBA playoffs. The comment placed the meeting in late May. Seven months earlier.

The boys-and-balls talk was ended abruptly by Sergeant Major Crockett's bark: "Gentlemen, the commanding general." This was followed by a scraping of chairs and somebody's knee popping. Johnson greeted the group. More scraping as everybody sat back down.

Fran tried to guess from the tape's acoustics where the recording device had been hidden. Somewhere to the general's right, she suspected. Never having attended a staff meeting, she wasn't sure where the general sat. That shouldn't be hard to determine. The king didn't pick a different seat every time he went in the throne room.

There were occasional cut-off sentences and blank spaces on the tape. Obviously, it did not include the whole meeting. Just enough to set the scene and give listeners an idea what was going on. This tape must be an edited version of the original. Whoever secretly set up the recorder had not been able to stop and start it during the meeting. Theoretically, the tape could have been stopped and restarted by remote control. But that was crossing into a James Bond technology that this operation, so far, did not feature. So, where was the original tape?

Fran eventually realized what the others in the room had probably known immediately. This must have been one of Johnson's first staff meetings after he took over at base. That explained why he began by making everybody say something about his own group. Much of this was deleted on the tape.

Colonel O'Dell went last, describing himself as "top cop." General Johnson followed up, seemingly as an afterthought, by telling O'Dell that some of the gate sentries were taking too long giving directions to motorists. What he was referring to, General Johnson said crisply, was the way some of the Marines seemed to "linger"—he rolled the word off his tongue suggestively—over the sweet young things who came through. Other voices on the tape responded to this with chuckles. O'Dell asked the general if he had any "pacific" incidents in mind. Johnson said he hadn't taken notes and it wasn't a big deal. In generalese, "not a big deal" meant, "Take care of it or I'll be on you like a lamprey with six heads."

The next section of the tape was a monologue. The general talked about the status of a project known as "Get the Lead Out." Lejeune's fifty-year-old pipes had been leaching lead into base water for years. In some areas, it was hazardous to drink. Johnson said that replacement of all compromised pipes was due to be complete within eighteen months. Another topic of the monologue was an enormous Capabilities Exercise then in the planning stages. Fran glanced at her calendar watch. That exercise would take place a week from Monday.

By this point, Boyette had tweezer-flipped the tape, and it had run almost halfway through the other side. The rapt expressions on the listeners' faces had disappeared. Colonel Petrie was crossing and recrossing his legs like a man in search of a sitz bath. Even Boyette was shifting uneasily in his chair.

After another pause in the tape came the sucking sounds of colonels bidding a commanding general adieu. Petrie stretched his calves in relief. They must be nearing the end of the recording.

On the tape, only General Johnson, Crockett, Knightdale, and the assistant chief of staff for logistics remained. The general remarked that Lee Goddard seemed to be adjusting well to his newly restructured duties. Fran knew he referred to the restructuring that would be the basis of Charmaine Roundtree's lawsuit.

"Of course, Ms. Roundtree isn't happy," the general said on the tape. "What do you hear, Bob? Is she supporting her new boss like she should, or setting up tripwires all over his office?"

It was difficult to understand Knightdale's response. Something about a "nose out of joint" and "adapting."

"Well, I know the type," the general said. "These civil servants think their careers are set in concrete the minute they're hired. Any change in the game plan sets off the waterworks."

Sergeant Major Crockett said something about Ms. Roundtree being too dried up to cry much. This drew a little perfunctory laughter but no glee. No one disliked Charmaine Roundtree personally.

"God knows, I've had to adjust to enough changes since I was a second lieutenant," Johnson said. "To shit I would have sworn could never happen. I've seen guys riffed that the Corps should have crawled under hot barbed wire to keep. But just try to unload one civil servant—especially a female civil servant—and you're the anti-Christ."

Background coughing. Crockett. Unintelligible remark from the logistics guy.

"Sometimes, I think I'm not a general at all. I'm really the city manager for a town where the people all dress alike."

Crockett coughed, then laughed.

"Hell, I spend half my time rearranging the egg money, trying to keep everything operational. If it weren't for Bob, I'd have run out of fingers and toes a long time ago."

A few sincere chuckles. Fran knew budgeting was a persistent headache for commanders. Military planners were expected to predict the state of the world, the economy, technology, and public opinion several fiscal years down the road.

Johnson's voice took on an angry edge. "More and more, readiness means readiness to change just for the sake of change. Well, this old dog can learn only so many new tricks. Right or wrong, I'm more comfortable dealing with veterans than with civilians who don't know a foxhole from an asshole. And I'm more comfortable dealing with men than women in command positions. I may be the last of my kind, but this general doesn't want any women commanders on his staff."

Pause. Then the tape repeated the last point: "This general doesn't want any women commanders on his staff." The person who edited it wanted to make sure nobody missed the punch line.

So, that was it. The room couldn't have been quieter if the ghost of Franklin Roosevelt had popped up and declared war on Toyota. Knightdale had sweat glittering on his upper lip. Petrie's legs were locked.

Boyette cleared his throat. "Colonel Knightdale, do you remember this conversation?"

Knightdale sat up in his chair and raised his hands defensively. "Honest to God, no. Pieces of it ring some kind of bell. The Capabilities Exercise. The water safety issue. But that last bit—about women commanders—I couldn't swear today that I heard him say it. I was already thinking about whatever was next on the day's agenda, I guess."

"Can you swear you didn't hear him say it, Colonel?"

Knightdale shook his head ruefully. "Sure, I was there. Why would I deny it? But nobody pays much attention to off-the-cuff remarks like that. If he said it and the tape hasn't been doctored. I either didn't hear it or it didn't make an impression."

An up-and-coming female officer like Rhonda Baptiste would know the potential impact of "off-the-cuff" remarks like that, Fran thought. *Or a female civil servant like me.*

Knightdale persisted. "Remember something, gentlemen, Special Agent Setliff. I'd seen this restructuring on paper. It is cost effective. I could quote you the savings line by line. If another result of that restructuring is that the general has an all-male staff—and likes it that way—so be it."

The staff judge advocate looked unconvinced. "Of course, another result was that a man was promoted and a woman who previously shared the same rating and responsibilities was put under that man's authority."

Nobody responded. Colonel Petrie, as staff judge advocate, had an interest in the Roundtree lawsuit. So did Knightdale, who worked for the defendant but might now be called to testify for the plaintiff about the tape. As could Boyette, Touchberry, and Fran.

Boyette asked them all to keep their meeting—and the tape—to themselves until he and Colonel Petrie decided on a course of action. Unauthorized discussion might compromise either of two federal investigations—one civil, one involving a death on-base.

The Naval Criminal Investigative Service was interested in the tape only if it was linked to the death of Ann Buckhalter. According to a newspaper reporter, she had known about such a tape and was about to turn it over to him.

The key question might be who had secretly taped the inflammatory comments. Who had access to General Johnson's office and bore him enough of a grudge to risk making his or her own career implode, if caught? Had the original plan been to give the tape only to Ann Buckhalter? Or did Ann's death necessitate a second plan, to give the tape to Fran?

Which led to Fran's own personal key question: *Why me?*

TWENTY-THREE.

SATURDAY 0900

"I'm the patsy Chicano and you're the patsy dame," Maldonado told her when she realized the two of them would be sacrificing a Saturday to chew the fat with fat-mouth civilians. Base had to offer up two bodies, and the CG had passed the word that they were it.

The event was an all-day outing to Raleigh with the county's Military-Civilian Cooperative Committee. Twice a year, the committee sponsored a trip to a college football game. The purpose, according to its promoters, was to "encourage cordial relations between the military and civilian business communities." And all this time, Fran told Vic, she'd thought that was what Tiddie-Winks Topless Massage was for.

Cynics said the outings mostly served as a chance for middle-aged businessmen to drop their tailgates and dangle beer in front of coeds. To counter charges that the committee traditionally excluded females and blacks, this outing would be the first to include a woman and an African-American. Fran and Vic's fellow hostage would be Colonel Mel

Hampshire, Combat Service Support Schools, Camp Johnson.

The happy group set off from the committee's downtown location in a red Econoline van. The van was emblazoned with the committee's logo, as well as the yellow ribbon that became synonymous with support for the military during Desert Storm. Most Jacksonville businesses were low-margin operations, and the massive deployment had left many hanging by their thumbs. But no one dared complain. Or forgot to put up that damn yellow ribbon.

The drinking began as soon as the van pulled out of the parking lot. Fran took a beer just to be sociable. She sat behind Vic and next to Colonel Hampshire, who was also sipping a beer. He looked like he was enjoying himself, probably because he was one of those sports fanatics who'd watch two teams of dung beetles push balls of shit up a hill if that were the only game available.

The patronizing of Hampshire began almost as soon as the drinking. References to Montford Point, the World War II recruiting site for black Marines. Colin Powell. Tina Turner. Most of the comments came from the same two guys. Fran would have thought they were on their way to an NAACP meeting. It all rolled off Colonel Hampshire like rainwater. He hadn't made colonel by being prickly.

Maldonado seemed to be enjoying himself, too. She caught bits of his conversation with a nondescript local lawyer and, across the aisle, a retired surgeon.

By early afternoon, she had to admit the day wasn't half bad. Good seats. Evenly matched opponents. She drank another beer with gusto, then left her seat a few minutes before halftime to beat the line into the ladies' head. She ran into Maldonado, who suggested they see if any of the chow slated for halftime might already be charred enough to eat. He'd skipped breakfast.

One of the committee members who'd pestered Colonel Hampshire, an overweight man in his fifties named Gifford Pfeister, had

stayed with the van during most of the first half. He was in charge of
firing up the portable grill. It took them awhile to find Pfeister in the
already raucous parking lot. When they did, he was wearing a Santa
Claus hat and trying to entertain a trio of students. The boy was sitting
in a folding chair. One of the girls was sitting at the boy's feet, twiddling
her hair. The second girl was perched on the van's tailgate, swinging
her long legs. She was wearing a thick sweater and baggy jacket, but
the sweater and low-cut jeans left her midriff bare enough to expose a
gold navel ring. Each youth had a can of beer. Two were smoking. Fran
thought they hardly looked old enough to drive, much less drink.

"Howdy, sports and lovers, I mean, sports lovers," Pfeister said, waving a spatula when he spotted Vic and Fran. "I've been makin' friends.
Don't worry. I checked everybody's ID." He winked at the girl with
swinging legs and patted her on the thigh. She hopped down immediately. "What's the score, Vic?"

Maldonado told him: 14–10, State over Georgia Tech. He grabbed
a beer, offered it to Fran, then, when she declined, popped the can for
himself. He opened a folding chair on the opposite side of the grill from
where Fran had sat, creating enough separation to baffle Miss Midriff.

"Are you with him?" the girl asked Maldonado, shading her eyes
with one hand. She was trying to put the old fat guy in context with the
good-looking young one.

"Yep. We go back a long way."

"Yeah? To where?"

"The Governor's Task Force on Underage Drinking," he said, deadpan.

She got it. Throwing him a sour look, she stood and brushed off
the seat of her jeans. "Nice meeting you," she grumbled, and herded her
friends away.

"Y'all come back, hear?" Pfeister trilled at their departing fannies.
He started peeling patties off a stack and slapping them on the grill.

Maldonado shot Fran a surreptitious wink. She was trying not to respond when she heard an unpleasantly familiar voice behind her.

"I figured you'd be the guy blowing the most smoke, Pfeister."

She twisted around in her chair. It was Lowell Mapp, shaking his finger at Santa. His clothes were wrinkled and shapeless, but the camera equipment strapped across his chest was top of the line.

"Hey! What's kicking, Lowell? Vic, this is Lowell Mapp. Bet you've heard of him. He reports on the base for the *Daily Observer*. His pap and I went to high school together. Oh, and this is Secret Agent Fran Heathcliff."

"Fran and I already know each other. What's crackin', Secret Agent?"

She was so amused by Pfeister's mangling of her name and title, she grinned at Mapp despite herself. Maldonado shook his hand. Santa slapped him on the back.

"Working today, Lowell? I know State isn't your team. You're one of those Tar Heel turds," Pfeister said.

"I'm just scoping out the competition," Mapp answered. "Got a comp ticket. So, what's the committee up to? Another field trip for over-the-hill rednecks with money?"

Pfeister laughed. "Just trying to attract new blood, Lowell. Young guys like you don't want to hang around old farts like us."

"Well, I see you have one politically correct addition," Mapp said, bowing toward Fran.

"We're way more enlightened than you realize," Pfeister said. "You know Mel Hampshire? Colonel Mel Hampshire? Runs Camp Coon. Sorry, Camp Johnson. Don't get any blacker than Mel without carrying a spear. A damn fine officer, too, isn't he, Vic?"

Mapp waited, amused, for Maldonado's answer.

"I think Mr. Pfeister has had a few and isn't speaking for the committee," the captain said.

I think Mr. Pfeister is a fucking idiot, Fran thought.

Mapp laughed, pitched his empty bottle into a trash barrel, and started digging through the council cooler for another beer. "Don't worry, Vic. You know what they say: 'What happens TDY stays TDY.' In this case, TDY means 'Tailgate Duty.'"

Ninety minutes and two touchdowns later, Fran offered to dump the doused charcoal into one of the oil drums placed throughout the parking lot for that purpose. As she steered the grill across the asphalt, she spotted Mapp getting into a Ford Explorer. The reporter's arm was draped over the shoulder and breast of a frayed-looking girl with dyed red hair. The couple was swapping spit with great abandon. She walked back to the council van through dust sent up by rows of departing vehicles, glancing left just as the Explorer turned in front of her onto an exit road. Mapp was too occupied to notice Fran, but she saw him pull the girl roughly by her frizzy ponytail and take most of her skinny neck into his mouth. She also saw what looked like a red enlisted sticker on the Explorer's windshield. If he had one of those on his vehicle, he could get on base without showing ID. Why was Mapp driving that vehicle instead of his Toyota hatchback with the vanity tag?

Shortly after the van started moving, Gifford Pfeister fell into a grotesque sleep, face flattened against his window. The noise he made sounded like a duck gargling mud.

Maldonado disappeared with one snappy wave as soon as they got back to Jacksonville.

Fran's Saturday-night plans included a Hail and Farewell she'd been nagged into attending. She'd already staged clothing and toiletries in her cubicle so she wouldn't have to drive all the way home in order to freshen up.

In the field office head, putting on lipstick for the first time in days, she wondered what kind of evening Ann Buckhalter had been looking forward to exactly one week ago.

TWENTY-FOUR.

SATURDAY 1900

Fran had agreed to attend the Hail and Farewell with a captain who had just checked into the Provost Marshal's Office. The provost marshal, Colonel O'Dell, made a big deal of the fact that the captain was also from Alabama. What was he thinking? The man was an Auburn graduate. Fran tried to make allowances for O'Dell. He'd enlisted at age seventeen and earned his commission after taking a patchwork of extension courses. He had no way of knowing that fixing up Bama and Auburn alumni was like trying to match-make across the Gaza Strip.

The captain had other liabilities. He was too damn quiet except for his compulsive gum-popping. At least the popping filled some of the gaps in the conversation. It would have taken a reading of the *Congressional Record* to fill all the gaps. This particular Hail and Farewell was subdued enough as it was. The son of the air-station provost marshal had died that morning in a Harrier crash at Bogue Field.

Hail and Farewells were enforced fun anyway. Official military functions at which everybody wore civilian clothes confused the troops. The people being hailed were uncomfortable because they didn't know their way around yet. The people being farewelled were just marking time until they were hailed at their next duty station.

Fran watched the captain load a frilled toothpick with three meatballs and wondered why she hadn't seen him remove the gum before putting the whole thing in his mouth. She grew fonder of him when he lifted his face out of his drooping paper plate and told her he needed to make an early night of it.

They were leaving when they ran into Rodney and Elva Walker. Fran had brought her own car to the Officers' Club, which meant she wouldn't be stranded if she accepted Elva's invitation to join them for a drink in the bar. The captain shook hands with everyone and departed, making her fonder of him than ever.

Fran paused at the threshold of the dimly lit bar. This was the last place Ann Buckhalter had been seen alive. Tonight, the barkeep was a female, an unnatural blond with hair spewing out of a banana comb.

Elva told Fran that she and Rodney had left their children home while they went to an R-rated movie. They'd come on base afterward so Rodney could drop some clean exercise gear off at his office, then decided to stop by the club for a tax-free Johnny Walker Red.

Elva and Fran chatted about what Santa Claus was bringing everybody. In Fran's case, Santa might have to slip some speed into the reindeer kibble to make last-minute deliveries. She hadn't bought a thing. Meanwhile, Rodney was unconsciously doing a seated soft-shoe routine, a half-smile on his face. He was dying to tell Fran something. She guessed he was waiting for Elva to leave the table. It was ironic that the agent with the least gossipy wife was the most cautious about conducting business in front of her.

Elva picked up the cue. She stood. "I'm going to call home and check on the kids. Oh, and I need to get the key to the Wives' Club office from Sandy O'Dell. God, I hope I don't have to listen to her Amway pitch again. I'm thinking of selling Mary Kay just so I'll have something to peddle when she starts in on me."

After Elva left, Rodney turned his chair to face Fran, whose back was against the paneled wall. She leaned over the table toward him. All his discretion would be wasted if she couldn't hear him.

"You won't believe who I talked to this morning. Commander Kevin Terry's girlfriend. You know, the real-estate agent. Jane Sherbourne."

An image of the handsome Navy doctor flashed through Fran's mind. Terry, who had an affair with Ann Buckhalter. Terry, who included Ann's daughter, Deirdre, in a psychiatric study without her father's knowledge. Terry, whom Ann telephoned the afternoon she died.

"I give you no jive, Setliff. You know that Elva and I are looking for an investment property, a place to buy and rent out until I retire. When we see something in the paper that appeals to us, we call the agent and arrange to see it. Just so happened that Jane Sherbourne was the agent we spoke to this morning. And it just so happened she brought up Commander Terry without any prodding."

"No!"

"Yes! She had a photo of the two of them under the glass top on her desk. Big old honkin' eight-by-ten. Taken at the Navy Ball. You described Terry so well, I think I would have recognized him even if their names weren't printed on the picture. I asked Jane Sherbourne how long they had known each other. It was like I'd pulled the pin on a grenade. I think the only reason that photo is still there is because she hasn't finished building a big enough pyre to burn it on. Just talking about him, she went so ballistic she could hardly keep it together."

"What do you mean, 'ballistic'?"

"That man done her wrong, Fran. Or that's the way she sees it. First off, the commander was lying, or in denial, if he told you Jane Sherbourne was so into her career she wasn't interested in a serious relationship. She thought they *had* a serious relationship. And from the kind of things he told her—which I'll get to in a minute—they were certainly more than casual friends. It's what he didn't tell her that soured things. See, Jane Sherbourne knew Commander Terry knew Ann Buckhalter. But Jane thought it was just a professional thing—you know, Ann's daughter being his patient. Terry must have finally told Jane the truth about him and Ann. However, he told Jane what he told you, that the sexual part ended long ago. Even if she believed him, Jane didn't like the idea that he was still communicating with this married woman he used to get it on with. And I think it upsets her that this other woman, who she just found out about, is recently deceased under mysterious circumstances."

"Hold it, Rodney. You're cutting way too many corners. Start with the important stuff. What does Jane look like?"

He cocked his head and squeezed his eyes shut. "Your fifth-grade teacher. Everybody's fifth-grade teacher. Polyester blazer. Just a little overweight. Dark hair. Glasses on a chain. Not bad, I guess, but I'm not sure I could pick her out of a lineup, and I spent a couple of hours looking at her. I don't know whether she was lying to herself or he was doing it for her, but Ms. Sherbourne definitely had the idea she and the commander had a future together. That's one mad woman."

"Mad enough to be vindictive?"

"You mean mad enough to spike Ann's drink and push her in the river? I'd say no. It's him she's mad at. Commander Terry slunk around the truth about something else, too. He may not be as coolly detached about the Buckhalters as he wanted you to think. Some powerful emotions surged through that cheatin' heart, according to Ms. Sherbourne."

"You mean feelings for Ann?"

Walker shrugged. "Don't know. But I do know one thing. Jane Sherbourne said Terry hated Lieutenant Colonel Buckhalter's guts. I wonder if that didn't add a little extra honey to the pot for Terry. Stick it to Buckhalter's wife, stick it to Buckhalter."

"Jesus, Rodney, you're going all obtuse on me. Why should Terry hate Gary Buckhalter?"

"Stay with me, Fran. Terry told Jane Sherbourne how he knew Ann from when he worked for Colonel Buckhalter—the dysfunctional family, et cetera."

"He told me all about that. The joint exercise. Et cetera."

"No, he told you only plot A. Plot B is much better. Terry explained to you that it was kind of a fluke, a Navy doctor working for a Marine engineer as part of a joint exercise. But fluke or not, it meant the Marine engineer wrote the Navy doctor's fitness report. That episode took place just after Buckhalter's son died of cancer. And not coincidentally, just after Buckhalter went on the wagon for good. Grief-stricken and sober, Buckhalter got a heavy dose of religion. Turned into a real Bible-thumper. It appears he did a lot of proselytizing on government time. Some of his people took advantage of it. When the boss is a Bible-thumper, the ultimate suck-up is to get born again. Must have created some awkward fraternizing. How does a staff sergeant ask the first sergeant for time off so he can pray with the CO? How does the first sergeant refuse the request? Still, Buckhalter's people rolled with it. Schedules are pretty tight on board a ship. Not a lot of time to brood about the boss's quirks."

"The crew that took down Captain Queeg would disagree."

"That was fiction, Setliff. Do you want to hear this or not?"

She made a keep-rolling motion with her hand.

"Well, Terry was just a little bit junior to Buckhalter, and he resented being preached to. Things came to a crisis in Guam. Some famous evangelist was holding a revival outside Roosevelt Roads. Buckhalter promised the evangelist he'd provide servicemen—in uniform—to serve as ushers. Buckhalter asked Terry to be one of them. Terry said no. And he wouldn't ask his sailors to do it either. So, Buckhalter approached one of those sailors directly. When the sailor told Buckhalter he was stomping on the line separating church and state, Buckhalter backed off. But he must have figured Terry put the words in the sailor's mouth. Buckhalter retaliated by offering up a special prayer during the revival. The prayer was for a certain Navy officer with a history of failed marriage who was also a doctor. This doctor's soul, according to Buckhalter, needed divine help if it wasn't going to end up in hell. Everybody knew who Buckhalter was talking about. The revival was broadcast over Armed Forces Television. That's how Terry found out. He went nuts. If that exercise had gone on much longer, Terry would probably have ended up in Leavenworth for murder. But it was nearly over, and he kept his cool. That would have been the end of the story except Buckhalter gave Terry the equivalent of two 'excellents' on his fitness report. And his written comments were, shall we say, terse."

Fran knew how damning those "excellents" were. Careers were made, got stalled, or went down in flames according to fitness reports. The competition for promotion was so tough, receiving an "excellent" instead of an "outstanding" in any category could be lethal.

"Well, maybe Buckhalter gave Terry what he deserved," Fran offered. "Just because Buckhalter was out of line about the revival doesn't mean he screwed over Terry's fitness report."

"Come on. A squid doctor? A shrink? Why bother to dump on one of those? But that's beside the point. Fair or unfair, it would account for Terry's dislike of Buckhalter."

"This Sherbourne woman told you all this?"

"It's what happens when good love goes bad. Next time, Terry better look for a woman who doesn't have a photographic memory." Walker hummed and beat out a few bars of "Baby, Please Don't Go" on the arms of his chair. "Don't go imagining things, Fran. Jane Sherbourne is not the type to push a rival in the river. Anyway, she has an alibi. She said she was showing somebody a house in Swansboro Saturday evening."

"At night?"

"She said the house was the last stop on a long list. She and the client were running late. Fran, if I had to pick one of those two as the most likely to help Ann take a swim, I'd go with Terry. He was in the area.

Ann would have let him in. And if she wanted to, she could have made big trouble for him. Adultery is still a crime in the military, and lately they've been prosecuting."

Walker cleared his throat and humped his chair closer to hers. "While we're talking about relationships, Fran, I'm going to stretch my neck out so far you might want to get your ax. You seeing Vic Maldonado?"

"What? No. I mean, not really. We've hung out a couple times. Spur of the moment. Unwinding after official business. Why?"

"Come on. I saw you guys in the parking lot. There was enough chemistry going on to jack up my Pfizer stock by twenty points. I just don't want you making any uninformed decisions. I guess you know the dude's got a fiancée back home."

Fran was more than a little annoyed. She was too old to need boyfriend advice. And although she knew Rodney didn't mean it that way, she didn't like having her nose rubbed in Maldonado's engagement.

"Of course I know he's engaged. Her name is Monica. How do you know?"

"Elva was at a coffee with the staff judge advocate's wife. Mrs. Petrie was talking about hosting a champagne brunch for Captain Maldonado and his bride-to-be. I think she's supposed to fly down after Christmas for her first look at Camp Lejeune. Don't you go clouding up on me. I know I'm out of line. I just don't want anybody messing around with my favorite snoop-mama."

"You know how I love it when you talk ghetto, Rodney, but butt out. I mean it."

TWENTY-FIVE.

It was almost midnight when Fran and the Walkers cordially parted outside the Officers' Club. After crossing the street under a lovely starry sky to where she had parked, Fran slumped behind the wheel with a sigh. She'd just spent the evening with a crowd of people and still felt lonely as hell.

Most of the houses she drove past on Seth Williams Boulevard were dark. On the other side of the road, the New River murmured against its banks. Impulsively, she turned into Marston Pavilion. She may as well milk her melancholy for all it was worth.

Marston had been Camp Lejeune's original Officers' Club. Its covered terrace stretched elegantly along a river inlet. A wide lawn sloped down from the terrace to the water and a broad, sturdy pier. Three hundred meters across the inlet was Gottschalk Marina. Fran could see the tiny bumper lights strung along the main wharf and the larger buoy lights at the end of the marina's piers.

The pavilion was now used by all ranks for special events: Lejeune High School graduation parties, unit cookouts, aerobics classes, craft fairs. Tonight, Fran had the place to herself. The area around the pavilion was dark except for the lighted exit signs over the doors and one floodlight in the main parking area.

She turned off her headlights and drove around to the far side of the building, not wanting to catch the eye of any cruising MP. She sat for a minute, thoughtlessly brooding, before taking the keys out of the ignition. Dangling them from her fingers, she grabbed her wallet from her purse and got out of the car.

Hanging ferns cast lacy shadows along the terrace. She idly hop-scotched between the shadows and meandered on to the lawn and down to the pier. The air was as warm as April.

The pier, wider and positioned in deeper water than the one at the B.O.Q., creaked under her feet. She gazed across the water. Downstream from the marina, the trees looked impenetrable, but Fran knew office buildings, locked up for the night, lay a hundred meters beyond.

During the day, Fran would have been clearly visible from Seth Williams Boulevard. At night, it was just she and the river. The wind rustling the marsh grass and the splash of a river otter making a catch were too soothing to bolster a case of the blues. Fran unbuttoned her jacket and the top half of her blouse and let the breeze fondle the rise of her breasts. Nature therapy. She stretched her arms over her head and felt the back of her jacket billow away from her body. Eyes half closed, she imagined a small orchestra in dinner jackets playing music on the terrace while women wearing spangled chiffon and wrist corsages danced with men in dress whites. It was 1943, and the orchestra was playing something sexy and heartbreaking, like "Moonlight Serenade." Fran did a box step at the edge of the pier, humming.

Later, she would kick herself for having her head so full of adolescent fluff that she didn't sense someone coming up behind her. All she heard was the hollow thud of somebody hitting her in the back. Hard. Hard enough to leave a bruise. Hard enough to pitch her head over heels into the chilly water.

She lost her shoes when she instinctively began to kick. Inexplicably, she flashed to Ann Buckhalter's high heels, lost the same way on the night she died. The water was only twelve feet deep at the pier, but with the wind knocked out of her, it seemed like she was underwater forever. She struggled to the surface, banging her head on a piling. Was someone standing on the pier, or was it just a shadow? She couldn't see. Her contacts were clouded by the silty water.

Fran realized how stupid she had been to go to Marston alone in the middle of the night. Among her panicked thoughts, she also realized this may have been how Ann Buckhalter ended up in the river. Damned if she was going to repeat that outcome.

She treaded water, afraid to climb out next to the pier. Unarmed, shoeless, nearly blind, she wouldn't stand a chance if whoever hit her was still there, waiting for a second shot. She sculled away from the pier on her back. What was she going to do? She rolled over and started swimming freestyle toward the only thing she could see distinctly: the buoy lights at Gottschalk Marina. Wasn't somebody there at night? If nothing else, she knew of an emergency MP call box there.

Concentrating helped stabilize her thinking. *Stroke, kick, breathe. Stroke, kick, breathe.* Thank God the water was calm. Thank God she was in good physical condition.

Halfway across, she started treading water again so she could slip out of her jacket. She felt it being tugged away even before she got her second arm free. A rippling vibration accompanied the tug. Something jostled her leg. Another jostle, then a definite nudge.

Something big was in the water nearby. A piece of driftwood? A scuttled fishing boat? An irrepressible gurgle of terror escaped her numb lips when she realized her decision to stay in the water might be the last stupid thing she ever did. Whatever was next to her wasn't floating with the current. It was propelling itself. And there was only one self-propelled thing that big in the inlet.

Alligator.

In panic, she swiped at it and made contact with a rough, resilient object that jerked away. A glittery eye, bright yellow in the moonlight, flashed above the water. She saw it clearly, though one of her contacts had washed away. She flailed and thrashed and tried to scream but only choked on a mouthful of water. Then she started swimming again. Faster than she knew she could.

Maybe she only imagined the gator was pacing her, one leisurely paddle stroke for every five of her frenzied ones. At some level, she knew she could not outswim the reptile. It would be smarter to make less commotion in the water. But she couldn't hold back. For the last fifty meters, she was strictly on automatic pilot.

She hit the boat ramp hard enough to leave a goose egg on her head, stopping so abruptly that something rear-ended her. If it was the snout of an alligator ramming her tailbone, she didn't want to know. She gave one last kick, and whatever it was withdrew into the water. She crawled up the ramp, bawling loudly. At the top, she curled up on her side and vomited.

"Holy shit, woman! What the hell do you think you're doing?"

The voice was angry, the outstretched arm as big as a pork shoulder. But the bearded face was full of concern. And it was familiar. Fran just couldn't remember his name. He put down his flashlight and tried to pull her to her feet, but she collapsed, gagging, on her hands and knees.

When she finished heaving and settled into a sitting position, he introduced himself as Steve Butcher, manager of Gottschalk Marina. He said she was lucky because a night watchman wasn't normally needed. The MPs made their rounds every hour or so. But both marina piers had been damaged by an August storm. And lately, there had been a problem with teenagers partying after hours. The damaged areas were posted, Butcher said, but he was afraid some kid would wander down to the pier, fall through one of the broken boards in the dark, and break his neck. But this was the first time he had pulled somebody out of the water in the middle of the night.

"This ain't the English Channel, you know," he chuckled, wrapping Fran in a tarp.

She sat back on her haunches and pushed the wet hair out of her face. His shocked expression told her she must look pretty bad.

"Um, listen, you weren't trying to get away from some guy, some . . . attacker, were you?"

A human assailant wasn't the first thing on her mind. "Alligator."

"What's that? Alligator? Did one of them suckers take a nip at you, ma'am? Jesus, you're not bleeding, are you?"

He swept a blinding flashlight over her soaked clothes and mud-streaked legs. She was wobbly but with a little help managed to get to her feet. She still had two of them, thank God. She turned slowly with her arms outstretched.

"No blood to speak of. Your head is banged up, but I don't see nothing looks like a gator chomp. Listen, I better call EMS. You're going to need a tetanus shot at least. That water's not fit for swimming."

"I'm so cold. Can I go inside?"

"Oh, sure. Sorry. Let me help you."

Butcher wrestled out of his zippered sweatshirt and wrapped it around her shoulders. He led her to his office and grabbed a plaid blanket off the couch, trading it for the now-damp tarp. He dragged a portable gas heater from under a table and switched it on.

"There's a head down the hall. Are you steady enough to go in and get your clothes off? I mean, you're gonna stay cold as long as you're in those clothes. I got extra sets of sweats here."

He foraged through a wall locker and brought out two thick wads of gray fleece. She accepted them gratefully.

Butcher was talking to the MPs on the phone when Fran latched the door to the small bathroom. She ran the water in the shower as hot as she could stand it and stood, then squatted, on the concrete floor, sobbing into the steam. She cried from relief and exhaustion and because she'd gotten a look at herself in the mirror. Muddy water and bits of debris swirled down the drain.

When she got out, she saw only one dubious-looking towel. Unable to bring herself to use it, she pulled handfuls of brown paper towels from the wall dispenser and dabbed herself with them. The sweats were much too big but clean. And warm.

She heard the approaching MP siren as she walked back into Butcher's office and collapsed cross-legged in front of the space heater. He handed her a cup of cocoa.

"Thank you so much." She smiled. "I didn't find any alligator bites. Why did they take down the warning signs if alligators are still out there?"

"'Cause General Johnson sent out an order telling us to. He said he didn't want so many negative signs on the base. Keep Off the Grass. No Parking. Don't Spit There. Don't Wear Jock Gear in the Exchange. We even had to take down some of the No Smoking signs. But I put 'em right back. We got fuel tanks in the shop back there. Kerosene. Gasoline. You think some people aren't dumb enough to light a cigarette and forget it's hanging out of their mouth when they get gas for their boat? At least with the sign, I can say at the funeral, 'Hey, he was warned.'" He topped off her cup from a badly dented saucepan. "Are you sure you ran into a gator? What were you doing in the water in the first place?"

"I'm pretty sure. Anyway, I'd rather save my whole story for the MPs, if it's okay with you. I just know I swam all the way from Marston Pavilion. About halfway across, I felt something bumping against me. Something that was moving against the current."

"What did this thing feel like?"

"Like the seat covers in my car. But alive. Oh, and I saw one of its eyes. I watch the Discovery Channel. I know what an alligator's eye looks like." She smiled weakly. "Reptilian."

"Might have been Effie. She's one of our regulars. Fifteen feet long, maybe."

"Effie?"

"Got her name after this pop-eyed private had his first look at her and said, 'That's one big effing alligator!'"

Fran giggled, then coughed up some brown phlegm.

"Mostly, the gators stay up Wallace Creek. But Effie likes to bring her babies to the marina in the summer because people feed them so well. Gators will eat anything. People think they're not good mothers, but Effie is. That's why we had to put up the signs in the first place. A gator can wreck a small boat. And a boat can wreck a gator. It's just too damn distracting. The boaters get excited and run into each other. They run over the baby gators, too. It's better to keep people and gators apart. But you don't have to worry much about being eaten by any alligator, ma'am. They're too fat and lazy to prey on people. Effie should be pretty sluggish this time of year anyway. She'd be flat-out hibernating if the weather wasn't so mild. She was probably just curious."

Fran was a little embarrassed when two corpsmen rolled a gurney into Butcher's office. She insisted she could walk, and they insisted she ride. The corpsmen looked surprised and skeptical when Fran said she was a special agent with NCIS. They'd have to take her word for it. Her wallet and ID were somewhere in the river. Fortunately, one of the MPs who arrived shortly after the EMS crew recognized her.

Fran's wits were returning. She asked for a breathalyzer test so there would be no question about her sobriety later, when she told her boss what happened. It was going to take some splainin', that was for sure.

After having her skull tapped and scanned, Fran spent the rest of the night in the Naval Hospital hooked up to an intravenous antibiotic and painkiller drip. She lost count of how many times her blood pressure was taken and how many times a thermometer was shoved under her tongue. As Grandmama Pattle would say, it was "irksome," but it was comforting, too. Almost as comforting as seeing Rumley's funny face poke through the door to her room after everyone else had been herded off the floor. She used her IV-free arm to gesture him in. He didn't turn on the overhead light but quietly eased the room's one chair close to the head of her bed. He leaned close enough to her face that she could smell his habitual breath mint.

"I may have talked to somebody today who saw Ann Buckhalter on that pier the night she died."

Reflexively, she lifted her head off the pillow. He pulled away, sternly hissing she must relax and listen, not speak.

"This buddy of mine from way back dropped by the base and invited me for a bite to eat. Since he was footing the bill, I suggested the O Club. Afterward, I walked over to the parking lot in front of the B.O.Q. building where Ann Buckhalter stayed. Everything was quiet. The pier was empty. I was leaning against a tree when I heard this voice from overhead: 'Have you seen him, too, mister?' I looked up, and there's this kid up in the tree, a girl about ten, wearing eyeglasses the size of saucers and holding a pair of binoculars almost as big as she was. 'Him who?' I asked her. 'The big owl,' she said. Really big. Seen him twice, she said. I was kind of tickled, so I said I thought owls were active just at night. 'Well,' she said, 'they have to hang out somewhere during the day, don't they?' She'd seen him twice, both times at night in that tree. I asked her how she knew it was a he, and she told me she was only guessing—that she knew it was a barred owl, and the males are bigger. Anyway, I asked if her parents let her come out there at night, and she said she didn't have to. She pointed at the B.O.Q. building across the street. Said she was staying there in a suite with her family, third floor front, waiting to move into quarters."

Fran sensed where this was going and forced herself to focus through the drugs. Humongous owl. Kid with humongous binoculars.

"I asked how long she'd been watching the area at night, and she said a couple of weeks. First hoot she hears, she rushes to her window. I asked if she was watching last Saturday, and—right on cue—she said, 'You mean the night the lady got drowned?' She said she saw some people sitting on the pier that night. I asked how many people, and she said she wasn't paying much attention, you know, because of the owl, but she was sure there was more than one. Then she narrowed her eyes and said, 'I was more interested in the man watching my owl.'"

Fran clutched the sheet in a rush of drugs and excitement. "What man? A man on the pier?"

"Shhh. I'm almost finished. No. Not on the pier. The kid said a man was standing close to the same tree I was under, but perfectly still. I asked what he looked like and she said, 'Cute. Like Dick Van Dyke, only not funny.' I asked how she knew who Dick Van Dyke was, and she said she had the video of *Mary Poppins*. But get this: I asked her what he was wearing, and she said a uniform, but not a Marine uniform like her dad wore. So, I asked if she meant a Navy uniform, like Popeye wears, and she said no."

Fran smiled unseen in the low light. *Oh, Rum! Popeye wears cracker-jacks. Sorta.* It could indeed have been a Navy uniform—service dress blues or khakis.

"I asked if she noticed what time she saw the man, and she said after 2130 and before 2200. She keeps notes of her Barry sightings."

"Barry?" Fran croaked.

"Shhh, for Christ's sake. That's what she calls the owl. Barry. A barred owl. Get it? She said the man just stood there for maybe five minutes, then sneaked—her word, not mine—away toward the club. Her mother came into her room about then to yell at her for having the window open. I got her name and her dad's name and rank but decided not to explain who I was. If she tells her parents about our conversation, they'll probably think I was Chester the Molester. But I'm betting she won't. Out of sight, out of mind."

He told Fran he'd shoot Boyette an email about the encounter and let him decide if any follow-up was needed. After all, "cute" as a description of the man under the tree was pretty arbitrary. And the child couldn't even confirm that a woman, much less Ann Buckhalter, was one of the figures she saw at the end of the pier that night.

Fran made Rumley swear to remind her of his meeting with the owl girl after she got off the drugs. He agreed, lightly patted her shoulder, and slipped out of the room. She thought she heard a nurse chastising him in a booming stage whisper, but she wasn't sure. Whatever the nurse had put in her IV line was wafting its crazy way through her brain, leaving her with just one sleepy thought: *Where do owls hang out in the daytime?*

TWENTY-SIX.

SUNDAY, EARLY MONDAY

Boyette was giving her a curious look. His wife, Abby, was peeling the blister pack off a toothbrush while Fran tried to rake a comb through the worst-looking head of hair ever seen on a living person.

She told them she felt fine, really. The doctor was releasing her, though he'd warned her that weeks from now, she still might develop pneumonia as a result of her experience.

It was going to be a busy morning. Boyette had arranged with the provost marshal to have somebody put together a new ID card for Fran. He'd also arranged for her car, fitted with a new key, to be driven to her house, and for the door locks on her house to be changed. There was a possibility she didn't remember events clearly and her assailant had taken her wallet and keys, although she could have sworn she lost them in the river. Boyette had also called in a favor at the state Division of Motor Vehicles to get somebody to burn her a new driver's license first thing Monday.

The doc had assured them that, for the most part, Fran would be back in business Monday. But Boyette insisted she stay home, just to be sure.

He told her he had sent an evidence collection team to Marston Pavilion, where it found her suit jacket snagged by a live oak downstream. Her ID folder was still in the pocket. Her badge was okay, but the ID card was not. One of her shoes was found floating next to a piling. Her purse, which she'd left in her car, appeared to be untouched. A zippered side pocket still contained a few bills and change.

The Boyettes had offered to let Fran stay at their home after she was released, but she declined. She also refused to call her parents. What could she tell them? "Hi, Pop. On a lark, I went out on this dark pier all by myself in the middle of the night about a mile from where this other woman drowned a week ago. Somebody pushed me into the water, and I got chased by an alligator, but I'm okay now. So, what's new with you and Mom?" She had done a foolhardy thing and hoped Boyette realized it was a fluke. He had enough four-alarm screwballs to deal with as it was.

They discussed the implications of the incident. Whoever had pushed Fran in the river either knew who she was or didn't. If he did know her, he probably hadn't intended to kill her, as it was a safe assumption a special agent would know how to handle herself in the water. Also, he'd have hit her on the head. Unconscious, she was much more likely to drown. If her assailant didn't know who Fran was, maybe he was some random wacko who saw an opportunity for mischief. Or maybe he mistook her for somebody else. Maybe some kind of drug deal was going on at Marston Pavilion, and the participants thought Fran was about to stumble on to something. Of course, the assailant could have been a female.

The alligator complicated their speculations. Even if the person who pushed her knew alligators were in the river, he couldn't count on one killing Fran. It was the New River, for Christ's sake, not the Amazon. The Boyettes agreed that it looked like Fran's assailant wanted to terrorize her, not kill her.

The most disturbing thing was the incident's proximity to the spot where Ann Buckhalter drowned. Had Fran been targeted because she was an investigating agent? Other agents were also involved, of course. But if somebody with a reason to worry about the investigation had a hatred of women, Fran was vulnerable in a way the other agents weren't.

She thought she was starting to look a little more presentable. Abby had brought along a makeup kit the size of a picnic cooler. She gently camouflaged Fran's bruises with concealer. And she brushed powdered color on her cheeks.

Fran wasn't shaky or coughing anymore, but the first twinges of muscle soreness were setting in. She hadn't done any distance swimming in years, and her deltoids knew it. Tall, rangy Abby had brought one of her own oversized poor-boy sweaters, some thermal socks, and a pair of stretchy leggings for Fran to wear home. *All I need,* Fran thought, *is a porkpie hat, and I'm ready to sell Depression-era newspapers on a street corner.*

It took more than an hour to collect the required forms and signatures for Fran's release. Halfway through the red tape, she bounced back enough to crave a cheeseburger. The best the hospital could do was a two-day-old chicken salad sandwich from a vending machine. Fran figured if she could survive a midnight swim with Effie, an overripe sandwich wouldn't kill her.

Riding home in the backseat of Boyette's car, she debated telling him about the Peeping Tom and the Foghorn Leghorn lighter. It had seemed a minor event after finding the tape in her mailbox. Now, she wondered if she'd underestimated its importance. What if the guy on the pier was the same guy who ran away from her carport after dropping the lighter? Still, she hesitated to tell her boss. Wouldn't bringing it up now make her look dopier than she already did?

It was late afternoon by the time Fran finally got home and locked the door behind her. She had primed herself to be nervous. But it was actually comforting to be among familiar objects, with a familiar cat on her lap waving his rear end in her face.

She sat in exhausted contentment for a while, then showered and shampooed her hair. She dried it while skimming the Sunday comics and listening to her phone messages. The world's shortest grapevine had done its work. Message one: Elva begged her to call, first chance Fran got. Message two: Rumley knew where she could get a Rottweiler. Message three: Hank Bunn sent his regards. Message zero: Vic Maldonado.

Fran got into bed at 1830, tummy telly tucked in beside her, fully intending to stay awake for *60 Minutes*. Her only concessions to the week's perils were the cordless phone on the pillow and the nine-millimeter on the floor.

She jerked awake with a gasp, painfully whacking her wrist bone on the TV, when the phone rang. She'd programmed it to forward incoming calls to her answering machine, but the cat must have hit the audible-ring button while boomeranging around the room. She reached down and swiveled the gun barrel toward the wall in case the cat had also figured out how to cock a pistol. Once she was sitting upright, it seemed reasonable to answer the phone.

At the other end was an unexpected voice that immediately identified itself as Captain Rhonda Baptiste. "I hope I'm not disturbing you, Fran. General Johnson is out of town, part of a seminar at the war college. I know if he hadn't been locked into doing it months ago, considering all that's been going on here, he'd have canceled. But Colonel Knightdale heard you were in the hospital and asked me to call. What can we do to help?"

Fran said the perfunctory things. It was nice, getting so much kind attention. Assuming that's all it was.

"Of course, I'm concerned about you, too," Baptiste said. "You were right. We women need to support each other. Frankly, I could use a little myself. I'm wearing extra hats at work, for a few days, anyway. Carolyn Holdsclaw is on leave, and Major St. Legere is buried in correspondence for next year's Reunion of the Stars. I'm pretty much running things. And to add to the chaos, I'm making travel arrangements for Colonel Knightdale. He's taking emergency leave."

"I hope nobody in the colonel's family is ill," Fran said. Emergency leave was never good news.

"Not in the family, no. The funeral of a friend, I believe. In Tennessee. But God, the timing couldn't be worse. Isn't that an awful thing to say? I just mean that so much is going on, it's a bad time to be short-handed."

Captain Baptiste paused. Fran sensed she was waiting for her to say something. What? Had Captain Baptiste gotten word about the secretly taped staff meeting? Was she fishing for details? Fran asked about Rhonda's son, Jeremy. He was fine. Her husband had insisted Jeremy get his first regulation haircut. Until now, Rhonda had trimmed the child's hair herself. Jeremy wasn't the least bit afraid of the clippers, she said. It had been more of a rite of passage for Mom than son. Fran chuckled politely.

Rhonda asked and Fran again assured her she didn't need anything. Something about the captain's effusiveness bothered Fran. It just didn't ring true for Rhonda Baptiste to be so back-fence friendly, especially with Fran.

After she hung up, Fran lay back down, but she was no longer sleepy. Her cat, the nocturnal boomerang, wasn't helping. He sprang from ironing board to chest of drawers, landing with all the grace and noise of a Huey. She got up to put the cat in the utility closet and considered whether hot cocoa or Jack Daniel's would be more soporific. Maybe she'd try a little of both.

Her mind kept circling back to something Rhonda said. Knightdale was taking emergency leave to go to a friend's funeral in Tennessee. When a general was away, his chief of staff assumed the general's responsibilities. For Knightdale to take leave during General Johnson's absence, especially when the general was juggling some serious issues, seemed as unnatural as Rhonda's gushiness.

Okay, people didn't die to suit the convenience of the military. Still, whoever died must have been a really close friend for Knightdale to take leave while Johnson was away.

Fran couldn't help herself. She looked up Knightdale's home phone number and dialed it. Her excuse would be to thank the colonel for his concern and offer condolences. Sure, he would think it peculiar, Fran's calling him at home. He'd probably attribute it to head trauma.

Fran punched the air in silent jubilation when Knightdale's daughter, Motor-mouth Marissa, answered. The teenager had no idea who was calling but didn't hesitate to volunteer that her mom was at the base chapel, supervising a potluck supper, and her dad was at his office, getting ready for a trip.

"Oh? A trip?" Fran asked.

"He's going to Memphis. Somebody's funeral. I didn't even know he knew anybody in Memphis. I wanted to go with him and see Graceland. That would be so cool. But he won't let me. I don't know why not. I mean, school's out and everything."

"Are you staying with friends while they're gone?"

"Huh? Oh, Mom's not going. I don't think she knew these people. She doesn't seem too thrilled about him going either. They didn't have a fight or anything, but I think she wanted to see Graceland, too."

Right. Fran took a deep breath. She was edging out on thin ice. If Boyette knew she was pumping the chief of staff's underage daughter for information, Fran would be deader than a Jeffrey Dahmer dinner guest.

"I used to live in Memphis," Fran lied. "I might know the person who died. What's his name?"

"It's not a he. It's a she. I think my dad said her name is Highlock.

Was Highlock? What I mean is, the person who called Dad to tell him about it was named Highlock. Maybe the dead person had a different name. All I heard was Highlock, like, 'Hi, Goldilocks,' only without the 'Goldi' and just one 'lock.'" Marissa giggled.

Fran tried to repress her excitement while easing out of the conversation. Her conscience pinched her only a little for deceiving the guileless little airhead. Thank God, Marissa never bothered to ask who was calling. If Fran was really experiencing some overdue luck, the girl would forget to mention the call to her parents. What had Rumley said about kids? "Out of sight, out of mind."

Fran pulled out her laptop and encrypted diskettes. She scanned two diskettes and six files before she found the right set of notes. There it was. Highlock. The name mentioned by the distraught child. The child who left a message on Ann Buckhalter's answering machine. The world was getting smaller by the minute.

She flipped through her phone book to find the area code for Memphis, then dialed 1-901-555-1212. The automated system failed to find the name. An operator came on the line and said there were no Highlocks in Memphis. She asked if Fran would like her to check the listings in West Memphis, Arkansas. Indeed, she would.

A second operator came on to announce the name and number of Michael J. Highlock. Fran dialed the number. The voice that answered was female, middle-aged, and unhappy.

"Please forgive me for disturbing you," Fran said, taking a shot in the dark. "Could you tell me the time and place of the funeral? I'm from out of town, and I just heard."

The voice sighed. "It's all right, honey. It's going to be on Tuesday. At two. First Methodist on Roxboro Road. We delayed it because her brothers are having to come so far. The visitation is tonight at the funeral home. Briggs and Weston. Who is this?"

"I was a friend of . . . the deceased. Please accept my sympathies. I'm so sorry." Fran feigned a choked sob and hung up quickly. This time, her conscience pinched her hard enough to draw blood.

She then called information and got the number for the funeral home.

"Briggs and Weston Funeral Services and Crematory. Your guide through life's most difficult hours. Patty speaking. How may I help you?" The voice was jarringly perky.

"I'm a friend of the Highlocks," Fran said. "Mrs. Highlock told me you folks are in charge of arrangements. I feel really dumb, but I need to tell the florist what to put on the card. I can't remember how to spell the deceased's name. Can you tell me?"

"Certainly. Her name was Nita—N-i-t-a—Highlock Donning—D-o-n-n-i-n-g."

"Thank you. Oh, and I'd like a copy of the obituary. Could you tell me what paper it was in?"

"The *Commercial Appeal*. Hold on a second and I'll get you that number."

Full speed ahead. Fran said good-bye to Perky Patty and called the newspaper.

"*Commercial Appeal*. Newsroom."

"Good evening. I have a favor to ask. I'm calling from out of town. Could you email me a copy of an obituary?"

Fran was relayed to the obit editor, who told her, in a patronizing tone, that the notice would be posted on the paper's brand-new website in a few hours. Was Fran able to access the World Wide Web?

Fran pleaded urgency and faked a sniffle. "It would mean so much."

The editor conceded.

She meant to stay awake until she got the email, but fatigue caught up with her. The next time she saw the laptop was in the daylight.

ooooo

Fran and the laptop both lay on their sides. She turned the screen toward her and saw the "New mail" message flashing. She also noticed it was 0600. Groggily, she blinked to clear her eyes of Sandman slime.

HARDYVILLE, ARK.—Nita Highlock Donning, 30, of 661 Mason Quarry Road, died Saturday at Shelby County Hospital. A graveside service will be held Tuesday at 2 P.M. at First Methodist Memorial Garden, Hardyville.

She is survived by a son, Paul Kelley Donning, 9; parents Michael and Sharon Highlock; grandmother Evelyn Highlock of Memphis; and two brothers: Marine First Lieutenant Roy F. Highlock of Camp Butler, Okinawa, Japan, and Jay M. Highlock of Cuila Bay, Alaska.

In lieu of flowers, the family asks that memorial gifts be made to St. Jude's Children's Hospital in Memphis.

Fran didn't know what to think. What was Colonel Knightdale's interest in this family? If he was so close to them that he would take emergency leave to attend the funeral, why hadn't his daughter ever heard of them? And why wasn't his wife going with him? Nita Highlock Donning was only thirty years old. What had she died of? Had the dead woman's brother, First Lieutenant Roy Highlock, worked for Colonel Knightdale?

She read the obituary again. This time, the name Paul Kelley Donning jumped off the screen. Nita Highlock's son was nine years old. The child who left the message on Ann Buckhalter's answering machine could have been that age. Of course, considering the quality of Fran's hunches lately, little Paul would turn out to be a deaf-mute.

Two dead women, a colonel, and a mysterious child's voice on one of the dead women's answering machine. Were they all spokes on the same wheel?

TWENTY-SEVEN.

When Peter Rumley came by her house to check on her, he had
no idea he was about to provide her a cover story for attending Nita
Highlock's funeral.

While they shared a pot of coffee, he told her about a briefing that
morning involving the Parris Island armory. The chief warrant officer
running the armory was in charge of issuing new M16 rifles and destroying the old ones when their barrels gave out. He got rid of the
weapons by cutting the rifles into pieces. The pieces later were dumped
in a river.

But it looked like the warrant officer had been destroying only the
stocks and barrels. He saved the bolt receivers and used them to build
the civilian version of the M16. He then either sold the weapons or
gave them to friends. One of those friends had bragged about it to his
company commander, who'd tipped off the Naval Criminal Investigative Service.

By then, the illegal guns were in the hands of a number of happy collectors, including a chaplain and at least one general. Fortunately, the bolt receiver was the part with the serial number. Investigators now had to interview every officer who might have crossed paths with the warrant officer while he was running the armory. Procedures at the armory had since been corrected, but it was important to get those weapons back. It would be a PR disaster if one of them turned up at a crime scene.

"They're everywhere," Rumley told Fran. "The guys still on active duty are easy to find, but a lot have gotten out. One retired general in Savannah is stonewalling. I don't think he's worried about getting in trouble. He just hates to give up that rifle. Savannah, New Orleans, Seattle, Memphis. There's probably one of those rebuilt weapons in every state in the country."

"Memphis? Who's handling that?" Fran asked.

"A resident agency there. But we serve as their field office. One of their agents is on medical leave, so we'll cover. They've already interviewed a retired colonel who admits having a rifle. One of our agents will have to blow a couple days picking it up and getting it to Washington."

Fran jumped to her feet, trying to remember where she'd stowed her under-eye concealer and hot rollers. She'd have to look real healthy to get Boyette to let her go.

"You going right back to work, Rum?"

"Sure."

"Tell Boyette I'm looking tanned, rested, and ready to fly. Tell him I want to go to Memphis."

"What the hell are you talking about?"

"Tell the boss a pilgrimage to Graceland is just what I need to complete my recuperation. And I'll be glad to pick up that weapon while I'm out that way."

And I might just take in a funeral, too, she thought. If the Highlock matter had nothing to do with Ann Buckhalter's death, neither Knightdale nor Boyette—nor Rumley—need ever know.

ooooo

Boyette was surprised and wary—maybe because her hair was looking unusually big. "I didn't know you were an Elvis fan, Setliff. Didn't I order you to take it easy for a few days?"

Fran hopped on the offensive. Would Boyette have ordered a male agent to take it easy for a few days? Anyway, what she was asking was really the same as taking it easy. A hunka hunka R&R, a change of scene, would do her more good than staying at home. Take her mind off things. She smiled, looking at him with a disconcerting intensity. It was the glasses. Through the thick lenses, her eyes looked like giant, shiny plums.

He sighed. Did she still have her issue American Express card?

She did.

ooooo

Her plane was scheduled to leave Jacksonville at 1700. She raced to the PX for a shower cap and a mini-tube of toothpaste and swooped back home to throw her gray suit in a garment bag and shovel out the litter box. For the first time since the Hail and Farewell, she put in a pair of disposable contacts. They felt okay. Matter of fact, *she* was okay, except for two red lumps, one on each temple at the hairline. The lumps looked like a baby goat about to sprout horns. Well, no need for that. She took a pair of manicure scissors from her medicine cabinet, sectioned off a chunk of hair over her eyes, and snipped bangs. She had to smother them in mousse to make them lie flat, but the result wasn't half bad. At least she wouldn't be going to a Southern Protestant funeral looking like the daughter of Satan.

Wired and impatient, she backtracked to the field office to pick up her new credential case and then headed to the airport. She finally relaxed upon tearing off a parking receipt at the entrance to the airport lot.

Fran had her choice of two flights. One included a two-hour layover in Charlotte, plus a stop in Atlanta. The other included a turbulence-prone propjet and ninety minutes in St. Louis. She opted for Charlotte, although neither route made any more sense than reaching over her shoulder to scratch her behind. From Memphis, she'd take a commuter to the Hardyville airstrip.

What Fran really hoped was that she wouldn't have to go to Nita Highlock's funeral at all. Maybe she could figure out what was going on beforehand by asking some discreet questions. At least she knew she wouldn't run into Colonel Knightdale on the way. With great reluctance, Rum had reconnoitered that for her. The colonel's flight was at 0700 Tuesday morning.

Fran wore a Navy peacoat over a baggy Aran Isle sweater and jeans. Too heavy for Lejeune, they might be needed in the hills of Arkansas. Her badge was clipped to her belt, hidden by the sweater. She had been "a suit" for so long, the outfit made her feel like an undercover NAS-CAR groupie. To bypass the extra paperwork and unwanted attention at the airport, she wasn't carrying her gun. She couldn't imagine needing it anyway.

She was seated between a guy in a Duke sweatshirt wearing earphones and a guy in a Cowboys sweatshirt reading *Consumer Reports*. The former had probably spent as much time at Duke as the latter had playing for the Cowboys. Both had the intentionally blank expressions of people who've passed too many hours having their personal space violated. Not that Fran was interested in talking. Her throat was growing painfully tender. She hoped that, if she avoided talking, whatever was incubating there wouldn't turn into something nasty.

Fran's flight plan hit a glitch in Atlanta. The connecting flight to Memphis had been canceled because of a mechanical problem. There was no other flight to that city until the following morning. For anyone who wished, the airline would arrange transportation to the bus station. Bus passengers would arrive in Memphis fifteen minutes earlier than if they waited for the flight next morning. Now the good news. Inconvenienced passengers would be refunded the price of their tickets, and the airline would arrange for them to stay at their choice of two area hotels. Plus, everyone would be guaranteed a seat on the morning flight.

Glancing around, Fran realized she was the only passenger particularly concerned about the news. A honeymooning couple actually squealed, they were so thrilled to have another hotel room to get naked in. A middle-aged woman with bags under her eyes told the airline rep she was returning home from a visit with a new grandchild. She'd welcome a break between housework there and more of the same waiting for her at home. Passengers starting their trips from Atlanta could just go home.

What should Fran do? If nothing else happened, the only real change in her schedule was that she'd spend the night in a luxury hotel in Atlanta instead of a stop-and-flop in Hardyville. She called Boyette to tell him about the change in plans.

When her room phone rang later that evening, that's who she expected to be on the other end.

"Hello?"

"Setliff? You okay? You sound like you swallowed a cactus."

It was Vic Maldonado. She folded up on the bed like a carpenter's rule.

"I've got a sore throat."

"Good. We've got a chance to set a real precedent here. I'll talk, you'll shut up. I heard you took a moonlight swim in the river and ended up in the hospital. Next, you get on a plane that can't fly. Is this some kind of survival test, Setliff? When I couldn't get you at home, I called Boyette. He gave me this number. Said you were in Atlanta boondoggling."

"Trust me. My boon is all doggled out."

"Jesus, you sound awful. Got any Chloraseptic? I thought you might get a kick out of knowing Major St. Legere wants to sue the University of North Carolina and every son of a bitch named Morehead."

"What? Why?" Fran was pressing the handset between her cheek and shoulder. If she could, she'd squeeze her whole body through those little holes his voice was coming from.

"You're not doing your part, Setliff. Shut up and listen. It's the major's son, Donald. You must have heard about Donald. He could slip that kid into a conversation about snow tires. Donald the scholar. Donald the distance runner. Donald the finalist for a Morehead Scholarship at UNC. If he gets it, it's four free years."

"Go, Donald," she whispered.

"Don't answer. Just nod."

She nodded.

"Anyway, Donald had his interview with the selection committee, which determines the winners. Guess what one of the interviewers asked this seventeen-year-old kid, the only finalist who's a military brat?"

Fran gave an interrogative squeak.

" 'Well, now, Donald,' "—Maldonado faked a simpering, affected diction—" 'how does it feel knowing your father's job is to kill people?' "

"No!"

"Honest to God. Donald gave the interviewer the evil eye and said, 'My father's job is not to kill people. It's to keep enemies of the United States from killing people like you.' Donald didn't add, 'you wormy little prick,' but it was implied."

Go, Donald, Fran thought.

"Unfortunately, the exchange rattled the kid, and he stumbled through the rest of the interview. The major said if Donald doesn't make the next cut, he's going to sue."

Fran coughed. It was agony.

Maldonado clucked his tongue in sympathy. "St. Legere could raise a stink, but there's no legal basis for a suit. The Morehead Foundation is private. They can screen candidates with a stripper's pole if they want."

Fran wheezed.

"Well, sweetheart, I'd say it's good to hear your voice, but I'd be lying. It is good, however, to know the rest of you is all right. Whatever you're up to, be careful. Call me when you get back, will you?" He hung up.

She touched her fingers to the mouthpiece. Had he called her sweetheart? She didn't want to read too much into it, but Vic didn't throw endearments around like many guys did. The important thing was that he cared enough to track her down. Unless, of course, General Johnson had told him to keep tabs on her.

She wouldn't believe it. If it turned out she was wrong, she'd join the first convent that took backsliding Baptists. Or she'd remarry Marlon. Either way, she'd put the old sex drive in mothballs forever.

TWENTY-EIGHT.

TUESDAY

Fran knew Hardyville's history as soon as she saw the place. It was like so many Southern towns that sank waist-deep in unemployment during the eighties. The town had always been dull as ditch water. Then came the nineties, when big-city people had enough money to look for places to get away from other big-city people. To them, Hardyville's dreariness looked like rustic charm.

The town still had a Main Street where cars parked perpendicular to the curb. It had a picturesque courthouse with a rust-streaked statue of a Confederate soldier. A little black girl was skipping around the statue, smacking the cold bronze to make a hollow pinging sound. The only eyesores Fran saw were the town's plastic chenille Christmas decorations, draped over every utility pole like caterpillars in drag.

If it hadn't been for the layover in Atlanta, Fran would have had time to pose as a mourner. Maybe she would have taken a couple of meals at Nancy Jean's Café and pumped Nancy Jean for information about the Highlocks. As it was, she barely had time to change into her gray suit in the restroom at Murphy's Gas 'n Go.

She quickly figured out that Hardyville had only two taxis. Both of them passed her more than once, coming up Main Street, picking up three or four people in front of the drugstore, then heading back the way they'd come. A funeral shuttle, Fran guessed. All the passengers wore dark Sunday clothes, and it wasn't Sunday. By the time she got into one of the taxis, she knew she'd be among the last to reach the cemetery.

That worked out okay. When she arrived, the mourners were engrossed in the words of a bald-headed speaker with the vocal quality of a kazoo. It was twenty degrees colder than at Camp Lejeune, but Fran had decided against wearing the peacoat over her suit. She tipped her cab driver to take the coat and her overnight bag to the ticket desk of the Hardyville airport terminal, which consisted of a windsock, a Quonset hut, and a double-wide.

Wearing dark glasses and a black wool scarf wrapped around her head and neck, she felt comfortably inconspicuous. Fran spotted Colonel Knightdale immediately. She positioned herself where she could see him but he couldn't see her. He looked different in his double-breasted civilian topcoat with just an inch of blistering-white shirt collar showing—very Wall Street, except that from his expression it appeared the market was about to crash. His sad eyes were fixed on the canopy sheltering a silver-gray casket blanketed with pink roses.

Fran eased her way around the edge of the crowd, handkerchief pressed to her nose. She found a spot from which she could see the people sitting under the canopy. From that vantage point, she realized Knightdale's gaze was fixed on a child. A little boy who looked enough like Knightdale to be his clone. Same dark hair. Same dark eyes, even

bigger and sadder in a child's face. The boy was fidgeting on a folding chair, scuffing his shoes in the green Astro Turf. The middle-aged
woman next to him held one of his hands, which he halfheartedly tried
to pull away. At his other side were two young men. The one with a
Marine haircut sat with his head lowered, hands clenched between his
knees. He repeatedly cut his eyes in Knightdale's direction. He could
have disemboweled the colonel with that look. The other young man,
almost as clean-cut but heavier, stared impassively at the casket.

Fran didn't need the Psychic Network to put this one together.
Colonel Knightdale was attending the funeral because the dead woman
was the mother of his nine-year-old son, Paul. Which explained why
Knightdale was standing fairly close to the canopy, although it made
him the target of those ugly glances. He wanted a good look at the boy,
Marissa's half-brother.

Mighty reckless, Colonel, Fran thought. *Nine years ago and today.*

Fran wasn't the only person hanging back from the crowd. A man
with an Adam's apple the size of a Granny Smith was also keeping his
distance. He was homely in an appealing way, his clothes neat, if ill-
fitting. The man dipped into the crowd only once, to wave quickly and
wink at the boy, Paul. The boy smiled and started to raise his hand, but
the young man with the Marine haircut saw the exchange and frowned
at the boy, downing his hand like an annoying fly.

Fran followed the homely man when he walked to a shady part of
the cemetery to smoke a cigarette. He tried three dud matches off the
sole of his shoe before he succeeded in lighting a fourth, struck off his
thumbnail.

"Could I bum one off you?" Fran asked, coming up beside him. "I'm
all out, and funerals make me nervous as a cat."

He squinted at her through the smoke. "Sure. I know what you
mean." He shook a cigarette out of the pack for her and went directly to
the thumbnail to light it.

She inhaled. Just like riding a bicycle. "Thanks." She exhaled smoke at the tail end of a deep sigh. "It's all so sad. I couldn't believe it, that Nita died. What happened? I hated to ask, not knowing whether it was, you know . . ."

"Female cancer. She never would get checked regular like women are supposed to. I guess she figured she was too young to worry."

"Are you a relative?"

He looked closely at Fran for the first time. She projected as much cow-eyed guilelessness as she could muster.

"Used to be. Nita and I were married for nearly five years. Name's Hugh Donning." They shook hands. "Yours?"

"Fran. How's poor little Paul taking it?"

He shook his head. "Well, cancer is a hard way to die. Anybody who saw her in the last three months would know she was real bad off. Even a kid. And he's not too little to know that if you get sick enough, you die. At least now he can start looking ahead to something besides his mama dying." Hugh Donning lowered his head into double-barrel streams of nasal smoke. "I'll probably never get to see the kid again. I figure he'll go live with his uncle Jay now. Jay and Roy both hate my guts."

"Why's that?"

"They think I should have stopped the divorce when Nita found out she was sick. Yeah, getting the divorce was my idea. But stopping it wouldn't have made no difference. I never could make her happy when she was well. What makes them think I could have did any better when she was sick? Her brothers never did think straight when it came to Nita. And dammit, I had found somebody I could make happy. I expect the Highlock boys hate me almost as much as they hate Paul's real father."

She wondered if Hugh Donning had any idea Paul's real father was less than a hundred yards away.

"Oh? Was Nita married to somebody else before you?"

He frowned at Fran, suspicious. "Where did you say you knew Nita from?"

Fran decided to take this one head-on. "I didn't know her. I'm sorry if I gave you that idea. I work with Paul's real father, Colonel Bob Knightdale. He's here, did you know that? The man in the double-breasted overcoat. See?"

He did see. With narrowed eyes, Hugh Donning looked long and hard, then turned back to Fran. "And what's your interest in all this?"

"I'm not his wife or girlfriend, if that's what you're thinking. Colonel Knightdale doesn't even know I'm here. That's all I can say about it."

"Oh, no, it ain't. Let's you and me talk, sister."

He steered her around to the far side of a mildewed monument big enough to screen both of them. Fran sat on the cold concrete. She noted that Theodore Flybold, beloved husband of Mary Hazel, had gone to glory in 1924.

"I've been curious about Knightdale as long as I've knowed about him and Nita," Donning said. He hitched up his pant legs and sat beside Fran. "I seen a couple of old snapshots and newspaper clippings Nita had. God knows, she talked about him more than I wanted to listen. What's he like? As lowdown as I always thought?"

"Truth is, by all accounts, he's a decent man, Mr. Donning. A good officer. Does he contribute to Paul's upbringing?"

"Financially, he does. Check every month. Never late. Set up an allotment through the bank. And I don't mind telling you, we were always glad to see it. I got a little company cleans up smoke and flood damage. Do all right most of the time. But when money's tight, the first thing people stop paying is insurance, and that's what pays me. Before she got sick, Nita used to work for the county. The problem was, her health insurance paid only 80 percent of the bills. That left her with 20 percent. Twenty percent of a hundred thousand dollars is twenty thousand. If she hadn't of died, she'd be broke. Now, her county life insurance will pay whatever else she owes. I don't know who paid for the funeral. They didn't ask me for nothing."

"Does Paul know who his biological father is?"

Donning shrugged. "He didn't know while Nita and me were married, I can tell you that. I was his daddy then. I never did legally adopt him, but he used my name. She told me awhile back she was going to tell Paul the truth before she died. I told her not to do it. I mean, didn't the kid have enough to deal with already? But Nita thought he had the right to know, and he should hear it from her. I don't know if she ever did." Donning leaned clear of the monument and looked at Knightdale again. "Lord, that guy's face will give him away soon enough if he don't do it himself. I hope Knightdale realizes this probably ain't a good time to make himself known to the boy, if that's what he's got in mind. Those Highlocks stick together."

"I don't think Colonel Knightdale is here to make a scene, Mr. Donning."

"Hugh."

"Hugh. Do you know how he and Nita met?"

"Sure. He was her teacher."

"What?"

"Teacher. Instructor. Whatever you call it. Nita was in college at Iroquois State. She got one of those NROTC scholarships that pays for everything. She said it was the best thing ever happened to her. Her ticket out of Polkaville, something like that. At the time, it ticked me off. She was so happy to be leaving. Nita and I went together through high school. I knew twelve years of school was all I could handle. But I was ready to wait for her if I had to. I thought she'd graduate college and be a schoolteacher or something. I didn't plan on her doing a hitch in the service. Anyway, Knightdale was one of her NROTC teachers. He's the one made her decide to be a Marine. A Marine! Hell, Nita was a homecoming princess."

Donning lit another cigarette and offered Fran one. She declined.

"Nita sent me a newspaper clipping about some training trip they all took on a boat."

"Summer cruise."

"Yeah, that's it. Sounds like a vacation, don't it? There was a picture in the paper, too. It showed Nita wearing a helmet and a big backpack. She was halfway up a wall, holding on to a rope. A man standing on the ground was giving her a boost. Nita said that was her commander, Major Knightdale. I never liked that picture. I mean, the only thing I saw was him standing there with his hands on her nineteen-year-old butt."

Fran stood and crossed her arms tightly over her chest. She felt a chill.

"Of course, she had to drop out of that NROTC program when she got pregnant," Donning went on. "It broke her heart like nothing you ever saw. Coming home, kinda in disgrace, after making everybody so proud. Nita kept saying she was going back to school after she had the baby. But they all say that, don't they? Paul had some health problems his first year, allergies or something. Nita lived with her parents so there'd always be somebody with him. Her folks were understanding, I guess, but her dad said he couldn't help her out with tuition on top of all their other expenses. I wasn't around at the time. It had hurt me so bad, knowing she'd do that with somebody else. Have a kid, I mean. When she always made me be so damn careful. Senior year, I poured half my money into that rubber vending machine at the Shell station. But then I got to feeling sorry for her. And to be honest, I still loved her. We got back together when Paul was two years old. The hardest part for Nita was facing up to the truth, that this Knightdale character didn't care about her. God knows, she was crazy about him. She protected him, too. Once, her brother Jay threatened to get Knightdale, and Nita swore she'd kill herself if he did. Only thing she let Jay do was see a lawyer about getting child support. That had just been set up when we started seeing each other again."

"But isn't Jay a Marine?"

Donning shook his head. "That's Roy. Jay's in the Army, but he's not an officer. Roy ain't been an officer for long. You could have knocked me over, Roy going in the Marines. The funny thing was, Nita acted proud of him, like there was no bad feelings. I wondered if Roy didn't do it for her. You know, to live out her dream." He chuckled softly. "On the other hand, I figured it would be more like living a nightmare, if Roy ever ran into Knightdale."

Fran hoped Colonel Knightdale appreciated Nita's loyalty—and silence. NROTC instructors were specially selected and trained at the United States Naval Academy. They taught naval science courses and supervised midshipmen during summer training sessions. It would be incredibly reckless for a married instructor to have sex with one of the midshipmen, many of whom were teenagers. It would be stupendously, incredibly stupid for a married instructor to knock one up. If Nita had chosen to make a stink, little Marissa Knightdale would be lucky to have a horsefly to play with, much less a horse. A general court-martial conviction for fraternization, conduct unbecoming an officer, and adultery meant dismissal from the Corps. Knightdale would have been forced to start from scratch, with zero retirement benefits and, at best, a general discharge. General discharge was code for "no-good shithead."

How old was Marissa when her dad was involved with Nita Highlock? Four? Five? Had Knightdale's wife known about the pregnancy? Did she know now?

"Hugh, you said Paul might know Colonel Knightdale is his father. Would Paul know how to contact him?"

"Can't say. He's a smart boy. In the gifted class at school. Maybe he figured it out. Then again, maybe Nita told him. She always swore to me Knightdale didn't mean anything to her except as Paul's father. But during the Gulf War, she got the newspaper from that town next to Camp Lejeune—Jacksonville, ain't it? Got it in the mail every day. Knightdale's name showed up once in a while. He was at Camp Lejeune then, same as now. Worked at a place called Moo something."

"The MEU. Marine Expeditionary Unit."

"Yeah. I told Nita, 'If you want to keep up with the war, watch CNN.' She said the Jacksonville paper was more personal. She liked to cut things out. Stories. Photos. She especially liked some woman columnist that wrote for the paper. As for me, I thought it would be good ole divine justice if Knightdale got killed over there. It's a shame how things worked out. He goes on with his hot-shit career, and she ends up dying young."

Some woman columnist. Ann Buckhalter was back in the picture. Fran made an educated guess about the chain of events. Nita told her son, Paul, about his real father, Colonel Bob Knightdale, and where he was, Camp Lejeune. After Nita died, the child found the columns his mother had kept, the ones with Ann Buckhalter's byline. If he called the paper, he would have been told she was living in Raleigh. It would be a simple matter for a smart kid to find her home phone number.

A more difficult question was why. Would a grief-stricken child look for revenge? Had his uncles told him a sure-fire way to get back at the man who wronged his mother? At nine, would he even understand what "wronged" meant in this case? Or was Paul just trying to find the man his mother had idealized, his father?

Fran stepped out from behind the monument. The service was over, the crowd dispersing. Colonel Knightdale was walking away briskly, head lowered. The casket trolley was empty. Nita Highlock Donning was in her grave.

Strange, Fran thought. Nita was the third person connected to the investigation who had died of cancer, counting General Johnson's wife and the Buckhalters' son. Considering the span of years the deaths encompassed, it probably wasn't much of a coincidence. Just another sad thread running through a sad story.

Paul, his uncles, and his grandmother were the last to leave. The boy sobbed uncontrollably against his Marine uncle's sleeve. It was a deeply disturbing thing to see. Hugh Donning's own eyes welled up.

After noisily blowing his nose, Donning offered Fran a ride to the commuter air terminal. She gratefully accepted but regretted her decision when the man started crying in earnest at the third stoplight on Main Street.

ooooo

Fran caught a red-eye to Washington after picking up the crated rifle in Memphis. The weapon traveled with its own fat folder of documentation.

In Washington, she was met by—surprise!—another female special agent, who took charge of the crate and the documentation. She let Fran off at the airport Hilton. Fran was so exhausted by the time she collapsed on her room's king-sized bed that she slept through her morning wake-up call and had to be roused according to her backup plan, a housekeeper sent to pound on her door.

She walked out of the Jacksonville terminal and headed to her car at 0834. That was one good thing about living in a small town. She could park her car within easy walking distance of the terminal. In fact, she could probably hawk a loogie on her car from the terminal if she had a mind to. Then again, hawking up loogies had about as much appeal as sharing what she'd learned about Knightdale. Fortunately, except for checking in with Boyette about the retrieved rifle, she had nothing to do the rest of the day but nurse her cold and think. The case was an ill wind that blew no good.

TWENTY-NINE.

THURSDAY

"No way am I going by myself to interview an old white woman with a chip on her shoulder," Rodney Walker told Fran when the two of them got in his car.

He was only half joking. He'd been slated to interview Charmaine Roundtree with Rumley, but as fate would have it, Rumley was among several agents suddenly laid low by the same respiratory bug that had struck Fran. Meanwhile, she had bounced back and was tapped to fill in. She didn't mind. She didn't plan to burden Boyette with the Knightdale bombshell until he could breathe through one or more nostril again.

As it turned out, Walker wouldn't have been alone with Charmaine Roundtree anyway. Her lawyer, a dandy little fellow from New Bern, was there, too. He looked like Jimmy Carter. No, the former president was too macho. The lawyer looked like Amy Carter. Fran assumed the

216

man was there to ensure Roundtree didn't say something that could jeopardize her lawsuit.

He was already aware of the alleged existence of an audiotape that might bolster his client's case. But Fran didn't think the lawyer knew the tape was real and had already turned up. He'd have to sort out that discovery stuff with SJA on his own. Fran also doubted the lawyer was aware that she and Walker wanted to talk to Roundtree mainly because of the tape's link to the late Ann Buckhalter. That link being her call to a newspaper reporter shortly before her death, in which she claimed to have the tape in her possession.

Mrs. Roundtree's demeanor was outwardly officious but evinced that little quiver of excitement solid citizens got when they did business with law enforcement. Her plain, shrewd face was topped by a mushroom of stiff gray hair. The chestnut eyebrow pencil she used had probably matched her hair fifteen years ago. Now, it looked like she had small, rusty horseshoes over her eyes. But she was smart. And would probably do better than Billy Graham on a polygraph.

Her repressed excitement escalated to repressed glee when Walker asked where she had been two Saturday evenings ago. She told him, enunciating each syllable, that she was volunteering at Onslow County's Interfaith Soup Kitchen, located in the part of downtown Jacksonville known as "the Combat Zone." She explained that once a month, volunteers rotated the duty of scrubbing the place down. That Saturday had been her turn. She would be glad to type up the names and addresses of people there with her. They could corroborate her "alibi," she gravely noted.

While Special Agent Walker jotted notes and feigned an interest in Roundtree's charitable efforts, Fran studied the pictures and awards on the woman's living-room wall. Apparently, she had been a world-class do-gooder for years. The previous commanding general had awarded her a silver tray for fifteen years' service to the Girl Scouts. She had plaques from the United Federal Campaign and the Red Cross. Ironically, her trophy wall also held a framed glossy showing Roundtree, General Johnson, Colonel Knightdale, Sergeant Major Crockett, and Captain Baptiste hovering over a sheet cake. Roundtree's new civilian boss was there, too. Everyone was beaming.

"Happier days," Roundtree sighed, noticing Fran's gaze. "That picture was taken on my birthday, the first week after General Johnson took command. He praised me to the skies in front of everybody. I had no idea all that praise was really a brush-off. Now, I feel uncomfortable even going into Headquarters Building."

The lawyer cleared his throat. Roundtree ignored him and came around the couch to join Fran.

"Oh, I understand the men sticking together. The traditional male franchise and all that. But the general's aide, Captain Baptiste, has had to compromise her principles so many times, I wonder how she lives with herself."

"She's a Marine officer, too, Mrs. Roundtree," Fran said gently. "I guess she sees working for General Johnson as a career opportunity, just like a male officer would."

The older woman snorted. "After what General Johnson did to her sister? Even Marines can have a little family loyalty, can't they?"

The lawyer jumped up like he'd been goosed by a couch spring. "Mrs. Roundtree and I have a number of things to discuss this afternoon. May I walk you two to your car?"

Roundtree took the lawyer's hint that the interview was over. She stepped back to allow Fran the shortest route to the door. Fran refused to take the hint.

"Sister? What are you referring to, Mrs. Roundtree?" Then to the lawyer, who suddenly sounded like he was coughing up a hairball: "What's the big secret, Counselor?"

"I'm not trying to be cagey," the lawyer said. "Mrs. Roundtree is bringing up a matter we talked about in private. Little more than gossip. Anyway, it's irrelevant to the matter at hand."

Fran sat. "If it's irrelevant, I assure you it will go no further."

The lawyer threw up his hands in annoyed resignation. "All right. Much of it is public record anyway. About five years ago, a former partner of mine was contacted by a Marine captain named Patsy Wilson. Until my partner filled me in weeks later, I had no idea the woman was a Marine. When I saw her, she was always wearing civilian clothes. No makeup. Neat. An ordinary-looking young woman. On one occasion, she was accompanied by another woman. This woman was younger, prettier, and also in civilian dress. I was told they were sisters. At the time, having just learned the details of the case, I wondered if the 'sister' label was just a figure of speech. It wasn't. They really were sisters. Granted, it's been awhile, but I'm 99 percent sure Patsy Wilson's sister and the woman in that photo—the general's aide, you said?—are one and the same. I've seen her a couple of times in the past year, at community functions where the general was a guest speaker. She either didn't see me or didn't remember me. We never spoke. Now, that's all I intend to say on the subject. If you want to know more, get the clips from the paper's morgue files. Better yet, why not ask the general's aide herself? If I'm mistaken about who she is, I'll give myself a good talking to." The lawyer smiled. "But I'm 99 percent sure Captain Baptiste is Patsy Wilson's sister."

Fran was 100 percent in the dark. None of it rang any bells with her. But all of a sudden, Walker seemed to want nothing more than to bolt out the door. What was wrong with him? Fran mimed his speedy adieus and trotted out behind him.

As soon as they were in Walker's car, he started chuckling and shaking his head in disbelief. "Patsy Wilson! How could I forget? Special Agent Setliff, we may have to set sail for the Isle of Lesbos!"

"Rodney, they closed that video place months ago. What the hell are you talking about?"

"Jesus, Fran, how did you miss hearing about that one? Patsy Wilson was the Marine captain accused of being part of a lesbian love commune that liked to party on some private island. Some thought she got the shaft just because the Marines wanted to make a point. Say, come to think of it, Rhonda Baptiste does look like Wilson. If you look at Rhonda through a butch filter."

"Start over. You lost me at the 'love commune' part."

Walker backed out of his parking space and tried again. Several years earlier, he explained to Fran, complaints had started dribbling in at headquarters about some of the female drill instructors at Parris Island. Those complaining were enlisted female Marines who had gone through recruit training there. They accused the drill instructors of openly promoting girls-only sexual liaisons. One woman claimed she and other recruits were photographed, without their knowledge, in the showers. When the recruits complained, the drill instructors told them to lighten up. It was only a joke, they were told. The pictures would be destroyed. The complainants later discovered, however, that the photos had made the rounds of the drill instructors' barracks.

Another woman claimed she had been caught in the gym sauna, where she was not authorized to be. As punishment, she was ordered to do fifty bent-knee sit-ups in the nude. The punishment was administered in the presence of three drill instructors, one of whom held her ankles.

The most serious charges accused drill instructors of coercing recruits into actual sexual activity. According to the complaints, those who willingly participated got special treatment, both on and off duty. Those who refused caught flack, both on and off duty.

And then one drill instructor came forward with a charge of her own. She told of a boat trip up Pamlico Sound. The boat, a big cabin cruiser, belonged to a wealthy Greenville woman who regularly hosted girls-only parties. The destination was her isolated beach house on the Outer Banks. The Greenville woman had been out of the closet for years.

The drill instructor claimed everyone on board was encouraged to strip and run their swimsuits up the flagpole as soon as the boat passed a certain buoy. Some did, she said, and didn't put any clothes back on until they passed the same buoy on the way back.

A few hours into the trip, she went into the cabin to lie down. The Dramamine she had taken to counteract motion sickness made her sleepy. When she woke up, the drill instructor who had invited her on the trip was performing oral sex on her. For the rest of the trip, she pretended to be sick and stayed by herself.

Fran avoided the predictable jokes about "cracks in the story" and the potential use of Dramamine as an aphrodisiac. "Where does Patsy Wilson come into it?" she asked. "Was she a drill instructor?"

"Keep your khakis on. No. But I'm getting to her."

A Colonel Amesly Johnson decided to go on a crusade, Walker continued. Two things had set him off. The first was a letter from a retired sergeant major whose teenage daughter wanted to enlist. The sergeant major, an old friend of Johnson's, had gotten wind of the rumors about the recruit depot. He wanted assurance that his little girl wasn't going to end up as some dyke's love slave. The second thing that set Johnson off was the name Patsy Wilson. In her statement, the drill instructor claimed her seducer had tried to calm her fears by telling her a Marine officer was on board. That officer was Captain Patsy Wilson.

The drill instructor told investigators she hadn't dreamed the woman who was introduced as Patsy Wilson was an officer. "She acted so normal," she said. She also told investigators she never saw Captain Wilson disrobe or do anything remotely sexual. More to the point, Captain Wilson had never been implicated in the Parris Island complaints. She had never even been stationed there. But Wilson was the only officer whose name popped up in the investigation.

Colonel Johnson was determined to make someone an example. The fact that Wilson was in his battalion when the report came to his attention didn't help her either. She was convenient.

"Johnson ordered Captain Wilson to appear before a Board of Investigation."

Those panels of two or more officers examined the conduct of other officers but had no punitive power. They were fact-finding bodies only. The Wilson board was convened to find out if the captain had participated in "conduct unbecoming an officer" by "consorting with known lesbians." Colonel Johnson did not foresee, however, that Patsy Wilson would retain a civilian lawyer who would call civilian attention to what was, to Johnson, a purely military matter. He was also naive not to have seen the possible political fallout. The Marine Corps was already perceived by some as being hostile to women and homosexuals.

"The ultimate disloyalty: airing dirty laundry," Fran said.

Walker nodded. "Under duress, the assistant commandant let civilian reporters sit in on the proceedings. By the time witnesses were actually heard, the original issue of recruits being intimidated was lost in the shuffle. Officers sitting on the board were defending themselves against charges that the military was acting out of homophobia and pure malice."

The owner of the cabin cruiser was asked to provide a statement. She responded, for the record, by saying "No thanks, and fuck you."

Captain Wilson, desperate, probably committed perjury when she denied being on the trip. But several of her bosses, past and present, testified she was an extremely good officer who never allowed her personal life—whatever it was—to intrude on her duties.

"The panel just wanted to get through the spectacle with their asses still attached to their backsides. The upshot was that Wilson was allowed to keep her commission but was subsequently passed over for major twice, which meant she had to leave the Marine Corps. It was like being on death row for three years, except she did get to leave with an honorable discharge."

"Jesus, Rod, that's quite a story. But just because General Johnson stuck it to Rhonda Baptiste's sister, does that mean Baptiste is out for his blood?"

"Think about it, Fran. Wouldn't working in Building One put Captain Baptiste in a good position to secretly record something that could sabotage Johnson's career? An eye for an eye, a career for a career?"

"You know, you might be on to something. Doesn't this whole thing boil down to people getting back at other people? We got Commander Terry wanting to get back at Gary Buckhalter, Jane Sherbourne wanting to get back at Commander Terry, Rhonda Baptiste wanting to get back at General Johnson. It's an endless tag-team grudge match."

"And think of this, Fran. What if Baptiste did plan to ruin Johnson? What if she told Ann Buckhalter about the tape, even gave it to her? What would happen if Baptiste changed her mind and decided it was too risky? The fallout could screw up her husband's career, too, you know. Would Ann Buckhalter say, 'Sure, let's just forget the whole thing?' I don't think so."

ooooo

Boyette had one working nostril when Fran hit him with the two barrels of ominous news.

Deciding how to proceed was easier in Baptiste's case. Boyette told Fran to talk to the general's aide, find out how Baptiste really felt about Johnson. Fran also had permission to ask Baptiste directly if she was the one who bugged the general's staff meeting.

Knightdale's situation, on the other hand, was enough of a minefield to leave the whole agency peg-legged. Boyette decided to think over his options. He didn't have much enthusiasm for digging brass-plated dirt.

Before confronting Captain Baptiste, Fran wanted to research the Wilson case. She reviewed the notes of her interview with editor George Griffin and reporter Lowell Mapp, looking for the name of the reporter Mapp had replaced. There it was. Aygarten. Vance Aygarten. She found Aygarten's Charlotte phone number through an Internet search. He was more than willing to discuss the Patsy Wilson case and volunteered that he had felt sorry for the captain.

"She was one sad little cookie, let me tell you. But I'll give the Marines this much. The officers Patsy Wilson worked for stood up for her. As for the board, she got a shitty deal from them. They should have told Johnson to cram his crusade up his bunghole before things ever got so far."

"But after all was said and done, she was never charged with anything," Fran pointed out.

"Yeah, but it was the kiss of death as far as her career was concerned, and God knows what it did to her family. The irony is that if this had happened just a few years later, Patsy Wilson would have been shielded by Don't Ask, Don't Tell. Say, is that what you're working on, some gay rights case?"

Fran demurred on answering his question, which Aygarten respected. In fact, Fran was confident Patsy Wilson's sexual orientation was irrelevant to the Buckhalter investigation. The important issue was whether or not Captain Rhonda Baptiste bore General Johnson ill will because of his treatment of her sister. And whether or not that ill will had anything to do with Ann Buckhalter's death.

THIRTY.

The general's secretary told Fran that Captain Baptiste was at lunch. Fran could hear Major St. Legere bellowing at her in the background.

"Special Agent Setliff, Major St. Legere says if you need to see the captain right away, she's at the French Creek gym," the secretary conveyed, unnecessarily.

Good. Fran and she could talk more discreetly at the French Creek gym. Unlike the main base gym, it didn't echo like the day shift at an anvil factory. It would be less crowded, too.

In fact, when Fran got there, the gym was empty except for Baptiste, a young Marine in headphones on an exercise bike, the woman working the desk, and the affable giant who ran the place. Sergeant Pilser was bulking up for an All-Marine power-lifting competition, probably with the help of the steroids that circulated illegally among gyms off and on the base.

Fran signed in. She had swapped her street shoes for running shoes, in concession to the gym floor.

Rhonda Baptiste was stretched out on a weight bench, pressing 135 pounds of iron. Fran was impressed. Baptiste would be capable of doing damage if she put her mind to it. When she sat up, her face softened into distinctly feminine planes. She was wearing high-cut nylon work-out shorts and a snug tank top over a jogging bra.

Fran, who could bench-press ninety pounds when incited by PMS rage, was more comfortable wearing sweatpants when lying spread-eagled on a weight bench. Maybe she was just a prig, like Marlon said. God knew, some men worked out in gear so skimpy their circumcisions could be graded from fifty paces.

Baptiste smiled uneasily when she saw Fran. Since Fran wasn't wearing workout clothes, it was clear she was there on business.

"Something up? Nothing wrong at the day-care center, is there?"

"Oh, no. But I do need to talk to you, Rhonda. I'm afraid it's not a subject—"

"Hold that thought until I do another set, okay? If you don't time it right, you lose the training effect." Rhonda lay back on the bench.

"Phone call!" the woman at the desk shouted, holding up a tele-phone receiver. She nodded in Fran's direction, then turned away to sign for a stack of towels. Fran walked to the desk, wondering who, except maybe Major St. Legere, knew where she was.

"Hello?"

"It's Steve. Listen, I forgot to tell you. You need to keep an eye on your oil gauge. I noticed . . . Is this Rhonda?"

"Oh, gosh, I'm sorry," Fran said. "Rhonda was right next to me. I thought the call . . . Hold on. I'll get her." Steve. Rhonda's husband, of course.

Fran told Rhonda the call was for her. Rhonda stripped off her workout gloves and walked to the desk. Heart pounding, Fran sat on the warm bench. She thought hard and fast.

Growing up, Fran had listened at closed doors while her broth-ers plotted their adventures. Sometimes, she overheard life-changing revelations. Santa and the Tooth Fairy lost their magic because of her eavesdropping. She had also learned where Rusty hid his Matchbox car collection and a few thousand euphemisms for jerking off. Being able to discern one voice from another had been a survival skill.

She was 85 percent sure she recognized Steve Baptiste's voice. It was the same voice that had told her to keep an eye on her mailbox. And of course, it was in her mailbox that she had discovered the audiotape of General Johnson's staff meeting. The tape that could send the general out the door with one fewer star than he'd hoped for. Knowing Fran would recognize her voice, the captain had asked her husband to leave the phone message.

Rhonda returned to the bench after finishing her call and getting two ten-pound dumbbells from the rack. She began doing curls. Her wrists and biceps were as powerful as her pecs.

"So, what is it you want to ask me about?" Baptiste said, grimacing at her flexed arm.

"Your sister, Captain Patsy Wilson."

The smile disappeared, but the expression that replaced it was more resigned than angry. Rhonda set the dumbbells down on the mat and stared at the floor for a moment.

"I've had enough. This workout's been shot to hell anyway. Let's go talk in the locker room."

Baptiste racked her dumbbells and walked ahead of Fran into the women's dressing area, where she sat and took off her shoes.

"I guess it was inevitable that you or somebody would dredge up that business sooner or later. I've never lied about my relationship to Patsy, but it's not an episode I like to reminisce about over cocktails either." She slipped on the wedding rings that had been knotted on her shoelaces for safekeeping.

"General Johnson doesn't know she's your sister, does he?" Fran asked.

"No." She laughed bitterly. "I bet he hasn't given Patsy a thought in years. Why should he? She wasn't any more important to him than what's in the trash can." Rhonda stood and tinkered with the combination to a locker. She removed a small canvas bag. "Give me five minutes, will you?" She stripped off her clothes and draped two towels around her neck before disappearing into the shower area.

While she waited, Fran watched the thin clouds of steam rising above the shower stall and sniffed the sweetness of herbal shampoo. She imagined a muscular, naked woman avoiding further conversation by escaping through the shower room's frosted-glass window.

Naw. Rhonda would never get to her car unnoticed. The Enlisted Club parking lot was on the other side of that window. A naked female would draw droves of happy onlookers.

Rhonda came out of the shower and spread her towel on a metal bench. She sat to cool off before putting her uniform back on, utterly unselfconscious as she applied deodorant and combed styling gel through her hair. Her body was sleek and well-proportioned except for the nipples, which Fran thought were too large. The effect was like putting Peterbilt wheel covers on a Honda Civic. *This is the first time I've interviewed a naked person,* Fran thought. *I'll have to give Rumley a beta blocker before telling him about this one.*

"Rhonda, did you request your assignment as General Johnson's aide?"

"That's a negative. I was transferred to base just before he took over. After the general picked Colonel Knightdale as his chief of staff, Knightdale recommended me. The colonel was my mentor, I guess you could say, while I was at Service Support School." Rhonda pulled on a pair of panties and covered the oversized nipples with a baby-blue bra. "General Johnson was in need of a token female. I fit the bill. I was reasonably competent. I was married. I was presentable looking, but not too sexy." She stepped into a half-slip and sat back down to unroll a pair of neutral thigh-high stockings. "I was someone who could be relied on to go home from any function before the drinking got too heavy or the jokes got too raunchy. Someone who had never rocked a boat—that anybody knew about—or expected any favors. So, you see, Fran, I was fucking perfect."

"You taped the general's staff meeting, didn't you?"

Rhonda smoothed her khaki blouse and snapped on her tie. She ignored Fran's question. "My sister is one of the nicest, most unselfish people alive. She's almost eight years older than I am. There's another sister, Emily, between us. Unlike a lot of older sisters, Patsy would take Emily and me to football games and movies. Sure, she loved us. But I realize that one reason she took us places was because she was shy and didn't have many friends. In college, she started coming out of her shell a little. Discovered she was a good lacrosse player. Her team played a series in Washington, and she got to see an Evening Parade at the Marine Barracks. Patsy was hooked. She bought a poster of the Silent Drill Platoon that's still hanging in her old room."

She drew a deep breath. "The whole family went to her graduation from Officer Candidate School. I'd never seen her so happy. 'Our Patsy has found herself,' Mom said." Rhonda zipped her A-line olive-drab skirt. "Four years later, when she was promoted to captain, I helped with her wet-down party. I was old enough by then to notice that some of her female friends were pretty butch. But I didn't expect female Marines to act like a bunch of sorority sweethearts. Why should they? Anyway, she had male friends, too. And married female friends. No boyfriend, but at the time, I didn't have one either."

Rhonda leaned against a locker while she put on her black pumps. "When I told Patsy I was thinking about joining up, she encouraged me. Said we should get Emily in the Marine Corps, too, make it the family business. The first year after I got my commission, they started questioning Patsy about that stink at Parris Island. I understood why they had to investigate. I would never try to rationalize the abuse of recruits. But Patsy had nothing to do with it, and they knew it. My sister was the victim of a witch hunt, pure and simple."

Fran watched the captain's face flush. Baptiste was getting wound up, losing her usual layer of restraint.

"Oh, yeah. By that time, I had accepted that Patsy was gay. We never talked about it, but I wasn't blind. And I knew that simply by being gay, she was violating the Uniform Code. But it was the hypocrisy that infuriated me. I've seen female lieutenants who thought they could build a career by sleeping with every male officer, married or single, who outranked them. And I've seen plenty of male officers willing to encourage that kind of career plan. But you know, I never saw a single officer brought before a Board of Investigation because of it."

Rhonda paced the row of lockers, jabbing each metal door. When she caught Fran's eye, she stopped and lowered her voice.

"General Johnson wanted credit for cleaning out what he saw as a bunch of oversexed predators. Patsy's reputation, her contribution to the Marine Corps, my family's feelings—all that meant nothing. My naive little mother, a Baptist Sunday-school teacher, was so upset she wanted to move away from the town she'd lived in for forty years."

"From what I've heard," Fran noted, "General Johnson didn't get a popularity boost from the investigation either."

Rhonda snorted. "Johnson was uncomfortable for maybe five minutes. But he's been promoted since and, I hear, is likely to be promoted again. Patsy is managing traffic for UPS." She chuckled coldly. "At least she's still in uniform."

Fran felt Baptiste's pain. A person under anesthesia could have felt her pain. So, how had she managed to keep all that pain hidden from General Johnson and Colonel Knightdale?

"Well, you got me. Yes, when I took the job, it occurred to me I might have the chance to trip Johnson up. But I wasn't looking for that chance. In a lot of ways, I even learned to respect him. Then I heard he was reorganizing his command staff, and sure enough, the only woman involved was going to get the shitty end of the stick. *Here he goes again*, I thought. I already knew where he was vulnerable. He says things in meetings he wouldn't dare say in public. I knew if somebody taped his conversations, it wouldn't take long for him to say something so politically explosive he'd have to retire. That would hurt. Johnson wants another star like China wants Taiwan."

"But what if you got caught?"

"Agent Setliff, I never said I taped anything."

"Rhonda, I recognized your husband's voice just now. It was his voice on an anonymous phone message I got."

"You must be mistaken."

"Not a chance." Fran thought a moment. "Okay, we'll play it your way. Let's suppose someone taped one of General Johnson's meetings to embarrass him. Why might that person give the tape to Ann Buckhalter?"

"I would assume that person didn't trust the chain of command not to cover up for the general. Maybe that person heard Ann could get the story out and still protect her sources."

"But what would happen if that person changed her mind and wanted the tape back? Maybe that person decided the tape could open old wounds for her own family. What if Ann refused to give the tape back? What if that person had a confrontation with Ann and got mad enough to shove her in the river?"

Rhonda laughed. "I'm sorry, but that's just too ridiculous. And your theory would really fall apart if the person who made the tape, along with her husband and child, was with her in-laws in northern Virginia the night Ann died. Jesus, Fran, I've got to go. Really. The general is expecting me back. Isn't he? I mean, you haven't told him I'm out to sabotage his career, have you?"

Fran shook her head. "I talk to general officers only when my boss makes me. Wait, Rhonda. Assume that some avenging angel gave a tape to Ann Buckhalter. But Ann died before she could do anything with it. What would happen then?"

"Then—if I was the person who made the tape—I'd make sure somebody else got a copy. Somebody who understood how hard it is for a woman to cut it in a man's world. Fran, remember the morning we talked at the Child Care Center? I got the idea you were an understanding person. Was I right?"

"Sure, Rhonda. I do understand it's not easy breaking through closed minds." Fran tried to sound sympathetic but not conspiratorial. "Oh, one more thing. The person who risked so much to make that tape would not have given Ann Buckhalter the original. Where might that original be, I wonder?"

"I'd suggest a safe-deposit box."

"That would mean there were three tapes altogether, right? One for Ann, one for me, plus the original."

"You're understanding *and* good at math."

Rhonda picked up her bag and pushed though the locker-room door. Fran followed. Sergeant Pilser stopped them at the desk and reminded them to sign out, which they did, not meeting each other's eyes once.

Parked next to Rhonda, Fran watched the captain start her car and back out. The child safety seat in the back cradled a Cookie Monster plush toy dotted with Cheerios. The floor was littered with Dr. Seuss books. *Captain Baptiste, they should give you a medal,* Fran thought. *Right before they court-martial you.*

ooooo

Fran edited her notes with one hand while steering with the other. At least she didn't do crossword puzzles behind the wheel like Rumley. So, what did she have for Boyette? Captain Baptiste had practically confessed to secretly taping the general. It would be hard to prove, however—Fran was no voice-identification expert—and it would mean reopening a can of worms the general himself wanted to remain closed.

She *had* clarified one point. There were three copies of that tape: the original, which was probably in the Baptistes' safe-deposit box; the one left in Fran's mailbox; and the one Rhonda had given Ann Buckhalter. That last tape: Where was it now?

THIRTY-ONE.

Fran was watching a vintage episode of the original *Superman* TV series, grimly noting the physical similarity between actor George Reeves and Vic Maldonado. That airhead Lois Lane wasn't worthy of either of them. She was flaky and wore head-pincher hats. And despite the tight suits, the woman was pretty much sexless. She and Jimmy Olsen were the two who belonged together.

"Gee, Chief," Olsen was saying to his boss, Perry White, "it would take Superman to get Lois to come back."

One fewer word and you'd have it right, Fran thought.

At Boyette's relayed insistence, Fran had bugged out early, fully intending to catch up on her sleep. But Vic called just as Superman's cape was waving beneath the credits. He asked about her sore throat, which she had forgotten until he mentioned it. And he asked for further details surrounding her mishap at Marston Pavilion, which she wished he had forgotten. She tried to spin the incident, hoping to give the impression she'd been up to something amusingly zany, à la Zelda Fitzgerald, instead of something stupid, à la Jethro Clampett. Lunatic or imbecile. Southerners had such great role models.

He asked her if she was up to meeting him at a comedy club in Swansboro. A mutual acquaintance, Private First Class Tony Quiera, was making his stand-up debut. A self-described Boston "brown blood," Quiera was naturally funny. To know him was to guffaw. Fran said she'd be there.

ooooo

The Chamber of Chuckles Comedy Club was a converted Mexican restaurant. The fake adobe walls in the main area had soaked up so much red pepper and grease, they made Fran's sinuses tingle. Quiera had a small but loyal following among his brother Marines. However, it was an off-payday Wednesday. Fran and Maldonado swelled the audience to a total of fifteen.

Fran thought Quiera was great. The act was mostly a self-deprecating PG-13, but the Marines in the audience hooted at anything that could pass for a dirty double entendre. Of course, Marines could put a bawdy spin on the contents of the Baptist hymnal.

Vic and Fran joined the throng that pounded Quiera on the back after the show, which included six other amateur comics, none of them as good as the Marine.

The captain and the special agent lingered in the parking lot afterward, mostly because Maldonado planted himself against Fran's driver's-side door. He folded his arms and looked everywhere but at her. A freight train shuddered by parallel to the highway, its whistle mixing with the music blaring from passing automobiles. When the red light on the last boxcar had shrunk to a pinpoint, he unfolded his arms and fished a piece of white paper from his jacket pocket. He looked at it, Fran thought, with an expression of distaste. But maybe that was just the bilious parking-lot lighting.

Wait. Had somebody sent Vic a nastygram about her? Like the time in third grade when Debbie Ledbetter passed a note to Trent Winkle saying Fran had head cooties? Well, she did have cooties. She caught them from Debbie Ledbetter. Trent Winkle had called Fran "Franken-cootie" until the day he dropped out of tenth grade.

"I want your opinion about something, Setliff," Maldonado said.

She doubted he remembered ever calling her sweetheart.

He handed the creased sheet to her. She looked at it. At the top was a swirly, indecipherable monogram. Typed beneath was, apparently, the wording for an engagement announcement. The engagement was that of Captain Victor Paul Maldonado and Miss Monica Juliet Burnside.

Terrific. Why the hell did Vic want Fran's opinion of his engagement announcement? Not only was Fran pissed at herself for letting an unfeeling Yankee lawyer bastard turn her emotions into tree sap, she was going to look like an ignorant hick. Again. All she knew about wedding etiquette was that the bride and groom weren't supposed to track mud into the sanctuary.

But she couldn't help herself. She was too curious not to read it.

Dr. and Mrs. Frederick Comer Burnside III, of Mamaroneck, are pleased to announce the engagement of their daughter, Monica Juliet, to Capt. Victor Paul Maldonado, son of Mr. and Mrs. John Maldonado of New York City. Miss Burnside is a graduate of Barnard College. She is director of marketing for Livingston-Hurley Enterprises. Capt. Maldonado is a graduate of New York University and the Columbia University School of Law. He is stationed at Marine Corps Base, Camp Lejeune, in North Carolina. A summer wedding is planned.

Fran flushed with irritation and dismay. The only glimmer of light was that the couple had not set a date.

"So, what am I supposed to be looking for, Vic?"

He crossed his arms and leaned against her, reading aloud, "Mr. and Mrs. John Maldonado."

"I'm still not following you." She drew up her shoulder so she was no longer in physical contact with him.

"My father's name is Juan." He said it with a nice, breathy whoosh.

She reread the paragraph and sighed. "Oh. Well, jeez, Vic, maybe it's just a mistake."

He shook his head. "Nope. Monica sent this to me, ostensibly to get my approval before it runs in the paper. I know better. She's testing me. When I reminded her, in a subsequent phone call, that my father's name is Juan"—he whooshed a small tropical breeze—"she said she only wanted to 'simplify' things. I asked her why she didn't go on and simplify the Maldonado to Du Pont."

Fran smiled despite herself. "Hey, give her a break. If your father's name was Levinson, she'd probably have renamed you Luther Calvin Wesley by now."

He looked at her sourly. "Yeah, Monica acted like it wasn't a big deal, too." He took the paper from Fran and returned it to his pocket. But he didn't walk away. He resumed his position barricading her car door.

"I don't know what you want from me here," Fran said with growing exasperation. "Do you want me to tell you to drop the superficial bitch while you've got the chance? Or do you want me to pretend it's not worth making a fuss over and maybe losing your once-in-a-lifetime shot at marrying a snotty princess?"

He ignored her questions. "I've got to give Monica points for frankness. It's not like she went ahead and ran this without asking me, then lied about it after the fact. Hell, if she'd told me it was some copyeditor's mistake, I'd have believed her. Maybe. But I keep thinking this is a pre-view of things to come. I mean, dammit, if she's uncomfortable with the name Juan, how's she going to feel about the mariachi band at the reception?" He glanced at Fran. "That was a joke."

Suddenly, Fran was genuinely angry. She hadn't spent ten minutes ironing a silk shirt so she could help him plumb the depths of his rela-tionship with Monica. She hip-bumped him away from the door hard enough to make him reach for the hood to steady himself.

"Leave me out of this, will you? Decide for yourself whether Moni-ca has enough pluses to make up for disrespecting your family."

He reached for her arm, but she snapped it away.

"You want me to be real? I'll be real. I'm past this kind of shit, Vic. You've sent me so many mixed signals, I feel like that shrink trying to deal with all three faces of Eve. Well, enough. Take your premarital angst to the chaplain and your etiquette questions to the protocol of-ficer. I'm out."

She drove away in a fuming, teary snit. But by the time she got home, the snit was morphing into something else entirely. Fran realized something. He hadn't shown her that piece of paper to get a second opinion of Monica's character. He'd shown it to her because he wanted her to know he was having serious reservations about the wedding. He was still hanging in there, but who knew? Maybe Monica was on her last blue-blooded leg.

THIRTY-TWO.

THURSDAY 2300

Fran sensed somebody was in her house as soon as she lifted a foot over the threshold. The cat didn't rush her legs like he usually did, and she was pretty sure she'd left a light on. Anyway, her living room was too small to hold another human being without giving off some evidence of that person's presence. Maybe the ambient air changed when somebody else was exhaling into it. But she knew.

She kept one foot outside the door while she reached for the light switch.

A man stood immediately from where he had been sitting on the couch in the dark. "I ain't gonna hurt you," he said, holding up both hands.

If there were ever words guaranteed to strike terror in a woman, they were "I ain't gonna hurt you." They immediately put the idea of hurt on the table.

239

He was dressed in utilities with the single stripe of a private first class. The tunic was too bulky for Fran to determine if he was carrying a pistol. He was a big, rangy guy. The wide shoulders came more from oversized bones than muscle. The face was good looking in a rough-hewn way, wide-set eyes counterbalancing a big jaw. His hair was dark and choppy with several overlapping cowlicks. He dropped his hands and started rubbing small, quick circles over the seams of his trousers. He looked nervous, which was as contagious as measles.

"Where's my cat?" Fran blurted out.

"I don't know. Uh, he run off somewheres. I didn't hurt him."

There he goes again, she thought. She could just back out the door and run for it. But having no idea how fast he could move, she decided to hold her ground until she had no other choice.

"How'd you get in here?"

He nodded toward the sliding glass door that led to the balcony. "I come up on a rope. The door wasn't locked or nothing."

Fran mentally kicked herself black and blue. She'd forgotten to put the broomstick in the door track.

"I didn't break nothing. I just had to talk to you." So far, his tone was wheedling, not pugnacious.

"Why didn't you just knock on the front door?" *Like normal people*, she thought, but decided against being needlessly combative.

"I didn't think you'd let me in, ma'am, once you knowed who I was. And you'd be sure to ask who I was if I come to the door, wouldn't you? But if I was already here, I figured you'd have to listen to me."

The "have to" bounced in the air like a hangman's noose. He lowered his head. He was wearing cheap athletic shoes instead of boots. He didn't have a hat. *This burglar is way out of uniform*, Fran thought. Only he didn't really qualify as a burglar, since he hadn't taken anything. And if he was telling the truth, he hadn't actually broken in either.

"Well, who are you?"

He restlessly shifted his weight from one long leg to the other. "I'm Private First Class Jervet Harriman, ma'am." He was looking straight at her now, his chest and chin thrust out in defiance.

Jervet Harriman. The Marine who Deirdre Buckhalter said had sexually assaulted her in a stall at the base stables. The Marine who was supposed to be confined to barracks.

"Um, have we met? Why would you want to see me?" Fran tried to look puzzled and ignorant. The puzzled part was easy.

"Ma'am, I know you know about me." He sounded reproachful. "I got this buddy works at the base stables. He overheard one of the girls talking about a lady from the Navy Investigating Service coming to see Deirdre." He pronounced the name "Dur-druh." "My buddy done told me about it when he come to visit me in my barracks. I figured you was talking to Deirdre because of, you know, what happened between me and her. That's why they sent you and not a man investigator."

Some of this was beginning to make sense. Harriman knew Fran had been in contact with Deirdre. He thought it was because of the alleged assault, not Ann Buckhalter's death. Fran wondered if the private even knew Deirdre's mother was dead.

"How did you know where I live?"

"My buddy followed you home from your office one evening. He come back here one more time at night, just to recon the area. He did it so I could get here, talk to you, and get back quick, without the duty sergeant knowing I was gone."

A bolt of mental lightning struck Fran. "Does your buddy smoke?"

"Yes, ma'am. He didn't burn nothing, did he?"

"No. Is he a fan of Foghorn Leghorn?"

The private grinned in surprise. "He sure is. Can talk like him, too. Now, how did you know that?"

"I nearly caught him in my carport. I thought he was a Peeping Tom."

Harriman bristled. "He'd never do nothing like that. He don't even keep dirty pictures in his room."

Fran was beginning to understand why this man, perhaps still a teenager, had not thought fifteen-year-old Deirdre Buckhalter was too young to fool around with. Their levels of sophistication were comparable. But it didn't take sophistication to commit rape.

"Did this same buddy drive you over here tonight?" That would explain why no unfamiliar car was parked outside.

"He was fixing to, but his transmission give out and he had to put his car in the shop. I thumbed it."

He took a step toward her, and she parried with a step backward. He noted her reaction with a frown and started rubbing his trouser seams again.

"I know you don't want me here. I'll talk fast and let you alone. I got to know about Deirdre."

"Know what?"

"How is she? Is she still mad at me? Is there any way I can talk to her?"

Fran was pop-eyed, drop-jawed amazed. He must have noticed.

"I know things are messed up right now, but I want to make it right. She don't mean those things she's saying about me. She's just scared. I'm all tore up about this, Miss Setliff. It's making me crazy, not being able to talk to her."

He was getting agitated. Fran tried to calm him.

"You've got the wrong idea, Private. I've spoken to Deirdre only a couple of times. I swear to God, she never mentioned you to me."

Now, he looked amazed. Then disappointed. Then skeptical.

"I expect she's been more concerned about what happened to her mother. Do you know her mother died?"

He sat heavily on the couch and ran his fingers through the choppy hair. "No! I . . . I . . . Poor little girl. That poor little girl." He snapped his head up. "I want to marry Deirdre, Miss Setliff. I done told the company captain that."

Fran repressed the urge to laugh. If she knew one thing for sure, it was that just-turned-sixteen Deirdre Buckhalter did not want to get married.

"I don't think marriage is on her mind right now, PFC Harriman. She's upset about losing her mother. She just wants to stay close to her family for a while."

He seemed to accept that.

"And frankly, Harriman, aren't you in kind of a tight spot yourself right now?"

"It's all going to get worked out, Miss Setliff. Deirdre will tell them what really happened. I know I had no business being with her that night. But God, she is so beautiful. I never saw nothing like her. And she ain't happy at home. I know that for a fact. I thought if we, uh, did it, me being her first, Deirdre would feel kind of like she belonged to me. She might even marry me."

Well, in a squirrely way, that explained the condom he'd been wearing. He had planned to have sex with Deirdre. Had he raped her as a kind of marriage proposal?

"She just turned sixteen, Harriman. Even supposing she wanted to, she couldn't get married in this state without a parent's consent."

"Jesus. I didn't know it was her birthday. I didn't get her a card or nothing. Well, maybe her parents wouldn't have liked the idea. I bet if Deirdre had got pregnant, they'd be glad enough to see me, all right. Sign those papers in a heartbeat." He frowned. "I guess she's got just one parent now." The PFC pressed on. "Don't you see? I got to fix things. The way she was that night, acting like she was scared to death of me, I can't leave it like that. I can't stand to think that for the rest of her life, every time she thinks of me, it'll make her scared. You can explain it to her, what I've told you. How I feel. Women are good at explaining feelings."

Fran decided to talk to Harriman like her Aunt Nanellen talked to people. Aunt Nanellen had a low, cooing voice and got along with everybody. She had never in her whole life offended a living soul. When she ended up in a state mental institution, she got along with everybody there, too.

"Time is what Deirdre needs to get over her fears. If you want her to be happy, you're just going to have to leave her be for a while. Anyway, you should be thinking about yourself right now. What's going to happen when they find out you're missing? Aren't you confined to barracks?"

Fran immediately regretted what she'd said. Planting a seed of anxiety might not be a wise move. His brow drew up into fleshy ripples, and he shifted restlessly on the couch.

"I'm supposed to be, but they let me do things I got to do, like go to work and get a haircut. Seemed to me, this was more important than a haircut, so I done it. My roommate is out in the field, training. Nobody's gonna know I left if I get back by 0600. Unless you report me." He plowed his fingers through his hair again. "I just want her to know I'll be there for her, if she needs me."

There where? Fran thought. *Leavenworth?*

"Which barracks are you in, Harriman?"

"HP 236. Room 211."

"You want me to understand," she said. "Now, I want you to understand. Whatever happened that night between you two, it upset Deirdre plenty. And now she's got something else to be upset about. Her mother just died." Was it strange, Fran asked herself, that Harriman hadn't asked how Deirdre's mother died? "Have you talked to a lawyer?"

"Yes, ma'am. They sent over Captain Newbold. He's okay, I guess, but he seems to want me to admit to doing something I ain't going to admit to doing."

"You haven't been charged with anything yet, have you?"

"No, ma'am. But Captain Newbold said if I don't admit to carnal knowledge, they might charge me with rape. He said I could go to prison for twenty years. I didn't rape nobody. Ask D—"

Fran's phone rang. She looked at Harriman. What would he do if she picked it up?

After the third ring, he looked at her, puzzled. "Ain't you gonna answer that?"

It was Vic Maldonado. He wanted to know if she was willing to accept an apology. He said he could tell by the tone of her voice that she was still torqued off at him.

"No, Vic. It's not that." She looked at Harriman. He was watching her, rubbing his hands together. Now or never. "There's somebody with me, Vic." She said it as Aunt Nanellen would have.

"God, Fran, who is it? Are you okay?"

"Private First Class Jervet Harriman came to see me. Yes, I'm fine."

When he heard his name, Harriman flopped backward on the couch and stared at the ceiling. "Well, the jig's up now for sure," he grumbled.

"I'll call the MPs," Maldonado said. "Hang up."

"No! Wait, Vic." She tried to think. "I don't want to get the MPs into this tonight. It's not necessary. Really. How about calling the duty sergeant at Harriman's barracks, HP 236, and telling them he's on his way back. And first, you might have to tell them he's gone. I think it'll work out better for him if he comes back voluntarily." She sensed Maldonado's reluctance. "Vic, if a male officer asked you to do this, you would."

Maldonado sighed. "Jesus, Fran, I hope you know what you're doing."

She hung up and faced Harriman. He stood, biting his lower lip. For the first time, he looked scared.

"Ma'am, they'll put me in the brig."

"I expect so. But the fact that you were gone only a couple of hours and intended to go back might take some of the stink off." She looked him up and down. "I'm going to do you a big favor, Marine. Are you armed? Gun, knife, lead pipe, candlestick?"

"No, ma'am." He patted himself resoundingly all over his shirt and trousers, front and back, to show this was true.

"Okay. When they ask what happened tonight, and they will, I want you to tell the absolute, 100 percent truth except for one thing."

"Yes, ma'am?"

"I want you to say I let you in. Understand? You didn't come in over the balcony when I wasn't home. I let you in." Which was not entirely a lie. If she hadn't forgotten to jam the sliding door with the broomstick, he wouldn't have gotten in. Ergo, she indirectly let him in.

He gnawed his lip again and swallowed hard enough to be heard. He placed his hand over his crotch, fig-leaf style. For a fraction of a second, Fran thought she might have made a fatal error in judgment about Private Harriman.

"Can I use your bathroom before we go?" he said, dropping the hand.

"Sure," she answered, beaming with relief. The gesture had been unconscious.

Once he closed the door, she started worrying again. Was there anything in the bathroom he could hurt himself with? Could he cut himself badly enough with a Gillette Trac II cartridge to do real damage? She didn't think so. Any dangerous pills? Nope. Only a tube of hairball medicine and a nearly empty bottle of Tylenol. She listened. Nothing but piddling, zipping, flushing, and a dry cough.

ooooo

During the drive to the base, Harriman was quiet. Fran couldn't think of much to say either. She turned into the barracks parking lot, where three Marines built like phone booths were waiting for them. She spoke sharply to her passenger.

"If you care anything at all about your mama, your daddy, or yourself, stay away from Deirdre Buckhalter. Don't call her. Don't email her. Don't send a buddy to give her a message. Don't ask anybody about her. Don't talk about her. Don't daydream about her. You hear me?"

"Yes, ma'am," he said softly. Harriman had spotted the three hulks. He made a series of throat-clearing noises. She thought she saw his hair starting to stand on end.

Fran put her car in neutral. She identified herself to the two corporals and one sergeant waiting for Harriman in a pool of yellow floodlight. "He's come back voluntarily, and he's got a lawyer," she said brusquely. "Keep that in mind, guys."

"Why, thank you, ma'am, we certainly will," the sergeant said, smiling like Aunt Nanellen's evil twin. "We do appreciate your giving him a lift. Now, if you'll excuse us, we need to get PFC Harriman to his room. Oh, and I promised a Captain Maldonado I'd let him know when you got here."

They opened the passenger-side door and waited for Harriman to get out. He threw Fran one last miserable look. She watched the trio accompany him, one on each side and one behind, to the stairwell. One of his escorts gave Harriman a jab to the kidney, and Harriman stumbled, but it was a pulled punch. Harriman didn't even grunt from the impact. Still, she'd make sure Captain Newbold checked on his client in the morning.

When she got home, her cat seemed to have put the whole home-invasion thing behind him. A message from Vic was waiting on her answering machine.

"I'm not going to call you again tonight. The sergeant said you dropped off your little hot potato and were on your way home. I'm hoping you'll stay put the rest of the night. Frankly, if you get yourself into another cliff-hanger situation before morning, I'd rather not know about it. Dammit, Fran, how am I going to get my trousseau together if I have to keep worrying about you?" A pause and some extraneous background noise. "I don't like mixed messages either, baby."

He did sound worried. Maybe even a little drunk. Good.

After futilely searching her bathroom cabinet, she opened her kitchen junk drawer, hoping to find a backup stash of dental floss. She spotted the cigarette lighter with the Foghorn Leghorn sticker and wished she had given it to Harriman to return to his buddy. For some reason, the damn thing made her sad.

THIRTY-THREE.

FRIDAY

During her drive to work, Fran dictated what she remembered of her encounter with Harriman into her tape recorder. Did she believe him, that there had been no rape? Maybe. The difference between intense making out and penetration could be a close call. When Fran was thirteen, Grandmama Pattle had told her girls could get pregnant from kissing. Two years later, she had rationalized her lie by telling Fran, "Well, too much kissing is like shaking a can of sody pop. You got no idea what's building up inside until it's too late to keep things under control no more. And then the girl gets pregnant."

Fran was surprised when Rumley met her at the entrance to the field office, steered her into Boyette's office, and closed the door. Boyette had developed viral pneumonia, he told her. Their boss had been advised to stay home for a few days to prevent his being exposed to something that might really complicate things.

"We're already short-handed," Rumley reminded her, "and I've got to look into a domestic at Watkins Village from last night that turned up pawn tickets for stuff the couple had claimed was stolen during a burglary. What Boyette wants is to wrap up the Buckhalter business before the rumor mill takes over the case."

"What does he want me to do?" Boyette and Rumley must have already discussed the priorities for the next couple of days.

Rumley paused a nanosecond, just long enough to make her uneasy.

"He wants you to talk to Knightdale. Informally. Boyette planned to do it himself, but now he can't. And after all, you're more familiar with the people involved in this than anybody. Knightdale knows we know about him and the boy. All you have to do is make sure there's enough distance between Knightdale and Ann Buckhalter's death that NCIS can exclude him from the case summary and we can close it."

Fran willed her face not to reveal how much she dreaded the assignment. "Okay, Rum. When and where?"

"Now. He's at the general's quarters, keeping an eye on things until Johnson gets back on Saturday. He's expecting you to meet him there. Neutral territory, he said. More privacy, too, probably."

∞∞∞

From the get-go, it was as unpleasant as Fran expected.

"Wally's out back," Knightdale said, meeting her at the front door of the general's quarters. "I didn't expect him to be here, but it's okay. Neighbors on both sides at work or away. We can talk without worrying about being overheard." He smiled his usual sad smile but avoided meeting her eyes, stooping to pat the whiplashing rear end of a black Lab. "This is Bilbo."

They walked through the house toward ceiling-to-floor French windows that led on to the back patio, an extensive lawn, and the drop-off to the river.

"My wife decided this morning to spend the holidays with my in-laws. She got an early start, took Marissa with her," he said tonelessly. "Not much point in my trying to dissuade her. It would just have made things harder for Marissa."

He stepped out on the brick patio and held the door open for Fran to follow. They could see Wally Johnson burning trash or yard debris in an oil drum. Thanks to the stiff breeze coming off the river, Fran could easily smell the acrid mix of charcoal starter fuel and burning vegetation, plus undertones of melting plastic. Strictly speaking, leaf burning was prohibited near quarters, and was also unnecessary. A yard maintenance crew took care of the leaves. But its schedule may not have suited the general's standards.

Knightdale was wearing generic sweats and a canvas barn coat with deep pockets. Fran had never seen him so casually attired. On the grass to their right, a dripping canoe was overturned, partially covering a large shrimp net.

"The CG usually walks Bilbo first thing. Wally's already been out in his boat this morning, but Bilbo's been cooped up. Do you mind if we walk while we talk?"

They followed the dog along the river's edge past the last set of general officer's quarters, currently unoccupied. Beyond that house was a narrow wood separating the residential area from the golf course. Bilbo disappeared down the utility road that cut through the trees, setting off a chain reaction in the surrounding brush. Fran could follow the dog's movement by the sounds of snapping branches and disturbed birds taking flight. She expected Knightdale to call the dog back, but instead he followed Bilbo's route until it ended in a small clearing. The clearing was littered with crumpled beer cans. A desiccated condom dangled from a tree branch. The party was long over.

Knightdale picked up one of the beer cans and threw it into the brush. "Come late July, these bushes are filled with wild blueberries. Before she got too grown up to hang out with her old man, Marissa and I would come here. She'd fill her bucket and then eat every one of 'em before we got home. Linda soon gave up on any plans for homemade blueberry pie."

Knightdale pulled off his glasses and pinched the corners of his eyes. "I saw you in Arkansas, Special Agent Setliff. I wasn't sure it was you until I got back and Marissa said she'd forgotten to tell me some woman with a *Beverly Hillbillies* accent had called." He looked directly at Fran for the first time. "This has been waiting to blow up in my face for ten years. I just don't understand why the Naval Criminal Investigative Service would be so interested in my personal life."

She was willing to put her cards on the table, too. "A child—I didn't know it was a boy—left a message on Ann Buckhalter's answering machine. He mentioned the name Highlock. Said something about the chief of staff. In view of Mrs. Buckhalter's death not long after, I felt it was something that should be looked into."

He missed the significance of the "I," instead of the organizational "we." "And Boyette couldn't just ask me?"

She didn't answer.

"The only question now," Knightdale said dully, "is what I can do to limit the pain this will cause. I told Linda about Paul last night. It's amazing I was able to keep it from her as long as I did. I guess it was because I was the one who took care of the family finances. The only time I sweated was when we filed our income tax. But Linda always signed at the X, no questions asked." He laughed bleakly. "Nita got an allotment, and Linda never gave my Leave and Earnings statement a second glance. What could go wrong?" He wiped his forehead, damp with perspiration despite the cool day, on the rough sleeve of his coat. "Funny thing. I sat there at her funeral trying to remember what Nita looked like. I couldn't."

But you won't have trouble remembering what your son looks like, Fran thought. *Just check the mirror.*

"I didn't even have the excuse of being in love with the girl. I wasn't. It was just a case of ego winning out over conscience. Linda didn't seem to find me exciting anymore. Nita did. That's all there was to it. Nita offered, and I didn't have enough character to turn her down."

"What happened when Nita told you she was pregnant?"

"She didn't. While I was on a long-weekend leave, she went to the Navy captain commanding the NROTC unit and resigned. By the time I got back, she was gone. The captain told me she resigned because she was pregnant. It shook me, sure. But to be brutally frank, I was relieved she hadn't brought my name into it. With Nita gone, I started thinking straight again. How could I have been so reckless? My marriage, my career, reputation. I'd risked everything. The possibility of AIDS scared me shitless, too. After all, what did I really know about Nita?"

Knightdale paused. "A few months later, one of her brothers came to see me. I honest-to-God thought he was going to kill me. I was so goddamn happy to learn Nita was willing to keep quiet, I never argued over the money." He smiled again. "And who knows? Maybe I had a few shreds of honor left." His expression turned oddly vacant. "You know, I hoped I would feel something for the boy when I finally saw him. But I didn't. I don't. He's absolutely blameless in all this, of course. But he's been a threat hanging over my head for so long, I can't seem to think of him as anything else. Maybe that's just as well. Nita's older brother has threatened to have me court-martialed. I could lose my retirement."

"Did you know the boy contacted Ann Buckhalter?" Fran asked.

Knightdale didn't seem to hear the question. His eyes swept over Fran's suit and pumps. "You aren't exactly dressed for the outback, are you? Why don't you head on back to the general's house, and I'll round up Bilbo. We'll finish talking indoors. I'm so sorry you had to get dragged into this."

Something in Knightdale's tone made Fran reluctant to turn her back on him. As it happened, it was Knightdale who turned his back on her. Stepping over some low shrubs, whistling for the dog, the colonel disappeared into the thicket.

Fran headed back toward the housing area. The whistling stopped, leaving a heavy silence. An ominous silence. She wheeled and, with a certainty she couldn't have explained, suddenly knew how Knightdale planned to extricate himself from his troubles. She started to run, shouting, "No! No!"

Her voice was obliterated by the sound of a single gunshot.

Oh, Jesus, no! No! Her heart mushroomed to fill her chest and throat.

Bilbo barked wildly. A golfer jumped, startled, from behind a tree thirty yards away. Still holding his club with both hands, he stared open-mouthed at Fran.

"Run, please! For Christ's sake, call an ambulance!" Fran screamed.

The man dropped the club, rummaged through his jacket for a cell phone, and shakily held it up so she could see him punching in 911.

Fran raised her hand in thanks, then turned to push through underbrush and pine seedlings, trying to reach the site of Bilbo's frenzied barking. She saw the black Lab jumping excitedly from side to side, as if he had cornered a striking snake. But it was not a snake riveting his attention. It was the twitching body of Colonel Bob Knightdale sprawled in the tall grass.

Knightdale lay twisted on his side, one leg doubled under him. A pistol was several yards away, thrown from his hand by the recoil. His eyes were closed, his open mouth full of frothy, dark blood. Under his head, a stew of blood and matter pooled on the leaves. He'd shot himself under his right jaw, at an upward angle.

Fran pressed Knightdale's cheek to allow some of the fluid to spill from his mouth. While starting cardiopulmonary resuscitation, she involuntarily imagined the bullet tumbling through his neck and exiting the back of his skull. His heart was, however, still beating.

The methodical Knightdale must have thought this all out, she realized. He shot himself in the woods so he wouldn't mess up his own or the general's house. He invited NCIS to unknowingly stand by so an agent, instead of some kid, would reach the body first. If he died, he wouldn't be court-martialed for his relationship with Nita Highlock. Linda and Marissa would receive his survivors' benefits. Hell, Knightdale had probably worn the old barn coat because it was the most expendable thing in his wardrobe.

Although the ambulance arrived in less than five minutes, Fran was liberally stained with blood. The emergency technicians initially thought she was injured, too. Spitting into the dust, she vigorously shook her head. She grabbed Bilbo's collar when the agitated dog started growling at the corpsmen. Two of them rolled a gurney out of their vehicle and unsnapped the litter to carry it into the thicket.

A pack of MP vehicles, sirens whooping, started arriving as corpsmen and litter reached Knightdale. Fran presented her credentials to an MP staff sergeant she didn't recognize, then identified the wounded man. The staff sergeant's head jerked back in surprise. He studied Fran for a couple of clicks, then asked if she'd like a ride back to PMO. Fran told him no. Her personal vehicle was parked at General Johnson's quarters, she said firmly, and she would drive herself back to her office as soon as she secured the general's dog.

Bilbo was trembling quietly and shaking his head as though his ears hurt. Fran wondered if the dog had been deafened by the gunshot. Bent over awkwardly, holding his collar, she was relieved as well as dismayed when Wally Johnson arrived and took charge of the animal. She told the stunned boy there had been an accident. Fran was wondering whom to contact on his behalf when a Latina maid arriving for work in one of the houses gestured toward them and shrilly repeated Wally's name until he began walking toward her. The woman seemed more wary of Fran than the dog, probably because of the blood on Fran's clothes.

Throwing a tarp she kept in the back of her car over the driver's seat, Fran congratulated herself on maintaining her composure as well as she had—even though it took three attempts at putting the key in the ignition before her hands were steady enough to complete the task.

ooooo

"I want you unavailable to the press," Boyette barked at her when she returned his call.

His voice was the loudest she'd ever heard it, pneumonia and all. Of course he was upset about Bob Knightdale, but surely he didn't hold her responsible. Her conscience pricked her only when she thought how she'd manipulated Marissa Knightdale to find out where her father was going. She hadn't told Boyette about that.

"Don't talk to anyone about this but me, Setliff. Do you understand? No one."

"Yes, sir. I understand."

She'd avoided being seen by any civilians except the Latina maid. And thank God, she didn't need to leave PMO to get a shower and backup clothing. The bloodied suit and pantyhose would have to be trashed. She flashed to Wally Johnson and his sulfurous burn barrel. That would be a fitting ending to her ensemble's hellish morning.

"I want you to get on the road to Raleigh as soon as PMO has taken your statement. Return the personal effects Ann Buckhalter left in the B.O.Q, as well as the microcassette tapes you took from her house. Tell Buckhalter that NCIS has nearly completed the investigation of his wife's death, and that the official determination will most likely be there is no evidence to indicate her drowning was other than an accident."

She was being given a thinly disguised bum's rush, but she understood Boyette's reasoning.

Fran gave her statement and cleaned up as quickly as she could.

Still, by the time she got on the road, two media vans equipped with satellite dishes were already parked in front of the base theater awaiting a press release about the "accidental self-inflicted shooting" of the chief of staff.

Worse, a fender-bender in the nearby roundabout delayed her enough to permit the surprisingly agile Lowell Mapp to trot up alongside her idling car. How did he manage always to be the first reporter on the scene?

She cut him off before he could speak. "Déjà vu all over again, Mapp. Everything goes through Public Affairs."

"And like I said before, you can't blame me for taking a shot. Sorry, poor choice of words." His smirk belied the apology. "This won't affect the Capex, will it? Still on for Monday? I found out this morning I get to go, and I'm just bustin' with excitement."

Capex? It took a second for that to register. Oh, yes. The big Capabilities Exercise. The ultimate in dog-and-pony shows, an extravagant display of military equipment and training, coming up in three days.

"I have no idea. But I bet Public Affairs does."

Weren't the non-transferable press invites issued weeks in advance? How had Mapp gotten in at the last minute? Not her problem.

She carefully accelerated away from him. As much as she longed to hit the gas and knock him off his feet, she'd seen more than enough blood for one day.

THIRTY-FOUR.

On the drive to Raleigh, Fran wondered if the family would be pleased that the investigation would soon be officially—if not definitively—closed. For Deirdre, at least, it might be some consolation to know her mother had not killed herself. Ann hadn't been so miserable that she chose to die even if it meant leaving her daughter behind. On the other hand, it might not be such good news for Gary. The implication was that Ann had died more or less as a result of her own foolishness. She drank and popped pills until she was too stupefied to keep her footing on the pier.

As it turned out, Deirdre wasn't home when Fran told Gary Buckhalter and his mother, Libby, the news. Libby informed Fran that Deirdre was spending the day with a girlfriend at Camp Lejeune and then staying for a sleepover. She quickly added that Gary had called the girlfriend's mother to confirm there would be adult supervision.

"I guess you just have to trust them at some point," Libby said with an unconvincing smile.

They listened to Fran without interrupting and didn't ask any questions when she finished. They were a stolid pair, mother and son, sitting side by side on a sturdy, nondescript couch, the woman's arm looped supportively around her son's.

Were they satisfied with the investigation's conclusion? Fran asked. Buckhalter nodded, expressionless. Libby glanced at her son, then nodded, too. He got up slowly, shook Fran's hand, excused himself to attend to some paperwork, and disappeared down the hall in the direction of what had been Ann's office. Fran picked up her purse, preparing to leave. But Libby seemed determined to stall her. She offered a variety of refreshments and, when Fran declined them all, dogged her all the way to her car, shifting the conversation from cookies to lawn treatments.

"Mrs. Buckhalter," Fran finally said, "I have the feeling you're trying to tell me something. For goodness' sake, what is it?"

The woman laughed nervously. "You're right. I don't know if . . ." She took a deep breath. "So, it's really over?"

"Yes. Well, there might be a few more details to clear up, but I think you can put any worries about foul play out of your mind."

The woman didn't seem satisfied. "Details? I see. It's just that . . . Gary told me Ann had taken a drug, a prescription drug, before she died. He didn't know anything about it. I just couldn't bring myself to tell Gary, but now and then I gave Ann a couple of my tranquilizers. I know I shouldn't have done it, but I just couldn't tell Ann no. I've been just sick, thinking I may have caused what happened by giving her those pills."

Fran decided on a merciful half-truth. "I can reassure you on that point, Mrs. Buckhalter. What you heard about the drug was true. But Ann had also been drinking before she died. That probably had more to do with it than the pills. Please don't torment yourself."

Libby Buckhalter grabbed Fran's hand and smiled. Convincingly, this time. Her eyes sparkled with tears. "Well, I'll try. Thank you, dear, for your help."

During the drive back to Lejeune, it occurred to Fran that dear, sweet Grandma had told her a half-truth, too. It wasn't a tranquilizer but an antidepressant that was found in Ann's body. Big difference. And anybody taking one or the other would damn well know the difference. Libby Buckhalter hadn't given Ann those pills. So, why would she go to the trouble of bringing them up just to lie about them? Who was she trying to protect? Gary and Ann hadn't been intimate enough to share a medicine cabinet, much less meds. So, who? Deirdre.

Fran massaged her temples, hoping to forestall a headache. She was sure Commander Terry had denied ever prescribing anything for Ann Buckhalter. Fran hadn't asked him, however, if he prescribed anything for Deirdre. She was willing to bet Ann had "borrowed" some of her own daughter's medication, maybe even with Deirdre's knowledge, and Grandma had just fallen on her sword to prevent further investigation into the matter. She didn't want Deirdre to have another reason to blame herself for her mother's death.

ooooo

Fran's plan for a quick zip back to Camp Lejeune was spoiled by an overturned tractor-trailer that made Raleigh's rush hour even more gruesome than usual. It took her nearly two hours to get off the beltline, after which she was delayed again when hunger and an overextended bladder forced her to stop near Warsaw. It was dark when she got back to Jacksonville.

Upon seeing the Buckhalters' pearl-finish Thunderbird parked outside the Rascal Ridge bar, her first thought was, *Oh, God, Gary is drinking again.* Then she reminded herself she'd seen Gary four hours ago, sober as a stick of gum. Her second thought was, *Somebody's stolen the Buckhalters' car.* Then she saw the "Hot To Trot" bumper sticker and remembered a horse-loving teenager also had access to the vehicle. *Deirdre, you little idiot. What the hell are you doing in a bar rough enough to sand sheet metal?*

She glanced at her watch. Twenty-two hundred. Friday night. Too early for much damage. She decided not to park in the bar's lot but on the other side of the low wall separating the property from an all-night coin laundry. She couldn't see anybody in the laundry, but she heard a washer lid slam and saw an empty detergent bottle hit the rim of a metal trash barrel.

The inside of Rascal Ridge was darker than the parking lot. Shaved heads looking like giant, glowing white mushrooms tracked her entrance. The heads must have reacted to the sudden onslaught of street light and fresh air because they could not have heard the door open. A large-screen television tuned to MTV and a smaller set mounted over the bar tuned to WWF blared intermingled gobbledygook.

She didn't hold the attention of any of the shaved heads. Her sour expression and the prim navy-blue suit were effective leer repellent. They probably figured her for a health department official.

The bar ran along the right wall. Three men sat there—a beefy guy with a pointy shaved head, a little wiry guy with a shaved head and Western boots, and a guy with a biker belly and a ponytail. The one with the ponytail had a Globe and Anchor tattooed on his forearm. A female waitress rotated listlessly between a stack of tapped kegs and the counter. High-backed booths along two other walls bracketed a pair of battered pool tables. At least three of the booths were occupied, judging by one outstretched leg, one enormous arm, and somebody's shaved head face down on a tabletop.

Fran started working her way around the room, glancing sideways into each booth. She was stopped short by a girlish squeal.

"Stop that! I mean it, I've got to go to the bathroom."

Straining to hear over the televisions, Fran guessed the squeal came from the booth with the enormous arm, which suddenly withdrew from view.

"Please. Puh-leese. Let me out." The voice had a whining urgency.

Fran still hadn't seen the face belonging to the arm when Deirdre Buckhalter popped out of the booth like a champagne cork. The arm shot out and grabbed her, pulling her onto a massive denim-covered leg tucked into a studded biker boot. The knee bounced her up and down a couple of times before the arm flicked her off. From the body parts she could see, Fran estimated the man was the size of a Clydesdale. Deirdre rebounded against a pool table and winced.

"You okay, baby?" Clyde asked, laughing.

Fran couldn't understand whatever Deirdre said back to him, but she got a good look at the girl when she turned around. She certainly wasn't dressed like a teen tart-throb. A pair of stonewashed jeans and a flannel shirt over a turtleneck. Not that it made any difference. Deirdre had the kind of baby-goddess beauty that would have radiated through canvas drop cloth.

Fran eased her way to an alcove with a sign indicating that it led to the restrooms. Deirdre walked toward her but with her shoulders hunched, eyes to the floor.

"Deirdre," Fran said when the girl came within a yard of collision.

Deirdre looked up, started, paled, flushed, and swallowed hard. "Oh, hi, Miss, uh . . . Ms. . . . ." She gave up. "What are you doing here?"

"That's my question, Deirdre. Let me give you a lift to wherever your father and grandmother think you really are."

The girl didn't look drunk, just a little goofy, but with a teenager, it could be a fine line.

She read Fran's mind and drew up stiffly. "I'm not doing anything illegal. See?" She leaned forward and puffed a moist, spicy-sweet cloud into Fran's face. Cinnamon gum. Grape lip gloss. French fries. Beer.

Fran tried to control her irritation. "Wrong. You're not even supposed to be breathing the air in here unless you're eighteen. Who's that guy you're with?"

"Why do I have to tell you what I'm doing? Are you investigating me or something?"

Fran replied with a look that could curdle spit. Deirdre curdled.

"Jeff . . . something. I forget. Please don't tell my dad. It would just kill him."

"You should have thought of that before you pulled this stunt." *And you should have parked your car more discreetly, you naive little twit,* Fran thought. *I'm too tired to deal with this crap and too much of a busybody to let it lie.*

From the corner of her eye, Fran saw a man approach. Clyde. Probably closer to thirty than twenty, she guessed, and truly monumental in size. He could haul freight in those shoes. He walked with one arm held behind him. He was either hiding something or dealing with anal itch.

"Hey, sweet cheeks, who's your . . . ?" He stopped smiling and narrowed his eyes when he saw the expressions on the two women's faces. With somebody else's personality, he might have been attractive. Even though the face had the first-stage mottling of a problem drinker.

"I have to get my purse." Deirdre was looking at the floor again.

"Is this your mother or what?" he said with a Freon-filled smile.

"No, she's . . . I better go, Jeff."

He pulled a floppy brown handbag from behind his back. "I thought you might need it in the wee-wee room."

Deirdre held out her hand. He raised the bag over his head, out of reach of anything but a cherry picker.

"Give me my purse, Jeff. Please?" She reached out again, but more tentatively.

"Not 'til I know what the fuck's going on."

"Give it to her." Fran spoke calmly.

Clyde visually raked Fran from hair to heels. "Let's see. You ain't her mother, and you sure as hell ain't pretty enough to be her sister. What are you, her Sunday-school teacher?" He didn't wait for an answer before turning back to Deirdre. "Don't let some tight-ass spoil our evening. Come on, baby. You still ain't told me how to use a curvy comb."

Deirdre smiled weakly. "*Currycomb*, stupid. Can I have my purse now? I've got to leave. Really."

He faked a quivering lower lip and took her outstretched arm, gently reeling her closer to him. And farther from Fran. Deirdre put up a flabby resistance by locking her knees after every step and staring fixedly at her purse.

"Let's talk about this, darlin'," Clyde cooed. "You convince me it's you and not your Sunday-school teacher who wants you to leave, and I won't try to stop you." Over Deirdre's shoulder, Clyde smiled at Fran and mouthed, "Fuck you."

Fran hesitated to smack Clyde with some official authority. Once she showed her ID, she'd have to write up a report about whatever happened next. And Gary Buckhalter would get another distressing phone call from NCIS.

Deirdre intervened by starting to cry. And it wasn't low-level blubbering either. She sobbed as if someone had shot her dog and was taking aim at her cat. Clyde looked surprised but didn't let go of her arm. The muscles in his neck knotted with frustration.

Looking on from the bar, the wiry little Marine wearing Western boots was suddenly overcome with chivalry. Carrying a plastic cup of beer, he came up behind Clyde, intentionally stumbled against him, then quickly sprang away, snatching Deirdre's purse in the process. It didn't seem to bother him that Clyde was twice his size.

The wiry little cowboy two-stepped toward Deirdre and tried to hang the purse on her free arm. "Here, miss. I think—"

Clyde, who'd been watching open-mouthed, his nostrils widening into caverns, snagged the cowboy's hand and bent it backward at the wrist. Way back. The purse dropped to the floor and skidded toward Fran, who quickly scooped it up. The cowboy yelped and tried to do-si-do his hand free, turning his back to Clyde in the process. Clyde snapped the cowboy's arm straight behind him and started cranking it upward at an unnatural angle while he wrapped his other arm in a half-hitch around the smaller man's shoulder and neck. It wouldn't be long before this freelance chiropractic resulted in multiple fractures. Concurrent to all this, the little cowboy's beer got tossed in Fran's direction and Deirdre quit crying and started screaming instead.

Fran grabbed Deirdre and jerked her back into the restroom alcove just as the cowboy's bar buddy, Pointy Head, joined the fray by applying pressure to Clyde's Adam's apple with the inside of his elbow. By the time Fran got Deirdre into the ladies' room—which stank of mildew, vomit, and counterfeit Giorgio—at least four men were in the fight. Fran instinctively braced herself against the door to keep the brawl at bay. Deirdre crumpled under the sink, sobbing onto her drawn-up knees.

On the way in, Fran had glimpsed the waitress at the bar making a phone call. To the cops, she hoped. In case she was wrong, Fran untangled her own purse from Deirdre's, took out her cell phone, and called the MPs. Why the hell hadn't she just stayed out of it? "You always got to be stirring up some shit," Marlon used to complain.

Fran thought she caught the hallelujah sound of sirens over all the grunting and yelling and body slamming. But she didn't ease up on the door until she saw red lights pulsing through the restroom's one small window. The loudest noises from inside the bar stopped soon afterward, replaced by coughs, groans, and retching.

Fran's next objective was to extricate Deirdre and herself from Rascal Ridge as quickly as possible. Thinking back to other bar brawls she had investigated, she bet it would take awhile for the police to get a coherent version of events from the participants. That might provide a window of opportunity for escape.

She pulled off her jacket and rolled it into a tight ball. Her blouse had beer on it, too, but not as much. One suit jacket ruined with blood-stains, another with beer, all in one day. She pulled Deirdre to her feet, planted her in front of a mirror, lightly slapped a few wet paper towels against her stunned face, and ran a comb through her hair. It must have hurt when Fran hit a snarl, but Deirdre didn't make any noise except for some post-crying hiccups.

"Okay, Deirdre. Let's go. We'll work our way out of the building as inconspicuously as we can and head straight for my car. Don't worry about yours right now. Don't look at anybody but me. Don't say anything to anybody. Anything needs to be said, I'll say it."

They caught a break when the only one to see them was a Jackson-ville police officer who didn't know Fran. He was checking the iden-tification of two men and seemed uninterested in the women coming out of the ladies' room. With Deirdre between her and the wall, Fran walked to the bar, flipped up the counter's hinged panel, and passed to the working side. She maneuvered Deirdre into position so the two of them were standing beside the waitress, who scarcely gave them a glance. Her lips were pressed into an amused little pucker as her eyes darted from one cluster of men to another.

"Did you ever see the like?" Fran said, Deirdre in tow. If they could slip through the kitchen door without being stopped, they were almost home free.

"Only a gazillion times," the waitress said scornfully. "It doesn't take but two things to get something started in here: enough beer and more than enough beer."

The waitress's interest shifted, but not to Fran and Deirdre. She bent to see herself in an unobstructed part of the bar's mirrored back wall, then repositioned some of the plastic clips jacking up her hair. She probably realized that, being sober, she would be an important witness. Might even make the TV news.

Fran sidestepped through the door leading to a small, crusty kitchen, pulling Deirdre with her. All that remained were six steps across a sticky floor and one more door, the one marked "Exit."

Outside, Fran saw an MP she knew. He did a double take when he saw her but kept his distance after she shook her head sharply at him. Maybe he thought she was part of an undercover operation. Or maybe he thought she was looking for love in some really wrong places.

She was amazed how easily they got to her car. She was glad she had parked in front of the coin laundry. A couple of women customers were standing on the pavement, watching what was going on in the bar parking lot.

Unless the incident involved firearms or a fatality, police weren't too interested in what started a bar fight. Their job was to restore order, note property damage, and sort out serious and minor injuries. Fran was indulging in a sigh of relief when she spotted another familiar face in the crowd. She wasn't glad to see this one. Lowell Mapp must have heard the call for assistance come over the newsroom scanner.

Mapp saw Fran at the same time she saw him. She didn't dare jump in her car and make a run for it. Acting evasive was a sure-fire way to step into it. Fortunately, he didn't see Deirdre, who was already obscured in the dark interior of Fran's car. She doubted Mapp would recognize the girl anyway. Ann Buckhalter didn't have the kind of relationship with Mapp in which she'd share family snapshots.

Fran positioned herself several yards from her car and waited for him to come to her.

"Well, well. Fancy meeting you here," he said with a smirk, taking in her wet blouse.

"Well, you know how it is. Stop to ask directions to the nearest

Christian Science Reading Room, and you end up watching a bunch of drunks pound each other."

He was still staring at her blouse, chuckling. "Jesus, Fran, you've got a real thing for impromptu wet-downs lately." Then the smile died a sudden death. He pitched her a quick, furtive look. "Well, I better get back to the police chief. See you around." He flung the words over his shoulder as he fast-stepped away.

She stared after him, heart pounding with righteous anger. *A real thing for impromptu wet-downs*, she thought. *You nasty little turd. You're the one who pushed me off the pier.* Fran mentally reprimanded herself to get it together. She could deal with Mapp later. And brother, would she ever.

As she slid in beside Deirdre, she took a last look at the half-dozen men shifting uneasily in the neon light of the Rascal Ridge sign. Things were so quiet now, the police radios and neon buzz were clearly audible. Everybody just wanted to go home or back to the barracks. The MP she'd recognized earlier had a man in the back of his vehicle, but he wasn't cuffed. A final EMS vehicle, siren off, arrived at a leisurely pace as Fran pulled out. The cowboy was probably on his way to orthopedics and a few weeks of light duty.

Fran smiled wryly at Deirdre, who was sitting in a tuck-dive position, her hair fanned messily over her knees. They'd soon be out of it. The whole incident was going to sound routinely stupid in the police reports. This big guy had his girlfriend's purse and was teasing her because she wanted to leave with this other girl and he didn't want her to. And then this little guy told the big guy to give the girl her purse back, and this buddy of the little guy got into it, and, say, where did those girls get to, anyway?

Fran eased on to Lejeune Boulevard. She thought of something. "Deirdre, you didn't give, um, Jeff your real name, did you?"

Deirdre cocked her head and uncoiled her left leg. She dug two fingers into a jeans pocket, extracting a peeling ID. Fran took it and, turning onto Holcomb, snapped on the overhead light so she could see.

"Ohio Bureau of Motor Vehicles. Arlene Nguyen, age twenty-two." The picture showed a round-faced woman with dark, straight hair. Fran sighed. "Okay, Deirdre. Where are we going? Where are you supposed to be?"

Deirdre sputtered and sniffled, then cautiously raised her eyes. She relaxed considerably when she saw they'd passed through the main gate. She must have thought Fran was taking her back to Raleigh.

"I'm supposed to be at the Madisons' house, on Wavell. Sandy and I are—were—in the same riding class. Sandy's mom is a nurse. She told my dad she was going to be home. But then she got called in to work part of a shift for some other nurse that got sick. Sandy's dad is in Norfolk. We were going to the movies. Then this jerk-face, Robbie, called Sandy and asked her out. She had the nerve to ask me to go to the movies by myself and then go back to her house and hang around until Jerk-face brought her home. I was really pissed. I told her if she did that, we wouldn't be friends anymore. It took her about two seconds to pick Jerk-face over me. Then I told her that when I lived here, Jerk-face asked me out more times than she'd been on actual dates, and I'd turned him down every single time because he was such a jerk-face."

"I see. And your only alternative was to go bar hopping?"

"No! It didn't happen that way! I went to the CD store and this guy, Jeff, started talking to me. He helped me set the bass on my earphones. At first, I thought he worked there. Honest. All I was going to do was hang around for a while, then go back to Sandy's. I was still pissed, but I didn't want to drive to Raleigh by myself in the dark. My dad wouldn't like it. Then he, Jeff, asked if I was hungry. I *was* hungry. And he didn't seem like any more of a creep than Jerk-face. So, I followed him to . . . that place. I'd never been in there before, honest to God. It looked okay from the outside. At least I knew better than to get in his car with him, didn't I? I'm not 100 percent stupid. I kept thinking, *As long as other people are around, it's no big deal.*"

"You couldn't just go over to some other friend's house?"

Deirdre snorted, then got sniffly again. "Ever since what happened to me at the stables, most of my friends, their parents won't even let them talk to me. I told only one girl about it, but now everybody knows. Even Beth Amans's mom acts like I've got some contagious disease, and she lets Beth have boy-girl sleepovers! She has no idea how much screwing has been going on in her breezeway. Beth told me her mother was mad when she heard we'd been hanging out together at the stables. Remember that day I saw you there? That's the last time I saw Beth."

Fran mentally debated the wisdom of taking Deirdre home with her. She decided against it. She must maintain at least a semblance of professional detachment.

"Listen, Deirdre, what if I check you into the guesthouse and call your dad and tell him you're with me and everything's okay? We'll say you and your girlfriend had an argument."

"I won't stay where Mom drowned!" Deirdre looked more frightened than she had when the Clydesdale was bearing down on her.

"No, no, of course not. Not the B.O.Q. The all-ranks Guest Lodge. You remember, next to the uniform shop."

The girl threw her head back against the neck rest. "Oh, I don't care. I'm such a fuckup, my dad should just write me off anyway."

"Maybe. But he won't. And neither will your grandmother." *I, however,* Fran thought, *am eagerly anticipating doing just that.*

THIRTY-FIVE.

But writing Deirdre Buckhalter off wasn't going to be easy.

After checking her into the Guest Lodge, Fran accompanied her to her room and called Gary Buckhalter. He was simultaneously angry, skeptical, and relieved—a common parental state, apparently—but he did not berate Deirdre when they briefly spoke. Neither did he insist on coming to get his daughter immediately. He'd pick her up the following morning.

Fran next called Rumley, who wondered why the Buckhalter case kept hanging on like a sticky booger. She told Rumley she was reluctant to leave the girl alone. Having come this far, she'd feel responsible if anything happened to her during the night. Fran looked over her shoulder. Deirdre was breaking open a package of cheap toothbrushes she'd gotten out of a vending machine.

"You may as well stay," Rumley advised. "If you don't, you won't get any sleep worrying about her."

"Are you going to stay with me?" Deirdre asked, jolting Fran with her intuition. "My mom used to say this place has roaches big enough to saddle."

That wasn't true. The teeny-tiny stirrups would drag on the floor. But it was the first lighthearted reference to her mother Deirdre had made. It sounded healthy.

Within a half-hour, Deirdre had taken a shower and was sitting on the bed farther from the door. Her hair, neck, and torso were wrapped in the room's entire allotment of bath towels. Fran would have to make do with a hand towel threadbare enough to sight those cockroaches through.

When Fran had cleaned up enough to pass inspection by her own nose, she fumbled for the switch on the bedside lamp, which was steaming slightly from the hastily rinsed-out blouse draped over its shade. She stretched out on top of the bedspread and covered herself with the spare blanket. Across the room, Deirdre was flip-flopping under the coarse bedsheets, making them crackle like canvas sails in a stiff wind.

"Good night, Deirdre," Fran said.

"Good night, Ms. Setliff."

Both were quiet a few moments before Deirdre spoke again.

"Do you want me to tell you what happened?"

"I pretty much got the picture," Fran murmured sleepily.

"No, I don't mean tonight. I mean the other thing. At the stables."

Fran's eyes snapped open. She had forgotten about Private First Class Jervet Harriman. She didn't much relish the idea of tiptoeing through an adolescent psyche right then—or at any other time. But she flashed back to Harriman's simple, desperate face. His laudable, if warped, sense of honor. Fran measured her words like gold dust.

"If you want to tell me, I'll listen."

Deirdre shifted on to her side, facing Fran, head propped on her elbow. "I've got to tell you something else first, if you're going to understand everything. I never told this to anybody except Dr. Terry."

Fran felt a "Don't!" rising in her throat. Jesus, what if Deirdre told her Gary had been abusing her? Or Dr. Terry? What would she do with that stink bomb? She hesitated too long. Deirdre was forging ahead.

"It happened when I was four and a half and Dale, my brother, was seven. He had these two friends that used to play at our house all the time. Sometimes, they'd play in this old tree house in the woods behind their house, down the street from us. Dale wasn't supposed to go there because the tree house was coming apart. But Mom wasn't as strict about things when Dad was away.

"I remember Dale getting only two hard spankings. One was when my dad caught him in that tree house the first time. He and those other boys were doing something dangerous, I think—playing hangman or trying to make a fire, something like that. I used to beg Dale to let me go up in the tree house, too. There weren't any kids my age to play with. But those other boys would always say, 'No girls allowed.' Dale told me they got to make the rules because they lived closer to the tree house.

"The time I'm going to tell you about, Mom had left us with the cleaning woman. I don't remember her name, but she was black and nice and didn't pay much attention to what we were doing. Dad had just gotten home from somewhere. He was asleep in his room with the door closed. We weren't supposed to bother him. I know now that he was probably hung over. But back then, it didn't seem strange.

"I sneaked through the neighbors' backyards to the tree house. Dale and those other boys were there. They were trying to keep quiet, and I just had to see what they were doing. I wanted to sneak up on them, but when I was climbing up, I caught my shorts on something, and they ripped at the front seam. I had a scratch that went right across my belly button, but I didn't realize that until later.

"The boys heard me. The two other boys were mad and told Dale to shake the ladder and make me fall off. But Dale pulled me the rest of the way up. He told me to go home or we'd both get in trouble, but I begged him to let me stay. Dale said okay and the other boys said okay, but only if I sat in the corner and didn't make a sound.

"They had all these little plastic soldiers and airplanes and trucks. They were moving them around these buildings made out of Legos. I sat still for a couple of minutes, I guess, but then I crawled over closer and sat cross-legged between Dale and one of the other boys. Suddenly, one of them started looking at me real wide-eyed, only he was looking at my . . . where my shorts were torn. I tried to pull my shirt down, but his face looked so funny, I started giggling. Pretty soon, they started laughing, too, and Dale pushed me away, trying to make me go back in the corner. I lay back and kicked, so he wouldn't be able to move me. The other boys started tickling me. I kicked harder.

"Then one of them, the one who'd been looking at me, asked Dale if they could pull my shorts down and see what a girl looked like. Dale said no. He said there wasn't anything to see. But the boy kept asking. I thought the whole thing was funny. I stood up and pushed my shorts and panties down to my ankles. I jumped up and down, laughing, until I tripped and fell, knocking Legos and plastic soldiers everywhere."

Deirdre fell flat on her pillow and sighed. "Dr. Terry asked me if I was scared when this happened. I told him no. Of course not. What was there to be scared of?

"By this time, my shorts were off completely and the boy was patting my . . . you know. Dale tried to grab my hand and make me get up, but I kicked at him some more. We had to go, he said, but not in a mad voice. He sounded worried, like he knew we were doing something wrong, but he wasn't sure why.

"The boys had toy guns. I don't know who did it first, but one of those other boys took his plastic gun and started poking it between my legs and saying, 'Bang, you're dead.' Then the other boy did it. When they'd say, 'Bang!' I'd hold real still and shut my eyes tight, like I was dead. Then I'd start kicking again. They did it faster and faster—'Bang! Bang! Bang!' One after another, getting closer and louder.

"I still wasn't scared or hurt or anything. But then the biggest boy came at me fast and jabbed the plastic gun barrel inside me, or at least it felt like it. God, it really hurt. I didn't even know I had a place to stick something. I know that sounds stupid, but it's the truth. Do you believe me?"

"For goodness' sake, Deirdre, you were four years old."

"That's what Dr. Terry said. Anyway, it hurt like crazy, and I screamed and started to cry. The two other boys got down out of that tree house so fast, one of them left his shoe. Dale tried to help me put my shorts back on, but he was crying himself by then. I was hopping from foot to foot, grabbing myself. I was bleeding a little, too, which really scared me, and then . . ." She stopped.

"Your dad showed up."

Fran saw the silhouette of Deirdre's head nod.

"The tree house didn't have a door, just an opening where the ladder was. Dad came up that ladder as fast as those boys went down. I cried even louder when I saw his face. I had never seen him so mad. Jesus, it was awful."

"Did you try to tell your dad what happened?"

"Not until that night. I didn't understand. I thought Dad was mad because we were up in the tree house. I thought that after he got us home and got me cleaned up—and maybe gave us a spanking—it would be okay."

"But it wasn't?"

Deirdre picked at her pillowcase. "He didn't spank me at all. He didn't even yell at me. But that was the second and last time I remember him spanking Dale. Dad made me stay in my room while he did it, but I heard everything. It seemed to go on forever. I was so upset, I threw up in my bed. He spanked Dale so hard, our cleaning woman came in from the kitchen and told him he better stop. And she hardly ever said any-thing to Dad except 'Yes, sir' or 'No, sir.' That seemed to snap him out of it. He went in the backyard and smoked about a carton of cigarettes.

"After Mom got home, she and Dad had a terrible fight. She said he was a monster and a drunk. They tried to talk to me, but I was so upset and confused, I probably made it sound worse than it was.

"After that, Dale didn't talk to Dad or me for the longest time. He never really played with me again. He wasn't mad at me. It was some-thing else, something I didn't know the word for then. But I do now. He was ashamed. I couldn't understand why he was treating me like that. I was so hurt, I told him I hated him, that I wished he was dead."

Fran heard her swallow a sob.

"And then he got sick, and after a while, he *was* dead. I thought I had wished it to happen. Even after Dr. Terry got me to realize it wasn't my fault, sometimes I still felt it was."

She flipped over on her back. "I thought Mom and Dad blamed me, too. All the time Dale was sick and after he died, they seemed to not love me as much. I thought it was because I made Dale die. Pretty stupid, huh? Now, I know they were just so worried and sad that they couldn't think about much of anything else. Not even their other child. Dr. Terry didn't tell me that. My mom did."

Deirdre flung her arm over her head and rat-a-tatted her knuckles against the headboard. "Anyway, after Dale died, Dad got real religious, and Mom got weird in her own way, too. She started thinking of Dale as this holy angel or something. I used to think he was an angel, too, but in my mind, he was still the same Dale, like a regular kid, only I couldn't see him or touch him anymore. I thought he had wings and could fly.

"Once, my uncle started telling about the time Dale and cousin Marty pretended to be pirates. Marty sneaked a steak knife out of the kitchen, and he had it in his mouth—you know, holding it between his teeth like a pirate. Dale and him started this sword fight, only the swords were paper towel rolls. Well, Dale accidentally hit Marty in the face with his paper towel roll, and Marty's tongue got cut. It was a bloody mess. Marty had to get two stitches. Dale felt so bad about it, he wanted the doctor to give him stitches, too. I remember it because Marty was always sticking his tongue out, trying to gross everybody out with those stitches. Before Dale died, it was just a funny family story. But when my uncle brought it up afterward, Mom went nuts. She acted like he'd accused Dale of murder. My uncle was so shocked, he didn't come visit for a long time."

Deirdre sighed. "After Dale died, it seemed like there was always somebody who wasn't talking to somebody."

Deirdre was more perceptive than Fran would have given her credit for. But how was this leading to PFC Harriman?

"Are you asleep?" Deirdre whispered.

"Lord, no, honey. I'm just thinking."

"I guess this stuff sounds pretty weird, huh?"

Fran smiled in the dark. She thought of her great-uncle, whose wife left him because he demanded she give up her place in their bed to his ailing bird dog.

"I've heard weirder."

"Yeah, sure." Deirdre punched her pillow into a neck brace and lay quietly.

"Deirdre, I expect you told Dr. Terry what you told me. How did your mother feel about that?"

"You mean the tree house? God, Fran, I didn't tell Dr. Terry about that for years and years. Not until a few weeks ago. About the same time Mom asked me to tell her everything I'd told Dr. Terry about Dale. But before I could answer, my dad came in and told her to leave me alone. He said some pretty cold things to her and reminded her she was the one who took me to Dr. Terry in the first place. He must have gotten through to her because Mom never said another word to me about the tree house or Dr. Terry."

Deirdre fell silent after a drawn-out sigh that evolved into a yawn.

Fran figured the night's confidences were over.

But they weren't.

"All the girls at the stables thought Jervet was hot," Deirdre said matter-of-factly. "Me, too, I guess. He was different from the other Marines that worked there. Even his name. Jervet. Don't you think it sounds French? And he was so good with the horses.

"Jackie Brewer came on to him every chance she got. But he didn't come on to her. Or any other girl. That's the truth. Then one day, I was in the stall with Manila Bay when he pinned me against the wall. The horse, I mean. Something had made him nervous, like horses get. He had his ears back and was stamping his feet and trying to turn around. I was afraid he'd hurt himself. Or me. Next thing I knew, Jervet was there, talking to him so soft and nice. Manila Bay just kind of melted. He eased into the stall—Jervet, I mean—and slid between me and the horse. We slid back out, sandwiched together, his body shielding mine. I just thought he was so awesome, so . . . powerful."

"Jervet, you mean."

"After that, he would come by when I was in the stall with Manila Bay and kid around. You know, he'd say something like, 'I've got my giant shoehorn with me, in case you get yourself in another tight spot.' And I'd laugh.

"Then he started showing up in the tack room when I was there. We'd just talk. He never said anything nasty. One day when there wasn't anybody else in the barn, he led me into an empty stall and kissed me. It was fantastic. I just turned into jelly. I've kissed a few other guys, but none of them were anywhere near as hot. Jervet was so . . ." Her voice faded into a melancholy sigh.

Fran cleared her throat to get the girl back on track. *You can get all squishy about your rapist later, dear.*

"I knew my parents would never let me go out with an enlisted Marine, not even if I was thirty years old. I told him so, too. He gave me a sad, big-eyed look and said, 'Well, are you going to let your parents keep you from seeing me?' And I said no. When that weekend came, Becky helped me set up this dumb plan. I was going to spend the night at her house. Becky's house was just up the street from the stables. I told Jervet I'd sneak out and meet him there. It seemed so perfect, you know? I'd walk to the stables, and Becky would cover for me."

Good God! Fran thought. Did parents ever know where their teenage daughters were at night?

Deirdre grew so quiet, Fran couldn't hear her breathe.

"Deirdre? Are you okay?"

"Sure. I'm just trying to remember exactly . . ."

"What happened that night?"

Deirdre cleared her throat. "I'm not sure. We were sitting—I guess lying, really—in a pile of straw, just talking and kissing. Like we'd done before, only lying down instead of standing up."

What a difference a change in latitude can make, Fran thought.

"Then there was less talking and more kissing, and then we were, you know, really making out. He was feeling around inside my bra and everything. He unbuttoned my jeans, I guess, and sort of lay on top of me. I heard him unzip his pants, but I didn't touch him—with my hands, I mean—and he didn't try to make me. I was uncomfortable like that. He was heavy, and his zipper was cutting into my skin. I arched up to try and push him away, and he turned on his side, just enough so he could pull my jeans way down and keep on kissing me. I guess he misunderstood, you know, the arching-up part. Then I guess I just freaked out. All of a sudden, I was four years old again and my dad was going to show up any second. I started pulling at the back of Jervet's shirt and twisting my head back and forth, trying to make him stop. I guess I could have bitten his lip or something, but I wasn't really thinking about hurting him. I just wanted to get away."

"Deirdre, did he, um, penetrate you?"

Monumental silence.

"Please don't laugh at me, Fran, but I don't know. I swear that's the truth. There was so much feeling around and pushing down there, I don't know what was fingers and what was . . . something else. I'd never done it. How do you know what it's like until you do it?"

She had a point. After all those years of horseback riding, Deirdre probably didn't have enough hymen to act as much of a gatekeeper. But the critical thing was this: If PFC Harriman really did ejaculate without penetration, he was a dumbass with a hair trigger, maybe, but not a rapist.

"Listen to me, Deirdre. Jervet is facing some serious charges. You've got to try and remember."

"But I do remember, I just don't know what happened. I tried to tell that woman MP what I told you, but I couldn't make her understand. I almost wish I got pregnant. At least I'd know for sure, then, wouldn't I?"

"Deirdre, you couldn't have gotten pregnant. He was wearing a condom. Didn't you know that?"

The girl gasped audibly. "No! But I don't remember him . . . Can you put one on with just one hand? How long would it take? I mean, could he have been wearing it the whole time?"

Fran was glad Deirdre couldn't see her face because she was trying not to laugh. How long *did* it take to put one on? She didn't think a boy could put one on single-handed. She had the idea it was like putting on pantyhose. If a boy tried to use just one hand, it would take so long, he'd miss the party.

Deirdre snorted indignantly. "Well, if he was wearing it when I got there, that means he was pretty damn sure of himself."

"Deirdre, whenever he put it on, wearing a condom was the only smart thing either of you did that night."

The girl fell silent. When she spoke, it was in a softer, more childlike voice. "I didn't want to get Jervet in trouble, Fran. I mean, I know he's older than me, but girls mature faster, so I felt like I was just as much to blame as he was. But at the same time, I thought maybe if it had happened, it would be easier for my dad if he believed I didn't want to do it. I couldn't stand to be a disappointment to him."

"So, what about tonight, Deirdre? Didn't you think about how you'd disappoint your dad if you were hauled out of a bar to jail?"

The girl's voice took on a quiver of self-pity. "Everybody thinks I'm so screwed up now, what difference would it make? I could get pregnant by an orangutan and people would say, 'Well, what else would you expect from her?'"

"You aren't any more screwed up than any other sixteen-year-old. You've just had a more screwed-up action plan."

"Dr. Terry said something like that. I told him I bet I was the most wacko kid in his study. He just laughed. He said I was really one of the most normal."

Fran's inner alarm went off. "Deirdre, did you and your mother ever talk about that study?"

Deirdre sat up in bed, a graceful, soap-scented shadow. "You know, for a long time, she wasn't interested in the study at all. But that was before she and Dr. Terry got into it. Man, she never even got that mad at my dad."

"You lost me."

"See, after I'd have my session with Dr. Terry, Mom would go in and talk to him for a few minutes. If my dad gave me a ride, he'd wait for me outside the hospital, but mostly it was Mom. While she and Dr. Terry talked, I'd sit in the waiting room or go downstairs to the snack bar. Dr. Terry always closed the door to his office, and there was another door between the hall where the offices were and the waiting room. So, I could never overhear anybody else's session from the waiting room. But I could hear what they were saying from the restroom out in the hall. If I put my ear next to the floor air vent."

"And you figured this out how?"

"Oh, I found out by accident. I got there early one day, and I was in the restroom brushing my hair. One of my earrings fell out and dropped through the vent. When I squatted to get it, I heard faint voices. Just curious, I put my ear down close to the vent. I could hear three people. I recognized Dr. Terry's voice right away. And there was a woman and another man. The woman was all bent out of shape because she couldn't have a baby and her husband wouldn't get his sperm counted."

"Deirdre!" Fran said reprovingly, knowing she herself would have had just about as much respect for strangers' privacy at Deirdre's age.

"Anyway, I started listening in when Mom talked to Dr. Terry about me. A couple of sessions later, he tried to talk to her about what happened in the tree house. I guess that was when she found out I remembered it. And that I'd discussed it with him. Mom's voice got real low, almost like a man's. Or that scary kid in *The Exorcist*. She asked Dr. Terry if he'd included that in the study. He said yes. She told him to show her what he'd written. He said no, and they started arguing. They must have both been moving around, so I couldn't hear everything, but Mom said something about making Dale sound like a child molester. He told her that was ridiculous, but she kept telling him to show her. I don't know how it ended. Somebody came into the restroom, and I had to get up off the vent. When Mom left Dr. Terry's office, she seemed okay, just kind of tense. We didn't talk on the way home like usual. I couldn't let on I'd been eavesdropping, and I wouldn't have touched that subject with a ten-foot pole anyway."

Did anybody in the Buckhalter family ever have a frank conversation? Fran envisioned the battle in Dr. Terry's office: the clinician fiercely protective of his decade-long study, the mother equally protective of her son's idealized memory. Ann apparently had not been rational about her son. To her, that study would have been a desecration.

Fran remembered the bits of paper clinging to Ann's body. Were they connected to her argument with Terry? Had she managed to get her hands on the commander's study after all?

The urge Fran felt to get to her files and review her interview with Commander Terry was so strong, she swung her legs to the floor. Then she pulled them back under the blanket. A few more hours wouldn't make any difference.

"Fran?"

"Yes, honey."

"Does Jervet blame me?"

There in the dark, Fran rolled her eyes. "I don't think so. I expect his lawyer will be able to work things out. You aren't thinking about trying to see Jervet again, are you?"

"No! No way! I'm never, ever coming back to Camp Lejeune after tonight. There's nothing happy here for me anymore."

What does "never" mean to a teenager? Fran thought. *Six months? Six days?*

"It would be a load off your dad's mind if you'd stick to that thought. He and your grandmother need you, Deirdre. Maybe more than you need them."

The girl lay silent a few moments.

"I'll miss Manila Bay," she said at last, a catch in her voice.

"Oh, I expect there are plenty of lonely horses in Raleigh, just waiting for somebody nice to give 'em a good going-over with a curvy comb."

Deirdre chuckled softly.

In a few minutes, she was snoring softly.

Fran put her thought processes on automatic pilot, hoping she'd wake up knowing what, if anything, to do about all that Deirdre had told her. If nothing else, she'd have to do something about that dumbass Jervet Harriman. But if anybody had put Deirdre Buckhalter through a psychosexual wringer, it was her own parents.

ooooo

Next morning, Deirdre looked like the freshest blossom in yonder garden and Fran like leftover scrambled eggs. That's how she felt, at least. She didn't have the guts to look in the mirror.

Deirdre smiled, but shyly, when they got up. Morning-after-too-much-shared-intimacy shyness. It wasn't just for one-night stands. But the teenager soon relaxed and grew downright bubbly while they dressed. Maybe it was watching Fran wash her underwear and throw it in the microwave to dry. Which setting was less likely to melt elastic, "Beverage" or "Popcorn"? Fran could live with getting back into the navy suit, but no way was she was stepping into dirty underwear. She stuffed her soiled bra into her purse. At times like these, B-cup gals had an edge over those overbearing Ds. No bra? No problem. Her polyester blouse was mostly dry, its collar—which was all that would show under her suit jacket—neat enough to pass for ironed. The jacket didn't smell so much like beer anymore. More like a hearty yeast bread.

The first business of the day was getting Deirdre's Thunderbird out of the Rascal Ridge parking lot. Fran called the MPs and asked to have the car driven to the lot at the Provost Marshal's Office. Gary Buckhalter could make arrangements to pick it up later.

The car and Buckhalter arrived at PMO within minutes of each other. A teary but calm Deirdre waved good-bye to Fran, then seemed to remember something and scampered back to her.

"I forgot to tell you something," she whispered. She held up a finger in her dad's direction, asking him for one more moment.

Fran stopped halfway into her own vehicle.

"Remember when you were at my house the first time, looking through Mom's stuff? You wanted all those little tapes of hers?"

"Yes."

"Well, you didn't get them all. There was another one. I took it. It was way in the back of a drawer by itself. I figured it was something Mom didn't want anymore."

"When did you take it?"

"A couple of days, maybe, before Mom died." Deirdre opened her purse and took out a microcassette tape with strands of long hair trapped in its spindles. "I meant to give it to you sometime." She put it in Fran's hand.

A tiny label was marked through with a swipe of felt-tip marker. But when Fran held it at a certain angle, she could read through the ink. "CG." Commanding general.

"Have you played it?" Fran asked.

"Yeah. I mean, I've played what's on there now. I guess I taped over whatever used to be on it."

"What's on it now?"

"See, this girl I know was going to a Phish concert in Greensboro. She told me if I'd lend her my recorder, she'd tape the concert for me. I know you're not supposed to do that—tape concerts, I mean. She hid the recorder in her bun. She said concert security guards never use the metal detectors on girls' hair."

Fran looked at her, expressionless.

"Phish. Fran, it was Phish! I swear I'll never do it again."

"Your list of never-agains is endless, Miss Buckhalter. Your mother never noticed the tape was gone?"

"I wasn't here when she left for Lejeune. Do you think she missed it?"

"Nah, you're probably right. I expect it wasn't anything important."

Fran turned the tape over in her hand. Captain Rhonda Baptiste's third copy. She gave it back to Deirdre.

"You keep it. As a reminder of all those things you're not going to do again."

THIRTY-SIX.

SATURDAY A.M.

While she was holding her breath until she was sure the Buckhalters were really and truly gone, her pager went off. Boyette, afflicted with pneumonia and cabin fever, was especially grumpy that she took five minutes to get back to him.

"Jesus, Setliff, I was about ready to call the police. I thought another PFC had dropped down your chimney."

"I spent the night at Lejeune, boss. It's a long story." She faltered. "Is Colonel . . . Did Colonel Knightdale . . . ?"

"Colonel Knightdale's condition is unchanged. I get the idea he's hanging in there, but just barely." Even for a naturally gruff man, his voice was clipped. "I'm glad you're on-base because there's something I'd like you to take care of this morning."

"Certainly, sir."

"At our request, Gary Buckhalter compiled a list of calls made to Ann's cell phone during the past thirty days. I want you to go over the notes of your interview with General Johnson and your personal recollection. I'm interested in knowing what he said about the last time he saw Ann Buckhalter."

"What's up, boss?"

"One rather lengthy call—fourteen minutes—was from Jacksonville, made the Thursday before the Saturday that Ann died. Buckhalter said it was the only number he didn't recognize, so he called it to find out who it was. A Miss Susan Ratchford told him she never knew Ann Buckhalter, but she did know who called Ann from the Ratchford phone. Brigadier General Amesly Johnson."

This one threw Fran for a loop the size of the moon's orbit. Susan Ratchford was Johnson's occasional significant other.

"Fran, we have to be absolutely certain before we confront him. Did Johnson tell you he called Ann Buckhalter two nights before she died? I've checked your report, and all I see is that he said he hadn't had any contact with Ann for months. Did that include phone contact?"

"I'll go through my notes right away, sir, but I'm sure he didn't mention a phone call."

They both observed a moment of deep silence before Boyette stated the obvious.

"If he didn't, that's a pretty big oversight. A fourteen-minute conversation with a woman who turns up dead in the New River, and he can't remember it five days later?"

Fran grasped at possible explanations. "Maybe this Ratchford woman doesn't have her story straight. Maybe she's got her own ax to grind."

Boyette snorted—although it could have just been phlegm. "I've left a message on the general's voice mail at his quarters and with the duty officer at Headquarters Building, in case Johnson gets there first. I made it clear we're not closing this thing down until NCIS talks to him again."

Fran had never heard Boyette refer to a general officer by his last name only.

No wonder she'd felt gauche and unsure of herself while interviewing the general. Johnson had been swinging her around like a cat with two tails.

As soon as she hung up the phone, she booted up her laptop. The download time seemed interminable. She pulled up the appropriate encrypted file and decoded it with her password, TOMBIGBEE.

There were his exact words, transcribed from the tape. Reading it with fresh eyes, she realized how pompous and unrevealing his remarks had been. He said nothing about a phone call, only that he'd glimpsed Ann from across the commissary parking lot some weeks earlier.

Fran jumped when the phone rang again. She must have accidentally shifted the ring volume to its maximum. It was Commanding General Amesly Johnson himself. That was surprising enough. Even more surprising, he sounded unsettled.

"Special Agent Setliff? I'm glad I caught you in. I just got back from Headquarters Marine Corps this morning. Looks like the whole goddamn place fell apart while I was gone. Unbelievable about Bob Knightdale. I, uh, I'd like to clarify a few things in connection with our discussion last week. Can you stop by my quarters, say, in an hour? I've already cleared it with Boyette."

ooooo

She combed her hair in the car, spritzing the bangs and flattening the cowlick at a succession of stop signs. She wanted to look halfway presentable in case Captain Vic Maldonado was called in again as legal observer. Of course, if Maldonado was there, it would confirm Fran's suspicion that his attention was a tactical diversion enacted on the general's behalf. She'd already left the captain a hostile phone message de-

claring her intention to avoid him in all unofficial capacities until the
case was closed, and maybe after that.

Maldonado was not there. The general met her with a fleeting
smile in the driveway of his quarters. He was wearing designer sweats
and looked winded and damp, as if he'd just finished a jog. He led her
around the house to the picture-book backyard. Bilbo barked plain-
tively from the sunroom.

She wondered where Wally Johnson was. Sleeping in, maybe, as
teens liked to do on weekends. Maybe that's why the general was putting distance between them and the house, leading her down a brick
path that stopped at the narrow strip of rock and crushed shell that
served as a private beach. The burn barrel now lay on its side, its wet,
tar-like contents trailing into the river. The green canoe was tied alongside a small private boat ramp, the shrimping net loosely folded in the
bow.

Fran double-timed her pace to keep up with his long strides. He
stepped onto a flat chunk of rock and stared out over the opaque water
a few moments before remarking on the mild weather and the number
of leaves still on the trees. She stood silently behind him, arms folded.
He didn't turn to look at her when he spoke.

"I understand you've learned I talked to Ann on the phone a couple
of nights before she died."

"Yes, General, I have. And it concerns me that you weren't completely honest when we spoke about the Buckhalter case in your office."

"You're mistaken, Agent Setliff. I was honest. You asked me when
was the last time I saw Ann, and I told you. You did not ask me when
was the last time I spoke to her."

Fran felt an angry flush rise to her face. He was not going to swing
her by either tail this time.

"General, you may think that kind of evasiveness can pass for cooperation. I don't. I think it's disingenuous, misleading, and just plain

shitty. In fact, some might see it as impeding an official investigation. And some might want to know what could motivate you to be disingenuous, misleading, and just plain shitty."

She expected him to respond with indignation. Instead, he backed off.

"You're absolutely right, Special Agent Setliff. It was presumptuous of me and unfair to your agency. Frankly, I hoped that the Buckhalter matter would be settled so quickly that my being less than forthcoming wouldn't matter. You may not believe me, but I've been increasingly uncomfortable about not telling you."

She didn't believe him. "General, you called Ann for a reason."

"We spoke briefly."

"Fourteen minutes, General. The Gettysburg Address took three."

"Fourteen minutes? Funny, I don't remember it being that long. All right. Let's put it all on the table. The Wednesday before Ann was killed, Public Affairs called me. They had gotten a query from a reporter named Lowell Mapp about a remark I allegedly made during a staff meeting. I wanted to know what was going on at the paper. I thought Ann would know. She told me Charmaine Roundtree's lawsuit was about to become public. She also told me someone she wouldn't name had given her a tape incriminating me. I was surprised to hear about the tape, but I told Ann I knew the lawsuit couldn't be kept under wraps much longer. I told her Mapp had known about it for months. That he had stumbled across it purely by accident. I clearly remember Ann's stunned silence. Then she sputtered—only time I ever heard her do that. She asked me, if that was so, why Mapp had kept their editor in the dark. I told her I made a deal with Mapp. He would sit on what he knew, and I'd grease a few minor skids for him here on base. In the meantime, maybe Mrs. Roundtree would decide to retire. Or realize that the only ones that profit from lawsuits are lawyers."

Fran blinked. So, that's how Mapp got his invitation to the Capex.

"Ann went absolutely batshit. She called Mapp names I haven't heard since basic. Apparently, sitting on a news story because the person you're writing about wants you to is like making a separate peace with the enemy." Johnson chuckled wryly. "I'm not sure which of us was supposed to be the enemy. Ann was always divided in her loyalties. I was aware Mapp was out of line, of course. But his professional ethics weren't my problem. Then I said good-bye and hung up. End of conversation. I didn't see any reason to volunteer the details to you. I knew I had nothing to do with Ann falling off that pier." He looked up at her. "And I bet Lowell Mapp hasn't been forthcoming about our little quid pro quo either."

Her aggravation was interrupted by the general's son, who looked little-boy disheveled and not quite awake as he walked past them to his boat, waving perfunctorily. He probably didn't even recognize her. The general ordered the boy to finish policing the contents of the barrel, to which Wally nodded without looking back.

"I saw your son do a handstand on a canoe once," Fran said. "Down by Mainside. He's quite the athlete. An impressive gymnast."

The general snorted. "Gymnast? What the hell kind of sport is gymnastics? He could be a fine quarterback, with all that agility. He's a decent runner, too. I think he picked a sport where the guys wear tights just to jerk my chain. But hell, if he gets into college on a circus-monkey scholarship, I'll be happy." He watched his son with narrow, appraising eyes. "It's been hard on him. Losing his mother. I have to make allowances for that. And now, this sad business with Knightdale." He turned away from the river and gestured her toward the driveway. "My professional problems are minor right now, compared to my concern about my son's emotional state. And my concern for my chief of staff, of course."

When they reached her car, he opened the door for her.

"I promise you, Fran, I'm one of the good guys."

"Yes, sir," she said crisply. "Nobody wants to believe that more than
I do."

ooooo

But she entered Autumn Oval mentally picking at the new loose
threads.

So, the general had done some insider trading with Mapp. Had
Mapp's boss, editor George Griffin, known about it? Of course not.
The only one at the paper who gained by keeping the story on ice was
Mapp. Griffin's instinct would be to beat the competition to the story,
wouldn't it? Didn't newspapers get good-conduct medals for scooping
each other?

And what happened after Ann Buckhalter found out about the
deal? Did she tell Griffin? No. Mapp would have been fired. Did Ann
confront Mapp herself? Did Mapp then try to shut her up to save his
job?

She'd fill Rumley in on the details later. But she did take a minute to
leave him a message, sharing her suspicions about which slimy civilian
had pushed her into the New River.

THIRTY-SEVEN.

SATURDAY 1300

If she hadn't absent-mindedly turned on to Brewster Boulevard to head off-base, a route that took her by the entrance to the Naval Hospital, she would have missed him. And if there hadn't been a large red vehicle ahead of her when he turned left on Brewster, he'd probably have spotted her.

It was his profile—hatless, hair longer than Marine-regulation—that caught her attention. He looked strikingly like a young Dick Van Dyke, just as Owl Girl had described him. "Chim Chim Cher-ee," Commander Terry.

Fran recalled his saying it was unusual for him to work on Saturday, but here he was again, a long drive from his beach residence. Her curiosity was further piqued when he turned on to Lejeune Boulevard in the opposite direction from the one he'd take to go home. She followed his BMW as he crossed Marine Boulevard and turned into a complex of unremarkable townhouse-style offices. Terry then cut left on a service road running behind those offices.

Fran idled alongside two parked cars until she was sure Terry wouldn't emerge from the other end of the service road and see her. He didn't. She slowly tracked his presumed route. By the time she caught sight of his parked car, he had already gotten out and gone—where? He had parked near a cluster of three offices. She noted the numbers on the back doors and parked her car before walking around to the front of the cluster, where she could match the tavern-style business shingles with the door numbers.

Dr. Mark Mercer, D.D.S. Locked up tight.

Dr. Alicia Gracida, Pediatric Dentistry. Open for business, but an unlikely destination for Terry, unless of course Gracida was the latest addition to his tryst list.

The third office was at the far end of the cluster. No tavern shingle here, just neat gold letters on the door. Dr. Crawford Ellings Stallworth, Psychiatrist. Artificial light leaked around the closed blinds of the office's one window. Fran pressed her palms lightly against the door, sensing the vibrations of human activity inside.

Why would Terry be seeing a civilian psychiatrist? Maybe for the same reasons anybody went to a shrink. But if Commander Terry needed professional help, why not see one of his peers at the Naval Hospital? She walked back to her car and leaned against the door, arms folded. Should she hang around? She could get into trouble with her boss for following Terry without prior permission. It would be her second foray into loose-cannonism. She decided it was as good a time as any to read that yellowed, coffee-spattered *Navy Times* crammed under her passenger seat.

The commander walked out of Stallworth's office exactly sixty-two minutes later. He looked much younger—vulnerable, even—wearing civilian clothes. When he saw her, his shoulders drooped, then sharply jerked back. His expression was angry, but he kept his voice low.

"Are you looking for me on official business, Special Agent Setliff, or do you just feel a special need for psychiatric care today?"

"I was about to ask you the same question." She nodded toward Stallworth's door.

"Unless this is an official NCIS matter, the answer to that is none of your business."

"Ordinarily, yes. But if this is part of your regular Saturday routine, and you gave me the impression you don't have a Saturday routine, it might make me wonder."

He laughed softly. "There's nothing suspicious or unethical here. My seeing Dr. Stallworth is simply discretion. I'm dealing with my own personal crisis—unrelated, I emphasize, to Ann Buckhalter—and I want that aspect of my life kept outside the military bureaucracy." He pointed toward the opposite end of the complex. "There's a little pastry shop and tearoom down that way. Let's talk there."

They were two of only four people in the cubbyhole-sized shop. The other two were elderly women speaking nonstop, overlapping Korean, which made them unlikely eavesdroppers. Fran grabbed a bottled water from the upright cooler by the cash register, and Terry ordered a cup of coffee after they sat at a tiny corner table. *Bumping knees again*, Fran thought.

"Well?"

"I spent years studying analysis," he began. "An approach to treatment that gets about as much respect as snake oil these days. Less, since I believe snake venom is being tested as a treatment for panic disorder. Being a psychiatrist requires little more than the thirty seconds it takes to write a prescription. The patient's history is mostly meaningless. If one medication doesn't get rid of the symptoms, there's always another to try, and more in the works. Dr. Stallworth shares much of my disappointment in our profession. Talking to him bolsters me for the coming week's charade. It's that simple."

"But why the secrecy? Wouldn't another military doctor be more sympathetic to your situation?"

He shook his head. "Military doctors are promoted based on fitness reports, just like any other officers. How career-enhancing would it be if my superiors found out I feel like a fraud? If anybody understands how little privacy is connected to a military medical record, you do. Stallworth refuses to bill a colleague. But if he did bill me, you can bet I wouldn't make a claim for reimbursement through the military. I'd pay in cash, just like a drug deal. Now, there's an irony."

"Like the irony of Ann trying to protect her family's privacy from the same system?"

He looked at her in surprise. She could see him fitting the pegs into the right holes.

"I see. Deirdre—it must have been Deirdre—confided in you. Hell, Ann wasn't trying to protect anybody's privacy. She was protecting self-destructive delusions about a dead child."

That's your diagnosis, Fran thought. *But you also said your profession is a fraud.*

"I came across Deirdre in the Rascal Ridge bar last night."

This time, his surprise was mixed with dismay. "What?"

"She was about to be eaten by a really big, really bad wolf. In fact, she was the catalyst for a barroom brawl. I was able to get her out before anything irreparable happened."

"Thank God. Is she all right?"

"I think so. Matter of fact, I stayed with her at the Guest Lodge last night. Darned if I know why, but she had the urge to confide in me. She told me about what happened in the tree house when she was four. And I know what happened at the base stables."

He swiveled the handle of his coffee cup, gently sloshing the contents. "I hoped to keep Ann under control until Deirdre turned eighteen and went away to college. I might have succeeded if it wasn't for Deirdre's experience with that young Marine. Harrison, was it?"

"Harriman. What do you mean?"

"Ann panicked when she found out Harriman's lawyer planned to subpoena Deirdre's psychiatric records if he was charged with rape. Her participation in my study, as a depressed juvenile dependent, is included in that record. I was as appalled as Ann. I'm pretty naive myself about military legal issues, but it's unthinkable that a civilian psychiatrist could be required to turn over a patient's treatment record. But in this instance, the lawyer claimed, Deirdre's medical record was government property needed to defend a Marine accused of rape. It was possible a military judge might open that door." He shrugged. "I was in no position to stop Ann from stealing Deirdre's file."

"Why?"

"I was told not to push Ann too far."

"By whom? Gary Buckhalter?"

Terry laughed bitterly. "Gary Buckhalter, Harriman's lawyer, Ann. They ended up being the least of my problem."

"Please, Commander, no more witty wordplay. Who ended up being the most of your problem?"

"The commanding general."

"General Johnson? What did he care? Is Harriman's father a four-star or something?"

Terry shook his head. "Ann talked to the general a couple of weeks before she died. She asked him to twist my arm. The general then summoned me to his office and told me to do whatever it took to placate Ann. I was stunned. I couldn't believe he'd interfere in a medical matter. And frankly, I was scared. If Ann told General Johnson about our affair, he had the ammunition to kill my career, in or out of the military."

"But why was General Johnson interested in this mess?"

"The study. Ann wanted Deirdre's part in it destroyed. Apparently, there was something in it the general wanted buried, too. If the study became part of a court-martial transcript, it would in effect be public record."

The study. The badass psycho-penny that kept turning up.

"Ann had a good idea what was in the study. She even proofread parts of it that didn't pertain to Deirdre. She'd worked as a medical transcriptionist before she took up journalism. And remember, before she found out Deirdre's tree-house experience was included, she was supportive of the study. I think she wanted to be able to blame Deirdre's problems on the military lifestyle instead of her own parenting. Anyway, she must have remembered reading something in the study she could use as leverage with Johnson."

He smashed one of the shop's dainty complimentary cookies with his thumb. "When Ann brought Deirdre to my office for the last time before her death, I intentionally left two partial files that had Deirdre's name on them in plain view on my desk. Decoys, you could call them. Of course, Ann took them. I had transcribed the original material on to compact disks long ago, so it was no great loss to me. It wouldn't have taken her long to realize she'd been . . . tricked. I expect that's why she called me the day she died, to vent her rage or demand the rest."

"But you didn't have to worry about that after Ann drowned."

He wearily massaged his eyebrows. "I had nothing to do with that."

"May I see the study?" Fran was careful not to frame her request as part of any official inquiry.

"Christ, can't you let it go? I doubt you could make heads or tails of it anyway. It's organized by the developmental age of the patients, and much of it is medical shorthand."

"Could I see just the parts Ann saw, then, that she proofread?"

He shrugged and leaned back heavily, bumping the wall. "If that's what it takes. I've got a set of the CDs in the trunk of my car. I no longer leave anything related to the study in my office. No patient is identified by name or date of birth, although I doubt a layman would be able to make much of it."

Now that she had a promise of the CD portfolio, she was ready to turn the final screw. A bluff based on Owl Girl.

"Why did you lie to me about going by the B.O.Q. the night Ann died?"

"Did I? Are you sure?" He responded so smoothly, he must have foreseen having to answer that question. "Are your recollections, recorded only after the interview, absolutely accurate? Was I under oath, or had I been notified I was making an official statement?"

"Let's skip the pissing match, shall we? You were seen that night at the B.O.Q. by a witness with an amazing memory for detail. Even noted how good looking you are. And that you were in uniform."

He flinched but then came up with an unexpected counterpunch. "If you want to badger someone who's been less than honest about their whereabouts that night, why don't you start at a much higher pay grade than mine? I did stop by to see Ann, yes. I was concerned about her emotional state when she called. But I didn't get any closer than the parking lot, as your witness with an eye for detail can confirm. I saw Ann walking onto that pier. And I saw someone join her. A man. He had a dog with him. I saw them sit at the end of the pier, shoulder to shoulder, almost cheek to cheek. As soon as I saw she was ... occupied, I left. They didn't see me, and I saw no reason to tell you I'd been there. I figured that, sooner or later, you trained professionals would figure out why and how Ann got into the river."

As soon as he said "dog," Fran's mouth went dry. "Um, you're positive of that man's identity?"

"Of course. It was the commanding general. Brigadier General Amesly Johnson. I don't remember the dog's name"—he gave her a slow, bitter smile—"but I expect he'd tell you."

ooooo

They did not walk back to the parking lot together. She intentionally let him outpace her, so his car was gone by the time she reached hers. Before getting in, she paused to finish off her water and toss the plastic bottle into a brightly painted oil drum labeled "Recycling."

She lingered near it, waiting for the niggling thought at the back of her mind to shuffle forward. Oil drum. Burned debris dumped into the New River. Now, why would a general who lectured his staff about dumping, a general with a cleverly designed compost heap in his backyard, tell his son to dump a barrel of burned junk into the river?

She must be crazy as a shithouse mouse even to think of such a thing. It was late Saturday afternoon at the end of an exhausting week, and she was seriously considering playing ninja. Fran was drawn back toward the senior officers' housing area like a moth that had learned nothing from being singed. Singed like whatever was in that damn barrel. She needed something concrete to place Johnson with Ann on that pier. Otherwise, it would be too easy for the general to claim Terry was mistaken. Or that Terry had his own motives for deflecting suspicion. The fact that Terry's initial statement hadn't mentioned seeing the general, that he had his own unsavory relationship with Ann, would ravage his credibility. Fran needed to take a look at that barrel. If it was still at the river's edge—which was a public area providing access to the waterway—she'd look like a fool if spotted. But she could argue that she was not actually trespassing.

Fran pulled into the small parking area next to the riverside tennis courts less than a mile from the general's quarters. She was prepared to sacrifice another suit and more pantyhose, but not her shoes. And she didn't dare shred the soles of her feet by navigating the rocky riverbank with bare feet. A pair of ratty Keds jammed under her passenger seat solved the one problem that could have deterred the moth from the flame. She slipped them on, locked her car, and clambered down the riverbank. Invisible to those at street level, she headed in the direction of Autumn Oval. It was alternately easy and rough going. In a few spots, she had to hold on to tree roots springing from the bank and walk sideways like a crab. A couple of boaters sped by mid-river but paid her no notice.

She knew she had reached senior officers' houses when the river-bank stopped dropping directly into the river and instead started dropping onto a pebble-strewn mini-beach. She rehearsed an explanation for her muddied, solitary presence—she was searching for a designer windbreaker accidentally tossed from a boat—should anyone question her. But she saw no one. It was so quiet, she could hear a muffled loudspeaker from the Naval Air Station across the inlet.

Fran inwardly cheered when she first glimpsed the barrel, then groaned when she got closer and saw its altered position and condition. Instead of being on its side, it now stood upright at the water's edge. The intriguing sludge-like trail she'd noticed before had been washed away and the barrel's interior swabbed. Only a viscous black layer coated the bottom of the barrel to the depth of maybe a quarter-inch.

Embarrassed by her thwarted recklessness, she decided she could at least take a sludge sample as a souvenir. There had to be some reason the mess was so meticulously disposed of and the barrel cleaned in such an environmentally unfriendly way. Maybe Fran was just clinging to an outside chance that she wasn't really as crazy as a shithouse mouse.

She took a Tylenol bottle from her purse and emptied its contents into her change purse. Improvised sample bottle in hand, she looked around for a long stick. The one she settled on had the proper diameter and sturdiness but required her to stretch most of her arm into the barrel in order to scrape the bottom. No matter. Her suit jacket was unsalvageable by then anyway. She dipped out a dollop of sludge and transferred it to the empty bottle. Whatever was in the glop had a peculiar smell reminiscent of rain boots left on a heating grate. She then ran the stick around the thick buildup on the bottom seam and brought up a thimbleful of the stuff. When she scraped it against the rim of the Tylenol bottle, something small but solid fell loose and dropped at her feet. *Ping!* A small, black, squarish piece of metal. She took a tissue from her purse and picked it up, rubbing it gently between her thumb and forefinger. The black soot flaked away, revealing tiny golden streaks.

It looked like a belt buckle for Barbie. What was it? The buckle from a watchband? Didn't those have a slot for the pin?

She froze when she realized what it was. The buckle from a shoe. More precisely, the buckle from a child's shoe, or the ankle strap of a woman's shoe. A single short strand of heavy thread, unidentifiable in color, clung to the miniscule prong. She struck her head with her sooty fist. *Think, Fran!* The shoes Ann Buckhalter wore. Did the ankle straps have buckles or elastic? Was that sludge the remains of Ann's missing shoe? The implications were enormous. If Commander Terry's statement put the general with Ann the night she drowned, this buckle might place him with her at the time she went into the water and lost that shoe. But how did it get here? And why would anyone hang on to it, then try to destroy it?

Fran realized that removing the buckle from the area could jeopardize its ever being used as evidence. She had no warrant to search that barrel, the general's personal property. Did she have the right to take possession of the buckle at all? She needed time to think. She needed to know what was in Deirdre's medical record that might have given Ann Buckhalter a hold over the general. So far, it didn't make sense. Every bit of dirt Ann might have held over the general's head was about to become public knowledge anyway. Something else was at play here.

Detecting a flicker of motion out of the corner of her eye, she was horrified to see a green canoe approaching from downriver, propelled by an electric motor. If it was Wally Johnson, he'd be coming her way and would see her within a couple of minutes.

She frantically duck-walked to a skimpy shrub growing out of the bank and stayed low behind it as she rummaged for a pen in her shoulder bag. She used the pen to pry a rock partially out of its perpendicular resting place, dropped the buckle behind the rock, and replaced it as undetectably as she could. Mangling a brand-new tube of lipstick, she made a red slash on a projecting tree root several feet directly below the rock.

Fran decided she'd better not leave the way she'd come. Better to gamble on the general and his immediate neighbor not being home than to gamble on Wally Johnson not recognizing her a second time.

She scrambled up the riverbank and raced between the two yards to the street, where she slowed to a normal, if breathless, pace. Except for Bilbo and a vigilant toy poodle, she walked out of the senior officers' housing area unnoticed, as far as she could tell. But once beyond it, she returned to the riverbank to finish picking her way back to her car. She still preferred not to be seen. She now looked worse than when she'd dragged herself out of the river at Gottschalk Marina. If an MP spotted her and word got back to Boyette, he'd put her on involuntary medical leave for sure.

THIRTY-EIGHT.

SUNDAY

The commander was right. The study was hard for a rube layman to follow. Fran had to keep referring to a medical terminology website. And the amount of information about every anonymous child was numbing. Did it really matter whether subject MC13 used a latex or silicone pacifier?

Unless she pursued a medical degree and took statistics courses, she'd never be able to wade through it. She thought she'd heard of a couple of the juveniles because either they or their parents had been part of an NCIS investigation, but they all predated her joining the agency. Her only *eureka!* moment was realizing Ann Buckhalter might have had the same reaction and ripped the paper copy Terry had given her into shreds in frustrated rage, flinging the pieces into the water. That would explain why Ann hadn't bothered to take the white plastic bag out on the pier. She no longer had any desire to protect what had been inside.

Fran decided she had no option but to call General Johnson's bluff, just as she had Terry's. The move would either lead her closer to the truth or get her fired. She and Lowell Mapp might end up mulling over the same help-wanted ads.

Johnson returned her call almost immediately. Fran told him she had spoken to Commander Terry and wanted to clarify a few final points with the general before deciding whether or not to pass on what she'd learned to Boyette. Fran estimated a fifty-fifty chance that Johnson would cut her off, call Boyette, and demand to know what the hell she was up to. The fact that he didn't confirmed her suspicion that Terry was right. Instead, the general asked Fran to come by his quarters late the next afternoon for a tête-à-tête.

ooooo

Even Bilbo seemed annoyed to see her two days in a row. The general ordered him to stop barking. And his first words to Fran were just as sharp.

"I thought this case was closed, Setliff." No ponderous thoughts to jump-start this visit.

He led her into the sunken family room, where he positioned himself against the white-brick fireplace and tinkered impatiently with a pipe rack. The room was dimly lit, accentuating the popping sparks and glowing embers of the small wood fire. His face was illuminated from below, exaggerating his scowl. Fran had the odd sensation that she was closeted with a jack-o'-lantern.

"And I thought we'd agreed I am not here officially," she said tartly. "You're right, General. On Boyette's orders, I've already told the Buckhalters. Accidental death. But this case is too much like one of those tricks where the magician keeps pulling out one scarf after another until you think the darn things are never going to stop."

Johnson flicked the air in annoyance. "Spare me your analogies. What did Terry tell you?"

"I've seen his study on depressed dependents." This was true, in the literal sense. "I have a good idea what Ann used for leverage against both of you. But I'm hoping you'll give me your version, and not make me use my imagination to fill in the blanks."

He shoved the pipe rack back against the mantelpiece. "I see. Do you mind if I let Bilbo in?"

She didn't. She was in civilian clothes. No matter if a little black Lab smell rubbed off on her.

Bilbo skittered in through the French doors, rump wriggling. He sniffed Fran enthusiastically, then, at the snap of Johnson's fingers, lay down at his owner's feet. Bilbo's was the only smiling face in the room.

"I've decided to retire, Setliff. Lately, I feel like there's a neon sign flashing 'This way out' over my head. The lawsuit. Ann's death. Bob Knightdale." He paused. "People have the idea it gets easier once you reach my rank. That's bullshit. It gets tougher. There's no room for error. No time to regroup if something goes wrong."

He sat. Fran did, too, although he didn't invite her to. A moment's silence, then he tapped his fingers idly against his forehead as he gazed into the fire.

"There was no way I could have foreseen what would happen in the Hoyt matter."

The Hoyt matter? It rang such a faint bell, she had no idea what he was getting at. But apparently, he thought she did. Fran gave him a look she hoped conveyed skepticism. How *could* he not have known what would happen? Whatever that was.

"But once Ann read about it—in that grab-for-glory Commander Terry calls his 'study'—she realized the decisions I made in the Hoyt case could look like an early indication of sexual bias. The survivors' families might even hit the Navy with another lawsuit. Lawsuits seem to be *my* scarf trick, Setliff."

Hoyt, Hoyt. Fran took a few whacks at her mental piñata. Where had she heard that name?

It came to her after she raced through the alphabet, tacking initials on to the name. N, O, P, Q, R. *Clang, clang!* R. J. Hoyt, ex-Marine. Hoyt had walked into his ex-wife's beauty salon while she was sweeping up a pile of hair and shot her in the head. While he was at it, he also shot and killed a customer and a FedEx delivery man. But what did a medical study about juvenile depression have to do with Hoyt's rampage?

Fran took a shot in the dark. "Hoyt's kid." She couldn't remember if the Hoyts even had a kid, but she spoke the words with knowing solemnity. And hit the bull's-eye.

Johnson smiled grimly. "I didn't know anything about that goddamn study until Ann came by my quarters a month ago. She had already called me once that week, in a near panic because she had heard some lawyer might subpoena her daughter's psychiatric records. Ann was coming unglued. I was able to calm her, but I knew it was temporary."

Ann had pressured Johnson to pressure Terry. It reminded Fran of a military Murphy's Law: If the enemy is in range, so are you.

"Ann knew Charmaine Roundtree had filed a sexual discrimination suit against me. Commander Terry's study gave Ann a weapon to threaten me with. The Hoyt boy's statements seemed to bolster Roundtree's claim that I'm some kind of woman hater. Terry never, never should have let Ann see that study. And he should have done a better job disguising the identities of his guinea pigs."

Fran was still 70 percent in the dark. "At what point exactly did the Hoyt child enter the picture?"

"Terry got his hooks in him as soon as Family Services sent Jimmy Hoyt to the psych clinic for counseling. Dr. Freud thought he'd found the perfect example of a dysfunctional military family. The boy told Commander Terry he was afraid his father was going to hurt his mother. Hoyt had written his wife from the Philippines, where he was doing an unaccompanied tour. He accused his wife of cheating on him. He wrote her what he'd do to her when he got home. I admit, some of it was pretty disturbing.

"The wife taught a step-aerobics class at the main gym. It drove Hoyt nuts thinking about her standing in front of male troops dressed in that tight, skimpy stuff women work out in nowadays. I never knew whether she really was unfaithful. It didn't matter. Depressed child in counseling. Father overseas. Perfect lab rat for Commander Terry.

"Hoyt was in my battalion. The wife complained about the threats, and I ended up reviewing the matter. I decided Hoyt was salvageable. I recommended anger management classes, which he attended like clockwork. That seemed sufficient. He could hardly hurt the woman from eight thousand miles away. He was due for discharge at the end of that tour. He was doing his job. Some men, their imaginations run wild when they're away from their wives. When they get back, they work things out.

"I was as stunned as anybody when, three years later, I heard Hoyt had been arrested in San Antonio for killing three people. By then, he and the wife had been divorced more than a year. Of course, I felt sorry for the victims. I hate it when a son of a bitch like Hoyt does something that reflects badly on the Corps. But I never felt a twinge of guilt personally. Why should I?

"The last phone conversation I had with Ann Buckhalter, she asked what I'd done about Terry, Harriman, base legal—her whole pile of personal shit. I told her the Harriman case would probably be put on hold until after the holidays, and that I hadn't gotten in touch with Terry. She demanded I talk to Terry immediately. I told her I would."

Fran tried to imagine Johnson taking orders from Ann Buckhalter. She couldn't.

"And did you?"

"Yes. I called Commander Terry, although I didn't know him from Adam. I told him it would be wise for everybody if he placated Ann however he could. That was my first and only conversation with the good doctor."

A regular daisy chain of butt-covering.

"I have no idea why she went out on the pier that night, but I'm satisfied she was not the target of violence. Certainly, her death was as shocking and unexpected to me as Bob's . . . accident." He glanced at the fire, his eyes raked by reflected sparks. Then he stood. "Well, Special Agent Setliff, have I satisfied your curiosity enough to get us through New Year's?"

Not by a long shot.

"I have reason to believe you were the last person to see Ann Buck-halter alive. There's a witness, as well as physical evidence that you were on that pier with her."

His response was delayed by the thump of an electronically controlled garage door opening beyond the wall to their left, followed by one of the pipes on the mantel clattering to the brick hearth as a result of the vibrations. Bilbo reacted with a tail wag and a woof.

Johnson retrieved the pipe and looked at her coldly. "You're bluffing."

"You had a dog with you, the witness says."

A subtle but distinct stiffening of Johnson's shoulders showed she'd struck a nerve. He glowered at her, unblinking, for one, two, three seconds, then walked to the room's one window. Whatever was beyond was obscured by light from the fire and a floor lamp reflecting off the glass.

"It's not impossible someone saw me walking Bilbo that night. I certainly wasn't trying to avoid being seen. I think I was even wearing a white sweater. Hardly dressed for anything incognito. That would be a wasted effort with a dog anyway, wouldn't it? I had no idea Ann was at the B.O.Q. If I did, I'd have chosen another route, believe me. I didn't notice her sitting at the end of the pier until she'd already seen me. I approached the area only because Bilbo ran ahead of me in that direction. I had his leash but hadn't attached it to his collar. I called him back, and Ann must have recognized my voice.

" 'Is that you, General?' she said. I had enough on my plate without another helping of Ann Buckhalter's melodrama. Nonetheless, I
had no choice but to keep heading toward her because Bilbo had run
out onto the pier. 'Don't worry,' Ann said. 'I'm not in the mood to twist
anybody's arm tonight.' Then, in that semi-flirtatious tone women affect
when they've had too much to drink, she said, 'But I wouldn't mind a
little unarmed company.'

"Ridiculous woman! She tried to threaten and browbeat me, and
now she was flirting? I thought it was wiser not to remind her she had
family members waiting at home to 'keep her company.' My problem
was that Bilbo didn't come when I called him because she was petting
him, hugging his neck. I went out on the pier, intending only to put on
his leash and leave. But Ann asked me to sit. I was wary but didn't want
to antagonize her, so I sat. That's all there was to it. I hardly glanced at
her. Couldn't even tell you what she was wearing. I think we exchanged
comments about the weather, our Christmas shopping. Oh, yes, she
made some joke about the MP with the worst breath always getting to
be the Toys for Tots Santa. I could tell she'd had a few drinks, sure, but
she wasn't what I'd describe as drunk. I lingered just long enough to put
on Bilbo's leash and not appear to be anxious to escape, which I was.
The whole encounter took ten minutes. Less, maybe."

He showed Fran upturned palms, the classic gesture of innocence.
"I swear to God, when I left her, she was as much alive as you are right
now."

He was convincing, she had to give him that. But she herself had
on occasion been convincing while being less than completely honest.
She'd take one more shot.

"Sounds reasonable. Except for one thing."

He frowned, more in exasperation than anger. "And what would
that be?"

"The shoe."

He looked at her in genuine—or amazingly convincing—bafflement. "What shoe?"

"Ann's shoe."

"What the fuck are you talking about?" Suddenly, his face relaxed into a half-smile that expanded into a grin. "Oh, I get it. This has all been a fishing expedition. You'd come over here tonight, throw out a few lines, and see if I'd bite. Well, okay, you're one for two. I admit it. You got me on the first one. The unnamed witness. Good work. What's next? Invisible ink? A secret door?"

Fran experienced a horrifying epiphany. He really didn't know anything about the shoe. A kind of sickening mortification rose from her innards and reddened her face. Maybe that hadn't been a buckle from Ann's shoe at all, but something left over from a piece of boating gear. An old life vest, maybe. They had buckles, didn't they? Jesus. She'd sacrificed her best Anne Klein suit in a muddy, slimy snipe hunt. What the hell had she been thinking?

He saw her waver. Gauged how unsure she was. Her rising embarrassment.

"I suggest we both deep-six tonight's conversation and continue whatever's left of our lackluster careers." Then, with a note of self-pity: "I expect Boyette will have to deal with your lack of professionalism at some point, but I probably won't be around to witness it. I'll be in a courtroom somewhere"—he gave a raw, bitter laugh—"apologizing for thirty years of doing my damnedest to serve the Marine Corps."

She didn't say a word as he opened the patio door for her and silently directed her outside and to the left, where a floodlight illuminated the end of the curved driveway. Adding to the brightness was the fluorescent light pouring from the now-open garage door.

Fran was walking past the garage, squinting in response to the stark illumination, when she heard a whirring sound and felt a sharp smack against her garage-side shoulder. It happened so fast, she thought for a moment she was under aerial attack. She looked down at her feet, where whatever struck her had dropped onto the cement floor of the garage. One edge of it had her by the sleeve.

"Geez, I'm sorry, ma'am. I didn't hear you come around the corner."

Wally Johnson jerked earphones off his head and scrambled forward to gather up the circular shrimp net he'd cast from the enclosed end of the garage. Fran giggled in nervous relief. Practicing his shrimping technique to a grunge beat, no doubt.

"You okay?"

He stopped, bent over, and peered up at her anxiously. She was clutching her chest, but the mock heart attack was purely for comic relief.

"I'm fine. But hold on a sec." She smiled and raised her free hand. "You've caught one of my . . ."

She reached down to free the section of net that had snagged a button on her jacket cuff. Then she froze, net clasped in unmoving fingers, and blinked hard over her contacts to make sure she was seeing what she thought she was seeing. Nearly invisible next to the dull gray metal of one of the net's small, kidney-bean-sized weights, its thin wire hooked firmly into the net's nylon strands, was a silver earring. A sterling silver earring with a small but distinctive marcasite dangle. She'd seen only enlarged photos of its mate, so she couldn't be absolutely sure. And yet she was. She gently worked it loose and held it up as she turned bewildered eyes on Wally Johnson.

"This belonged to Ann Buckhalter. How did it get in your net?"

A shiver ran down her neck when she saw him shrink back into the interior of the garage, dragging the net with him in clenched fists. His eyes darted frantically from wall to wall, seeking an exit. The earring was in the boy's net because he'd been there when Ann Buckhalter lost it.

Suddenly, he fixed on something behind her. She whirled around to see the general standing just beyond the spillover light from the garage.

"No invisible ink, General," she said. "No secret doors. Just a dead woman's earring."

He stepped into the light with a deep intake of breath, coming within feet of Fran but not looking at her. He was staring at the cowering boy with disdain and pity.

"Don't say anything!" he snapped. "Not a word."

His father's words acted on the son like the blast of a water cannon. He jerked upright, shaking with fury.

"No more fuckin' orders, General! None of this would have happened if you hadn't treated Mom like garbage."

A stunned silence, then a hiss of outrage in response: "You little fool. You don't know what you're talking about."

"How many others besides that Buckhalter woman were you fucking while Mom was dying?"

"For Christ's sake, Wally, shut up! I was never unfaithful to your mother. Never. Especially not with a screwball like Ann Buckhalter. And it wasn't from lack of opportunity, let me assure you. Women not much older than you, privates up to—and including—a full-bird colonel. I've had offers most men wouldn't have turned down. Do you hear me? I never cheated on your mother."

The boy gave his father a look that twisted Fran's heart. His voice quavered as he spoke.

"You took her for granted, Dad." He glanced around the garage. "Like . . . your fucking golf clubs. Your pipe collection. Your car." Long pent-up resentment stiffened his spine. "You think you deserve some kind of medal for not driving somebody else's car?"

"How dare you blame this mess on me? That earring"—Johnson shook his finger at the object in Fran's upraised hand—"ended up in your net because you bought dope that night. It had nothing to do with how I did or didn't treat your mother."

Fran was now completely lost. Dope? Cheating? This thing was going off the rails faster than the wreck of the Old 97.

"You both were on the pier that night?"

"Lady, you'd never—"

"Shut up, Wally. You're talking to a criminal investigator."

"What the fuck do I care?" The boy chuckled uncontrollably. "All I did was try to drown my father. You gonna press charges, Dad?" His near-hysterical state made his voice break. He laughed again.

Johnson tacked toward the rear of the garage, trying to corral his son into a corner. But the boy evaded his father's grasp, ducking and twisting, shouting to Fran around his father.

"I paddled up to the O Club, where I know a guy who sells weed."

The spacey busboy, Fran thought.

"I can paddle so quiet, nobody knows I'm there. I was turning around to come home when I heard my dad call Bilbo. I stood in the boat and watched him follow Bilbo to the end of the pier and sit by some woman. They didn't see me or hear me glide up underneath the pier. At first, I was scared he'd catch me with the shit—you know, the grass. But I didn't want to ditch it unless I had to. Then I heard the way she was talking to him and started thinking how they seemed to know each other really well, and how she had this sexy voice."

The general abandoned his pursuit and collapsed on a lawn chair. He stared at the ceiling as Wally bobbed in front of him, talking in crazed elation.

"I kept thinking about the way he talked to Mom, like she was some private that cleaned out the head, and how she always made excuses for him. I just wanted to do something to hurt him. Like he'd hurt us." Abruptly, he squatted on the cement floor, simulating his posture in the canoe. "I held on to a piling and quietly pulled the bow out from under the pier, just far enough so I could stand. I looped up my net like I've done a million times and threw it out toward him. I wanted to scare the holy shit out of him. I don't know what happened," he mused, poised with arms positioned to one side, the follow-through to an invisible thrown net.

"You missed," Fran suggested.

"No!" He glared at her, offended. "I didn't know he'd move. My dad must have heard something, and he leaned forward to look under the pier just when I let the net fly. At the same time, the woman must have leaned back, I don't know why. My net, it . . ." He swallowed hard. "It caught her instead of him. She made this funny little squeak but didn't yell or anything. She grabbed at the net covering her face, and I started pulling up on the casting rope to get it back, and she fell into the water."

That explained the crosshatch marks on Ann's face. Rope—or net—burns.

"My dad and I jumped into the water and tried to get the net off her. She was thrashing and kicking, but we managed to do it. Her face came up above the water next to me, and she gasped. Then my dad came up between her and me. He shoved me away from the pier and told me to take the net and get in my boat and paddle the hell away from there as fast as I could. I was so scared. I had to turn the boat around to get clear of the pier. The water was low, and I tried to push off from the pilings with the paddle, but it was dark, and I think I hit her. . . . I kept hitting something, but finally I got out into the current."

And there was the final piece of the puzzle: the wounds to the back of Ann's head. The blunt instrument that caused her injuries? A canoe paddle.

"My dad swam out toward me and told me to stop paddling and use the electric motor. I steered us home, with him in the water hanging on at the stern and Bilbo running alongside on the bank. It didn't take us more than ten, fifteen minutes to get there."

Fran stared at the general, stupefied. "You just left Ann?"

"No, no! It wasn't like that!" Johnson struggled to his feet from the depths of the chair. "I saw her surface a couple times and heard her gasp for air. I swear she was alive and conscious when we left. I admit, my first thought was to get Wally out of there before she recognized him. I don't think she even realized what happened. She must have panicked or become disoriented when her hair got caught"—he sputtered—"in that goddamn crab trap. I was as stunned to hear about the trap as anyone. I had no idea, I swear. I guess the more she struggled, the more she entangled herself."

The expression he gave Fran was a plea for understanding she couldn't muster.

"She was within arm's reach of a pier piling," he insisted. "My God, a couple of feet closer to the riverbank and she could have waded out."

"She'd been drinking. She was hit on the head. It was dark," Fran said matter-of-factly.

He nodded. "Yes."

A moment later, he whipped his head around to look at his son, anger rekindled. "I didn't find out about the marijuana until we pulled the canoe out of the water. He'd forgotten to dump it." The general spoke to her but continued to look at his son. "I still can't believe he was using marijuana and I had no idea."

Fran shook her head in amazement. "So, using weed is unthinkable, but not checking on an intoxicated woman your son forced into the river doesn't keep you awake at night?"

"You've got it wrong. I did return to check on Ann, in my car. I circled the B.O.Q. parking lot. No, I did not get out. But the pier was empty, the water still. Everything was perfectly quiet. The lights in Ann's suite were on. I assumed she'd gotten herself out of the river and returned to her room. I fully expected an enraged phone call from her, if not that night, the next morning."

She directed her next question to the boy. "When you realized you had one of her shoes in your net, why didn't you just dump it in the river?"

He gave her that "Duh!" look teenagers favor when confronting idiots. "I didn't find it until the next day. If I'd thrown it in the river anywhere near our quarters, there was a chance it would come ashore somewhere between here and the B.O.Q. It would be obvious it was moved on purpose, wouldn't it? If it was found upstream of where she drowned? I thought about taking it downstream of the 'Q' in my canoe, but that was risky, too. What if someone saw me before I got rid of it? Anyway, it floated like a cork. I decided the easiest thing was to burn it."

"And your father didn't object to this plan?"

"My dad didn't know anything about the shoe. It was dark when we got back that night. I crammed the net up under the deck plates. The first thing on Dad's mind was for me to get rid of everything in the house that was connected to weed. I didn't have much. That's the truth. A clip. A pipe. The baggie I bought that night. He told me to burn all that the next morning. The clothes I'd worn, too. And the paddle. I used his band saw to cut it up first. I burned all that stuff along with leaves from the compost—and threw in the shoe, too, when I found it. That really freaked me out. I kept that fire going until nothing was left, as far as I could tell. Then I dumped the whole burned mess in the river and washed out the barrel. I didn't know about any earring."

Six eyes were drawn to the small, glittery item Fran still pinched between the thumb and forefinger of her left hand. She reached across her body with her other hand to unzip her purse. She'd tuck the earring into a small interior pocket and decide what to do with it tomorrow. She would have delivered a pithy parting line to father and son, but frankly, she was out of pith. Better to leave quietly.

Wally had been in a loose-limbed teenage crouch for so long, he took Fran by surprise when he sprang up, snatched the earring out of her fingers, and swooped past her toward the river. She did her best to pursue, but holy shit, the general was right: The boy had speed. And he knew the terrain. She stumbled over unfamiliar brickwork she could barely see.

He took the steps to the pier in one leap and the pier itself in three giant strides, hitting the canoe with enough force to set it in motion even before he unhitched the line and grabbed the paddle. Fran flashed to the image of a Polynesian war canoe zipping by in a blur.

"Wally, stop!" she yelled, windmilling ridiculously at the edge of the pier to keep from taking a second unintentional tumble into the New River.

But the boy didn't even glance over his shoulder as he headed straight to the center of the channel, almost vanishing into the glare of the setting sun, paddling so ably he made no visible splash. Between his paddling skill and the current, that earring would be downstream in minutes. It would end up exactly where it could be expected to end up had it disappeared into the water next to the B.O.Q. Not that it would ever be discovered. Fran certainly had no intention of demanding a pointless dredging of the New River for a sterling-silver trinket that would probably be declared inadmissible as evidence anyway.

ooooo

Had there even been a definable crime? Simple assault? Negligent manslaughter? Maritime hit-and-run? The cannabis, she supposed. Fran had worked her way through so many questionable legal and ethical strands with this case, she felt like she'd spent two weeks weaving the world's biggest, ugliest potholder.

She thought the general, peering fixedly into the dusk after his son, was oblivious to her resigned movement toward her car until she felt his arm shoot across her midsection, blocking her with nearly enough force to double her over. But he still did not look at her as he spoke.

"He doesn't know it yet, but I've arranged for him to be admitted to a residential school that specializes in teenagers who . . . act impulsively and don't make healthy decisions. I don't want you to think I expect all this just to go away."

"Will anybody treating him be aware that one of his unhealthy impulses led to a woman's death?"

The general actually flinched. Then smiled bitterly. "I won't be surprised if he tells them himself, like he did you." When he finally turned his eyes to hers, he looked old. "But if not, I will. I won't hobble his healing with any half-truths."

She drove away wondering if—and to whom—she would ever confide the truth about Ann Buckhalter's death. She might have to sleep on this one long enough for her pillow to fossilize. She just hoped wherever Wally Johnson ended up, he'd have access to a canoe. Supervised access.

THIRTY-NINE.

TUESDAY

Things were looking up. Knightdale was hanging on, Boyette was back, and Fran had an alligator taking up most of her cubicle.

The tipoff to the origin of the cheapo pool toy was an attached sticky note written in Rumley's back-slant scrawl: "My coworker went to Marston Pavilion, but all I got was this Effin' Alligator."

Rumley himself wasn't there. He'd probably headed home after the Capex. The whole field office was unoccupied, in fact, except for herself and Boyette, who was ranting endearingly on the telephone from behind his closed door.

She kissed the alligator's rakish vinyl smile and scrubbed her cheek against its belly until static electricity made her hair crackle. A few things to gather up and shut down, then girl and gator would slip out to claim an afternoon of preapproved comp time.

Another uplifting indicator: Maldonado was leaning against Fran's car door when she reached the parking lot. The Miata, topless and tempting, was two spaces down.

"New interrogation tool?" he asked.

"Yep. Standard-issue replacement for rubber hoses."

"Hop in." He jerked his chin toward the ragtop. "If we time it right, we might see something that's sure to make your day."

"Can I bring my alligator?"

"I normally draw the line at inflatable companionship, but as a personal favor, sure."

Her first clue something official was afoot was the MP cruiser that pulled out behind them on Seth Williams Boulevard and stuck with them. Her second clue was when Vic turned into the B.O.Q. riverside parking area immediately beyond where the cruiser had just parked in a discreet side space at the O Club entrance. The giveaway, though, was the black sedan Fran recognized as an unmarked NCIS vehicle.

"What's going on, Vic?"

He said nothing but gestured for her to get out and follow him down a narrow path leading to the rear of the unit where Ann Buckhalter had spent her final evening. There, he positioned Fran and himself under a porch overhang. He faced her, arms crossed, as though they were engrossed in conversation and paying no attention to the tall man in a blue suit accompanying a slump-shouldered youth through the O Club's empty back patio and toward the parking lot where the cruiser and unmarked sedan waited.

It was such a subtle collar that if Fran hadn't recognized both Rumley and the pimple-faced busboy and instinctively looked for the flex-cuffs, she might have assumed the agent's arm—casually draped over the teen's back, obscuring the restraints—was friendly. The busboy, ashen-faced, dragged his feet.

"NCIS questioned the suspect yesterday in his home," Maldonado told her. "He was so eager to ingratiate himself, he offered investigators a joint."

Fran was puzzled. She didn't take any pleasure in the kid's coming misery. "This isn't exactly the thrill I was expecting, Vic."

"Only the warmup act, my dear. After Rumley puts this one in a holding tank, the next warrant will be executed at—"

Click. "The *Daily Observer.*"

"Yes, indeed. One Lowell Raymond Mapp is to be charged with the trafficking of illegal drugs on federal property."

"Okay," she admitted, "picturing that does give me a tingle. But be prepared. He's going to claim he was working on an investigative story, undercover."

"A story his boss didn't assign and JPOA didn't clear? Besides, our suspect here may have flunked math, but he kept a spiral notebook full of laughably coded but detailed records that would make Ernst & Young proud. Know why Mapp was at Marston Pavilion that night? Getting his supply of weekend weed, according to the busboy. He says he and Mapp did some dealing pretty regularly. And on nights when too many people were at the club, they transacted business at Marston. My guess is, you showed up at a bad moment that evening, and Mapp took the opportunity to vent his annoyance at you for interfering with business."

Maldonado didn't seem to notice how her smile drooped when she realized it probably wouldn't take long for the busboy or Mapp to bring up Wally Johnson's name. She hoped Wally's exit from base into a mental-health facility might preempt any criminal charges, which would likely lead to rehab anyway.

"Thanks, Vic, but I've had enough. Let's duck into the back bar and have a drink, okay?"

She hoped a little chitchat with a chipper waitress and a couple of Blue Moons spiked with orange slices would put a period to the subject of law enforcement. But Maldonado seemed to feel otherwise.

"I can't say I'm sorry it's over." He was squinting out the window toward the New River, expression unreadable.

"Me neither, I guess. Still, there are things about Ann Buckhalter's death that are going to bug me for a long time."

"What? Oh, that, too. But I meant my engagement. Monica dumped me."

Fran cocked her head at him. He was clearly stifling a grin.

"Your broken heart is putting up a mighty good front."

"Only a flesh wound." The grin broke loose. "It's okay. Really. I was in love from afar. Up close, not so much."

She smiled back. "And that's supposed to be the best part. Speaking of confrontations, please disregard any unfriendly phone messages I may have left you."

"All your phone messages are unfriendly, Setliff. But no, I've been in Jersey getting dumped. Haven't checked my messages. What, wasn't it unfriendly enough for you? Want a do-over?"

"I'll save it for something we haven't done yet—bowling, making out, whatever. Just disregard any messages, okay? And don't question anything I might do in the next half-hour."

He didn't. Not even when she swiped a votive candle and a pack of matches from the main dining room. And not when she led him onto the empty B.O.Q. pier, inflatable alligator tucked under her arm, as dusk deepened around them.

Without hesitation, he sat beside her and let his Corfam-shod feet dangle over the edge. And he looked on with nonjudgmental solemnity as she placed the candle on the alligator's back and lit it. Wordlessly, he helped her lower the float into the river and nudge it toward the channel, where it made one leisurely turn, flashing them a parting vinyl grin before heading downstream.

If something like an impromptu eulogy for Ann Buckhalter flitted through Fran's mind, she kept it to herself. They watched in silence while the flickering light grew dimmer in the distance.